T0071156

Return to Travers Corners

Return to Travers Corners

STORIES

Scott Waldie

Skyhorse Publishing

All rights reserved. No part of this book may be reproduced in any manner without the express written consent of the publisher, except in the case of brief excerpts in critical reviews or articles. All inquiries should be addressed to Skyhorse Publishing, 307 West 36th Street, 11th Floor, New York, NY 10018.

Skyhorse Publishing books may be purchased in bulk at special discounts for sales promotion, corporate gifts, fund-raising, or educational purposes. Special editions can also be created to specifications. For details, contact the Special Sales Department, Skyhorse Publishing, 307 West 36th Street, 11th Floor, New York, NY 10018 or info@skyhorsepublishing.com.

Skyhorse® and Skyhorse Publishing® are registered trademarks of Skyhorse Publishing, Inc.®, a Delaware corporation.

Visit our website at www.skyhorsepublishing.com.

10 9 8 7 6 5 4 3 2 1

Library of Congress Cataloging-in-Publication Data is available on file.

Cover design by Owen Corrigan
Cover image credit Bud Kanouse

Print ISBN: 978-1-62914-756-7
Ebook ISBN: 978-1-63220-106-5

Printed in the United States of America

To my wife JANE with special thanks to CAMRON COOPER and JIM HOUSE and dedicated to the memory of DOLLY CARROLL

Time passes slowly up here in the mountains,
we sit beside bridges and walk beside fountains.
Catch the wild fishes that float through the stream,
time passes slowly when you're lost in a dream.

Bob Dylan

CONTENTS

~

Introduction 1

It Ain't Over till the Fat Man Sings 9

Invisible 51

Wretched Access 103

No Fishing Aloud 131

Woodrow Dickey 169

Your Name in Lights 215

Afterword 275

~

Introduction

TRAVERS CORNERS, IF visited by a dedicated urbanite, would be
seen as nothing more than a windblown gas station of a town
that would make the Middle-of-Nowhere look like Metropolis.
To the naturalist, artist, and poet, Travers Corners is a small picturesque
western town. But what the town lacks in amenities it more than makes
up for in the essentials—quality of life leading the list. Travers (the locals
tend to drop the *Corners* part) is an outpost for the celebration of all
things wild and beautiful: rivers and creeks, wildlife, cattle ranches,
glaciated benchlands sweeping to the timbered mountains.

Fly fishermen, the few who live here and the scores of anglers who
travel to the Elkheart Valley, see Travers as a paradise, the ultimate destination, home to the finest trout waters on this or any other continent: the
Elkheart River, Carrie Creek, the East Fork, to name a few.

Naturally, to the 329 residents, townspeople and ranchers, Travers is
home. Though it's not much more than Main Street, the locals would
object to its being called just a *gas station of a town*. There is other commerce besides Ed's Garage and filling station. There's McCracken's General Store, the Tin Cup Bar and Cafe, Elkheart Valley Bank, Webb's
Insurance, Dolores's Beauty Parlor, the Roxy Theater, and the Take 'r

Easy Motel. There are: side streets and residents, one flashing light to regulate the traffic, one Baptist church to regulate sin, a school, and the county fairgrounds across the river. And, of course, the main reason for many of those visiting Travers, the Carrie Creek Boat Works and Guide Service—Judson C. Clark, proprietor.

But to the historians, Travers is known because of the journals. A town that was documented from its discovery.

The Journals of Traver C. Clark, five ledger-sized volumes in all, span fifty-three years to the time of Traver's death in the fall of 1926. State historians value them as the best historical diaries in Montana for their details, illustrations, and candor. The journals are more than the daily depiction of the American West. They are a multilayered collection of a life's entries, the writings of an educated and moneyed man, the history of a family, of their times—turn-of-the-twentieth-century ranch life, wilderness times. The journals tell everything. They are both the accounts and the daily diaries for the Carrie Creek Ranch. They are the cattle prices, the feed and seed costs, the cow and calf counts, the price of the new bull, a new hammer, a sack of flour, a new buggy, the family budget, the cost of doing business. And mixed in on these same pages are the Clarks' stories, the family's triumphs and tragedies; Traver's everyday anecdotes from life on the ranch, the birth of his two sons, as well as the sad entries—the death of the oldest boy to pneumonia; the bitter chronicles of the killing winter of 1888; a December that turned his cattle empire into a struggling ranch.

You can find copies of these journals in most Montana county libraries. The originals are under glass at the one-room library in Travers Corners.

The journal's entries begin in 1873 with Traver leaving Boston on a business trip, his first assignment with the family fortune. He was sent west by his father to check on the family's shipping and banking interests in San Francisco and to look into the possibilities of future timber interests south of Denver. But Traver wasn't cut from the same commercial cloth as his father and grandfather. He was not a businessman by nature. Money was not, as it was with the rest of his family, his main directive, the only goal of his yet-determined occupation. His field of expertise would be more that of preoccupation. In short, Traver was a dreamer.

On that fateful trip west Traver never made it to San Francisco. In fact, he never got any farther down the Union Pacific rail than O'Malley's Bar in Denver, where, as fate would have it, he befriended the infamous D. Downey and D. Downey's sister, the lovely Carrie whom he fell in love with on first sight.

D. Downey was larger than life, certainly larger than Traver's life, and larger than any life Traver had met before. There was something infectious about the man, this wonderfully crazed Scot, this wickedly charismatic Highlander, this giant of a man, that it wasn't long before he had persuaded Traver to abandon his ideas of investigating the family's business. Instead he thought what Traver needed, after being stifled by the East Coast establishment since birth, was an adventure, to do a little wandering just for the sake of wandering, and because he and Traver shared a passion for trout fishing, he thought it would be best for the two of them to head for Montana where the land was wild and where there were trout as long as your leg. And he assured Traver that the timber in Montana was second to none. The fact that D. Downey had never been to Montana and knew next to nothing about the trout fishing or the timber there didn't deter him in the slightest.

To D. Downey, Traver was the answer to his prayers. A fellow angler, wanting an adventure and never having one, a man so in love with angling that he traveled with his own bamboo rod. And Traver made the perfect traveling companion—a man who had lots of money with access to more, where D. Downey had none and no more was coming his way.

The two of them left Denver, hired a guide (a man known only as Albie) in Jackson Hole, and headed north. Albie, the son of a trapper and his squaw, led them into a valley seldom seen and its Elkheart River, Montana Territory—where the only interest D. Downey and Traver took in timber had to do with those trees that provided shade over a likely trout pool.

From The Journals of Traver C. Clark

October 1, 1873—
We have been on the trail for two days, and there is nothing to write about but long days in the saddle. Albie assures us we will make Missoula and hopefully the stage sometime late tomorrow.
I am convinced of it now—I shall return to the Elkheart and with Carrie as my wife, if she'll have me, I'll build a cattle ranch on the bluff above the river. I am delirious by the thought of it. I have also decided to give D. Downey my Leonard fly rod. He admires it so.

The following summer Traver did just as he had written—he married Carrie. Then with two dozen hired hands, many of whom stayed on to wrangle, Traver built the Carrie Creek Cattle Company at the edge of the Elkheart Wilderness, overlooking Carrie Creek, its confluence with the Elkheart, and what would become the town of Travers Corners. With Carrie, Traver ran the ranch up until their son Ethan and his wife, Anna, could take over. Carrie died in 1925 and Traver the following year.

Albie, a mountain man and trapper by trade, would pass through the Elkheart Valley twice a year, and visit for a week or more. When he became too old to trap he settled in town. He died in 1930.

D. Downey was never to return. He headed back to Scotland, where he married into wealth. But the letters between him and his sister continued until his death in 1921.

The three men, best friends for life, came into the Elkheart and left their names affixed to it. The tallest mountain in the Elkheart Range, Mount D. Downey; Albie Pass is the southern route into the valley. Traver's name became a town, and Carrie's, a creek. But they left their names behind in the more traditional way as well by having families.

Those descendants, chiefly Judson C. Clark and Henry Albie, are still in town and carrying on the friendship.

So for those of you who haven't been here in the Elkheart Valley before, welcome. For those of you who read the first collection of stories, welcome back to Travers Corners, a place far from reality and blessed is that distance.

From The Journals of Traver C. Clark

July 2, 1887—

Carrie and I returned from Missoula yesterday. We picked up the bell for the new carriage house, spent the night at the Carlton, then came home. Making it home in two days with the new road. For the most part, the carriage house is done and the belfry is ready for the bell.

The reason for the bell is twofold. The peal of that bell will be heard for miles signaling an emergency on the ranch, and it will be rung on Sunday mornings because Carrie misses the church bells of Sunday morning in Scotland. "There is something so joyous and rousing about the sound of a bell—and at the same time peaceful," she always says.

Beautiful ride from Missoula. The wildflowers were everywhere. Carrie never looked lovelier.

Missoula mercantile (strapping for the bell) - - - - - - - - - - - 2.45
Lodging and dinner - 4.25
Livery - 1.00
General supplies -22.27

~

It Ain't Over till the Fat Man Sings

NEVER BEFORE HAD Jud seen the town busier, and he would be a better judge of this than anyone else around Travers Corners. From the side yard up at the Boat Works Jud had a high hillside view of Main Street, the side streets, and most of downtown Travers. The fact that the town was crowded came as no surprise. Traffic and people were expected, planned for, and counted on.

This was *the* Saturday of the year, the Saturday of the town's annual fair—D. Downey Days, a five-day event centering on 4-H clubs, livestock auctions, a rodeo, a demolition derby, jam and jelly competitions, ring-toss and guess-your-weight sideshows, with events, demonstrations, exhibitions, presentations, programs of every description, hot dogs, cotton candy, souvenirs, rides for the kids, including a Ferris wheel, and culminating tonight, with *the* Saturday night of the year. The thought of it made Jud's neck cramp.

Everybody in the Elkheart Valley was here. Day-trippers and hard partiers in from Helena and as far away as Missoula; ranchers and cowboys from all over the state, here for the auction and the rodeo. And anyone who wasn't here already would be here with his brother and two of his friends tonight. These numbers, added to the modest numbers of visiting fishermen, turned Travers from not much more than a whistle-stop into something of a city for one night, and with this came both the delights and consequences that a metropolis, however ephemeral, can bring.

Tonight Travers would shed its sleepy small-town visage and its adopted adage of *Travers Corners—where nothing much has happened since Herbert Hoover stopped for gas.* For four or five hours of cowboy bacchanal Main Street is closed to traffic but open for dancing, and every cowpoke and rancher worth his salt would be getting in his licks, two-stepping down Main. A D. Downey Saturday night was the kind of carnival Jud couldn't wait for as a boy, almost looking on the fair day with Christmas-like status. He'd enjoyed it as a younger man as well, all the pretty girls in town for the street dance, the music, the buzz. But now at forty-nine and a few months away from being called fifty, Jud never saw midnight even on a Saturday. Midnight, the hour in which the town would be at its most fevered pitch, would find Jud sleeping or trying to with his windows closed. He knew from previous years that no precautions would work. The loftier notes, and guitar riffs with drumbeat, would float their way up the hill over Carrie Creek and seep in through the old log walls.

But D. Downey Days came just once a year. Jud could deal with it. He would have to or leave town. One thing was certain, Travers Corners had a perfect day for its fair. Sunny and warm.

Jud had spent most of the morning putting the final touches to a new driftboat, a custom-built dory for an Oregon steelheader who would be by in the morning to pick it up. In his usual varnishing outfit, suspenders, a long-sleeved blue cotton shirt, an old vest, baggy pants, Jud looked thinner, if not slightly poorer than normal. The clothing had years of varnish, hundreds of coats around the upper legs where the varnish had been wiped from his hands. Gray hair spilled out from beneath his cap and when the sun caught it, it turned pure white, making him look older than his years. In one hand he held a small brush, in the other a half-pint of thinned varnish. He was moving slowly but that was completely normal, slow being Jud's only speed.

But there was one thing that was unexpectedly abnormal about this day and this boat—Jud, and this was a true rarity, would have this river dory ready on time. In fact twenty-four hours ahead of schedule. Normally he could be working well into the night getting a boat ready for a client, and there had been more than a few instances where the customer would need to spend an extra night in town waiting for his driftboat to come together. Rarely did they mind. Jud's boats were well worth any wait.

Being a craftsman, he moved at a craftsman's pace. Jud could take the purposeful and methodical pace of an artisan, and easily halve it, and then when you added what else was going on in his head, other than the brushwork at hand, you would need to halve his speed once more. Jud could outslow a sloth. His thoughts revolved around lunch, a cold beer, a nap, the next boat, an airline hostess from fifteen years ago. But mostly about escaping town and the fair's madness by doing some late-afternoon and early-evening fishing. He did this while at the same time supplying his own running narrative to the rodeo speakers from over at the fairgrounds. The sound of the announcer, after crossing the river and town and being muted as it traveled through the surrounding cottonwoods, reached Jud as just an unintelligible mechanical drone to which he applied his best rodeo commentary.

"In chute number two motorin' down from the Triangle Nine Hereford Ranch in Seeley Lake is Little Skeeter Johnson and he's gonna be ridin' a bull out of Pocatello, Idaho, named Critical Condition. This cowboy, who don't weigh a hundred and twenty pounds with his boots full of water, is climbin' aboard a twenty-two-hundred-pound Brahman bull who's either maimed or mutilated seven out of his last eight riders. The eighth bull rider was bucked so high and so wide he has yet to be found. He's a bad 'un, this 'un. But Skeeter says he's a wrangler up to the challenge and says his rodeoin' has been improvin' steadily since he had the metal plates installed in his head."

Cowboys and ranchers he understood; in fact, admired. But *rodeo* cowboys riding the circuit from one fracture to the next was a psychosis all on its own, and it was something Jud couldn't quite get his mind around. He remembered Henry's rodeo days when they were younger. He didn't understand it then either.

Watching the varnish leave his brush in liquid ridges that flattened to glass over the red cedar, he thought about Doc Higgins and how he would be sitting on the tailgate of his pickup parked in the same place as every year, near the loading chutes. He was there in case of injury, which, when factoring in Brahman bulls, was a given. He glanced up from his work once more and looked down on the chaos that was town. A crowd of young cowboys was crossing the street heading for the Tin Cup Bar and Cafe, and he thought about Sarah. He could easily imagine her in her Yankees cap and Hawaiian shirt serving up hamburgers as fast as she could fry them while Sal tended the back bar where it would be smoke, jukebox, cowboys five-deep, ditches, and beers.

A crowd of kids came out of McCracken's and headed for the fairgrounds. The general store would be filled with people wanting everything, and Jud laughed at the thought of Junior McCracken running at fever pitch trying to wait on all of them. Jud was glad that he was safely away from the fracas. Tall and thin by description, angular and slow by movement, protracted and sidetracked by temperament, he took a step back to inspect his work and in doing so seemed to unfold, elongate, then somehow, in his baggy and well-varnished pants, reassemble. He pulled the pocket watch from his vest to verify his hunger. It was ten to twelve or thereabouts. He was never too sure with his grandfather's Waltham, a watch that lost around one hour out of every four. He approximated the remainder of the day. After a long lunch and a short beer he would take a nap of indeterminate length. At whatever time he awoke he would do those few things that still needed doing on the driftboat and that would take about an hour, give or take. Then, in all likelihood, he would head to the meadow stretches of Carrie Creek in the late afternoon, more or less, and be there sometime in the early evening at the very latest, an hour or two either way.

It could be said of Jud and his pocket watch that in these digital days of atomic chronometers, he and his Waltham would enter into the time continuum within a few moments of one another, *más o menos.*

Work and sleep took up most of his calendar, save for Tuesday evenings and Saturday afternoons this time of year. It was summer, it was Little League. Travers had a good team this year, and he was the assistant coach. But baseball was always called off this weekend because of D. Downey Days. Otherwise he would be down at the fairgrounds with Sal and the team right now and somewhere in the second inning.

All morning he had been stepping around Annie. This time as he stepped back, he stepped on the Wonderlab and she gave a yelp. "Oh, jeez, I'm sorry, girl. I know. I know." He bent down to pat her head and rub her ears. The loudspeakers, the sound of traffic, the crowds, the general bu-z-z-z around Travers had Annie upset enough without having to be trod on as well. Being a Labrador and possessing easily ten times the acumen of man, Annie was always made nervous and underfoot by D. Downey Days.

Thoughts about getting out of town, camping out tonight up in the meadows crossed Jud's mind but that was out—the man from Oregon would be here to pick up this boat first thing tomorrow morning. Continuing to rub Annie's ears, he headed for the house and lunch, realizing he and Annie reacted the same way when the fair came to Travers—he didn't pant or get overly nervous, but there was a definite tightness in his neck.

Being a bachelor he had few plans, and he generally took each moment as it came. This included meals. Lunchtime came and at the same moment he took his first step toward the kitchen, Jud remembered that continuing would be pointless. There was nothing to eat. Having been so high-centered on getting the dory finished he'd forgotten about going to the store, about the general necessities—groceries and the like. Now he had no other choice but to face the music. He would have to go down to McCracken's. But he did have cold beer in the fridge and he decided to have one, maybe two if he had to face town. He heard the sound of a car coming up his drive.

"There it is, Martha. There's the sign, 'Carrie Creek Boat Works and Guide Service—Judson C. Clark proprietor.' And there he is standing over by one of his boats, the old craftsman himself."

"All right, Father. Now please remember. We have a plane to meet in Helena."

"I know. I know," he answered as the car rolled to a stop. The man was quickly out of the car and over to introduce himself to Jud.

"I'm looking for Jud Clark."

"I'm Jud." The two shook hands.

"My name is Harlan Anderson, that's my daughter, Martha, over in the car. She sits there for two reasons: one, she has little interest in fishing, and two, to remind me that we are in a hurry."

Though Martha couldn't hear what they were saying she could have easily added a third reason for staying with the car—watching Jud, *the old craftsman,* bending and moving with his clown pants and white hair. It reminded her that she had a week of old people coming, aunts and uncles, parents, their friends, a family reunion with a median age in the seventies. The previous two months to this *vacation,* and she snorted at the thought of that misnomer, had been the most brutal in her corporate life, complete with hostile takeovers. Hardball at its most vicious. She wanted a week in Venice or Paris, but what she needed was a year off in St. Bart's. What she was going to get was a week on Flathead Lake with Uncle Elmo and Aunt Edna.

"My your little town is busy."

"D. Downey Days. Big rodeo in town," Jud explained.

"Ahhh. I was wondering if you could take me fishing next week, on the twenty-fourth. That's a week Tuesday, I believe."

~

"Well, I know that sign says guide service, but it's a pretty old sign and I only guide a few times a year these days—and just for some of my old clients," Jud said.

"Once in the boat I *would* be a client, and I certainly qualify as old." Jud smiled and nodded. Harlan took off his dark glasses and cap. It was then Jud got a sense of the man, a man in his seventies with wavy white hair and owlish eyebrows, the kind that sweep up at the sides. Beneath his brow were the most electric eyes he'd ever seen, big blue eyes under a pair of casual lids that opened and closed erratically, lifting to open on those words he thought key, embellishing them by stretching them out for emphasis while the remainder of his remarks were met with eyes nearly closed. It was as if his dialogue was being simulcast in semaphore. But while they were open his eyes were keen and piercing, not only observing all that was around him but taking a full inventory. "Your boats are beautiful."

"Thanks. I could give you the name of another guide, or give him a call for—" Jud offered but was cut off.

"Your home is absolutely lovely. The logs are huge, fir of course, and I would think they had to be brought from some distance, seeing mostly pine on our drive in. Was it once a barn? And it looks very old, I would say 1880 at the very earliest. Would you mind telling me its history?"

"Well, my grandfather was one of the first people in the Elkheart. *Traver* Clark—*Travers* Corners. He had the first ranch here, the Carrie Creek Ranch—built it in 1874 so you weren't far off. Fir trees, you bet. You'll find stands of fir farther up Carrie Creek. This was his carriage house and all that's left of the ranch. The ranch house sat farther up the hill but it burned down in 1968. When I bought the carriage house back from the city, twenty-six years ago, it was falling down. Bottom logs all the way around had to be replaced and it seems like I've been working on the place ever since. Lots of work. Had some help from a friend."

"The cupola is wonderful—just wonderful. Now," he said with his eyes fully open, "I was told by a dear friend, Terry Pearce, that you were the man to hire. No other guide will do." But he only talked at Jud since the carriage house was gaining his full attention. "Would you mind if I looked around inside? Just for a moment since we really have to get going, I suppose."

"No, go ahead. I'm just going to go over and change into some other clothes." In the time it took Jud to walk over to the workshop, Harlan was back out the kitchen door and waving madly for Martha to join him.

"Oh, no," Martha said, slumping in her seat and shaking her head. She recognized that enthusiastic wave. All her life she had been both blessed and cursed by her father's undying enthusiasms, and now she was *once* again being beckoned to yet another *one* of her father's finds. Her father loved people and he loved life, she thought, and then muttered, "The man loves everything." Harlan's gusto for life and all its inhabitants, animate and inanimate, sometimes wore a bit thin, especially when there was a plane to meet. Then she shook her head and laughed at the uselessness of fighting it. He drove her slightly nuts, but she loved him dearly and she had always envied him. Martha may have had her mother's beauty, but she would trade it all and easily for half of her father's zeal.

Her childhood had been one enthusiastic wave after another, and here she was forty and he was still waving for her. Unlike his daughter, and unlike most people, adventures however small were a constant for Harlan Anderson. Around every corner came the possibility of a whole new frontier. Everything held revelation, epiphanies were an hourly event, and anything new, anything adding to his already vast knowledge, excited him. The carriage house thrilled him.

Clipping her cell phone to her belt, she turned off her laptop and opened the door, sighing with every move.

Inside the workshop Jud hung his old varnishing clothes back on their hook. Tucking a clean shirt into a pair of clean Levis (his cupboards might be bare but he was well laundered), he slipped into his boots wearing a pair of socks that were out at the heels. Heading for the door, winding himself around two dories in different stages of completion, he happened to look out and see shapely legs stepping from the car. Wearing blue shorts and a white blouse, Martha was beautiful even at a distance, even through windows laden with sawdust. He wasn't planning on it, but he combed his hair. He buffed the toes of his boots on the backs of his pant legs and watched her cross the yard, long strides for a woman, and he followed her without her notice to the house.

Opening the screen door, Annie beating him through and nearly knocking him down, he was met by Harlan at the height of one of his enthusiasms. "This is wonderful, did you see, Martha, did you see? Look at this spiral staircase made out of wagon wheels. Look, everything is made from wagon parts, buckboard siding for the cabinets and countertops and look, a wagon's tongue to hang his pots and pans. It's all ingenious." Standing on the first step of the stairs, "I know this leads to the cupola, but what goes on up there?"

Jud found himself staring at Martha. Embarrassed that he had to struggle free of her beauty to answer. "Not too much, it's a small space. Room enough for an easy chair and a book. I call it the observatory. Great place to be at sunset. Originally it was the belfry. In case there was an emergency on the ranch, they would ring the bell and it could be heard for miles. And it still can be heard for miles—hangs down at the Baptist church now."

What happened to the old gray and bent craftsman? Martha was wondering. This man was handsome, talented; had a kind face and warm smile. About his staring—she didn't mind. She was used to being stared at. Most of the time she ignored it. This time she was enjoying it.

"Would you mind if I went up to see?" Harlan asked.

"No, go ahead."

Harlan went up the steps light of foot, nimble as a young man.

"This place really is amazing," Martha said, noticing mostly the dust and the dirty dishes and general dishevelment. A clock on the windowsill prompted her to look at her watch. The clock was forty-seven minutes slow. She couldn't imagine how someone could stand to have a clock out of time. For her such an anathema registered as complete discord—fingernails on the chalkboard. But then she couldn't have known its hands were set by Jud's pocket watch—a timepiece as reliable as a sundial on a rainy day.

"This is wonderful up here. Martha, you must come and see. What a view—the fair, the rodeo, the river. The mountains. Oh, this is something." Harlan's voice echoed down from the observatory.

"I'm sure it is, Father, but we really *need* to be going." Still, there was something about the way Jud looked at her that made her want to stay.

"Okay, okay." Harlan descended the staircase, took two steps, and discovered the photographs on the wall. "Oh, look at these, Martha."

Jud stood to one side so that Martha could step around and see the photographs. Walking within inches of him she smelled of perfume, what brand he hadn't a clue, but it was a smell he couldn't have described anyway. His neck stiffened and his mouth went a bit dry. She caught his smell as well—varnish, sawdust, and sweat. She liked it.

Along the wall above the table hung Jud's three favorite photographs. "This was taken in 1887," Jud said, pointing to a photograph showing a gathering of cowboys standing stick-rigid for the exposure, lined up in front of a buckboard. "That's my great-grandfather Traver, my great-grandmother Carrie, and Albie their guide who first brought them into the Elkheart. I don't know who the rest of the men are, but you can see the carriage house." His hand went to the next photograph.

"This is the carriage house in the spring of 1973. That's what the place looked like when Henry and I started on it. That's Henry Albie there on the left with the saw. That's me on the right, well, a thirty-year-old me." Jud smiled. "During my bearded era.

"And this is the carriage house from a few years ago, restoration nearly completed with almost twenty years into it," he went on, wiping the dust from the frame of the third photograph. "Everything being made from wagon parts sort of stretched the renovation." Straightening the photo, he looked at it again. The carriage house completed and standing in the doorway. Driving the last nails, there was Henry twenty years later and looking the same: strong, square-shouldered, expressionless. He could have been happy or sad in either picture, but it was a difference a camera could never capture.

As long as Jud could remember and before—there was Henry. Jud imagined it would take an additional lifetime to explain a lifelong friend. But with Henry it might take even longer, for they had their lives in common, and three generations in Travers before them.

Jud went to the bookcase and grabbed two more photos. "This picture is one of my great-grandfather Traver, my great-grandmother Carrie, and her brother, D. Downey—taken in Denver in 1873. And this is a picture of what the ranch looked like in 1903," Jud said, handing the second photo to Martha, a picture of men lined up on horseback in front of the original homestead.

"What a beautiful home. What happened to it?"

"Fire. Burned to the ground in '68."

"Shame. D. Downey. D. Downey Days is the name of your fair. And Albie is the name of the pass we crossed coming here. Tell me about that."

"A man known only as Albie, a man who was mostly Nez Perce, led my great-grandfather and D. Downey into this place. Henry is his great-grandson."

"And you and Henry are friends?"

"Best friends since birth."

"What an incredible story. And Carrie Creek—of course. I need to hear more about this and, because we have to leave soon, you will now *have* to take me fishing."

The phone on Martha's hip rang, and there was something so lovely about Martha's hips that Jud nearly took the call. "Hello," she answered. "Okay . . . sure, that will work out . . . okay . . . right. All right, Phyllis. Good-bye." She clipped the phone back on her belt and explained the call to her father. "That was Phyllis. Their plane has been delayed in Salt Lake. They're going to be two hours late." She set the alarm on her watch.

"Splendid," Harlan nearly shouted. Then turned to Jud and eyed him up and down. "You look to me like a man who might be hungry. Have you had lunch?"

'Well, no, but I—"

"Martha, let's you and I make Jud some lunch."

Even within Jud's lackadaisical schedule for this afternoon's fishing, a two-hour delay would have him leaving too late. "No, really, I—"

"Jud, what you don't know is that in the backseat are coolers," Harlan explained. "Very big coolers, filled with food, New York fresh this morning. Things you can only find at Genoa's Grocery on Ninety-seventh. Greatest deli in the world. Maryland crab, corned beef, shrimp." Jud's stomach, now angered by hunger, rolled at the mention of each entrée.

"I think I should explain," Martha said. "We're not gluttons. We're on our way to a family reunion on Flathead Lake and we've brought some of the food. Genoa's makes a pollo alla scarpariello to die for."

"Look at this lamp, Martha, made from an old hand brake. And judging by its size it came from a large cargo or ore wagon. Did they find much gold around here?" He didn't wait for an answer. "Okay, let's get to eating. We've brought some bottles of chianti. Do you like chianti?"

"Well, sure but—"

"Splendid."

In the time it would have taken Jud to open a tin of soup, Martha and Harlan were out to the car and back again with cartons of food. Lunch was instantly under way. Jud's kitchen, notable for its inactivity and lack of stores, was suddenly filled with delicacies and all of it prepared that morning in New York. "My favorite kind of cooking. Gourmet and ready to eat. Try the pasta, Jud."

The conversation centered mostly on Harlan's constant questions, questions about to the local history and geology and anything else that popped into his head. But most of all he asked about the fishing and hit on the recurring theme of how Harlan needed to fish with Jud for a day. While Jud did his best to steer the conversation away from fishing: "Hey, this is wonderful bread."

"Comes from a little bakery around the corner from where I live on Lexington. Have you ever been to New York City?" Martha asked.

"Once," Jud smiled. "Ought to last me a lifetime."

Martha laughed. "It's a bit of heaven and hell. But the food . . ."

"Not to mention the delivery service," Jud toasted, sitting back in amazement—amazed at how fast they moved, amazed at how fast they talked, and even more amazed at how, ten minutes into his life, they had totally taken over. He wasn't complaining. He'd gone from starvation to gluttony in minutes, an instant feast with food he couldn't believe and some he couldn't pronounce. And he was quite certain that Martha was flirting with him, and *damn* it felt good.

Reaching into his pocket pulling out a small book, Harlan checked his dates. "What about next Saturday? Could you guide me on Saturday?"

"Impossible," Jud replied.

"Old clients coming in?"

"Little League game."

"You have a boy who plays?" Martha asked. Seeing no signs of domesticity in Jud's home, she was sure no woman was about. She hadn't thought about a son.

"No, I'm the assistant coach. Playing Reynolds on Saturday. Biggest game of the year—Reynolds being our archenemy," he explained and reached for another shrimp, another piece of bread.

"Perhaps I could move some things around at the beginning of the next week," Harlan mumbled, still looking at his schedule.

"Listen, Harlan, and I know this sounds ungrateful from a man with a mouthful of your food, but I just can't do it. I have boats to build. I really—"

Martha interrupted, "Father, I think you're forgetting your own number one Anderson's rule of business, and I quote, 'If it's worth getting, then get it at all costs.'" Martha smiled and turned to Jud. "How much is one of your guided trips worth?"

"I get two hundred a day."

"I'll pay you six hundred and let's do it on Sunday?"

"What time?" Jud smiled. He'd just been bought and he didn't mind. The triple pay more than influenced his decision but the part of her proposal that iced the deal was the "let *us* do it on Sunday." *Us* would mean Martha as well and he would take her down the river, or anywhere else she might want to go, for free.

"Splendid, Sunday it is," Harlan shouted and poured himself another glass of chianti. "Well negotiated, dear."

The next two hours fell into easy conversation. Jud learned the best way to counter Harlan's barrage of questions was to get a question off first, then sit back, listen, and enjoy the stories. The man had been everywhere and knew everyone. Retired from corporate business, steel and manufacturing, Harlan had an apartment in New York and a home in the Bahamas. He knew senators and presidents and was good friends with Walter Cronkite.

And he knew a bit more about Martha—big business as well, computers, on the boards of several companies that Jud had never heard of. "Haven't joined the computer age just yet. I'm still kinda coming to grips with the industrial revolution," Jud smiled. "I'm making my boats in much the same way these boats were made a hundred years ago, and you can't computerize handcrafting."

"Perhaps not, but there's always marketing. Every business needs to have more customers."

"Right now, I'd like to have a few less. I'm working overtime to keep from being more than a year behind." Martha laughed and her hair drifted down across her face. There was no doubt about it—she was flirting with him.

"So, Judson C. Clark," Martha said with a certain coyness, "are you going to the big doings tonight? According to the banners around town there's going to be a street dance."

"Used to go when I was younger but not now. Actually I'm going fishing this evening. Gotta get Annie out of town as well. The noise from the band and the fireworks at the fairgrounds really put her on edge." Lying at his feet, Annie rolled over on her back at the mention of her name and Martha leaned down to rub her tummy. The alarm on her watch sounded, ending the afternoon. "We have two hours to get to Helena. That's it, Father, we have to go." Then a genuine sadness came into her eyes. "Now, ain't that a shame." Martha was looking at Jud in a way no woman had looked at him for a long time.

Falling to his feet to help Martha and her father pack up the food cartons, Jud felt satiated to the point of pleasant discomfort, warm from the afternoon wine, and aware of the inner glow of very certain urges resulting from the way she said *Ain't that a shame*. His heart fell into Fats Domino chord progressions, boogie-woogie, and joyous bebop, knowing this woman would be back and in his boat on Sunday.

Out at their car Jud helped Martha with the coolers. Harlan was already in the passenger seat with a pair of binoculars in one hand while his other hand quickly thumbed his Peterson's Guide. "What kind of bird is that?"

"Bobolink," Jud answered and helped Martha slip the cooler into the backseat. "So, I'll see you on Sunday."

"Not me, you won't. Unfortunately I'll be on the plane home Sunday. Board meeting Monday. It'll just be my dad."

"Oh, I thought you would be coming as well," Jud said, wondering if his outward appearance had caved in anywhere; his heart was still playing Fats's chords but had dropped an octave to "Blue Monday."

"It's a bobolink," Harlan looked up from his Peterson's and went back to his field glasses.

Jud smiled and Martha laughed. "His hearing isn't very good these days and he misses some things because his mind is processing so many things at once. When he was younger he missed nothing, has an I.Q. of one eighty-four. Sleeps four hours a night. In our family he's known as the Wizard. It's pretty annoying sometimes. I mean, everyone knows someone who thinks he knows everything, but with my father, well, he *does* know everything." Jud laughed. She reached over and touched his arm in a gracious and kind way. "Judson C. Clark, I wish I could have stayed and I wish I could have gotten to know you better. Right now my life doesn't allow such pleasures."

"Maybe next year." Jud shrugged.

"That would be wonderful. Of course, if you're ever in New York . . ."

Jud with a slim smile told her what the chances were of that happening.

Opening the cooler once more, she pulled out two cartons. "Here, you take these. They'll get you through a couple of dinners."

He hesitated at first and was about to refuse when he was interrupted by Harlan asking, "What flies will I bring on Sunday?"

"I'll have all that you'll need," Jud smiled.

And with that Martha said her good-bye, and Harlan waved his. But for Jud the good-bye had left him feeling hollow. It was a strong, but not an uncommon sadness, and not because he had fallen in love with Martha—he'd only known her for two hours—but a loneliness brought on by the prospect of being forever alone. Martha's being here just reminded him all the more about his want of a woman. Her good-bye was more than a farewell, it was the latest in a lifetime series of farewells, another fascinating woman, another ill-timed chance. Marriage was something he'd tried once and failed at, but as of late it was something he wanted to try again.

The muffled loudspeakers and a roar from the rodeo crowd replaced the silence he was feeling. He went out to the back porch and gathered his waders and fly rod. On his return he pulled two beers from the fridge; the kitchen suddenly felt empty. Only moments ago it was filled with laughter and promise. Annie barked. He was not completely alone.

Down at the bottom of the hill, Martha had met Henry's truck on the one-lane bridge crossing Carrie Creek. Henry had waited on his side for her to pass, gaining a good long look at the comely blonde at the wheel who, in turn, noticed Henry long enough to smile a thank-you through her window without really seeing him. But she was distracted. All she was thinking was that her one chance at some good times and maybe a little romance on this so-called vacation had just slipped through her fingers. Jud, the country craftsman, was certainly not the cultured, high-priced urbanite she was used to seeing, and she guessed that's what interested her most. In Jud there was a man of substance without effort; a man somehow seemingly happy without any apparent wealth. Her usual fare were men of substantial wealth, men who went to great effort to make their wealth very apparent in the hopes that this might somehow make them happy. She liked Jud, it was a real and mutual attraction, of that she was sure, but where would she be tonight—at Elmo and Edna's. Shrugging her shoulders in a gesture fitting her internal dialogue, she acquiesced to her fate—the longtime-planned-for family reunion, a family as large and as dysfunctional as anyone's. Martha wheeled onto the highway and headed north.

Pulling into the yard Henry could see Jud coming from the house with fly rod and waders in hand. At first Henry had no intentions of stopping; he was just coming by to extend an invitation for supper. Hot and dusty from helping out at the fairgrounds, he stepped from his pickup and walked to the hose for a drink. He wanted to know more about the woman he'd met on the bridge, and, after fifty years of seeing each other nearly every day, best friends in a small town, there was never a need for greetings between the two of them. Most of their conversations started with a question. "So who was the blonde?"

"Martha," Jud answered, putting his fishing tackle in the back of the Willys.

"She was about the best-lookin' woman I've ever seen in real life," Henry reckoned as he tilted his hat back to show a lighter skin line.

~

Water dripped from his mustache. Jud always marveled at the size of the man's hands, hay-hook hands hanging from the ends of his sleeves, heavily muscled hands from a lifetime of ranch work.

"Yeah, I'm pretty sure I'm in love again. She's been here for the last couple of hours. Fed me an incredible lunch," Jud said.

"I fell in love with her and all I did was pass her on the bridge. Who was the guy with her—didn't get a good look at him—her husband no doubt. That kind of woman always come equipped with a husband."

"Nope, that was her father. Going to take him fishing Sunday."

"What about her? She coming to do a little fishin', too? I'd be more than happy to row her if'n you got somethin' else to do," Henry leered and the devilment danced in his eyes.

"Nope, she'll be back in the Big Apple. Important board meeting."

"Ain't that a shame."

Jud nodded in agreement and Fats played some sad chords.

"The main reason I stopped by was to tell ya that Dolores wants ya to come over for some supper tomorrow night."

"I'll be there," Jud smiled, thinking that he wouldn't have to worry about cooking for several nights running.

"Where you gonna go fishin'?"

"I was going to go up to the meadows, but I'm getting a late start. Now I think I'll go down to the river, fish the braids."

"Like to go with ya, but I'm running a little behind and I gotta take Dolores dancin' tonight. See ya tomorrow."

"See ya," Jud waved. "C'mon, Annie, let's go." Annie jumped in the back of his Willys, barking twice. Then, panting and wiggling, she settled into the passenger seat.

That night, after an evening of fair fishing, under fair skies, downstream from the fairgrounds, Jud was feeling surprisingly sort of okay, kind of all right, well, in a word . . . fair. He wasn't blue, exactly, just more alone than he'd like to be, and his loneliness was highlighted by the fact that it was Saturday night and people everywhere had somebody.

His best friend was out on Main Street dancing with Dolores. He could picture them now and just as easily picture them thirty years ago, dancing and laughing.

And Martha's appearance didn't help his loneliness much either. She was a beautiful, engaging, and most current reminder of all the wonderful single women out there, *out there* being the key words, because there were no single women *around here*.

Sitting on a log Jud watched the trout feed in the still water of the Elkheart, where the river ran quiet and flat before it tumbled away. There he waited for nightfall and the darkness needed for fireworks. The first rocket flared over the cottonwoods, and its ephemeral fires lit the low-lying heavens and the pool in front of him, reflecting every chaotic display of gunpowder and dazzle in a sky-wide pool—fireworks above and below him. The reds and pinks of each explosion flickered in the riffled waters like dusk's own brushstrokes.

Annie was back in the Willys, curled up in the passenger seat, oblivious to her old pyrotechnic nemesis. The slightly different murmurs of rolling water and gentle breezes muffled the distant whistling and cracking missiles. Her eyes closed, Annie missed the show and awakened only when Jud turned the key on the jeep for the ride home.

Back at the Boat Works, windows closed, Annie curled up on the foot of his bed, Jud imagined the two-stepping crowd on Main Street. He stayed awake until the music stopped at two.

Sunday, D. Downey Days were over. The tents were being folded at the fairgrounds, the streets were being cleaned, the cowboys had been leaving since daybreak. The steelheader from Oregon came and picked up his boat, paid his balance, and was gone. Jud spent the rest of the morning moping, finally working himself up to some nonproductive fiddling around by the early afternoon, followed by a late afternoon of blatant goofing off. His underlying melancholy stayed with him for the day and finally surfaced that evening at Henry's.

After a few ditches and while Henry was out tending to some irrigation before dinner, Jud talked to Dolores about how much he would like to have a woman in his life. It was his usual social lament, one that Dolores had heard many times, but this time she felt as though Jud had hit a new low and she was worried about him. And, as with all her private conversations, Dolores was able to share her concern with Monday's patrons, one of whom was Pam McCracken, postmistress and gossip to the world. On any given day nearly the whole town came to McCracken's for their bulk mail and bills and, of course, Pam's most recent edition of town hearsay.

Now with the beauty parlor and Pam McCracken both dispensing the gossip, the hearsay was not only spread with the speed and efficiency of the U.S. Mail, but it got curled, twisted, and colored at Dolores's. So by the time the rumor reached the outlying ranches and reverberated back again, Jud's condition had progressed from blue, to depressed, to manic.

But in truth, by Tuesday and Jud's first sojourn into town since the fair, things were looking very good. That morning his yearly order of cedar had arrived, and it was the best-looking wood he'd seen in years. Later in the day he had received another boat order. But his best news had come the night before. Around eleven Sal had called. Jud had just fallen asleep.

"Jud, I got some sad news," Sal said, "and I am hopin' you are sittin' down."

"Better yet, Sal, I'm lying down."

"Yeah, I know dat it's late, but dis is such sad news that I had to share it with youse right away—a guy from Reynolds just came into the bar and he tells me dat Kirby Long broke his collarbone dis afternoon whilst foolin' around on some other kid's skateboard."

Sitting straight up in bed, not fully awake but smiling from ear to ear, "Oh, damn, now I hate to hear that," Jud laughed, feeling only the slightest twinge of guilt from the joy given by the boy's misfortune. But Kirby Long was the best hitter and the best pitcher Reynolds had or for that matter anyone else in the league had. He had a rocket arm and not a kid in Travers or any other town could hit his pitching. Without Kirby "the Curve Ball" Long on the mound, Reynolds would be facing Travers on a level playing field for the first time all season. Reynolds and Travers had played twice this summer—the scores were 13–1 and 11–0, respectively—and both times it was "the Curve Ball" on the mound.

"Anyways, dat's what I got to report. Good night there, Judson C." Settling back into his pillow, hands behind his head, eyes closed, Jud could see Sal behind the bar pouring himself and everyone else at the rail a tall beer. Jud went to sleep grinning.

First thing Tuesday morning Jud was down the hill to McCracken's to pick up his mail and restock his stores. Naturally, being one of the topics of yesterday's conversations, Jud's appearance drew attention but not so that he would have known it—at first.

" 'Morning, Pam," Jud greeted the postmistress.

"Oh, Jud," Pam greeted him a bit flustered. "And how are you feeling today?" she asked in a strange way, like a doctor might ask a young patient.

"Couldn't be better," Jud replied, puzzled by her obvious concern. Gathering his mail, she let out a heavy sigh, thinking what a brave front he was putting on.

Mail in hand, Jud left the postal part of McCracken's, grabbed a cart, and started heading down the aisles, filling his cart with supplies and necessities. Etta May Harper looked at him curiously from the produce section. He nodded and smiled. Just past the baling twine and liquor department he ran into Junior, who was stocking motor oil on top of a crate of oranges. Merchandising was not one of Junior's strong suits.

"Hey, Jud," Junior greeted. High strung by nature, he wasn't sure how to look at his old friend now that he had been reported as mentally disturbed. He did think that Jud looked very chipper for a manic depressive. Being the town's pharmacist and the closest thing to a doctor the town had at the moment, with Doc Higgins away at a medical conference in

Billings, he thought it would be best if he broached the subject gently, get around to Jud's insanity slowly. "So, you been fishing lately?" Junior asked.

"Went Saturday night. It was kinda slow," Jud answered.

"Well, I went Sunday and didn't do too well, either." This of course came as no surprise to Jud, Junior being quite possibly the most unsuccessful fly fisherman in the history of the sport. It was a motor skills problem for Junior. Casting, mending line, walking were problems for Junior. But the man could talk about fly fishing forever. Vicki Whitehead appeared at the pharmacy counter. "And there's something else I wanted to talk about . . . so hold on a second, Jud, I'll get Vicki's pills and I'll be right back."

But Jud took advantage of the interruption and headed for the checkout counter. Junior got hung up on a phone call and Jud escaped McCracken's without having to listen to Junior tell long stories about short trout.

Back at the Boat Works Jud spent the afternoon sorting and stacking his shipment of cedar in a three-sided shed at the rear of the workshop. With every piece length he stacked, he thought about how strange the morning had been, and he asked himself the most commonly asked question when living in a small town, *Was it me or was it everyone else in town?* And he thought about practice this evening. He couldn't wait to see the team's faces when Sal gave the news about Kirby Long.

Just before practice started that evening four of the team's mothers and one of the aunts, having heard about Jud's severe downheartedness, brought him food—a casserole, a loaf of bread, cookies, and one apple pie were delivered with encouragements such as, "everything's going to be all right . . . cookies always cheer me up . . . I've got a cousin in Helena who's single . . ."

But before he had time to ask as to what all the attention meant, Sal arrived with the bats and balls and practice was under way. "Okay, all of youse, listen up." Eleven uniformed boys gathered around him. "I got some good news and I got some bad news. First the bad news . . . we gotta play Reynolds again Saturday." Sal, a shortstop in his day, now in his sixties, bald and bellied, his Italian eyes about to water from the sweetness of this forthcoming bulletin, then added, "And now for da good news." He smiled over at Jud. "The good news is dat Kirby the Curve Ball broke his collarbone yesterday." The team, the Travers Corners Yankees, went wild. In a sentence they were back in the game.

"Infielders take your positions. Jud, why don't you hit 'em some pepper. Outfielders come with me." The practice took on a whole new meaning with the news about Kirby the Curve. Without him Reynolds became like any other team. Everybody that evening was hitting and fielding well; there was snap and fire in their play. In fact Jud had never seen them all play so well— except, of course, the McCracken brothers, who unfortunately inherited their father's hand–eye coordination. But they gave it their best.

Near the end of practice Sarah came to watch her team, see her Uncle Sal in his element two thousand miles from Brooklyn, and check on Jud. But as soon as she saw him laughing and joking with the boys, working on the double-play ball, she could see that all reports in Travers of his pending insanity had been embellished. Being a lifelong fan of the sport, she loved coming to the games.

Sal blew his whistle and signaled for all the kids to huddle around him. "Remember dis, and remember it all week long—we're gonna beat dees guys." With that practice was over and the team slowly dispersed in rounds of laughter, horseplay, and chants of *We're gonna beat dees guys.*

While Jud gathered the bats and balls, helmets and bases, Sarah talked to some of the mothers. Sal was on the mound with Saturday's pitcher, Ricky Underwood, imparting some final knowledge on breaking pitches. Loading the collected equipment in the back of Sal's station wagon, Jud was interrupted by Nancy Hicks, who handed him a pan of her meat loaf. "Just something to show how much we appreciate what you and Sal are doing for the boys." She patted his hand, smiled, and joined her son, Lyle, the Yankees' star left fielder. But the thanks for his help in Little League was a euphemism, just Nancy's way of avoiding the subject. Her way of saying... *It's tough to go through life completely loony tunes and maybe this meat loaf will ease your mania.*

With the team and parents leaving, and Sal giving Rick a lift home, Sarah and Jud, still holding his meat loaf, were the only ones left on the field. "All right," Jud asked, "now maybe *you* can tell me what's going on in this town? This morning at McCracken's everybody was weird, Junior was stranger than normal, and in the last two hours I've been given enough food to start a shelter."

Sarah laughed, looking at the pan of meat loaf in his hands, and then asked, "Haven't you heard?"

"Heard what?"

"That your lackluster love life is driving you to the depths of depression. Half the town has it that you've gone around the bend for some blonde, and not any ordinary blonde."

"Ah, it all comes clear. I had a few too many bourbons with Dolores the other night and, Dolores being Dolores . . ."

"I talked to Dolores about it this afternoon. She told me you were blue, but hardly ready for hari-kari. She did say she told Pam, and there's a woman who can take a rumor and run with it."

Jud smiled and shook his head. "Small towns. If there isn't any news—make up some. Hey, did you hear about Kirby the Curve Ball?"

"Did I hear about the Curve Ball? All day long that was all I heard. All day long Sal was whistling and singing. One thing for certain—if we ever have a chance to whip Reynolds it's going to be Saturday."

"We're gonna beat dees guys."

The week passed. Jud was busy at the Boat Works, the start of another boat, but his mind kept going in and out of work. He thought about the game, had some long metaphysical discussions with Annie, and thought about Sunday and guiding Harlan, but he thought about Harlan's daughter more.

Saturday at seven the T.C. Yankees and the Reynolds' All Stars took the field.

"Hey batta, batta, batta, hey no batter." The chatter from the infield carried out from the diamond over the outfield and down the Elkheart River, which carved its way behind right field. The crack of the bat, the snap of well-hit line drives could be heard on a quiet night down to the city limits. The score, after three, was tied two-all.

In the stands sat much of the town, parents of the team, baseball fans without kids, and citizens of Travers who knew nothing or cared very little about baseball but had showed up for the possibility of Travers beating Reynolds in anything. Junior McCracken was hawking hot dogs for the Rotary Club, Henry was in the stands with Dolores, Doc Higgins had even stopped by but had to leave during the second inning. A stranger entered the stands at the bottom of the third. The lights came on in the sixth.

Throughout the middle and late innings the score staggered back and forth—Travers up by a run, Reynolds ahead by two, and at the end of eight and a half the score was 5–4, the T.C. Yankees holding on to a very thin one-run lead. Very thin because Lyle had been throwing heat all night and the arm was tired. The first hitter grounded back to Lyle; the second hitter popped it up. Both boys had stretched Lyle to long counts. Then in three bad pitches came two blistering hits and the All Stars' centerfielder was now the tying run and safe on third. The winning run, their shortstop, was standing on second. The third batter, the All Stars' first baseman, had gone three for four on the night against Lyle.

Lyle had held the All Stars to four, something no other team in the league had done all year, but his arm was gone. Sal, on a normal team, would have put in a reliever, but Lyle with a rubber arm was better by far than the reliever's best stuff. Lyle would have to pitch it out. The infield chattered, "C'mon Lyle . . . fire that thing . . . fire that rock-a-honey-baby-seed . . . C'mon Lyle . . ."

While the All Stars heckled from their dugout, "Hey, no pitcher . . . no pitcher out there."

All Lyle had was what was left of his fastball. The world was watching. He reached down deep for the pitch he needed and his long, leggy thirteen-year-old frame unwound from the mound, sending a fastball as fast as anything he'd thrown all night . . . but the batter had it timed.

Crack! The ball was hit well, as high as it was deep. The boys on base were heading home. Deep in right field and running in uncertain circles ran Bobby McCracken. All night long not one ball had been hit to him (something Sal and the team were thankful for), and now the game-winning hit was driving Bobby back, back to the fence. Stumbling once, he lost the ball in the lights. He gave his best guess as to where the ball might be, stuck up his glove, closed his eyes, and hoped for the best. Sal, Jud, everyone in the stands knew that all was lost. Sal's heart sank.

The ball hit Bobby's glove just as he started to stumble once more. He landed hard. On the ground he looked to his glove, and more to his surprise than to anyone's, the ball was there, half in and half out of the webbing. He raised his glove to prove the catch had been made.

Travers Corners erupted from the stands. The T.C. Yankees left their positions running, throwing gloves and hats in the air as they descended upon Bobby in a pile. Jud was out there and running with them. Sal just stood there numb. Everyone was hopping around and slapping on Bobby's shoulders. A chant broke out—*We're gonna beat dees guys, we're gonna beat dees guys* . . . Bobby McCracken, who had never done an athletic thing in his life, and given his talents was almost sure not to do another one, was basking in the moment. Junior McCracken just stood on the sidelines, tears rolling down his cheeks.

Sarah ran across the diamond and jumped into Jud's arms and gave him a big smooch, then ran on to Sal and did the same. The victory celebration ran at fever pitch for a minute or so then settled into mere exaltation. Collectively the Yankees couldn't believe it. Bobby was hoisted on the team's shoulders while Reynolds gathered their equipment, gave their two-four-six-eights, loaded their bus, and left. Sal was relishing the moment. And Jud believed he couldn't have been any happier—that nothing could make this moment any better. He was wrong. Suddenly out of the crowd of parents, players, and fans Martha appeared.

"Congratulations, Coach. It was a great game." She greeted him with a handshake and smile.

Jud, still a little weak in the knees from the victory, nearly buckled at the sight of her. "When did you get here?"

"Been here since the bottom of the third," she smiled.

"Where's Harlan?"

"Father couldn't make it. So you have to guide me tomorrow. Hope that will be all right?"

"That would be fine." Fats Domino put a whole new rhythm into his heart. "But I thought you didn't fish?"

"Who said anything about fishing?"

With the entire outfield tugging at his sleeve—"C'mon, Mr. Clark, C'mon Coach"—Jud could hardly speak as two of the infielders climbed onto his shoulders.

"Listen, if it's all right, I'm going to go up to your house," Martha said. Jud could only nod in agreement, as the chant *we're gonna beat dees guys* had started up again. "I've brought some food and wine if you'd be interested in a late supper. When you're done here, head on home. No rush."

"Hey, Coach, c'mon, let's go." Lyle was pulling on his arm. They were lining up for the team photo. Martha blew Jud a kiss as he was being dragged away. He looked over his shoulder and watched her walking to her car. Martha couldn't go anywhere unnoticed. Henry had noticed her when she came up into the stands and had spent the rest of the game trying not to notice her because of Dolores. Dolores had noticed her in the way that one beauty always notices another. Sal had noticed her the way an old man notices a younger woman. Sarah had only noticed her as she was walking away, but it was long enough to know it had to be *the* blonde. Junior missed her entirely.

And Joan Pearson noticed her as well. She had brought Jud her three-bean casserole to help his spirits, but anyone who had a blonde like Martha batting her eyes at him and blowing him kisses was doing better than anyone else on the field, save Bobby McCracken, and Joan kept the three-bean for herself.

It was tradition that the team always went to the Tin Cup after home games where they would be treated to ice cream on Sal—one scoop for defeats, two scoops for victories. Tonight there would be triple scoops all around. Normally a win over Reynolds would have been enough to satisfy Jud's night, but now he had Martha, the flirtatious bright and beautiful Martha, without her father, waiting for him with a bottle of wine at his house. An hour glaciated past.

"I remember the days when ice cream did it," Sal said over the clamor of eleven Yankees spread out at the counter. "But I like being 'dis age right now, because I got a twenty-year-old bottle of Scotch waiting for me at home 'dat I been saving for 'dis very occasion." Sal hadn't stopped grinning since the catch.

"I got a good-looking woman at home waiting for me, and believe me *that's* an occasion," Jud muttered under his breath.

Cones in hand, everyone scoring a triple, the Yankees took their victory and horseplay outside onto Main Street. Small-town heroes, the young princes in pinstripes owned Main Street at this moment in time, and Main Street being the world, they owned it all. Jud remembered, if only for a moment, the feelings of such a night from his youth and baseball. But, his mind could not be clogged by memories when something as current as Martha was waiting.

"So, was that the blonde of the *infamous* blonde fame?" Sarah asked.

"Yep," Jud replied. "I can't believe she's here."

"And you thought you'd never see her again," Sarah smirked. Knowing Jud's charm, knowing that she herself would have fallen for Jud in another lifetime, the blonde's arrival came as no surprise to Sarah.

"Listen, I better go," Jud said a little nervously.

"Oh, yeah, I think you'd better," Sarah laughed. Jud went out the back door with a wave to Sal, who was standing at the front window of the café watching the boys—lost in horseplay and victory—moving as a team down past the Roxy.

Annie barked as Jud pulled up in front of the Boat Works (Annie was not allowed at the games, Annie being a retriever, and the game being baseball . . .). All the lights were on. Martha was still there.

She was standing at the sink as he came through the door. She greeted him with a glass of red wine. "Quite a team you have there, Coach." Jud looked into the sink to see water running over four lobster tails. He just smiled—mostly from disbelief, lobster and blondes not being part of his usual Saturday night.

"That kid's catch, bottom of the ninth, what a hero . . . I hope you like lobster."

"That was Bobby McCracken, the worst player on our team by a large margin, who made that catch. I don't think he's made three catches all season. I love lobster."

"And the team was so excited. You, too. It was so wonderful to watch."

"Well, Reynolds is a town seven times our size. We lose to them every time we play them. Every once in a while, every ten or twenty years, we either get lucky or we field an extraordinary team and we beat them." He then explained about Kirby the Curve Ball but then noticed that the words seemed to be falling out of his mouth and he found himself staring at her—Martha had that effect. She was elegant yet easy at the same time, like he'd known her a long time, like she'd just stopped by as usual, like an old friend from down the street.

Her cell phone rang. She looked at her watch. She checked the pager in her purse. "I need to make a quick call." She dialed. "John. Martha. I've read Johnson's proposal and I agree, it's bullshit. My vote is no . . . Montana is lovely . . . Okay . . . 'Bye."

She poured herself another glass of wine and one for Jud. "All right, Judson C. Clark, before we take this evening to the next level, there is one thing I want to understand. When I was here last time, your fridge was bachelor empty, a two-condiment-and-one-stale-beer kind of refrigerator. This time I come in and the thing is packed with food, cookies, and pies. Now, you have either a doting aunt who's taking a cooking class or a string of girlfriends. So come clean, who's the woman?"

Jud laughed. "Well, in a way *you* are." He then continued on to explain about the gossip machine around Travers, about the too many bourbons with Dolores, about Pam, about how the mysterious blonde had broken his heart, and about how Montanans treat all illnesses with food. Jud mimicked, "Did you hear about poor old Charlie? Well, he just came back from the hospital. The doctors told him that he has clogged arteries, that his cholesterol was about nine thousand, and that he's diabetic. I'm going home right now and make him my chocolate cheesecake to cheer him up."

Martha laughed. Annie came over with her tennis ball and dropped it in her lap. "Okay, one more question—who was the woman at the game who ran across the infield and gave you that kiss?' "

"Sarah."

And Martha didn't need to ask who Sarah was to Jud; her eyebrows arched with enough suspicion to do that for her. "I don't mean to be so nosy. It's just that my last attempt at some kind of romance turned out to be a blind-sider—an unforeseen triangle that included a friend, and I never wish to be anywhere near a situation like that again."

Jud nodded then explained Sarah. "Sarah is one of the most amazing women I have ever met. She moved here with her Uncle Sal about twenty years ago. Sarah and her husband were both schoolteachers in New York City. One day her husband and their little boy were coming back from a playground and were caught in a war between two gangs. They were both shot and killed. After that she wanted to move as far away from a city as possible—she and Sal settled in here. Sarah is as good a friend as I have, but it's far from romantic."

"I'm sorry, I'm sorry I asked. God that's a horrible story."

The evening settled in over lobster and wine. She talked about her life, her early years at private schools, then Wellesley, corporate life, New York City and the fast track. Constant travel to places he'd only read about. Never at home if she really had a home. Rich, busier than anyone should be, mostly unhappy when she had time to notice. A man in her life was out of the question—no time.

And he told about his forestry scholarship to Cal Berkeley, the 1960s, his moments of moderate rebellion, his dropping out, his time spent with a Zuni shaman in New Mexico. He talked about his early years mostly, because for the last half of his life he'd been back in Travers Corners at the Boat Works and doing the same thing year in and year out. Comfortable, and pleased with his home. Poor, busy as he wanted to be, and pretty happy about most things. The right woman coming into his life would make things better, though it didn't seem likely, but only time would tell.

A marriage apiece, a divorce apiece. Both single forever, both had flirtations and love affairs, offers and considerations, and that was where any similarity between the two ended. But they were having a great time and the laughter came easily. Right now they had adjourned to the living room where Jud had built a fire and they were defending the other's life choice . . .

"I mean, look at this place, this setting on Carrie Creek, it's not only the path less traveled but it's on ancestral ground," Martha said, standing with her back to the fire. "You live a one-of-a-kind existence in a one-of-a-kind home of your own making. I don't know anybody who gets to do that. And look where you get to live."

"Yeah, but look at you. A honcho. A big-time executive. You can have nearly anything you want and when you want it. Great restaurants, plays, museums. Of course, there is that living in New York City part—a major subtraction."

"I never wanted to live in New York. When I was young I envisioned myself in Vermont and owning a small bookstore. But I was under a lot of pressure from my father to join in the corporate world. You know what Father is doing right now?" she asked, looking at her watch. "He's having cocktails with Walter Cronkite and Glenn Close at a ranch near Whitefish."

"Oh yeah, well I'm doing a *whole* lot better than that and I'm eating lobster."

"You say the kindest things." Martha leaned in and kissed him softly on the mouth.

Look at me I'm in love again, ain't had no lovin' since I don't know when. Fats pounded out a rhythm Jud hadn't felt in years.

From that point in the evening there was more kissing than talking, then there was no talking. Then there was talking again and then no talking. They made love in front of the fire, then worked their way to the bedroom, taking advantage of any flat surfaces they passed along the way with time spent on the kitchen table. There is no passion like older passion, wizened, well practiced, and without the pretense passion. Passion after years of longing, seasoned passion, where the gymnastics of young passion, kitchen table aside, are replaced by a softer, slower passion.

Night turned to morning.

"So, what do you want to do today?" Jud asked slightly blurry-eyed, showered, dressed, and smiling.

"More of what we did last night," Martha said, just out of bed wearing one of Jud's T-shirts and joining him now in the kitchen.

She was beautiful in a T-shirt, Jud thought, and she had been more than beautiful without it. "Well, you know, money did change hands. I *owe* you a guided trip."

"If last night wasn't a guided trip then I don't know what was. God, you would have thought we were teenage newlyweds the way we carried on." Martha blushed, which Jud thought was wonderful because she hadn't last night. "But if I must be guided, where would we go?"

"Well, let's see . . . do you want to fish?" Jud asked, pouring himself another cup of coffee and thinking strongly about a piece of apple pie for breakfast.

"No, not really. But let's go someplace where you could fish and that we could take Annie." Hearing her name and sensing inclusion Annie gave Martha a cold nose under her T-shirt, making her jump. "You want to know what I really want? I want a piece of that apple pie." Then she giggled like a schoolgirl who had just heaped another sin onto an already wonderfully wicked night.

"Great minds," Jud began to say . . .

Her cell phone rang. She looked at her watch.

It was decided after the phone call, after the pie, and after three more phone calls, three pages, and a check of her e-mail, not to float the river as had been the plan with her father, but to spend the day up in the far meadows of Carrie Creek. There was another decision made by Jud—to leave all forms of electronics, cell phone, pager, and laptop, at the Boat Works. She was also told to leave her watch.

The upper meadows of Carrie Creek were Jud's favorite places on earth. There was something much more than the fishing when wandering up Carrie Creek. Carrie's Creek. His great-grandmother's own creek. It was more than just magical, or memorable; it was somehow maternal, nourishing, like going home. The meadow grasses had been bent and yellowed slightly by the first frost, still covering everything in shade. The aspen leaves had been tipped in gold by autumn's first call and their stands, patchworking the knolls and climbing the mountain canyons, stood haloed by the midmorning sun. The day was windless with clouds spread thinly over the southern skies. Deer, an eagle, antelope, and one moose at a great distance had marked their drive, and now the creek glistened as it made its lazy bends through First Meadow. They drove the extra three miles to Second Meadow and Jud's preferred water.

As he pulled the Willys into a spot he had parked a thousand times, a shaded spot near the ruins of an older lumber mill known as Second Meadow Mill, Martha was ecstatic. "Oh, this is perfect, look at the wildflowers." She was out of the car and smelling the air. Annie joined her and gave two requisite barks, securing the area from any possible vermin. Then, being a retriever, she promptly picked up a stick and dropped it at Martha's feet, and before Jud had a chance to stop it Martha had tossed Annie's stick right into the pool he always fished first, his favorite pool, the Morning Pool in Second Meadow. Now there was seventy pounds of Labrador swimming through it. The trout would not rise there again until October. Normally that kind of thing could spoil the better part of a man's day. But not today because hearing Martha's laughter was better than fishing.

The day drifted past. Jud would fish for a while then they would talk for a while. They returned to the Willys and had sandwiches, a bottle of white wine, more apple pie included. Then after a skinny dip, when the talk returned to the activities from the night before, the passion was rejoined on a blanket in the shade.

Two hours later, with Martha and Annie off to inspect the ruins of the old mill, Jud was alone and fishing the ancestral waters, water flowing from one undercut bank to the next, with seven fair-sized rainbows landed and released since lunch. Full from a second piece of pie, glowing slightly from the wine, still dining intermittently on yesterday's win against Reynolds, and smiling from time well spent on a blanket, Jud waded quietly on to the next bend, one of his favorite bends in the meadow, and with it came a sudden hatch of mayflies. But only one trout was rising to take them . . . luckily it was a large trout, larger than anything landed all day and by pounds.

Clouds had been building steadily, and shadow and light had sailed mountain and meadow all afternoon. Now the valley was all in shadow.

~

The black feathered edges of rainfall spread over the southern sky. The wind, which had been gentle all day, was coming in strong gusts followed by long calms in which he could cast. Martha and Annie reappeared out of the willows just as Jud was about to send his dry-fly offering to the fish.

The trout, a large rainbow, was feeding just ahead of what Jud called cauldron water, roiling water returning from the undercut banks to the stream in tremendous boils, and these mismatched currents made it a difficult cast to gauge. The fly had only a second or more to drift before his line would be swept away and under. This, of course, made the fish all the more enticing, all the more prizeworthy, and nothing pleased Jud more than a large, problematic rainbow. Another strong rush of wind. Waiting for the calm, he finally made another cast and a rainbow took his line, but it was far from the fish he was trying for, proportionately and geographically. A five-inch brook trout had taken his Adams at the very end of its drift, fifteen feet away from his trout, which was no longer feeding since all the mayflies were gone on the wind.

Martha and Annie were now standing on the bank just behind him and as Jud released his fish Martha was going to say something rude about the size of his catch, but the wind was up again and this time it was not another gust. This time it was the storm, and with it came the rain. In one more halfhearted attempt Jud rolled a cast to where his trout had been rising, the spot he had sent his fly a dozen times before, but this time his fly, bewitched by currents and tailwinds, drifted slowly over the once feeding rainbow; slowly enough to make him feed once more. As he was turning to find Martha he saw the rainbow take from the corner of his eye. Surprised, he was late to strike, and when he did it was with a very slack line. But the rainbow still got a taste of the hook and took to the air in one high leap, twisting silver against a gray day. Rolling midair, the great trout spit the fly and hit the water free. Jud laughed at the ridiculousness of the whole thing but also regretted that he hadn't been paying attention—it was a very large rainbow. Looking back to Martha,

~

he realized she had missed the brief battle. In fact Martha and Annie were on the run and halfway to the Willys. Jud ran after her.

Wiping the water from her face Martha was laughing as Jud plopped down behind the wheel, closed the door, bumped the jeep into neutral, and turned the key in one fluid motion. Not soaking wet but wet, Jud spit rainwater from his lips with the first few words, "You missed it."

"Missed what?"

"The biggest fish of the day," Jud answered, turning onto the road. "Just as you turned away this giant rainbow ate my fly."

"Is this a fish story?"

"No, really. I had started to climb out of the creek and I flipped one more cast and damn if he didn't take it. A fish in the four-pound category, mind you. Twice as big as anything I caught all day."

"Naturally. To what advantage is it to lie about missing a small fish?"

"I promise you," Jud laughed, knowing that he was up against not only Martha's doubt but the skepticism of the ages—an almost inherent mistrust of fishermen and their tales. A fisherman, telling of his catch, is automatically portrayed as a liar, because it is known with a certainty that there is no other kind of fisherman. Jud was also up against her highly qualified smirk, a Myrna Loy smirk, and against the mocking indulgence on a beautiful face there is no defense. "Honest." Jud decided to try once more even though it was clear he was losing. "I was looking over to find you and he took the fly. Jumped four feet out of the water."

She slid across the seat and kissed his ear. "Jud, you know you don't have to lie to impress me," she cooed. The patronization lying in the back of her throat formed a slight vibrato.

"If I'm lyin', I'm dyin'," he quoted from his boyhood.

"Gee, a one-that-got-away story and we hardly know each other."

Jud sat there a minute then looked over to her and shifted into third. "No, I think when my lifetime is tallied, *you* will be the one that got away."

"That was a sweet thing to say." Jud's eyes had returned to the road and the ruts ahead of him, so he didn't notice the tears form in her eyes. She wiped them away, then shivered. "It's cold."

Jud pulled the knobs for the heater. "Takes a while for her to warm up but she gets there."

The drive home offered almost every weather—heavy winds, rain, sleet, distant thunder, and finally hail. As they rolled into Travers the streets and yards were as white as winter. At the Boat Works, Annie was the first one out of the Willys and rolling in the hailstones. Martha went inside to check her messages, pages, e-mails, and she needed to make several calls. Jud fed Annie then grabbed an armload of split logs. Last night's fire had been romantic; tonight's fire would be a necessity.

But tonight it was Annie who was stretched out in front of the fire. Jud, with Martha curled up on his lap, was sitting in the one and only overstuffed chair up in the observatory, the old belfry. They sat watching the storm pass, leaving behind slate-colored clouds now parading past a half-moon, stars in every opening.

"If I live to be a hundred, these last few days will still be a memory. Carrie Creek was so beautiful. I can only begin to understand why the place is so special to you. And lucky you, you can visit Second Meadow whenever you wish."

"Well, you're welcome back anytime. I wouldn't mind it much if you stayed another week or another few months or so. Fall. You should by all means stay for the fall."

Martha laughed. "I wish." She reached over and held his hand. "I really *do* wish. Someday I hope to call my life my own. But not now. According to the last e-mail, I'm leaving for Hong Kong on Thursday."

"I've never been to Hong Kong. I'm sure it's fine and all, but my best guess tells me that Carrie Creek in the fall is better," Jud smiled.

"I wish changes in my life were as simple as snapping my fingers, but the truth is I'm up to my neck in my work, and there's no way out."

Jud fell silent for a moment, staring into the darkness; looking at his life in Travers as a life and a place from which he would never wish to escape, and, at the moment, feeling sorry for Martha—the beautiful rich woman with wit and charm trapped in a corporation. She was the kind of woman men fell in love with at a distance, and Jud had known her as close as man and woman can get. But Jud, older and wiser with each romance, recognized the impossibility of a relationship: a boatbuilder and guide from Montana wouldn't make it a minute in Manhattan, and a Wall Street CEO wouldn't last long in Travers.

The wine finished, they went downstairs to find the fire a bed of embers and Annie still curled where they had left her. Jud threw on more logs. Martha took a bath. Jud scrubbed her back. They talked about dinner but never got around to it. In the morning Martha was gone.

That afternoon Jud was at the ball field shutting the diamond down until next spring—digging up home plate, covering the scoreboard, boarding up the concession stand. Most years Sal was there to help him but this time he was shorthanded at the bar. Jud was in the strangest mood. He wasn't lonely. He wasn't sad. He was smiling, though he was sure he wasn't happy. When all was winterized he walked over to his great-grandfather's memorial and stood there watching the river flow. Looking at the names on the marker without reading them, he laughed at the modern problems of love—the difficulties in finding the right other, the perfect one, the hardships, the hazards of maintaining a relationship in a comfortable and convenient world. Traver and Carrie only carved out a life in the wilderness, survived winters, survived true hardships yet stayed together, and as the journals tell us happily, for fifty years.

On the road, Martha was thinking only of Jud. Jud was as fine a man as she had met in a long time. Ships in the night. She was already alone and she was crying. Her cell phone rang. Next stop Hong Kong.

Jud drove to the Boat Works glad not to have seen a soul, but tomorrow at the Tin Cup Sarah and Dolores would be wanting to know who the blonde was and where he'd been the last few days. Henry would want to know that and a whole lot more.

It was Monday, not a Fats Domino "Blue Monday," and even though

It Ain't Over till the Fat Man Sings

～

the Fat Man's bluesy rhythms were playing in his heart, Jud found himself feeling pretty good. The win over Reynolds helped a great deal. He would get Christmas cards from Martha even after she married, and he would never go to Second Meadow again without thinking of her.

Though we're apart you bother me still . . .
for you were my thrill at Second Meadow Mill.

From The Journals of Traver C. Clark

October 14, 1918—

Had a long talk with Johnny One Pony today. What a life he has led. Once a warrior, now the head wrangler on the Mohler Ranch on land his forefathers hunted. Johnny stands apart from his tribe, his reservation, as he stands apart from most men. I went to Harvard, and have traveled to Europe, and I consider myself a well-read man. But I know next to nothing when standing near Johnny. He is intuitive—a Blackfoot perspective—Indian logic. He understands anything and everything and when studying something he seems to somehow see through whatever it is to a simple and ingenious solution, while all the white men in town seem to stumble all around and only complicate things.

I wonder how many other great Indian minds are being wasted because of our bigotry.

Invisible

IT WAS A cool kind of an evening that invited a stroll. A chance to saunter along and take the evening air. A chance to finally be enjoying the day rather than merely enduring it. Of course, Jud's normal gait was no more than a stroll, so the people of Travers Corners who saw him coming never knew if he was just out for a lazy walk around town, or if he was running late.

He'd spent the afternoon hand-pegging the decking. It was hard work, and he had a few more days of it ahead. The two hottest days of the summer had made it even more difficult. There were more modern, and certainly easier ways of doing the decking than the way they had done it one hundred years ago, but he liked incorporating some of the old ways. He liked the time-honored approach to his work, and whenever he could craft a dory by hand he did so.

Naturally, as you might expect from a man so steeped in tradition, Jud had chosen his usual route for the evening's amble: down the hill from the Boat Works, across the bridge on Carrie Creek, then on into town. He loved his summertime constitutionals, and though this path was repetitive, it was the routine he enjoyed. Jud was most comfortable with the familiar.

He passed the Millers' house, the Boardmans', the Allens'—the first three houses on the outskirts of town. Jim and Mary Boardman, both now retired, were predictably in their garden. They were forever pruning, mowing, edging, digging, planting, or clipping something in their yard during the long summer evenings. Jud waved. Mary waved back, but Jim was oblivious. He was lost on the shaping of a shrub at the corner of their house; hesitating and worried over what must have been a precision trim. Jud smiled, thinking, *Ya ain't cutting diamonds there, Jim. Let 'er go. Go with your cut instinct. Prune it, ol' timer.* The old man finally snipped the critical branch, then stepped back smiling at his work just as Jud disappeared behind the windbreak of the Allens' lilacs and Russian olives.

It was this particular stretch of his walk and the next half mile that he treasured most. It was where the Hourglass Ranch narrowed as it crossed the highway—the waistline. The Hourglass (so named by one of the original homesteaders, Hezikiah McHale, because of the shape of its fence lines) was at one time one of the largest ranches in the Elkheart. The top half of the Hourglass, off to Jud's left as he strolled along the two-lane, fanned out into expansive holdings on the East Bench ending where the forested slopes of the Elkheart Range began. On his right the bottom half of the Hourglass became open meadows, hay fields, willow thickets, and finally cottonwoods down to the river.

The grasslands of the bench were bleached nearly white, but now appeared almost a deep gold in the last light of day. He watched irrigators move through the lower fields carrying the long water pipes that flashed as they caught the sun. He heard the hum of distant engines, but there wasn't a car on the road. The blackbirds were balancing on the cattails and singing as the first shadows of sunset crept across the highway. And although tired and a little stiff—the cedar doesn't bend as easily when you're fifty—Jud was relaxed and comfortable; taking solace in the fact that everything was as it should be, and all things were in their place.

The long brick wall of McCracken's General Store was still in sunlight,

⌒

that last beacon, that final color-drenched ray shining in just before the sun calls it a day. It was only in this light that you could best see the faded outlines of the Coca-Cola girl.

He remembered her as a boy when her colors were bright. When her long blond hair cascaded back as she tilted her bottle of Coke toward her laughing smile. She used to lean back against a brilliant red ball on which COCA-COLA was scripted in white letters. She wore a blue top and a white pair of shorts, and her long legs stretched out nearly the full length of the building. So joyous was she in that moment, that "pause that refreshes," that ecstatic first sip that one of her legs was kicking up slightly. There are few things clearer than a boyhood memory.

It was only at this time of evening that you could best see the outlined remains of the faded mural. Forty years of exposure to Montana's elements saw to that. If you knew how she looked in 1956, when Miss Coca-Cola was brand new and beautiful, you could make out her vestiges: traces of her long hair, part of her hand still there, and a little of the neck on the bottle. All that was left of her long shapely limbs was part of a thigh and the foot of the kicking leg. The white lettering was long gone, but the bright red ball was still there—now no brighter than the bricks.

As a boy, Jud remembered, that big red ball was the first thing he used to see coming into Travers. He and Henry used to watch it slowly come into view on those summer afternoons as they bicycled back from fishing out on Miller's Bend. They knew once the red ball was visible, it would be about another ten minutes of hard and hot pedaling, as this last mile into town was slightly uphill. Soon they would be at McCracken's lifting the lid of the Coke machine and dropping in their nickels.

They usually had a mess of trout dangling from their handlebars. Long cane poles were taped to the frames of their bikes and hung out far behind them. It was on a hot day like this one that Jud and Henry first saw Jed Thomas . . .

* * *

"Hey, Jud, I'll race ya to McCracken's. Coke's on the loser," Henry shouted as he stood hard on his pedal trying to get the advantage.

"I'm not racing nowhere. It's gotta be a zillion degrees out here and you wanna race—uphill?"

"Okay. Okay," Henry agreed. He settled back in his seat and they pedaled steadily on. Henry wanted the race because he normally won. He was parched beyond measure, and he didn't have a nickel to his name.

They didn't talk. The June heat and the uphill grade took away any extra wind they had for conversation. The letters on the red ball became readable as they crested the incline and the best part of the ride—two hundred yards of downhill on into town. They each gave a few hard pumps, causing their trout to sway from side to side, then they let gravity take over. Coasting and laughing, they came sailing into town. They didn't notice the stranger until they were nearly upon him.

Sitting on his briefcase, directly below the red ball, sat a man in a suit, a white shirt, and a tie. A city hat was cocked back on his head. He was carving on a piece of wood. Now, a stranger in town was always worth a look, especially a stranger in a suit and tie. But a black man sitting right there beside McCracken's, sitting right where the bus had left him, a black man in downtown Travers Corners—well, that was worth, and it received, a stare. As the boys rolled past him, Henry in his amazement crossed tires with Jud, and nearly knocked him from his Schwinn.

The man was sitting in the shade exactly where they usually parked their bikes, so they leaned them a little farther down the wall. The man looked up from his whittling and said, "Nice mess of fish you fellers gots there. You catch 'em on worms, did ya?"

At age ten, Henry, to that very moment, had never seen a black man, except on TV, and now he was not only seeing one, he was about to talk to one. But his mouth froze.

"Yep," Jud answered, and he and Henry walked by the man. Jud had seen black people while on vacation in San Francisco with his parents when he was seven, and he saw two in Missoula once.

"Where did you catch 'em?" the man asked, then blew the shavings from his whittling.

"Down on the river. Down on Miller's Bend," Jud answered.

"Well, them sure are some fine-lookin' trout, now. I plan on catchin' me a few sometime soon." The man went back to his whittling.

The boys went inside. The Coke machine stood in the corner of the general store between the front door and a window looking out onto the street. Jud loaned Henry the needed nickel and they dropped their coins into the slot and cranked the handle in front, which set about a series of loud clanking and thumping noises that finally produced their Cokes through a metal flap. The bottles, as always, were ice cold. Jud held his to his forehead while Henry pressed himself against the coolness of the machine. Then they went back to the window to watch the black stranger who would, now and then, take time out from his carving to look up and down Main Street.

"What do ya think he's doing here?" Henry asked. Jud shook his head.

Two young cowboys came into the store and old man McCracken hollered from the warehouse where he was stacking sacks of flour. "Hey, you fellers, I'm back here. What can I do for ya?"

They walked past the two boys as if they weren't there, craning their necks to take another look at the man sitting on his briefcase. "I don't know who he is, Vern," Jud could hear one of them saying to the other. "Are you expectin' any visits from one o' yer relatives?" Both the cowboys laughed. Jud kept watching them as they walked back to the storeroom until he felt Henry tugging on his sleeve. Out front John Rosso had just pulled up in his brand-new station wagon.

John worked as a real estate salesman when he wasn't hiring out as a ranch hand. He had distinguished himself in real estate by being the only Realtor in Travers Corners and by having the name of his company, Elkheart Realty, painted on the driver's side door. The two-tone red-and-white Mercury, which was also his office, had set him back more than he'd imagined, and he couldn't afford to paint his sign on the other side of the station wagon—so he was careful which way he pulled into McCracken's.

The way John got out of his car told the boys that he was late for an appointment. Ordinarily John didn't move very fast, but the car had barely rolled to a stop before his short, stocky body was out the door. Tucking in his shirt and smoothing down what was left of his hair, he quickly looked around. He noticed the stranger sitting on a suitcase, and the anomaly of a black man in Travers did slow his search down long enough for a double take, but then he was back furtively looking for whoever it was he was supposed to meet. His eyes took him up and down Main Street and other than a few trucks parked out in front of the Tin Cup Cafe there was nothing going on in town. Checking his watch, he headed for the general store. But he was stopped short by the stranger, who was lifting himself slowly from his luggage and calling John Rosso's name.

The man walked over to where the Realtor had been frozen in his tracks. John awkwardly shook the man's hand. Jud and Henry were on the other side of a dusty window and forty feet away, but they could see John turn pale. The two men talked briefly. John opened the tailgate and the man loaded his suitcase. They looked over a few pieces of paper. Then John Rosso and the black man climbed into the Mercury and drove away.

By dinnertime of the following day there wasn't a conscious soul in the Elkheart who hadn't heard the news, that a fellow named Jed Thomas had bought the old Halloch place, and that Jed Thomas was a Negro.

The next morning in the conference room at the bank an emergency meeting took place among Mayor Hearn, the mayor's wife, the town council, some neighboring ranchers, a few busybodies, John Rosso, and a couple of very anxious bigots. The purpose of the meeting was to get an explanation from the real estate agent who had made it all happen.

"Listen, it's like I already told you," John Rosso answered from his chair, which was centered in the middle of the conference room at the

Elkheart Valley Bank, "I didn't know the guy was colored. Everything was done by mail. I received a letter of inquiry from this guy, this Jed Thomas. He was from Virginia. He was looking for something to buy. The only land I had that would fit into his price range was the old Halloch place. One hundred and forty-nine acres with a house and barn. It does have a good stand of fir and a good-sized spring."

"Tell us why again," asked the mayor, who was outwardly confused, "why didn't Halloch just sell it to the Hourglass. I mean it pretty much surrounds the place."

"Yeah, except old man Halloch hated the McHales. Something between him and Hezikiah that went way back. He said he would never sell to him no matter what he offered. And he didn't."

"Didn't you never talk to this Thomas on the phone," one of the anxious bigots asked from the back of the room. "I means dey does talk different from us'n." He said it as Amos might have said it to Andy. Everyone in the room laughed. Well, nearly everyone.

"No, I didn't talk to him once. All the title searches, the deed, the escrow, the money, everything was handled in the mail."

"We got a leg to stand on here, Ben?" the mayor asked of Ben Wilkens.

"Everything has been recorded in due process. The land is legally his and that is that." Ben answered rather quickly for a lawyer.

"What did he pay for that land?" asked the mayor.

"Fifty-two thousand dollars," John Rosso answered. "Cash."

A murmur passed through the crowd mixed with some laughter. Everyone gathered knew that fifty-two thousand was way too much. It was a house and barn with 149 acres—granted. But the house was no more than a old trapper's cabin that was about to fall down and the barn wasn't much better. There were no more than twenty acres of tillable ground while the rest of the Halloch place was pretty much straight up and rocky. True, there was a pretty good-sized spring on the place, and the timber would be worth quite a bit. But by even the roughest calculations, benchland going for a hundred dollars an acre, the house and barn worth next to nothing, and the stand of trees valued at perhaps twenty thousand, Jed Thomas had paid double what it was worth.

One of the bigots from the back was heard saying, "Now that figures. About the only person dumb enough to pay that kind of money for the Halloch place would have to be a ni—"

A rear door swung open. Noah McHale was now at the meeting. His presence drew the sort of attention that the wealthiest man and one of the largest landowners in the Elkheart might. Most of those assembled liked Noah. Some in the room didn't, but that was mostly envy. But no one in the room would dispute that Noah was the hardest-working and most fair-minded man in the room.

"Morning, Noah." The mayor stood. "We were just discussing the—"

"I know the purpose of this meeting," Noah said, removing his hat. He was thinking how strange it all was that everyone in the room, and up and down the valley, were meeting the news of Jed Thomas's arrival with so much concern when in fact, it was he and he alone who was directly affected.

Noah openly addressed those gathered. "Now, I can't for the life of me figure out why a Negro would bring himself to this country and buy himself a place. One would think such a move would make even less sense to the Negro—this Jed Thomas. I mean, there isn't any of his kind here. Hell, I don't think there are more than a couple of other colored folks in the whole state of Montana. But he's here now. He owns his land. And that sums it up.

"I share a fence line with the man, but I don't plan on sharing anything else. And not because he is colored, mind you, but because of the way he snuck in here. A man ought to own up to who he is and what he's up to. That's all I've got to say. Now, if you'll excuse me, I've got some cattle to move." Walking to the door, he pulled on his crusty and torn hat. He didn't say another word. He didn't look back. He did nod to one of the ranchers standing by the door. Crawling up onto the seat of his pickup, Noah was moving slower these days; arthritis had settled in through his hips, the result of being crushed by a bull in his rodeo years, his younger and crazier days after college.

"People gathered in the middle of the day and accomplishing nothing. Flapping their gums. Getting all lathered up about something they can't do a thing about. Don't they have work to do?" Noah mumbled as he backed away from the bank. Shaking his head and looking at his watch. He felt as though the morning was wasted. He wouldn't have come at all if the mayor hadn't been so insistent. Shifting gears, he headed for the Hourglass.

One of the bigots from the back used the sound bite from Noah: "I think McHale is right about one thing, *those* folks are sneaky." This triggered a wave of prejudiced murmuring, and racial stereotypes went around the room in whispers: worries about the safety of the local women, real estate values, concern that more of *them* could be on their way.

"Gentlemen, gentlemen." The mayor raised his hands and the din died down. "John, is there anything else you can tell us about this man? What does he plan on doing for a livelihood? A man's gotta know more about the fat hog he just cut than you do." The room laughed.

"Now, I am telling you"—John was getting a little worked up about cracks going around the room about his sale—"I worked hard for that deal. I mean I really did. That Thomas fella wanted to know everything there was to know about that place. I had to take pictures of the foundations. I had to remeasure the boundaries. I had to have soil samples taken. I had to have the water tested. I had to count every tree on the place. I must have sent over thirty letters back and forth to this man— and about ten rolls of pictures.

"But I don't know any more about him than that. I mean, I asked him what he was gonna to do on the place and he said he was gonna fix it up and that was the only plans he had." Then he added, "Well, there is one more thing. When I drove him up out there, two big truck and trailer rigs were there waiting for us. I never saw what was in the trucks."

"I know something about Jed Thomas," Edgar McCracken stepped forward. This was not the kind of meeting he would normally attend, but he had something to say. I've only dealt with him a few times. His orders all come by mail. Yesterday, he ordered eleven hundred dollars worth of tools and materials and a few appliances. He wanted everything delivered. In fact I'm going out there later today with the first delivery. He doesn't own a car and said he probably wouldn't for some time to come. And he asked me if I wouldn't mind delivering everything he'd be needing. I also know that he has purchased two draft horses from Deer Lodge, and he just bought a used tractor from someone over in Missoula.

"I know nothing else—but if his purchases are any sign of his character, well, this man intends to work."

"How do you know he's good for all this?" asked the mayor.

"He refused credit and he wants everything sent C.O.D. And I have one more thing to add. Jed Thomas seems like a real gentleman, and I think we owe him the same respect we would pay any of our neighbors."

John Rosso had to agree. "The man is real polite and real friendly. I think Edgar is right."

"Well, that's a fine and very understandable sentiment coming from a couple of guys who have made thousands off this man. I don't care if this Thomas has money or not. I don't care what Edgar McCracken thinks of this man's character. He don't know nothin' about nigras," Bobby Lee drawled and stepped from the back of the gathering. "I was born and raised with these people. They don't have no character and they're a threat to the community," he continued from his piglike mouth. "They ain't got any morals."

Edgar walked slowly to the center of the room so he could better his view of Bobby Lee. Though he couldn't see him at first, Edgar knew for certain it was Bobby Lee who had said it. Just as he knew for certain how much Bobby Lee hated him since his credit at the general store had been cut off.

"Well, if character were money, Bobby Lee, you would live as a pauper," Edgar said. The two men glared at one another. Hating each other for what they were in one another's eyes: a high-tone, churchgoing, liberal do-gooder extending a phony helping hand to a common nigra; and a moronic, fat racist of KKK caliber who wasn't worth his salt. Edgar McCracken then made his way through the meeting. His pulse was racing and his neck was visibly red. He'd come to have his say. He'd said it. Now there were prescriptions to fill and he made his way to the door.

The meeting adjourned in a mumble of disgruntled, concerned, and sympathetic voices. Within seconds the minutes of the meeting were distributed, via gossip, around Travers Corners.

That evening the lights of the old Halloch Ranch could once again be seen from the main ranch house on the Hourglass, a fact that had a disquieting effect on the general mood of Noah McHale. The Halloch place had stood empty for more than four years and he'd grown used to not having to look at it at night. Now the lamps were lit once more, but now they belonged to a black man.

Noah owned, in the shape of an hourglass, from tree line to town and then on to the river, twenty-five thousand acres. But he didn't own one quarter-section that sat right at the very top of the Hourglass. He'd wanted that land his entire lifetime. Now he'd never get it, and all because of some water dispute fifty years ago between Grandfather Hezikiah and old man Halloch.

Grabbing the daily paper, he left the kitchen grumbling while looking up the hill once more to Jed Thomas's lights. He then walked to the living room and eased his long angular frame, bent by work, down into his overstuffed leather chair looking out over the Elkheart River Valley. From there, as was his way every evening, he could read the paper and look out over more comforting lights, the white lights, the distant glow of Travers Corners. It was a window onto a beautiful world: the valley, the distant mountains, the sunsets, and miles of Carrie Creek, shadowed by aspens, meandering and tumbling for the river. It was a sight he had shared with Emily for twenty-four years until the cancer took her six years ago. He'd been alone since Emily's death, sharing the view with no one. Now he was sharing it with a Negro. He snapped the paper open.

Noah read, but not a word of it was registering. Dropping the paper every once in a while without realizing it, Noah would stare out the window without seeing a thing. His mind was that filled with the events of the morning. There was one thing he'd said at the meeting that troubled him over and over again—when he told the mayor and the rest that he didn't care about this Thomas being colored, and how the only thing bothering him was the way he stole into the valley without telling anyone what or who he was. That was a lie.

Noah had dedicated his life to doing the right thing, being honest and God fearing, and a lie just wasn't in his nature. But contrary to what he'd said at the bank this morning, he did hold a prejudice for Jed Thomas and colored people and it wasn't a bias based on any personal experiences, for he had never even talked to a black man for more than a minute in his whole life. It wasn't a hatred for Negroes with Noah as much as it was mistrust. For his grandfather, Hezikiah, and his father, Liam, it was hatred.

Hezikiah's rancor was born in the South where he had been raised, where he had fought for the Confederacy, and where he had lost his right arm at Antietam. His bigotry was deep-seated and bigotry being a characteristic that is passed along just as assuredly as a dominant gene and the family jewels, it was a part of his legacy. As his cattle, his deeds, and the Hourglass were handed down to Liam, then on to Noah, so was Hezikiah's hatred.

But Noah never thought in terms of hatred. He was too right-minded to hate someone based on skin color. He always referred to them as Negroes or colored and nothing derogatory. He just disliked what he'd been taught by two generations: that they were lazy and they couldn't be trusted, and if there were two things in this life that Noah could not tolerate, it was laziness and dishonesty. His life had always revolved around hard and honest work.

Eventually, as was Noah's custom, his glasses slipped down his nose as his head drooped to one side, and the paper fell to the floor. He would awaken at ten and go to bed. He would be up at five.

Everyone in Travers Corners was preparing for their first meeting with Jed, figuring, like everyone else, they would have to run into this Jed Thomas somewhere along the line. Certainly he would have to come into town now and then for the things everyone had to come to town for—but they were wrong. They didn't see him those first few weeks. They didn't see him the first few months, and when a year had passed, still no one had seen him—save Edgar McCracken. For everything, without exception, that Jed Thomas needed, Edgar personally delivered to his cabin. He was paid fairly for the service, it being thirty miles out there and back.

People around Travers were eager to know what the black man was up to, and though Edgar drove out there at least twice a week with the mail, groceries, and supplies, he could tell no one what was going on because he didn't have a clue. All he knew was that the man paid for every delivery—cash on the barrelhead—and that everything he'd ordered was figured out right down to the last screw and nail.

He could report as well that the cabin, now being referred to around town by some as "Uncle Thomas's Cabin," was still very much in need of repair. Not a bit of work had been done to it. Jed had cleaned up the yard. A few of the trees had been chopped down. Some necessary work had been done to the barn, but nothing much more extensive than a new roof. All Edgar could tell anyone was, "Everything that's going on at the Thomas place is going on inside the barn. When I ask him what he's doing in there, he just says he's fixing the place up a little."

Even Sue Stillings, who ran the switchboard in Travers Corners and

~

was able to listen in on any phone conversation up and down the Elkheart, and usually did, was of no help. Jed had no phone.

On May 29 Noah saddled up and rode the fence lines. He'd done this with his father, as his father had done it with Hezikiah. It was an Hourglass tradition. "On May twenty-nine, you ride the fence line," they would say. He and Emily had but one child, Susan, now a woman who had no love for ranch life. She lived in Phoenix with her husband. So Noah rode the boundaries alone. It took him two days. He'd ride the top half of the Hourglass back to the house one day, and the bottom half the next. He would make minor repairs himself, and mark those places where more serious work was needed.

The only sounds heard that first morning were mule deer crashing through the underbrush, the bawling of distant cattle, his horse's hooves, and the creak of the saddle. Now and again Noah would ride over to a familiar pool on Carrie Creek and see if the trout were feeding.

The fence lines, other than minor repairs, were in good shape until he came to the top of the Hourglass, where his property shared fence with Jed Thomas. A line that came within a few hundred yards of Jed's cabin. There, a couple of posts were down, and the wire was lying flat. He made a quick repair with branches and rocks, but it gave him ample time to evaluate any progress made by his neighbor.

Sure enough, all the junk had been cleared away, and there was a new roof on the barn just as Edgar had reported, but other than that nothing else seemed to have been done. The cabin was the same as old man Halloch had left it—about to fall down. Nearly a year on the place and this man had finished about three weeks' worth of work. Shiftless and lazy—*their* reputation held. Noah rode on.

Two cattle came up missing on the next head count, and it often crossed his mind if there wasn't some connection between the downed fence by Thomas's cabin and the two rustled heifers. He wondered if maybe Mr. Thomas wasn't dining on Hourglass beef. Another two months passed.

~

It was in the middle of July, on a Sunday, shortly after five, and Noah was in the kitchen about to have his first cup of coffee. It was just getting light. The phone rang. "Good mo—er—hem—ning," he said. His voice was still gravelly from sleep, and his answer was froggy and partly missing, so he repeated himself. "Good morning."

"Mr. McHale?"

"Yeah."

"This is your neighbor, Jed Thomas."

"Uh, well . . . er . . . Mr. Thomas." The surprise of the phone call made him spill his coffee.

"I was wonderin' if maybe you could come down and sees me sometime today. I been workin' on this old cabin lately and I found somethin' the other day that I thinks you might be interested in."

"Well, I . . . er . . . guess I can. I was going to town anyway a little later. How would eleven o'clock be?"

"That would be fine. Ummm, Mr. McHale?"

"Yes."

"Is the sound of the phone good? Is it workin' fine?"

"Just like regular, I guess. Sure. Why?"

"I just had the thing installed two days ago. You're the first person I called. Just wanted to make sure I gets my money's worth. Never had a phone before."

"Oh."

"I'll see you around eleven."

"Eleven o'clock sharp. Good-bye, Mr. Thomas." More than a year on the Halloch place without ever seeing or hearing from the man, and now from out of nowhere he was inviting him down. Pouring another cup of coffee, he reminded himself to be careful with these people. You never knew what they were up to.

At eleven o'clock Noah, being a man of his word on every level and never having been late to an appointment in his life, drove onto Jed Thomas's land. But this time the log cabin, which was just two rooms and a bath, was in the full throes of remodeling. There were saw horses and tools about. New windows and doors, still in their crates, were stacked in the shade of a giant willow. The logs had been rechinked. New foundations had been poured. A new roof was in place. "Well," Noah said aloud, even though he was riding alone, "it looks like he's slow but sure." He'd been told that these people were slow. "Just think, in another five months or so he just might have another window or two in. Hell, a place that size could be done in two months by a fair hand. Anyway, he should have tore it down and just started over again."

Swinging his truck around to the front of the house and rolling to a stop, he looked down on a new-mowed lawn. Surprisingly, flowers grew along a stone walkway. A large corn patch and a garden were planted on the other side of the cabin. He climbed down from the pickup.

In the doorway, holding a tattered screen door open, stood Jed Thomas, and though he'd been his neighbor for a year, Noah had never laid eyes on him. Smiling like he was glad to see him, with his hand outstretched, Jed said, "Welcome to my home, Mr. McHale."

"Er . . . ah . . . thank you," Noah said, walking up and shaking his hand. It was the first time he had ever touched a black person, and it sort of unnerved him. He became very businesslike, as he had always done when he wasn't sure what to say. "So, you have something for me to see?"

The gray hair around Jed's temples told him that this man might be as old as he was. Noah really hadn't given any thought to the man's age, and for no reason, he'd imagined him to be much younger. He was slim, seemingly fit, and of medium height. He was dressed in bib overalls and a long-sleeved work shirt. A short-billed cap sat on the back of his head. A gold tooth flashed when he smiled, and he hadn't stopped smiling since Noah stepped from the truck.

"Yessir," he said. "But ya gots to come inside to see. Can I get you a cup of coffee?"

"No, thanks."

Noah, following Jed, stepped around tools and a ladder bridging a torn-up floor. Through the hole he could see jacks holding up the joists. They walked into the other room where new pipes and fittings were stacked in one corner waiting to be plumbed, and in the other corner all the new electrical fittings were stored ready to be wired.

"Last month, I was tearin' down this here wall, and stuck inside the wall, and stuck in there purposeful-like, I found a metal box. Inside was a bunch of old letters," and he said it as he took a pipe from one pocket, packed it with tobacco taken from another. He lit the pipe. "I also found this old contract," he said, reaching for a piece of paper inside a toolbox resting on a chair beside him.

"This here is an agreement," he continued, unfolding the papers, "all wrote up and dated on April twenty-second, 1893. What it says is that Hampton and Hezikiah McHale agreed to share the spring. It's signed by Hezikiah, but it ain't signed by Hampton. But the water rights is all recorded in Helena and the water all belonged to Halloch—now it all belongs to me. Now, I'm guessin', but I'm bettin' that somewheres along the line, Halloch cheated your granddaddy out of the water?"

"Well, that's exactly right. And there was bad blood between the Hamptons and us ever after."

"Yep, that's what John Rosso said when I was tryin' to buy this place." He relit his pipe, and fussed with it until it was drawing to his liking. " 'Course, I ain'ts no lawyer, but I did read up on it some. The spring falls under somethin' called decreed water rights and decreed rights are rights written in stone. So what I guess I'm tellin' you, Mr. McHale, is that half that springwater is *rightfully* yours." He took a long puff on his pipe then, slowly regaining his smile, he added, "but *legally*, it's all mine." The two men studied each other for the first time. "I means you can calls a lawyer and has it all checked out, if'n you wants."

"I don't have to call any attorney to know that you're right about decreed water. I've had enough dealings with water rights over the years to know that for certain.

"So that kind of brings us full circle, Mr. Thomas. But something tells me that you didn't call me down here to share in this little historical find of yours, now did ya?" Noah, an old horse trader and a good one, had recognized the gleam in the black man's eye. It was the twinkle of a man looking to effect a trade, looking to make a deal. Trading as many horses as he had, Noah also recognized that the gleam had a smirk to it, that certain glint a man gets in his eyes when he's about to get the better end of a bargain.

Jed knew from his conversations with John Rosso that Noah McHale was a smart businessman, and he'd made a lot of dollars from common sense. He would go about his proposal slowly and surely. "Well, I was wonderin' if me and you might works out ourselves a little trade?"

Noah moved his hat around his head a few times then pulled it down into bargaining position. Jed saw the spark of a man who loves to barter arc across Noah's green eyes; another trait passed along from Hezikiah was his love of dickering. Hezikiah had bargained and traded his way into half the Hourglass's holdings. Jed also noticed the reluctance at the edges of the spark, that glimmer of mistrust he'd seen a thousand times in white men's eyes whenever they were about to do business with a black man.

"What is it that you have in mind?" Noah asked.

"Well, that spring's got more water than I'll ever need. Fact is, that spring has about enough water to irrigate maybe a hundred and fifty acres of land. I want to trades you for that water."

Noah knew the spring to be a good one and had always estimated its irrigation potential slightly higher—closer to two hundred acres. "I'm listening."

"Yessir, I'd like to trades you the water, minus o' course what I'll be needin' for my own personal self. That would be the needs of one man with a big garden—and I'll be needin' some water, not too much now, up in the barn. But that won'ts amount to no more'n a trickle in that stream of water. I'd like to trade you that water for the privilege of goin' fishin' on Carrie Creek anytime I want."

Repeating it like he hadn't understood what he had just heard, Noah asked, "You want to trade me the right to go fishing on my land for water?"

"Yessir."

Noah kind of shook his head like he still hadn't heard quite right. Anyone who wanted to fish the Hourglass could, and for free. All he needed to do was ask. Now this colored man wanted to trade about eight thousand dollars in hay crops for something he could have had for nothing but the asking. "All that water for a little trout fishing. And that's all you want?"

"No, that's not *all* I want, I wants somethin' else."

Here it comes, Noah thought. He had been warned for a lifetime that these people were sneaky and underhanded. He raised his eyebrows and noticeable tones of suspicion crept into his voice when he asked, "And what would that be?"

"Well, of course I'll be wantin' twenty percent of the profits from whatever the land produces." He smiled and the gleam of his gold tooth didn't hold a match to the glow in his dark eyes. "I means I'm all for rightin' any old wrongs, and I do thinks the water should kinda flow back to its rightful owner and all, but I think I should be compensated for my honesty, not to mention my water. I mean, Mrs. Thomas didn't raise any fools." His grin quickly turned into a laugh. Even Noah laughed a little, something he'd never done doing business.

"I tooks the liberty of drawin' up this here little contract," Jed said, handing Noah an envelope. "You has your lawyer look at it. He can put it in fancy writin', as long as it says the same thing—I don't mind. But I think it's pretty straightforward. And I knows that you got a great deal 'cause you'll be gettin' eighty percent return on that land and that's eighty percent more than you woulda ever got."

"All right, I'll give you an answer tomorrow."

"Take yer time. I know, why don't you come down this next Friday?" Jed stopped and thought for a moment. "No, makes it Saturday. You can give me your answer then, but I can't imagine anyone sayin' no."

"Neither can I."

"Anyways, the barn will be finished on Saturday and I would likes to show it to you."

"Okay, I'll stop by Saturday morning. I should be here by . . ."

"Don't makes no difference when you gets here, I'll be here or out in the barn. You come when you like."

Driving away, Noah started smiling and shaking his head. He looked into the rearview mirror to see Jed sitting down on a stump and lighting his pipe. "No wonder this fella hasn't got hardly anything done the last year and a half. Look at him. A thousand things to be done, and there he is sitting down smoking a pipe.

"He was a pleasant enough feller just greeting him, though," Noah conceded, talking to himself as he always did. "Nothing uppity or put on about him. But," he shook his head, "they truly aren't as smart as white folks. Trading the profits of two hundred acres of irrigated land for the right to go fishing. I mean, I like my fishing as well as the next guy, but . . ." He then started to feel unexpected pangs of guilt. Here was a man who had been swindled on the land to begin with, and now all he was asking was 20 percent, when 50 percent was fair. Colored man or no colored man, fair is fair and honest is honest. He would have to offer Jed Thomas more.

Jed looked on as Noah's truck disappeared almost immediately behind a cloud of dust, and he could watch that plume of dust roll from its wheels for miles. He puffed on his pipe. Tears formed in his eyes, joyful tears, and he slapped his knee.

The week passed.

When Saturday morning rolled around Noah could be found at the back of McCracken's General Store loading a brand-new metal gate.

~

"Going on up to Jed Thomas's later today. You know if he needs anything up there?"

"Nope. Just made a delivery up there day before yesterday," Edgar said, helping Noah lift the gate into the back of his truck. "The order was just like one of his regular orders, except this time he ordered up a bottle of the best champagne I could find. I never have delivered any spirits to his house before." Though he knew he had promised Jed not to talk with anyone about what was contained in any of his orders, a promise up to that moment he had kept, Edgar also knew Noah to be tight-lipped about everything. Not that there was anything really peculiar about any of his shipments—fittings mostly, specified hardware. Nothing really out of the ordinary except for some of the large quantities. Since the day after he arrived, Jed had been one of his best customers.

The contents of two shipments did leak to the locals. But these were shipments Edgar had nothing to do with, as they rolled through Travers and were taken directly to Jed Thomas's. One was a semi loaded down with new brick. The other was a delivery of copper, in sheets and rolls. Both came shortly after Jed's arrival. If those two truckers hadn't stopped at the Tin Cup Cafe, then even those shipments would have remained a secret. The drivers innocently divulged the contents of their loads as part of their idle lunch-counter chatter.

"Bricks and copper, now what else is a darkie gonna do with bricks and copper, but build himself a still," Bobby Lee was heard to say late at night from his usual stool at the bar. "I don't know what's wrong with this here town. Everybody's all curious about what this nigra is doin', but nobody goes and looks. But I can tell you for a fact what he's doin' up there, and what he's doin' is makin' moonshine. One thing, and about the only thing I figure that coloreds are good at, and that's moonshinin'.

"I think I just might give Sheriff Johnson a call tomorrow over in Helena. See if he might want to hear about Uncle Thomas's still." This, of course, was Bobby Lee just being boastful to the other ditch drinkers at the rail. Everyone knew he didn't have the energy or the ambition to do much of anything, never had and never would. Bobby Lee, as anyone in Travers would be glad to tell you, didn't have any more gumption than what it takes to buy drinks for his fellow bigots at the bar—bigotry needing company, and hating being no fun if done alone. Bobby Lee would buy himself the needed listeners with money he owed elsewhere and regale them with his experiences with the coloreds in the South, mostly about what a lazy and untrustworthy lot they were.

Bobby Lee was right about one thing—no one in town had gone to Jed's cabin. No one had welcomed Jed Thomas, no one other than Edgar McCracken. Not even the Travers Corners Welcoming Committee sponsored by the Baptist church. Naturally, the Baptists would be the very first to meet new residents, being First Baptists and all. But the church, under the Reverend Mathis, made no effort to greet the newcomer. Normally the Baptists were at the door before the moving van had rolled to a stop, welcoming the new neighbors with a basket of homemade jams and baked goods.

But with Jed Thomas's arrival, the Baptists did nothing. Though it was only whispered, the truth of the matter was that the good Reverend Mathis, the only man to guide the religious right and social conscience in this one church town, was a bigger bigot, albeit a quieter one, than Bobby Lee.

"Hey, Edgar, order me in another one of these gates, will ya?"

"Sure thing, Noah," Edgar said, and he pulled a pad from his apron pocket and wrote it down so as not to forget. Edgar and his wife, Leslie, had invited Jed down to their house several times, but he would always, and very politely, refuse. Leslie did, however, send an apple pie up with one of Edgar's first deliveries.

It was late in the afternoon when Noah drove onto the Thomas place, later in the afternoon than he'd originally intended, but the gate went in a little slower than he had planned. He'd put the gate in alone because he liked working alone. It would have gone much quicker if he'd brought along one of the young hired hands, but he'd gotten so that working with others drove him crazy. Twenty years ago he would have had that post in, the south forty plowed, and had the space to do a little fishing in the same time it took to hang that gate. This was bothering him—getting older and having less time to fish. He never seemed to have the time for fishing anymore. It was contradictory to rational thought not to have time for this pleasurable pastime, but work had always come first.

Jed was walking from the house to the barn when Noah came driving up. Jed was all cleaned up. He was still in bibs, but a brand-new pair. He had on a white silk shirt, a suit coat, and a string tie. He was wearing a bowler. And he was smiling a smile you could hang your wash on.

"What the Sam Hell is he all dressed up for?" Bone-tired from the afternoon's work, Noah was looking forward to getting on home. He'd make his proposal, offer Jed what was right on the water deal, and leave the legal papers for him to sign. "And I gotta look at this guy's barn." He'd promised.

"Hello, Mr. Thomas," Noah greeted, climbing down from his truck. "Sorry to be rolling in here at damn near suppertime, but I've brought the necessary papers. I have made some changes to the initial agreement, but I think they should be to your liking. I had my lawyer draw up a lease that—"

"Uh, excuse me. Mr. McHale, can we please gets to that business in maybe just a few minutes, or somethin'? I want to show you my barn."

"Well, uh . . . sure, I guess," Noah said. Unused to be interrupted by anyone since his wife died, he was slightly taken back. But seeing the barn right away suited him fine. The quicker he looked at whatever there was to look at, the quicker he could go home. Anyway, how much could there be to see in the barn, if the progress on his house was any indication?

"I don't means to rush you, Mr. McHale, but I been workin' my whole life to get to this point, and I don't mean to sound prideful, but I just gotta show my dream-come-true to somebody, or bust. And seein' as how you is my closest neighbor, and my future business partner, I wants to show it to you first."

Noah followed him through the door to the barn, thinking that never in his life, certainly that he could recall at the moment, had he seen a happier man than Jed Thomas. Once inside, Noah looked around and saw why.

The barn was no longer a barn, but a factory. A factory with three floors of machinery and saws linked together by conveyors, trolleys, motorized tracks, catwalks, and landings. Ladders and contraptions zig-zagged everywhere, and everything was made of wood and edged in cop-per, except for the chain powering the conveyors. Giant beams and posts crisscrossed, supporting it all. And suspended on hooks all along the three-story assembly line were pieces of furniture in various stages of construction: table legs, the backs of chairs, the arms of chairs, and all hanging by the dozen.

"What the Sam Hell are ya . . . I mean where did . . . what . . ."Noah was nearly staggered by the complexity and ingenuity of all that sur-rounded him.

Jed opened the giant barn doors and motioned for Noah to follow him outside.

"Ya sees, what I does is I takes the draft horses and I pulls down a tree from my mountain there, and I run the timber through that big milling saw over there, cutting it roughly to the lengths and widths I need. Then I dries it in that kiln," Jed explained, pointing behind Noah. Noah turned to see a long and narrow brick kiln running along the back wall of the barn. "When it dries enough so I can work it, I brings it back in here." Jed led Noah back inside to the middle of the factory's floor. "In here is where I does the final sawin' and millin'. Then the rough cuts is sent along on the track to the different machines for shapin' and squarin'. My saws, routers, the lathes, drill presses, and everythin'. All that copper edgin' is to prevent wear on certain parts. Then it all gets taken to the second floor where I does the finishin' and gluin' then on to the third floor, where it's varnished and sealed."

Through the open stairways and wide landings Noah could follow his tour without having to climb the stairs. "Then the furniture gets dropped by block and tackle into crates out back and it's ready to be shipped. Yessir."

Noah was just bowled over. It was not only remarkable, but it was beautiful because of the copper and wood. Everything was lacquered; everything was in its place and spotless.

"I calls it my one-man mill. And it's all powered by that one small truck engine over there in the corner. Gots somethin' else to shows ya." Jed walked over to the table saw and grabbed a magazine. It was already opened to the right page, and he handed it to Noah. Reaching across Noah's outstretched arm, he pointed to an ad. "Right-hand corner, there ya see. That there is me."

Noah reached into his shirt pocket for his glasses, then read aloud, " 'Jed Thomas—Fine Mountain Furniture. Made in Montana. Available only at Pearson's Home Furnishings.' " He had to hold the page out a little farther, for even with his glasses, the print was too small. " 'Eighteen-fifty-seven East Sixtieth Street, New York, New York.' " The ad pictured a table and chairs of a simple and functional design, almost Shaker style, straight backs and straight lines. Noah looked to the chair in the picture then to the milled pieces hanging above him. "Well, I'll be a . . ."

The closer he looked at how much work had been done, the more he was amazed by this man. Noah had a keen eye for estimating the work and effort it takes in the doing of something, and this was incredible. He asked, taking off his hat, "You did all of this yourself?"

"Every stick, Mr. McHale."

Noah could actually feel his long-held beliefs eroding, and it was an uncomfortable and shaky feeling. Nobody but someone who was damn clever could have masterminded the complexities of all this, and nobody but a hard worker could have accomplished it. Shiftless, lazy, and dull, his preconceived misconceptions, left him at that moment never to return.

Suddenly he was no longer tired. He now, and for the first time, wanted to know more about this man. Noah was impressed, and it took a lot to impress Noah McHale. It was an odd feeling, certainly, after a lifetime of prejudices, but he felt an admiration for this man, albeit a guarded admiration. After all, the man was colored.

"Now on accounts that this here advertisement won't even be out for another week, and I already has orders for three tables and twelve chairs, and on accounts that my one-man mill here, something I've been dreamin' for years, is all done. And on accounts that at moments like this folks usually has some kinda party or something, I think we should have ourselves some kinda toast." Jed walked to a cramped corner of the barn, to a space Noah hadn't really noticed. It was Jed's living quarters: a bed, a refrigerator, a chair, a table, a sink, and a woodstove. He pulled a bottle from the fridge. "I boughts a bottle of champagne, and it would be a privilege if you shared a toast with me."

"Uh, well . . . you bet, I will. Only I don't know if a toast is gonna handle it. I mean, drinking to a feat such as this, and that's what it is—a goddamn feat—might just take the whole bottle," Noah answered, thinking that if Jed would have asked him before showing him the barn, he would have surely refused.

Jed unwound the wire wraps and thumbed the cork until it popped. He poured the champagne into water glasses, and handed one to Noah. "I would likes to make a toast. A toast to my wife, Clara," he said, taking off his bowler. "Without her I never woulda made it here. Without her I woulda never made it anywhere." Tears formed in his eyes. "She worked side by side with me for twenty-two years. She's been dead nearly two years now. All this was her dream, too."

"To Clara, then." Noah raised his glass.

The taste of the champagne took Jed by surprise. He tried another sip, then another. "Hmmm . . . this stuff ain't half bad," and he laughed. "Clara and me used to talk about this here moment all the time. How we was gonna get all gussied up and open ourselves a bottle of champagne, and then we were gonna dance all night."

~

"Well, I'll drink with ya, but don't go asking me to dance with ya."

They both laughed. Jed laughed harder and more tears formed in his eyes.

"I lost Emily—been six years now. Hardest thing I ever been through. Cancer got her. So, I kinda know what you went through."

"I lost my Clara in a fire." With that said their eyes met, and Jed's eyes held Noah's for no more than a second, but in that moment, and in no uncertain terms, Jed told Noah that he had no idea what he went through.

Feeling slightly embarrassed for being emotional, and emotional in front of a white man, Jed straightened himself up and put his bowler hat back on his head. "You know I never has had champagne before. Clara and me didn't allow for no luxuries. Didn't allow for no children, either. For years we worked two and three jobs a day. We took all the work what was given to us. Lived in small mill towns in the hardwood forests of Virginia. On the walls we had pictures of Montana and we had this dream—this dream we is standin' in. A home in the wilderness. We both had this dream, kinda likes a fairy tale, of living high in the mountains, and the wide-open spaces.

"We saved every penny. We were puttin' away every penny, but a black man's wages were less than a third of a white man's. So, the savin' was goin' slow.

"One night a few years before Clara died," Jed started to explain, then gestured for Noah to follow him. They stepped around a lathe and a drill press, and walked to the center of the barn. "Anyways, one evenin', I was goin' on about our wrongful slave wages. Rantin' and ravin' on about how I was worth more than any white men in the mill. I was always goin' on about how I was ten times handier, twenty times a harder worker, and about fifty times better lookin' than any white man anywhere." Noah laughed, for he said all this with his wide smile. "That always made her laugh, too.

"So anyway, I was rantin' and ravin' and Clara told me to stop my spoutin'. She said, 'If you is so handy why don'ts you prove it. Why don't you invent somethin'.' Well, that put a bug in my head, and I started looking aroun' for things in the mill that maybe could be improved on. The first thing I came up with was this thing here." He pointed to a metal swing on the great saw blade. "This is called a Sawyer's Middle Arm. It allows the sawyer to adjust the blade without having to stop the saw.

"Well, that little invention, not exactly the lightbulb, or the telephone, mind you, became a pretty popular item and every sawyer in every mill wanted one. The royalty checks started comin' in, and all of that money went into our savin's. And our savin's is what got me here. But it was all Clara's doin', don't ya see?"

He slapped his pipe against his palm, letting the ashes tumble into the sawdust on the floor. Packing it and relighting it, Jed added, "And the nicest thing about them royalty checks was that they was color-blind and I gots paid just like a white inventor." Noah was fascinated. Jed was wound up a little bit with the champagne, his accomplishment, and the fact that he hadn't talked to anyone at length in more than year.

"I drove mules and skidded lumber. I worked the saws. I spent five life-times in those hellhole mills. I knows the lumber business.

"Then one day I was lookin' at a magazine, and they was advertisin' furniture. 'Send for a catalog. We ship direct,' the ad said. Then it comes to me that the mail-order business, well, it was like the inventing busi-ness. Mail orders, like them royalties, were color-blind.

"We both worked hard and I gots my royalties. And when we had the money we started to shop around. We looked in Idaho and Wyomin' and Montana. This place was just what I was lookin' for. I knows that the folks aroun' here think I am some kinda ol' fool Negro, spending the money I did on this place. Edgar McCracken sort of let that slip one day. But I knew that the money I lost in the buyin' I would more than make up in the timberin'. Ya see, cuttin' down trees from my own personal for-est, I eliminate lots of the middlemens. I is the logger, I is the skidder, and I is the miller. Then I changes my hats and I is Jed Thomas—Furniture

Maker. So I paid, and I figured it pretty close to right, I think, forty percent more than this place is worth to gain about another ninety percent on my cost of goods."

The tour continued with Jed talking of his life in the mill towns. The second glass had gone down and the champagne was having its effects, and while Noah was enjoying listening to the man, he was also feeling tired and his routine was now being interrupted. He wanted a shower, a little supper, and his big easy chair. "Say, listen, I gotta get goin'. I'm gonna leave those papers for you to look at, Mr. Thomas. I couldn't take advantage of you on the that deal of yours, 'cause the going rate for a land and water exchange around here is fifty-fifty. So, that's how I had Ben Wilkins draw them up."

"No sir, Mr. McHale. I only wants the twenty, and I wants my fishin' privileges put down in writin'."

"What?"

"That's the only way I'm gonna sign 'em."

Noah, incredulous, agreed, and together they made the necessary changes. When everything was initialed and signed, Jed asked, "Now when do the terms of this here contract go into effect?"

"Soon as the ink dries."

"Then tomorrow I am goin' fishin', and I am gonna fish all day. On Monday through Friday I'm goin' to get up at eight o'clock. I'm gonna quit at five. And come next Saturday I'm gonna be fishin' again, and that's gonna be me for the rest of the summer, and for the rest of my life. Saturday and Sunday I'm fishin'." The champagne bottle now empty, as was his glass, Jed added, "You know this champagne stuff is pretty good."

"The best fishing is lower down," Noah said as they started walking toward his pickup. "Smaller fish up here. Brook trout, mostly."

"Nope, I's gonna go fishin' right out my back door. Gonna walk down to Carrie Creek and sit down on some big hole and I'm gonna fish and watch the clouds go by. That was another part of me and Clara's dream.

~

Lazin' around on weekends, fishin' and such. Me a-fishin', and Clara tendin' to her garden."

"Well, have it your way. Just know that there are some good-sized rainbows and the odd brown down by my calving sheds. It was a pleasure chatting with you, and thanks for the champagne. And your factory is a true wonder." Then Noah was just tipsy enough to ask something that had been bothering him since Jed came to the valley. "But why were you so darn secretive about coming here, and what you were up to? Everyone in Travers Corners thinks you're making moonshine up here."

Jed laughed, and slapped his knee. "Well, Mr. McHale, I'm about the onliest black man in this white man's Montana. And I knows I was kinda sly, sneakin' into the Elkheart like I did," he said, "but I always find when workin' with Whitey that it's not always best to tip your hand when it's holdin' a promisin' idea. I had my second invention stole from me by a white man—cost Clara and me lots of money and lots of time. Naturally, I fought my case in court—a white man's court. I lost. I means some white folks are okay, now don't go gettin' me wrong, but you has to admit there are some that are pretty damn sneaky." Then he raised his eyebrows and his smile widened into an exaggerated expression summoned to make Noah laugh, and it did.

"I means we wouldn't has to travel far to finds ourselves a crooked white man. No farther than the walls of that old Halloch cabin yonder."

Noah laughed, and shook his head. "One thing for sure, Mr. Thomas. You would have to travel a good deal farther to find a dishonest black man."

Jed laughed even louder at that and relit his pipe.

Noah drove home thinking about Jed Thomas's work and accomplishments; thinking that even though he'd just spent two hours with a colored man, he now knew less about Negroes than his father had taught him. Noah genuinely liked this man and respected him. One thing was set and dead certain in his mind: If Jed Thomas said he was robbed on his invention by a white man and a white judge, then that was the way it happened. Noah prided himself on reading the truth in another man's eyes.

The next morning after a late breakfast Jed, dressed in his hip boots and bibs, with a fishing pole waving over his shoulder and a small bucket full of nightcrawlers swinging in his free hand, went fishing for the first time in twenty-two years. How he had loved it as a boy. Bobbing worms in the backwater ponds, fishing for bass and bream. But what he loved most was fishing for speckled trout as a young man when he was logging in the Appalachian Mountains where he first met Clara.

The air was cool but sure to warm once the sun broke around the southern shoulder of Mount D. Downey. He would be on the creek at that golden moment when first light hits the water, when morning becomes electric, when everything that flies and swims moves to the warmth.

Stepping over the fence that divided his land from the Hourglass, Jed walked out onto the sun-yellowed grassland of the bench. Following no trail, he headed downhill for the trees that lined Carrie Creek. The morning was dead calm, and after he'd covered some ground Jed stopped walking just to hear the silence. He looked back to see that his cabin was hidden by the trees, but the barn could be seen clearly. Below him he could see Noah's house, no more than a dark spot and a roofline off in the distance. Far beyond that, and in full sunlight, lay the town of Travers Corners, no more than odd shapes and unnatural colors amid the muted bands of greens and grays that followed the river. Above him the aspen groves staggered their way to the tree line and the first rock faces of the Elkheart Mountains. He filled his lungs and chills ran the length of him. He was free and at the end of his dream. No longer shackled and slaving in smelly company towns, he was free and standing alone on a windswept plain—standing between his home and one-man mill, and a trout stream within walking distance.

The sun crested D. Downey, and light flooded the benchlands as Jed entered the first grove of trees. The stream was small here and tumbled quickly, spilling over rocks into a beaver pond below him. He accidentally jumped a pair of mallards, and they left the pond in a clatter of quacks and wingbeats sending ripples across the pond's mirrored finish. The white bark of the aspens, their leaves, the sky, the mountains, and Jed Thomas were among the glassed reflections as he settled himself in against a log. He had worked a lifetime and more for this moment.

He looked through his bucket for a promising worm. He baited his hook, adjusted his red-and-white bobber, and slid a small split shot up the line with hands that looked too large for the task. They appeared swollen almost broken, and nearly white where the large round knuckles drew the skin tight. The hands of hard work. He bit the lead into place. With the new pole and reel delivered from McCracken's the week before, he tossed out his first cast, which sent bobber and worm to the middle of the pond. Small rings scurried for the shore. Then the pool was like glass once more. How beautiful the water and all that it mirrored. He thought of Clara.

Watching the clouds go by, Jed set his mind adrift. He wondered. He invented and redesigned, always with one eye on the bobber. He recalled good times and bad moments—things he wished he'd never said, and things he didn't say. Jed had most of the silent conversations a man will have when left to himself, but because he was fishing most of his thoughts were good ones.

The Elkheart Valley and Carrie Creek were heaven on earth. He had made it. This was the day he'd dreamed of. The moment he'd seen with closed eyes a million times.

When the first brookie took his worm, when that bobber dropped from sight, when he could feel the pull of the fish, this was a joy he hadn't felt since he was a young man. The delight of his pole bent, his hand reeling instinctively, his line taut to a fighting trout, washed twenty-two years away. He said a quiet prayer and gave thanks as he brought the trout in and guided it into his hands. The sheer beauty of the fish and the moment brought tears.

But the moment was more than this. While he felt that same giddy rush that he had as a boy, this happiness held so much more. This was the final dream in his and Clara's vision. The very last wish come true. These seconds were the culmination of everything they had lived for, and a pride went through him. A sense of fulfillment he'd never felt before. A wave of elation rolled over him so strongly that he felt short of breath and he gasped for air. A searing loneliness was also felt. If all had gone exactly to their plans, she would be in her flower garden now while he fished.

Whitey had changed their plans.

All of his life he was taught to hate Whitey: taught by his parents, who started their lives as slaves; taught by the neighbors at every turn and corner in the shantytown ghettos in Whitey's lumber towns. He'd known a few good ones, but for the most part Jed hated white people, and not just because of all the prejudice from which he was born, but for their cowardice in not letting the black man have a chance. But there was a quality about this Noah, to Jed's thinking. He was a man of his word. No question. He liked the way the man looked him in the eye and was grateful to have him as a neighbor. Neighbors had been his biggest concern in coming to the Elkheart.

Tears of joy, tears of thanks, tears of loss, but most of all tears of freedom rolled down his rounded cheeks. Some fell into the pond and were lost in the splashes of the struggling fish. Others fell into the corners of his trembling smile. He let the fish go as a symbol of his intentions. Brightly marked of red, black, and white, the trout was quick to leave his grasp and shot back into the deep water. The feeling of all this was overpowering and he leaned back, almost falling, against his log.

He sat motionless under the weight of the moment. Yet at the same time he felt almost weightless, as if the twenty-two years had lifted and disappeared. His hands shook as he tried to reach for another worm. He took a deep breath. A resolve was reached when he said what Clara always said: " 'Things will be as God wills them to be.' " Looking around at the pond, the morning light on the bench, the distant mountains, his smile broadened. "This here, and right now, is just about as free as a man can get." He kept two small brookies, which would be dinner.

The summer went by. Every weekday would find Jed making furniture. Every weekend would find him at the pond he fished that first day, or the two ponds above it, or the creek below. His business grew. In fact, it had grown much more quickly than he had counted on. He was keeping up with the orders, but his eight-to-five workday had turned into seven-to-nine and later. His weekends would be kept free at all costs, at least during the fishing season.

The orders came in from his New York dealer. Tables with chairs mostly, but by fall he had added a small dresser and an end table to his selection. The money was good and he soon bought a car of his own—a brand-new Oldsmobile Rocket Eighty-eight. He also bought an old pickup from one of Noah's ranch hands, which he used for his everyday errands. No longer did he ask Edgar McCracken to deliver his mail, supplies, and groceries. He drove into town for all the things he needed. On Sunday he fired up the Eighty-eight and went to church.

Now, his initial appearances in Travers Corners startled some people. They'd gasp, not knowing what to do or say, and their children would stare. But his first appearance at the D. Downey First Baptist Church— that was a gospel stopper. The good Reverend Mathis was leading the church choir, page 119 in the hymnal, and the congregation had just joined in the chorus when Jed, who was late for services, tried to go unnoticed as he sat down, alone in the very last pew.

Those who saw it said that the word of God stuck in the reverend's throat like a fish bone. The sight of the black man seemed to tighten his collar, and he choked. He went bug-eyed with disbelief at the latest parishioner in the back row. This in turn made the choir look up from their songbooks to follow his stare, and they slowly groaned to a stop. As the congregation turned their heads they all stopped singing, all but John

McMurray, who was caught up in the spiritual, hymn number 119 being his personal favorite, and finally had to be elbowed to a halt by his wife.

There was a frozen moment that to Jed's recollection seemed like days. But it was only a matter of seconds before Edgar McCracken stepped down from the choir. "For those of you who still haven't had the pleasure of meeting Jed Thomas," he said, walking past the reverend and down the aisle, "I'd like to introduce him now, and welcome him to our church. I've been inviting him down here for over a year, and I'm sure glad he came." Edgar shook Jed's hand.

Bob McQuade stepped out from his pew. "Uh, there's some room up here, don't have to sit in the back there, Mr. Thomas. C'mon up here with me and the kids. Slide over for the man, Doreen." His daughter, with eyes bigger than offering plates, slid over. Bob had had his life saved on Iwo Jima by a Negro soldier. He had no problems with his color. Jed walked up and took the seat offered to him, and the reverend, though rocked and a little wobbly, continued.

Jed was to never miss another Sunday, and he slowly evolved, by varying degrees of acceptance, resignation, and resolve, into just another part in the everyday life around Travers Corners. Within a few months people were used to seeing him around town. When bumping into Jed at the post office or on the street, most people would smile, or nod, or engage in weather-related conversation. Some would say nothing and look the other way. Etta Mae Harper would avoid Jed at all costs—to the point of crossing the street if she saw Jed coming—and not because of bigotry. Etta Mae didn't have a bigoted bone in her body. She just got so flustered when she saw him coming she didn't know what to do. But then Etta Mae flustered easily.

Bobby Lee knew what to do. He sneered at Jed from a safe distance and seethed at the sight of him. Hate mumbled easily from under his breath.

Jed's visits with Noah grew more and more frequent, and by the time

~

autumn rolled they had fallen into a once-a-week routine—playing cribbage on Friday nights. Noah had just purchased his first television, and the marvel of it captivated them. The evening centered on Sid Caesar and the Friday Night Fights.

It was the last Friday of September. Jed had just arrived and was shuffling the cards. He was tired and he shuffled without looking. The work at the one-man factory had outgrown what one man could do, and he couldn't keep up with the orders without working nights and weekends. The business, much to Jed's astonishment, was in a few short months more successful than he'd ever imagined it would be. He shuffled the cards once more looking out the window as the first snow of the season was just starting to fall. It was a lazy snow and the flakes were lit by the living room lights.

"You know I has to make a business decision, and I wants to have yer opinion on it," Jed said to Noah as he entered the room to fresh beers and a bowlful of potato chips. "The furniture makin' is doin' a whole lot better than I ever expected it to. Fact is, it's doin' too damn well. Ain't no way I can keep up with the orders. The way I sees it I has two choices. I has to either turn down orders, which ain't no good for business, or hire me some employees. It's either that or I starts workin' the weekends, and I ain't gonna do it. I'm too old and I ain't gonna cut into my fishin'."

Noah was delighted, but not surprised at the business doing well. He'd seen the freight trucks coming up the road with regularity to pick up the shipments. He also felt honored that Jed wished to ask him for advice about his work. "Well, that's great, Jed. Sounds like too much business is the kind of thing a businessman would love to complain about. You know, there are lots of folks around Travers who would jump at the chance at picking up some work. Finding good help won't be a problem."

"Yeah, but I'm afraid that sort of thing might bring about troubles."

"What do you mean?"

"Well, white folks don't mind havin' colored folks work for them, but they kin git awful touchy when they have to work for a colored man. I seen it happen. It turned into somethin' real ugly one night in a mill outside of Harrisonburg. A Negro was made a foreman—first one ever."

"What happened?" Noah asked, setting the bowl of chips and his beer on the table next to his big easy chair.

"Well, a handful of the Klan got wind of it, and they done burned down a church. The two women inside were killed."

Jed had never mentioned Clara's death since that first day at the mill. But Noah knew she was lost in a fire, just as he knew from the rage and anger that flashed in Jed's eyes that Clara was one of those women. How odd it seemed to see that much hate in an otherwise peaceful and lineless face. But Jed was reliving the horror, seeing what he always saw in the memory: the church an inferno, the walls crumbling in sheets of flame, women screaming, children and men crying, the burning crosses left by the Klan. He went to the window and stared out over Montana. Noah said nothing. When that old terror had once again left him Jed returned to his chair.

Suddenly Noah's befriending of this black man fell into a new perspective. Once unimaginable and for all the reasons that a white man could condescend to call this black man his friend, Noah was now hit with the realization that Jed's befriending of him was an act of monumental forgiveness. He wanted to say something, but Jed said, without saying, this was something he didn't want to talk about.

"Hell, Jed, nothing like that is going to happen here. Those folks who won't want to work for you, won't, but that'll be all. Hells bells, I know fifteen men I can call—hard workers everyone of them. And they'd be here ready to start in the morning. Things have been pretty tight around here since they cut back at Rossiter's Lumber Camp." Noah was still reeling from the realization.

"You really don't think nothin' will happen?" Jed asked, sitting down in the rocker that had become his usual ringside seat.

"How many men do you need?"

~

"I figure two. Two mens who is handy at workin' wood but also can work with the machines—and someone to help me with my book-keepin'."

"Tom Alexander and Mark Evans. Good workers both of them. Nancy Stoops helps me with my books. She'd be glad to help you with yours. I can give them a call if you want." He opened his beer and handed Jed the opener, then he clicked on the television.

"Well, let me think on it some."

"You know, this snow isn't going to amount to anything more than a dusting. Tomorrow it'll be warm and Sunday is going to be even better. Why don't you come down and go fishing with me?" Noah asked.

"Here I been invitin' you to go fishin' for two months runnin'. You is always too busy. And now all of a sudden you wants to go?" Jed laughed. "White folks."

"I'm telling you some of the best fishing on Carrie Creek is down here in the meadows behind the corrals."

"All right. I'll be there right after church."

"Good. You know I haven't taken the time to go fishing since the summer before last, and here I live not two hundred yards from some of the best fishing in Montana. And I love fishing."

"Well, that's just contrary thinkin'."

The announcer took over the room. "Tonight's championship fight between Sugar Ray Robinson and Carmen Bascilio is brought to you by Pabst Blue Ribbon and Gillette . . . Feel sharp, look sharp . . ."

Saturday, because he was far behind, Jed worked. This went against the promise he'd made himself. The problem of whether to hire more people or to cut back on production bothered him all day, and he went to bed that night tired from both work and worry.

But by Sunday afternoon Jed was his smiling self again. Driving back from church he was feeling good for all sorts of reasons. He'd been asked to join the choir, and for that he was feeling a little more welcome. He'd wrestled with the problem of employment and decided to take Noah's advice to hire the extra men, and now he was going fishing. New water with a new friend—the first white friend he'd ever had. He was also still gloating a little because Sugar Ray had won the championship.

This was his second fall in the valley. The first one had passed, not without notice, but certainly without participation. This one he was going to savor color by color, leaf by leaf. These were the moments he and Clara had lived and worked for. The aspen groves painted the benchlands and mountains in long sweeps and strings of spangling gold, as his new Olds Eighty-eight rolled down the two-lane out of Travers. His mind was active with a design for a rocking chair that would have to be more comfortable than that thing he always had to sit in at Noah's.

Life had been hard, but right now life was feeling fine. He drove home, changed clothes, had a bite to eat, and switched vehicles. He was pulling into the Hourglass a little after noon.

Noah was in the yard helping one of his wranglers load a wagon when he saw Jed's dust lifting up the road and the glint of his windshield. He looked at his watch then looked at the sun to confirm the time. He walked over to the front porch, slipped on his hip boots, grabbed his creel, his rod, and his reel. And to his surprise (and with some delight) he realized he had left the cowboy to continue the work alone.

Jed stepped from the pickup and reached in the back for his can of worms and pole. "'Afternoon, Noah."

"Hello there, Jed."

Jed followed Noah as they walked through a series of gates in the corrals. Noah opening and closing each one as they went. "You knows you ain't near dark enough to be no doorman," Jed said. Noah laughed. Jed was always making Noah laugh.

Walking through a narrow field edged in willows and cattail, they followed a beaten path over a natural bridge of firm earth with marsh all around them and into the shade of the cottonwoods bordering Carrie Creek. As they walked they chatted easily about one another's lives—a contrast of more than just color.

~

"Would you just look around you now." Jed stopped and turned himself full circle. "Have you ever seen anythin' as pretty as today. Mmmmmmmmm. Look at that sky goin' on forever."

"Fishing today is going to be unbelievable."

"And how does you know that?"

"Well, I've been fishing this place my whole life. The first couple of days after the first snow is always the best. The trout feed like crazy because they know winter's coming."

"Bream fishin' in Virginia is abouts the same—only, o' course it's completely different," he said with his smile.

The stream first appeared as sparkles through the underbrush. Stepping out from the red willows onto a high bank above the water, Noah pointed with his rod. "This hole here is about the deepest hole on the creek. Great spot for a worm. I've caught a few monsters here. I'll be just up ahead. I can see trout rising from here."

Settling into a comfortable place on the bank, Jed baited his line and tossed worm and bobber into the current, but he couldn't take his eyes off Noah who was midstream and casting his fly. Wading into the shade, at the head of the pool Jed was fishing, Noah worked his cast out into the light. Floating it back and forth until it had reached the desired measure, he then settled fly and line onto the water. The beauty with which Noah handled the rod and line was absorbing. The fact that Noah had taken two fish almost immediately also caught Jed's attention. He'd seen pictures in magazines of fly fishing, but this was the first time he'd ever seen it done.

When Noah had hooked and was playing his third trout, this one a fair-sized fish, it sparked something inside Jed had long forgotten—the imperative curiosity of a young boy. Fly fishing was something he now *had* to try. Wanting to see the trout Noah was reeling in—it was easily three times bigger than the brookies he'd been catching—Jed tossed his pole on the bank and went to view Noah's fish firsthand. Of course, if Jed had been paying any attention to his own bobber, which had gone up and down as many times as it took a two-pound brown to pick his night-crawler clean, he would have had a trout of his own.

"My Land o' Goshen, that there fish is a dandy," Jed said, watching the fish jump, marveling at the bend in the long rod.

"There's a couple bigger ones up ahead," Noah whispered over his back, and quickly brought the rainbow in and released it.

"I seen pictures, but I never seen nobody doin' it for real. You just tossing out that tiny little ol' fly. Oh, I am gonna have to try that."

"Well, here," Noah said, trying to hand Jed his fly rod.

"No, let me watch you some more."

Noah blew the water from his fly and cast again. Jed looked on, watching the line become longer with each false cast, and he broke down the cast into the laws and principles of motion. He thought out loud, "Now, the force of Noah's arm is turnin' his old fly rod into a lever, with a kinda parabolic effect caused by a handheld fulcrum. And once that power is applied into that backcast the lever changes its mechanics and it becomes a spring, and that spring is storin' the energy in the resistance produced by the bent bamboo. It finally releases that power when Noah is bringin' the rod forward, and that energy is used to accelerate the weight and mass of the line." Physics was something that he'd needed to learn once he decided on becoming an inventor. So Clara bought the books and he taught himself.

With equations and Newton's laws of motion still being worked in his head, Jed sat and watched as Noah landed another rainbow. "Well, that there is about the cleverest thing I've ever seen a white man do," he said.

"Go ahead, you try it." Noah attempted to hand Jed his rod once more.

"Now, Mr. McHale, I don't wants to be cuttin' into your fishin' none."

"You won't be. I don't . . . wait a minute. You wait right here. I'll be right back." Noah handed Jed his fly rod and headed quickly back for the house.

Jed was left to admire the inner workings of the reel and the crafts-

~

manship of the bamboo rod. The cork was black with wear. The wraps were red and faded—some had started to fray. He looked upstream to watch the trout rising, and he lit his pipe and relaxed. Noah was on his way back in the time it took Jed to have his smoke. He watched him coming through the corrals, carrying something in his hand.

"My daughter gave me this rod and reel for Christmas," Noah said, scrambling back down the bank. "I never gave it more than a wiggle. I don't know why she spent the money. I mean, I've already got a fly rod. But she insisted that this was the latest and the greatest. I know she paid a pretty penny for it, but that woman was born to spend money. Good thing she married a doctor.

"Made out of fiberglass. Abercrombie and Fitch—top of the line," Noah concluded. The two exchanged their rods and Jed went about examining the new one.

Wiggling the rod from side to side, Jed laughed. "It feels fine to me. It's so long, but it's so light. Fiberglass, eh?"

"I've got some extra leaders and flies. Let me show you how to rig that thing."

So Noah set Jed's rod up and afterward gave him some casting lessons. "It's just timing and rhythm. A kind of four-four time," he explained while he made false casts. The line sailing back and forth above him as he counted, "One-two-three-four. One—two—three . . ."

"Well," Jed said, "as all you white folks knows, us coloreds gots rhythm. All 'ceptin' me. I would has to be the one Negro left out. I can't dance. Very embarrassin', you know, to be colored and uncoordinated. I was no Satchel Paige in baseball, neither."

"Who?"

"Satchel Paige?"

"I don't know who—"

"Satchel Paige was onliest the greatest baseball player of all time. That man could pitch, now. He had a curveball that would pick the buttons right of the batter's shirt, then it would break and cuts the outside corner. Why, one time Clara and me saw him play in Charlottesville and . . ."

And so they started their afternoon, leapfrogging and laughing from riffle to pool up Carrie Creek. They fished, and chatted about the fishing, and about baseball, furniture, trees, cattle, the Deep South, the Far North, rocks, crops, birds, beer, childhood, Ford versus Chevy, FDR, and anything else that popped into their minds. All the time Jed's slow and easy movements were coupling naturally with his understanding of physics and motion, and he was turning out some very tidy-looking casts with the new Abercrombie and Fitch. He'd missed several fish, and he'd had two on but failed to land either of them.

Noah was catching quite a few. All day he kept thinking about how much fun it was being around Jed, and how much he enjoyed watching him reveling in the day. Noah grew up fishing these holes, like his father and his father before him, and he couldn't help being jaded by their familiarity and proximity. While Jed just kept looking around him and smiling, and if he said it once he said it twenty times: "Mmmm-mmmmm, would you just look at this day? I never seen such colors."

Everywhere Jed looked and everything he tried took his breath away. He was fascinated by the rising trout and at the ease with which Noah was taking them. He'd had a taste of success by fooling a couple of fish, and now he wanted to land one before the day ended. In awe in every direction and lost in the fall spectacle, he was like a kid with a new pair of skates—anxious to get better, and never wanting the day to end. Goose bumps and joyful tears were taking their turns.

Jed was having the time of his life. The sky was clear and vast. What amazed him most about this moment was that he was sharing it with a neighbor, his business partner, and a white man. The implausibility of it all made him giddy. There was no doubt about it. This was a friendship, the best he'd had in many years.

They fished until the last of the day. The long shadows had fallen, and the sun was close to setting. Jed was still to land a trout, and the fishing had slowed way down. There were no rising fish. Noah had only taken two in as many hours, while Jed continued to practice and improve his cast. They'd worked themselves a few miles up Carrie Creek when Noah said, "C'mon, we'll walk on over to the road. It's an easier and shorter walk back."

"Noah, would it be all right if we just sits here on this log and watch the sun go down?"

"Sure."

"You know this has been one of the best days of my whole life?" Jed said as he packed his pipe and lit it.

"It's sure been a good one," Noah agreed.

"Well, I'd like to makes it even more special," Jed said as he reached into his creel to pull out a pint bottle. It had no label and the liquid inside was clear and slightly yellow. He pulled the cork.

"What the Sam Hell you got there, Jed?"

"You know that day you came up to the barn and told me that the people in town thought I was makin' moonshine up here?"

"Yeah."

"Well," he said a little sheepishly, "they was right."

Noah was taken aback for a moment, "You made this?" he said as Jed handed him the bottle.

"Just seemed kinda natural. I means I had the copper, the wood for fire, the corn to make the squeezin', and the kiln for a place to hide it all—and to account for all the smoke. Brewin' shine makes a lot of smoke. That's how the Revenuers always caught a shiner—by his smoke. My daddy made shine. His daddy before him."

"You really did make it?"

"From my own little garden, and I don't minds tellin' you that this is fine shine, now."

Noah laughed, then laughed even harder as Jed transformed his face to one of exaggerated guilt. Then Noah took a swallow. Jed was right. It was as smooth as the corn silk it came it came from, and from the slow but increasing warmth radiating from his stomach, he knew the spirits were strong.

Surprised at just how easily it went down and already anticipating what a few more sips might feel like, Noah said, "Tastes good, but I can kind of sense that it wouldn't take very much of that to make a man drunk."

"That's why they calls it sippin' whiskey."

They sat by the creek and they sipped a few more. They watched the sun seemingly balance on the faraway peaks. Then Jed saw a fish rise. "Lookee there. There's another trout nosin' around."

"All right, you spotted him. Now you go get him."

"Okay, I will," Jed said, taking one more sip on the whiskey. "I knows one thing for certain—I ain't never gonna fish with worms again. Tomorrow I'm callin' Junior McCracken and I am gonna have him order one of these here fly rods."

"You don't have to do that," Noah smiled. "Why don't you keep the one you have there?"

"Well . . . I . . . I . . . that's about the nicest present I believes I ever did receive." Noah, knowing much of Jed's life, could tell in his eyes that it very well could have been the nicest present he'd ever received.

Tapping the pipe into his hand then slipping into the bib pocket of his overalls, Jed set about measuring the line needed to reach the rising fish. The fish was joined by another, then another, then by two more. With every new arrival he felt his pulse increase. He was tingling, alive in the moment, and glowing from the moonshine. He could feel his cheeks flush as the alcohol reached his capillaries. He added a little Mucilin to his fly as Noah had taught him.

The trout were coming to a late-evening hatch of small mayflies, but Noah recommended, "Just stay with that old Royal Coachman you got tied on there. They'll take it."

Each dimple and every wave's trough across the stream, every swirl of the current, all the ripples being sent by the rising trout were rimmed in the fiery orange of last light. Jed cautiously moved into Carrie Creek and safely behind the fish. He made his false casts then delivered the fly smartly and gently. It landed in a likely spot. A trout took it. First cast. Jed lifted the rod and the rainbow was in the air. The silver and whites of her sides and underbelly caught the colors of sundown, and the trout for the briefest moment flickered over Carrie Creek like a flame. She dived. She ran to the head of the pool. A second and third jump. A few shorter runs then she tired. Slowly Jed reeled her to his side, where he kneeled down and brought her into his hand. Marveling, Jed cradled the trout as Noah joined him.

"That's a dandy, Jed. Seventeen inches—pound and three-quarters, maybe two." Noah leaned in for a closer look at the trout.

Her back was coal black in the fading light, her belly an iridescent white. Her sides sparkled with all the colors of the rainbow. Jed plucked the fly from the fish's mouth. Once the trout had regained her senses, she swam easily to the freedom of the deep water.

"That there was the icin' on the cake, now. Mmmmm—mmmmm. That was just only the best."

They walked back to the log, where they sat down and enjoyed a few more sips from Jed's bottle. They talked of the day's fishing. Then it was time to walk on home, and as they gathered their gear, Noah started to stand, but then sat back down. There was something he'd always wanted to ask and now the corn liquor made it easier, "Jed, don't you miss being around other colored people? I mean I know you moved here to be in the woods and all, but don't you miss family or friends or—"

"Noah, when you is a black man in America you is pretty much invisible, unless'n course you wants to use the white man's toilet or sit in the front of the bus. Then you is visible—oh, highly visible"—Jed laughed—"and more than likely a little bruised." Then he stopped laughing, and in a rare moment he stopped smiling. "Bein' invisible in a white man's world is a pitiful feelin'. Ya ain't nothin'. Just ain't much hope of bein' somethin' or havin' anythin' when you is invisible.

"Clara and me sort of figured that the best place for us to live would be somewheres that you don't has to go through the pain of bein' invisible all the time. And the only way we could sees to stop bein' invisible was to move someplace where you don't has to be seen by many people. That was the wilderness. That was Montana. That was freedom."

Jed stood up and Noah followed him, but his standing came with an audible crack in his hip. Jed and Noah exchanged smiles; they were both starting to get their share of creaks and cracks.

"And, as far as family and friends, well, Clara was my family. And friends, well I miss some, but not many. I gots to tell you somethin', Noah, right now, in my life, you is abouts the onliest and best friend I has."

Noah nodded. "Gonna be another fine day tomorrow, Jed. Just exactly like the one today. And I'll bet it stays this way for another couple of weeks."

"Gonna be mighty hard to keep from fishin' weekdays with my new Abercrombies and Fitch fiberglass fly rod," Jed replied.

"Damn near impossible, Jed, damn near impossible."

They walked down the dusty road to Noah's as the first few stars came out for the night . . .

Jud had walked to the river, down to the old train station, back past McCracken's, and was once again walking the waistline of the Hourglass Ranch. He looked back over his shoulder to McCracken's General Store. There was no trace of the Coca-Cola girl, not even the big red ball as the old building stood mostly in shadows, the brick a pale and lightless pink. The sun, though set, still lit the peaks of the Elkheart Range.

He remembered the immediate success of the rocking chair design Jed had come up with for watching Sid Caesar in comfort on Friday nights. In fact, the demand was so great he added another four people, and a night shift of six more just to build rockers. He also added Friday to his fishing week.

Noah began giving more and more work to the hired hands and less to himself.

Jed and Noah weren't rich, but they were doing quite well, and with every passing summer their workweek dwindled and their angling hours multiplied.

A smile appeared slowly on Jud's face as he walked from the highway and started up the hill to the Boat Works. It was the kind of smile you see when an absurdity is remembered. He shook his head as he thought of it—the first, the last, and the only racial incident in the Elkheart.

Jed's hiring of four more white men was the straw that broke the bigot's back. Bobby Lee, after hearing the news of Jed's new employees, spent most of the week in the bar. The thought of a black man hiring whites had always infuriated him. But when Jed became the largest employer in Travers Corners, it sent him into a rage. On a Saturday night, drunk and full of hate, Bobby Lee set a cross on fire at the corner of Jed Thomas's land. A west wind came up that night to fan the flames of the crucifix. A half mile of fence line, a beaver slide, and two stacks of Hourglass hay burned to the ground before the fire department, Jed, Noah, and the hired hands could contain the blaze. The mill wasn't touched.

The next morning Sheriff Johnson found Bobby Lee's Ford upside down in a barrow pit with Bobby Lee still drunk at the wheel. In the truck the sheriff found gasoline, a hammer, a saw, some nails, plus a diagram of how to build a cross. Bobby Lee went to the county jail for four months and had to pay for the damage.

Stopping at the top of the hill, looking over the tops of the aspens to the valley, Jud remembered the countless times Noah and Jed were seen over the next twenty-some-odd years: heading for the Elkheart; heading for the Bitterroot, the Big Hole, the Missouri, the Yellowstone; heading somewhere with their fishing rods poking out the rear window of Jed's long black Oldsmobile. Noah's acceptance of Jed as a friend, and ultimately as his best friend and fishing partner, was recognized and respected right away by some of the people around Travers Corners. It came slower to others, but they came around. Then there were those in town who found it impossible to forgive.

Noah died in '75, Jed in '78. Their friendship was legendary.

From The Journals of Traver C. Clark

November 12, 1922—

Heard today in town that the Luthy Ranch sold. Not to ranchers but to some people from the East. That's the third ranch this year. These people come to the Elkheart for a month or two then leave and never work the land while they are here. I don't know but something seems wrong about this.

Case of nails - *2.50*
Gloves - *1.00*
100-foot roll of bracing wire - *4.00*

Wretched Access

ABOUT HALFWAY BETWEEN Travers Corners and the headwaters of the East Fork lies the Ashton Ranch. The Bar A. Two thousand acres and change, the Bar A owns, on both sides, about six miles of the East Fork River—the best six miles. The ranch has been owned by the Ashton family for a hundred years, and the Ashtons are regarded by all the inhabitants up and down the Elkheart Valley as a good family, hardworking and honest, except, of course, for its most recent generation.

There is John Ashton, whose father homesteaded the place. He was born on the Bar A, working it his entire life, a life now well into its eighties. John still helps with the irrigating, but the general operations of the ranch are up to his son, George, and his wife, Anita, both nearing sixty. Then comes George and Anita's highly unlikable son, Kenny.

Kenny is a shallow shell of a man; a rather useless sort of worm. These are about the kindest words you are apt to hear about him. Thirty years old, he is closing in on being the town's leading drunk. He hasn't worked in years. His only contribution to the ranch is trying not to be too loud when he comes home plastered, and that would be nightly. So because of his cocktailing, he ain't worth a shit, and that would be daily.

~

The Bar A is a rarity amid many cattle ranches—it's successful. Successful because of its location, the best bottomland on the East Fork. Successful because of the richness of its soil and good water. And successful because George and his father have run the ranch like the labor of love that it was for them. Unfortunately it's a clock whose time is running out, for when it comes Kenny's turn, he will "Sell it to the highest bidder and then it will be wine, women, and song for ol' Kenny." That's what he says after the liquor hits him, and after more liquor hits him he is reduced to sitting at the end of the Tin Cup's bar, talking to an ashtray or to Lyle "the Fish" Smith, who at present is the true and reigning town drunk. Lyle will surely be abdicating this position soon, and not because he is in any danger of taking the cure, but because when sitting at the bar, Lyle's liver requires a separate stool. The ashtray of this trio, around closing time, would be the one judged most coherent.

The Bar A being the best ranch in and around the Elkheart Valley is an opinion held unanimously by Jud, Henry, Junior McCracken, and Doc Higgins. Not because of its cattle production, but because of its river—home to the best fly fishing in the valley. The oxbow water on the East Fork.

This story begins several years ago, down at the Tin Cup, late on a rainy Tuesday night . . .

"Yep, when we sell the ranch, I'm gonna do some real movin' and shakin' then, Lyle old buddy. Gonna have me some capital. Then the folks around here will apree-*hic*-shheeatate—apppersmminate—mmmmm—*hic*—me more," Kenny slurred from his usual stool at the end of the bar. "Another round for me and my—*hic*—friend, Lyle," he ordered, waving his arm loosely over his head to gain Sal's attention.

Tending bar on a Tuesday night is something Sal hated to do, because on a weeknight, and a rainy one at that, he knew there would only be two customers near closing time and he knew which two they would be.

~

The only good thing about the evening was a preseason double-header coming over the TV.

Two men came into the bar as Sal was mixing up two more ditches for Lyle and Kenny. The first man was a short, fat man dressed in outdoor gear—Patagonia, L.L. Bean kind of outdoor gear. Dressed as if he'd walked into Orvis and told the clerk to dress him like the guy in the window. The clothing looked not just wrong on the stranger, but comical, and not only because it was all brand new but also because he had the pasty look of a man who had spent very little time outdoors. The second man was thin, tall, very pale, and he followed behind. He had a nondescript face, very thick glasses, and his eyes darted around.

"A couple of beers, bartender," said the short guy as he threw a hundred-dollar bill on the bar. "And let me buy a round for those guys," nodding to the two drunks in residence. Sal nodded.

Having the drinks already mixed, he delivered them to Kenny and Lyle. "These two are on those guys," he said, shoving the drinks in front of them. Lyle and Kenny both rubbered around, and though the two strangers at the bar were completely out of focus, as was most everything in the room, Kenny said, "Thanks for the drinkshh, mish-ter."

First bringing the beers, Sal then gave the stranger his change. Sal had taken an instant dislike to the guy. He didn't like the way he threw his money on the bar. Resuming the business of washing up for closing time, Sal returned his attention to the seventh inning of the second game.

"See those guys down there? Those are the guys you look for in places like this. I'll go down and see what they know," the short one said out of the corner of his mouth, and walked down to stand behind Kenny and Lyle. "Hey, how are you guys doing tonight?"

Lyle replied first, looking confused, because he didn't *know* how he was doing tonight. "Mmmmm. Ribbberverifin, an-r-yurshelf?"

"Fair to middlin', and how'shh about you?" Kenny answered.

"Well, we've been traveling all around your great state of Montana, chasing the wily trout. Haven't had too much luck, though. You wouldn't know a good place to go fishing around here?" the stranger asked. He directed his question to Kenny, who was definitely the less drunk of the two, as Lyle blurted something delusional and then fell facedown into his practiced, waiting, and folded arms.

"Mishter, you come to the right place, becaushhe I jushht happen to own the beshht fishin' around here."

The stranger waved his friend down from the other end of the bar. Sal checked his watch. There was another thirty minutes left to closing time and time for a another couple of innings.

"My name's Belson, David Belson, this is my business associate, Herschel." Herschel nodded timidly with a rabbit's smile.

"Thish here ish Lyle, and I'm K-K-Kenny—*hic*—Ashhhton."

Lyle mumbled something into his sleeve.

Sal was interrupted, bases loaded, once again by Kenny, who obviously forgot he had just received a round of drinks. "Another round down here—all around.

"Yeshhsir, if there ish one thing I know about it's fishing, and our ranch on the Easht Fork is better than anybodyshhh."

Sal was pulling down the bottle of bar bourbon but was stopped by David, "No, not that stuff, bartender. Give my friends the good stuff." He pointed to a bottle of twelve-year-old on the back bar. He threw another hundred on the bar. Lyle, near comatose, rallied for the better whiskey and slid his glass to the edge of the bar—instinctively, blindly, and without raising his head.

Sal delivered the drinks and, spotting the second hundred, raised his eyebrows. "Could ya give me somethin' a little smaller there, pal?" Belson tossed a twenty at Sal without looking.

"Fifteen minutes, boys, and I'm closing," Sal said.

It didn't even take Belson the full fifteen minutes before he had invited himself to come and fish the Ashton Ranch, secure directions, and establish the best time for him and Herschel, who wouldn't be fishing, to arrive.

"I'd shay you should come up tomorrow around ten. Fishing will be good. I shaw a bunchhh of fish—*hic*—risin' all week. And you'll have the whole ranch to yershhhelves."

"Everywhere I go it's the same thing: I should've been there yesterday, I should been there the day before," said Belson, laughing a long fake laugh. He laughed out of a mean mouth in the middle of a round and horrible face. He then stuck a hundred-dollar bill in Kenny's pocket, gave him a hearty slap on his shoulder, and said, "Thanks for the invitation. See you tomorrow."

"You should have been here, never," Sal whispered to himself switching off the game. "Okay gentlemen, I'm closin' her up."

"C'mon, wake up. We gotta go," Kenny said, standing down from his stool onto a pair of tenuous legs. He shook Lyle's shoulder.

Lyle pushed himself away from the bar. In a split second he was vertical and ready, but walking was going to be a problem. His first step was a failure. Luckily Kenny was there to catch him, and, stumbling into each other, they headed for the side entrance. "We'll she-e-e you guysh in the morning," Kenny said as Lyle careened off the poker machine, only to go headlong into the door. "I'm pretty shhit-facsshed, there, Lyle ol'd buddy—you be-be-better drive. Good night, Shhal."

"Good night, Kenny," Sal said, shaking his head. Belson and Herschel left without saying a word.

The next morning the air still had a chill to it, but it was warming. Henry and Jud had been waiting for such a day and for quite some time, a day of dry-fly fishing on the Bar A. They met for breakfast down at the Tin Cup. The breakfast crowd gone, Sarah had joined them at their table. Other than Jud and Henry, the café was empty, except for the waitress, Sally, who was still cleaning up.

"Doc fished the East Fork yesterday and called me last night just to rave about it," Jud was telling Henry as he was finishing his stack of cakes, "and Junior fished it the day before and caught fish all day."

"Well, if Junior McCracken was catchin' fish," Henry said with his very slight smile, "it has to be some kind of fishin'."

"Hey, Sarah," Jud asked, "what's been troubling Sally? She hardly said hello to us this morning." Sally was a new waitress, twenty years younger than either Jud or Henry, but both enjoyed flirting with her. Jud because he enjoyed watching her blush, and Henry because it was in Henry's nature to flirt. He gave everything a tumble. "You never can tell" was his outlook. Of course, if Dolores ever got wind of any dalliance, his life would become a living hell.

"Well, she was doing just fine until this bozo came in a while back and gave her a hard time," Sarah explained. "This guy didn't like the coffee. Didn't like the way his eggs were cooked. Wanted a special kind of marmalade. Then he puts his moves on her. Asks her if she'd like to go out tonight. She says no. He then says something so graphic to her that the poor thing could hardly talk. It made her cry. Then he leaves her a fifty-dollar tip clipped to his business card."

"Who was this guy?" Henry was steamed.

"I never saw him before. Ugly little man."

"Where's the card?" Jud asked. Sally reached into her pocket and handed it to him.

"Belson and Associates, David Belson. Washington, D.C."

"Never heard of him. Hey, look at the time. We better go fishing," Jud said, reaching for his wallet.

"Do me a favor, Henry?" Sarah asked, standing and wiping her hands on her apron. "Tell Anita that I'll be coming up for a visit real soon. And tell her I'll bring those books she's been wanting to borrow. She and George sure don't get to town very often. All those two seem to do is work."

"Okay, I'll do 'er," Henry said, slipping on his hat. Then, as he passed the counter, following Jud, he sort of leaned in on Sally who was putting away silverware. Her eyes were still red and her mouth still pouty. "You know, darlin', there're differences in men." Henry said it with his notorious wink and smile. "There're men that're worth gettin' all *bothered* about"—that's when he applied the wink, changing bothered, meaning annoyed, to the state-of-the-heart, emotional kind of bothered—"and there're men who ain't worth botherin' about." He kicked in his mischievous grin, which put Sally at ease. It even made her laugh.

"Put that guy out of your mind, kid," Henry said, leaving the money and his check on the counter. "That's for Jud's, too."

"Thanks, Henry," Sally said with her wonderful blush.

He understood as he went out the door he had just imparted fatherly advice, not designed to do anything but comfort her and make her laugh. And he'd given her a little flirt to build her esteem, a little comfort. Still, another part of him wouldn't mind showing her that difference in men.

He turned to Jud as they stepped from the café. "Forty-eight is sure a strange age. Definitely my weirdest year to date. I'm too old for young women, too young for old women, and all the women my age have got my number."

Jud laughed. "I've got to run into McCracken's real quick and get some leaders."

"I'll wait in the jeep," Henry said and walked over to sit in Jud's Willys, parked at the curb in the shade of the café.

Inside McCracken's Jud was relieved to see Junior busy with Maudie Albright, who was past hard of hearing and bordering on deaf. Junior was shouting his instructions on her prescription to her so loud it carried down the aisles. Jud grabbed his leaders, paid at the register, and waved to Junior on his way out the door.

A little miffed at Maudie's timing, as he wanted to talk to Jud about fishing, he was somehow enjoying the yelling. Maudie's prescription being a suppository made little difference to Junior, as he was in a bad mood anyway and had been all morning. Ever since that short little jerk, the first customer of his day, came in to buy flies.

Junior had spent his entire life at McCracken's, raised into the business; the store bore his name. So you can imagine how well he handled this guy's opening line—"Hey, you have a pretty good selection of flies for a little jerk-water shop." This was followed by, "Are you kidding me? A dollar fifty for dry flies? Hey, I never pay more than a buck back east, and I don't give a shit who tied them." Then he had added his parting comment, "Yeah, eat your heart out, shopkeep. We're going to go fish the East Fork—on the Ashton Ranch. If these flies you sold me don't work, you'll be hearing from me."

Junior spent the day sick to his stomach. Even though he was a pharmacist, it was a malady for which he could prescribe no cure. The thought of that ugly little man fishing some of his favored water visited him with waves of nausea until quitting time.

"Elkheart's lookin' real lush there, Judson C. Could be some fine fishin' today," Henry said as Jud made the turn from the highway, steering the Willys up the East Fork turnoff. Seventeen miles to the Bar A.

Belson, with Herschel, stepped from their Cadillac at the appointed ten o'clock. "This place is beee-yooooo-tiful," Belson said to a rather blasé and certainly disinterested Herschel. He was busy swatting at the deerflies and was clearly a man uncomfortable with the great out-of-doors.

"Just the kind of place I'm looking for, that is if the fishing is as good as that drunk from last night said it was," Belson snickered. He grabbed his fly rod.

The Ashton Ranch was a showplace, a beautiful ranch house with log outbuildings, painted barns, buckrail fences. All nestled into a grove of aspens and a sizable stand of fir, planted as windbreaks when the Bar A was nothing but a homestead. Belson, dressed again like an advertisement, a catalog caricature of a fisherman, walked to the front door. He was already in his still-immaculate waders and boots, plus a spotless fishing vest with every fly-fishing gimmick known to man dangling from its every pocket. A large black Stetson hat was balanced on his pointy little head, and a red kerchief divided his fat neck like a tourniquet trying to suppress a goiter. He knocked on the Ashtons' front door.

~

Old man Ashton answered. Opening the door he hobbled right past Belson, pausing for a moment to study him. "Son, you look like you jest stepped out of a box." He laughed and shook his head at the sight, then kept right on walking, his old and bowed cowboy legs, brittle wishbones in boots, taking him toward the barn. He was followed to the door by his son, George.

"What can I do for you, mister?" George greeted the stranger with a smile.

Belson took off his glasses and rubbed his beady little eyes. His face had no character, and neither did the rest of him, as any number of businessmen in and around Washington, D.C. could have told you. Belson had made his money in Florida's real estate boom of the 1970s—that was in the real estate above the high-water mark and below.

"My name is Belson, David Belson," he said through a thin-lipped smile. "Last night I had the good fortune to meet Kenny Ashton in Travers Corners, and he invited me up to fish his ranch. Is he around?"

"Kenny is around, but I'm sure he ain't up yet. And Kenny don't own this ranch, Mr. Belson, I do."

"I see, well, would it be all right with you if I fished *your* river today? Just myself. My associate"—he pointed to Herschel, still sitting in the car—"won't be fishing."

George really didn't want to talk about this any further, as his arthritis had been acting up lately, and if his son had promised this dude a day of fishing then it was up to him to fulfill an Ashton promise. "It ain't my river. It's God's river." He paused to rub his face. "Well, if Kenny gave his permission, go ahead and go fishin'. Park yer car over by that corral and you can fish upstream or down. Catch and release."

"Absolutely, and thank you very much," Belson said without any discernible appreciation, as if all that was just granted to him was something he deserved. He drove the car to the corral and headed for the river with the most expensive rod and reel made in his hand.

Two miles downstream Jud had just wheeled the jeep into the middle fields of the Bar A, deciding they would check in with Anita Ashton and give her the message from Sarah when they had finished fishing this evening.

Getting out to open a gate, Henry spooked several whitetails. They bounded, tail flags a-flying, across the hay meadows, spooking three sandhill cranes to flight. High over their heads a pair of hawks soared.

"This place is great. You know, I'd give anything to own a place like this," Jud said, shifting into first while Henry climbed back into his seat.

"Yeah, well, enjoy it while ya can there, amigo, Kenny's gonna get his grubby little hands on this place someday, and everyone knows what he's gonna do with it. And some rich asshole from out of state is gonna buy it, and that will be the end of our fishin' days at the Bar A."

"Bite your tongue."

"Well, it's gonna happen. And speaking about bitin' yer tongue," Henry said lecherously, "ain't that Sally a cutie, though."

Jud laughed. "I know, I know, you'd like to be twenty years younger again."

"Can you imagine some guy comin' and bein' mean to that sweet young girl?"

"No, but I *can* imagine an *old* guy lusting after such a sweet young girl."

"I ain't lustin'," Henry said grinning with an exaggerated, whimsical, far-off smile, "I'm just rememberin'."

A short time later they were heading for the river. Dressed for the fishing in their hip boots and vests, they threaded their rod tips carefully through the rose hips and willow. When Jud stopped to ask, in a tone mockingly incredulous, "I wonder why it always is—that when middle-aged men see some bright, interesting, young, attractive woman, they instantly wish they could be twenty years younger. Never do you hear, 'Boy, isn't she something, if only she were twenty years older.' "

"Judson, fer a guy who most of the time I regard as purty darn bright, sometimes you kin miss the point by miles."

The East Fork was in perfect condition, and even though it had rained the night before, the water was flowing low and clear. The cottonwoods and birch trees were all leafed out, and the trout, as predicted by Doc and Junior, were feeding as if there would never be another hatch. Gusts of wind came and went, but for the most part it was calm. As soon as they began fishing they started catching trout—brown trout. Henry managed to take a sixteen-inch brown on his first cast. Now, a fish taken on a first cast is oftentimes looked on as an ominous beginning, as often that first fish on that first cast is the last action of the day. And make no mistake about it, Henry was superstitious. But as it turned out, that first trout was just the beginning of an unbelievable afternoon of fishing.

It was a day to make up for all the days when there are no rises. It was a day to make up for those days when there are no hatches. A day to make up for the days when it's too windy, too cold, too bright, too hot. It was the rarest kind of an angling day, a day when a fisherman would not have to make up any excuses. Nor would he have to make up any lies.

It was a day of two lifetime friends fly fishing the oxbow water on the East Fork; fishing one of their old haunts, one of their favorites, and it was being most kind to them.

The trout were up after a long cold spring and openly dining on all passing mayflies, of which there were plenty. By late afternoon Henry had taken two nineteen-inch browns and Jud had several in the seventeen to eighteen-inch range. Brown trout of the fifteen-inch variety were being caught at will. The rainbows, though just as plentiful on the Bar A's stretch of the Fork, were yet to be seen.

Climbing up on a high bank, Jud paused to watch the clouds drifting and forming; the winds aloft caught their great white feathered edges to contort and stretch them in compliance with his imagination. They flew across the narrow corridor that was the valley of the East Fork. Light and shadow whirled around him. From where he stood he could see the mouth of Jeppson Canyon, three miles upstream, where the East Fork carved its way through the giant limestones. At the mouth of the canyon he could see the final fence line, easily marked by the straight edge where the cultivated land ended. Where the western boundary of the Bar A met the rocky beginnings of the mountains.

He had just left Henry on the last bend where, in one sweeping turn of the river, there had to have been forty or fifty trout up and feeding. Henry, he knew, would be there for quite some time. Jud moved upstream.

He waded quietly, heading for a long-remembered hole, remembered for a rainbow caught on a day such as this when he was still a young man. It was a large pool formed where the river made a hairpin bend. Moving with a more guarded stealth than on previous bends, he was stepping slowly because just ahead he could see rings forming in the back eddy. A few more steps. Two blue-winged teal took flight, giving him a start. *Oh, good,* Jud thought, *I'm sneaking up on duck rings.*

Another two steps and he was in a position to make a cast. The rings formed once more. They were not duck rings, but heavy rings made by a heavy trout that thankfully had not been frightened in the least by the hasty and rather noisy exit of the teal. The trout rose and rose again as she swirled for every mayfly in sight, every mayfly in the window. With every take, the fish turned to the light and a silvered side flashed beneath the water. *This one is a rainbow.*

It was a difficult place to fish. To achieve a tempting drift to his cast, he had to stand on the right side of the pool, casting to its left side and over a wide and rather swift and boiling current. The cast had to be high, long, and mended, only to be mended again. A two-or three-second drift would be the best he could expect. Distance could only come from one strong forward cast. The backcast—almost a steeple cast, needed to clear the willows behind him—would have little power.

There could be no false cast. He could get no closer. Any closer and he would be in over his boots. A step or two farther than that and he would be in over his head. *But,* Jud said to himself, *if I time it just right, two or three seconds will be all I need.* He stripped the line he needed from the reel.

"Fucking ducks," Belson said through a clenched mouth. All day he had been spooking ducks. He'd missed quite a few chances at some fish because of their splashy departures. He was, however, still having the best day of fishing he'd ever had—landing eight. One trout would easily have been in the eighteen-inch range. He would lie, of course, and tell everyone it was twenty-two inches long, as he would lie about the number fish he'd caught at his very first chance.

Belson was not a fisherman, nor would he ever be a fisherman. He couldn't cast. He had watched all the videos, but he just couldn't cast a fly line. Given his coordination level, he was lucky he could cast a shadow. Although he *had* perfected one method. A method that never failed him: the downstream dry-fly dead-drift cast, which, as Belson applied it, was no cast at all. Positioning himself far upstream, he would center himself in the feeding lane, strip off the line he needed, and feed the fly down to the rising fish. He let the current do his casting for him. It's perhaps the oldest method of fishing known to man; comparisons could be made to fishing with a kind of floating bait, and, like bait fishing, this downstream presentation is highly effective. It's deadly accurate. It's always drag free. But, it's considered by all true fisherman as a no-skill nonsport. In a word—cheating. In fly fishing, lying is almost an accepted practice, but cheating is an abomination.

As adept as he was at both lying and cheating, Belson was even better at downstream drifting, and he was about to apply this expertise on easily the largest trout he'd seen all day. Centering himself well above the rising trout, he started feeding out his line and bouncing his rod tip to add exactly the amount of line needed. The fly was dead on target, floating as well as the naturals. The fish would take. Just a few more feet now. Belson could taste it. He'd kill this one. If she was big enough, and she certainly looked big enough, he'd hang it on the wall in his den.

So intent was he on his line and his fly that the arrival of another fly in the midst of all those in the air went unnoticed. This fly landed just inches in front of his. The fish rose, and he struck. He leaned back against the strike, but there was nothing there—an air set. Planning on that resistance, but getting none, Belson bumbled over backward and was waist-deep, on his ass, in the muddy goo.

Looking through a pair of mud-splattered glasses he could just make out the shape of a wondrous trout. Water dripped from his Stetson and streamed down his face. He couldn't see well, but he could see well enough. He could see *his* fish fighting a line . . . but it wasn't *his* line. It was a line angling downstream. The chrome of an angler's rod tip sparkled above the willows. It was the only part of this trout thief Belson could see for the underbrush. Jud was laughing, just out of sight, on the blind side of the bend.

"Some son-of-a-bitch has my trout!" Belson's lips quivered. He was red hot and hopping mad. Grabbing his fly rod, he hissed, "I am not going to let that bastard get away with this." As he crossed the creek, he stumbled, and the Stetson rolled off his head and into the current. "To hell with it." He stormed into the willows and began thrashing his way through the underbrush toward Jud. Blinded by mud and by rage, and about twenty feet into the thicket, Belson's lack of regard for body or belongings was made audible by a crisp, brittle *snap*. His fly rod was now a three-piece. "Goddammit! I'll sue this son-of-a-bitch for damages." Making a wrong turn, he was lost in the willows for a time and managed to follow a game trail through a mucky bog—twice. On his second go-round he successfully ran into some barbed wire.

Jud heard a muffled cry. *Henry must have a good one on.* His trout, in the meantime, was tiring, and tired she should be after all those fantastic leaps. Bending his rod back, Jud brought the large rainbow gently into his net. Pinching the fly, he removed the hook from the fish's jaw. Then

~

he cradled the trout, net and all, upstream until she had calmed. She swam in the netting and the current as one. Looking down on this fabulous creature, he thanked Whoever it is who's in charge, and not only for the gift of this trout, but for the clouds, and this bend on a river. *The East Fork—if this ain't vana, it's near vana.*

A hat tumbled past him four feet underwater. He didn't see it. He heard what he thought to be a deer in the willows, and went back to admiring and reviving the rainbow. All was well in the world.

"That's *my* fish, asshole!"

Jud looked over his shoulder and nearly jumped from his hip boots. A bald, short, fat man lurked dripping wet and holding a mud-covered three-piece. His neoprene waders were in shreds. Jud, startled out of the serenity of the moment, now completely shattered, tried to ask, "How's that . . . wha . . . who? . . ."

"You stole the fish I was fishing for. You stole it right away from me."

"Well, mister, I sure am sorry about that, but I had no idea that you were there. I—"

"Never mind that—that's my fish."

"Now, calm down, mister. There's nothing that can be done about it now." *What is this guy doing in the middle of my day. How did old man Ashton let something this ugly on the ranch.*

"Well, it's my fish. You can give it to me now. You didn't happen to see a hat float by, did you?"

"I saw no hat and I'm not about to give you this fish, mister. In another few seconds, I'm going to let her go."

This brought Belson down the bank and in a hurry. "You will not let my fish go, or I shall sue you for theft."

"You're gonna *what*?" Jud laughed. *Here I was, near vana a second ago, fishing in paradise, and now I am in the middle of lawsuit with some little puke.*

"My name is Belson, David C. Belson. I am an attorney at law. I know of what I speak."

Jud, still kneeling over the fish and seeing that she was ready to go, let her do just that. "Say good-bye to your trout, Mr. Belson." The rainbow's fins feathered her from his net, and quickly she disappeared into the river.

"No!" Belson screamed. "I wanted that fish for my den. You moronic asshole." Belson went crimson with rage as Jud stood up, towering nearly a foot above him.

"I'm hardly a violent man, Mr. Belson, but if you call me an asshole once more, I'll be more than happy to knock you down."

"That's it," Belson said, stepping back two paces, but still pointing his finger. "Now you've threatened bodily harm, bodily harm by a thief, and an obvious trespasser. Oh, I can make a complaint out of this. I paid money to fish here. I paid one hundred dollars and was guaranteed, by verbal contract, to have the river to myself. Maybe I'll have you and the Ashtons both up on damages. Now, who are you and where do you live? How would you like your subpoena served?"

"Well, my name is Clark, Judson C. Clark, Mr. Belson. I live back in Travers Corners. I'm easy to find. And you can take your subpoena and . . ." Then the penny dropped. *Belson . . . the card left by the creep back at the Tin Cup. The little pervert who upset Sally so much . . . Belson.*

"That's all I need to know." The lawyer turned to leave.

"Say, Belson," Jud said calmly, blowing the water off his fly with one hand, while the other hand reached over and grabbed Belson by the suspenders, stopping him in his tracks, "you weren't by any chance down at the Tin Cup Cafe having breakfast this morning, were you?"

Struggling against Jud's hold, he answered, "What of it? Let me go or I'll add aggravated assault to your charges."

Jud whistled loudly, and a return whistle was heard from downstream.

"Who was that?" Belson asked nervously.

"Uh, that would be Henry," Jud said, letting him go but continuing to blow on his fly. "Anyway, like I was telling you before, Mr. Belson, I'm not a violent man. But, Henry downstream there, well, he's not a violent man, either—unless, of course, he's riled. Then Henry can be downright menacing. Practically the strongest man I ever knew. Great believer in vigilante justice, Henry. Oh, and you should also know this, Mr. Belson. Henry's a close friend, almost a father figure you might say, to that young waitress you were so crude to this morning? You really upset her, and that, of course, riled Henry."

Belson started to run, but Jud grabbed him once more. "I'm not a lawyer, it's something I sort of pride myself on, but which offense do you think would carry the heaviest fine in a court of law? I mean between stealing another man's fish, and sexual harassment?"

Belson wriggled free and ran, turning long enough to threaten, "You haven't heard the last from me."

Jud waved the man away. Then he stood with his hands on his hips, staring out over the valley. *What the hell just happened? That guy was awful. I should have socked him one. I'll be hearing from him . . . Hearing from him is one thing, but I sure do hope I don't have to* look *at him, too.*

Belson promptly got lost on the game trail, went through the bog once more, and managed to get back to where he had crossed just as the female skunk he had frightened from her nest on his first time through was returning to her young. This time she was poised and ready. She did what she had to do.

A muffled cry was heard in the willows.

Henry must be getting closer. "Over here, Henry."

Henry cut across the bend and Jud could hear him coming through the thicket. When he finally appeared on the opposite bank, he was holding a Stetson hat. "Waterlogged, but hell, the thing's brand new. I just found it pinned agin' a log. It don't fit, though—too big. It's a seven and five-eighths. Musta belonged to some kind of fat-headed monster?"

"It belongs to a monster all right."

"Yeah?"

"Yeah, in fact he just left my sight. He was this horrible little man.

Ugly. I mean butt-ugly." Jud's voice was so angry, it cracked from disbelief. The wind shifted. "I mean, there I was having a great time, near vana, and I had just landed this beautiful rainbow when this ugly little jerk jumps out of the willows and . . . Whooooweeeee." Jud was suddenly waving his hand in front of his face. "Now, that's a nearby skunk."

Deciding that it would be best to retreat to less pungent ground, they crossed the river. Heading upstream, Jud told Henry what had happened. Ending with the punch line, ". . . and the guy's name is, and this should fill in everything else you need to know about this guy, the guy's name is Belson."

"Belson? Belson—that's the guy who gave his card to Sally."

"The same guy."

"How'd he ever git on the Ashton Ranch?"

"Well, we'll tell George about him, and he won't ever get on the Bar A again. Wanted to kill my rainbow for his den. Man . . ."

"I woulda liked to talk to that creep, myself," Henry said with a grimace. "Maybe I could catch up with him?"

"Naw, he's long gone. He took out of here like a rabbit. He ran pretty fast for a fat man."

"Why was he runnin'?" Henry asked.

"I told him you were coming," Jud said with a smirk.

"Me?"

"Yeah, I told him how mad you got this morning when you heard what he had done to Sally. Told him that Sally was your girl." Jud smiled. "Told him that you would naturally have to kick his ass."

"I wouldn't beat him up," Henry laughed. "I mighta dog-slapped him a few times, though."

They fished the rest of the day away. Jud tried to regain the fine time he was having before it was destroyed by the Belson, but couldn't. And even though the fishing remained a constant, even though the afternoon warmed into the balmiest of the year, the wind died down to nothing, and he caught another big rainbow around seventeen inches, Jud just couldn't get rid of the image of Belson and his ugly little face screaming at him.

By the time he and Henry called it quits, walked back to the car, and drove to the ranch house, it was around seven o'clock. But the Ashtons were nowhere to be found, so Jud left them a note:

George—Ran into a guy named Belson by the middle field. Don't ever let him fish your ranch again. I'll tell you about him next time I'm up.

Anita—Sarah says she's coming up for a visit soon. Says she has some books for you to borrow.

Thanks from Henry, and me, too, for the fishing. It was great—
Jud

A few months passed. Jud never heard anything more from the Belson. No subpoena. Nothing. Henry had assured him that this would be the case. "That guy was all bluff," he would say.

Then early one July evening the word spread, and for Junior McCracken, Doc Higgins, Henry, and Jud it was a moment they would remember as they would remember where and what they were doing when Kennedy was shot.

Sal was tending bar and was among the first to hear the news. He felt as though he should call Jud; he would find out soon enough anyway. "Yeah, Jud, it's Sal . . . Yeah . . . Good. Listen, Kenny's down here on his way to a world-class bender. He's buyin' drinks for everyone . . . Hey, drunks are coming from all over the valley . . . Well, I got some bad news for ya—the Ashtons sold the Bar A. Some big corporation bought it. Paid four million for it . . . I don't know . . . Anyhow, the first thing these new owner-guys have done is paint nearly every fence post on the ranch bright orange. 'No Fishing' signs are posted everywhere . . . Yeah . . . Yeah . . . Sorry there, buddy, but I thought you should know . . . Yeah.

Hey, pal I gotta get goin' here . . . dis place is startin' to look like a fair night . . . Yeah, sure. I'll be seein' ya."

Jud took the news like the loss of a good friend. He called Henry. Henry called Junior McCracken, and Junior called Doc Higgins. Henry took the news like one might take a bullet. Junior was depressed. He paced and he ranted, as the East Fork on the Bar A was about the only place Junior had much luck fishing.

But of the four, the news might have hit Doc the hardest. He fished the Ashton Ranch more than anyone. It was his favorite. For days after hearing about the sale, Doc was moody, snappish to everyone in sight; he walked around town for weeks looking like someone had just kicked his dog.

Between the four of them they had more than a hundred years of fishing the Bar A. Now not one of them could fish there, and perhaps never again. They decided they would not give up without at least an inquiry. Two of them, Doc and Jud, would go see the new owners when the time presented itself. It didn't take long.

The day after the sale was final, two weeks after the Ashtons, John, George, and Anita, left the East Fork for a new life in Arizona, and one week after Kenny moved into his brand-new doublewide, the gossip reached Doc. One of the new owners was in at the Bar A.

Doc and Jud made the drive up the East Fork. They brought their fishing rods just in case. "It feels so damn strange. I mean after all those years of coming up to the Ashton place, thirty-nine years to be exact, that now I have to go up to some stranger, with my hat in my hand, and ask permission. I mean it gravels me." Doc packed his pipe while he was driving. "I wish George and Anita had never sold out, but things change and you can't stop it. I hate change."

"Me, too, Doc. Me, too," Jud replied. He, like Doc, had come to think of the Ashton water as his own, and certainly not in the sense of possession, but his own by way of the soulful attachments that grow from a favorite fishing haunt.

"I wonder how they're doing down in Arizona?" Doc asked, striking a match to his tobacco.

"Sarah's heard from Anita. All seems to be going fine. They love their new place, and George and her have taken up golf." Doc laughed at the thought of George Ashton in a pair of golf pants.

Later Sarah would receive a letter telling her how the decision to sell the ranch had come about. "It came after a series of events," Anita wrote, "all happening early one morning. George got up with his arthritis nearly crippling him. Poor old John was having his usual problems that come with being eighty-five. And I threw my back out trying to do work I used to find easy, but now it was too hard. Then Kenny came rolling in from a night drinking and he'd wrecked our new pickup.

"About an hour after all this, George got a call from a man representing a huge corporation. He said he wants to buy the ranch. Quoted George a price that was unbelievable. It all seemed like it was meant to be. George said send me the deal. When it came there were some changes to be made, and D&B Enterprises, that's the company that bought it, met all our requests. For some kind of tax reasons, they gave us fifty percent down. They also donated land to The Nature Conservancy.

"We were sad to go and happy to go. It was a good life, but it came to be a hard life. I wish Kenny was the man to take over, but he isn't."

Doc turned his car through the gates of the Bar A. The Bar A, after first being a homestead, then one of the showplace ranches in the Elkheart, was now a tax write-off. There were several cars out front. "Well, it looks as though someone is here, at any rate."

Knocking on the front door, and feeling uncomfortable about it, Doc stood waiting. Jud was still coming from the car as he had to go back and grab the cake he'd forgotten from the backseat. A cake made by the Travers Corners Welcoming Committee.

A woman came to the door. "May I help you?"

"Yes, my name is Dr. Thomas Higgins and I was wondering if I might have a word with the new owner of the Bar A?"

"What is your visit concerning?" the lady asked, acting and certainly looking like a secretary.

"Well, I . . . er . . . we"—he pointed to Jud, still coming up the walk—"we're wondering if it would be possible to do some fishing?"

"Please wait here." She left the front door open.

"Are they here?" Jud asked as he came to the door.

"Yeah."

A shape appeared down the hall. Though the hallway was dark, and he was looking through the mesh of the screen door, the shape looked familiar to Jud. It made him uneasy. The phone rang in another room and the shape shouted, "No calls. No visitors. No matter who it is—I'm not here." That voice. Jud felt his stomach drop. The voice and the shape were a match.

"Who are you? What do you want?" It was Belson at the door.

"Well, as I was saying to the lady, we were wondering if we could do any fishing? Oh, excuse me, my name is Dr. Thomas Higgins, and this is my friend Jud Clark."

Jud's name was shouted over by Belson. "Can't you people read the 'No Trespassing, No Fishing' signs? Does all that orange paint, orange paint everywhere, not mean anything to you? What is it with you country bumpkins, are you stupid? Nobody fishes here except for me and members of my corporation. I cannot believe th . . . Jud Clark?" The name had rung a bell. *"Judson C. Clark? The fish thief?"*

"That's right, Mr. Belson," Jud answered. He would try his best to smooth things over for Doc's sake and though it stuck in his throat, he thought it best to start with an apology, "Look, I'm sorry about our last run-in, but I wasn't trying to—"

"Not the same Jud Clark who caused me to break my brand-new fly rod, who made me ruin my brand-new waders, and who forced me into the path of a skunk after threatening me with bodily harm? And all this after he *stole* the biggest fish I have ever *seen?* It couldn't possibly be *that*

~

Jud Clark. Get off my property. *Get off!* And if I ever catch you anywhere near the Bar A, I'll call the sheriff."

"You ugly little puke. How can you, or anyone else for that matter, own a river?" Jud asked through tight lips.

"Because I have lots of money," Belson laughed, and slammed the door in their faces.

Doc turned and looked up at Jud. Then he smiled, the kind of smile you see at funerals. Belson, though he'd met him just seconds before, was no stranger. Doc had heard the story about the great fish robbery from both Henry and Jud. He'd also heard about the fifty-dollar tip and the business card. Belson was everything he'd been told and more.

The shock of what had just happened to him was leaving him with every step he made back to the car. Doc had that capability. He hadn't had much hope to begin with. The orange paint should have told him everything he needed to know, but he had to try. Just like he had to try with patients and friends, even when he knew death was imminent. And losing the dry-fly water on the East Fork was a death of sorts. Another death he was powerless to stop.

Jud, on the other hand, was steaming, even madder than the first day he'd met Belson. He had tried politely. Now we wanted to sock that little son-of-a-bitch. He wanted to pitch a rock through his window, but that would get him nowhere. He was glad Henry hadn't come along, for right about where Belson called them "country bumpkins," Henry would have gone through the screen door and dog-slapped Belson to the carpet. Then Belson would have him up on assault charges. He felt helpless, helpless to do anything. All he could do, like Doc, was face the realization: All those years on the East Fork were now gone.

Nearly at the car, Doc paused and couldn't help but laugh. "Judson, my boy, got a question for you. Why, with all the trout in the river, did you have to steal Belson's?"

Jud laughed as well. Sticking his finger in Sarah's cake and licking the icing from his finger, he answered, "Well, regardless of my stealing his trout, I don't think he was about to let anybody go fishing. Is that an ugly little man or what?"

"Ugly," Doc agreed, as he stood taking in the views from the lower fields all the way to Jeppson Canyon. "To paraphrase a famous line from Winston Churchill, 'We now can pack up and take the pleasure of our fishing elsewhere, but Belson will be ugly forever.'" A sort of resolute joy crossed his round face.

Jud laughed. "And on top of being ugly and mean, he fishes his dry fly downstream."

"Unspeakable."

Not much was said on the drive back to Travers Corners. But Jud, years later, could still remember his thoughts from that afternoon clearly . . .

How can a man own a river? How can he own the ever-changing, eternally flowing river? It's tantamount to owning the flight of a thunderbolt, a place in time, the paths of clouds, the wind itself, the will of nature.

Man cannot own something more powerful than he is.

There are those who would agree, but defend and retain their ownership of the river by contending that they own the land beneath the river and the streambank that holds the river. Isn't this the same as someone saying, I own the cradle therefore I own the life of its child?

No one can own life, not the life of a river, a life unto itself, nor the lives of all that inhabit it. How does anyone own the otter, the teal, the mayflies, the crayfish, the trout?

The thought of owning land was ridiculous to the last sane people to inhabit our land. They held the soil as sacred, and revered the rivers as spirits.

No one can own a spirit.

No matter what deity you choose, there can be no arguing with George Ashton . . . "It ain't my river. It's God's river."

Jud and Doc ended their day fishing the public water on the Elkheart. The day might have finished there, but the story, the Belson Saga, was far from over.

The first year after the Ashtons sold, things went along in Travers Corners as usual. No one heard or saw much of Belson. He built a landing strip in the middle fields, and he flew in and out of the Bar A.

There was only one incident, and that was when Belson, on one of his very rare appearances in Travers, stopped in at McCracken's to buy some more NO TRESPASSING signs. He timed it badly. Henry was inside buying some horseshoe nails. Henry, in deference to the ladies who were shopping, neither dog-slapped nor confronted him in any way. But he had to do something. What he did was quintessential Henry.

He'd been fishing that morning and had kept a few whitefish for his cat. His truck was parked next to Belson's Cadillac. He took the largest whitefish and shoved it down deep in Belson's backseat. Word got back to Junior that Belson then drove to the Bar A for a two-week stay. He parked the Caddy, left the windows closed, and didn't use the car once during his visit. It was the hottest part of August.

But in the second year, Belson was again making news in the valley. He had sued The Nature Conservancy. He'd found loopholes in their contract. To everyone's disbelief and dismay, he won the lawsuit. Belson then decided he would subdivide the Bar A. Twenty-acre ranchettes.

Several more months passed. Then Sarah received a letter from Anita Ashton. To Sarah the letter was good news, but to Junior, Henry, Jud, and especially Doc, it was music to their ears. Belson had lost the Bar A. Ownership had returned to the Ashtons by default. Anita wrote, ". . . seems like old Belson sued the wrong people back in Washington, D.C. Sued the kind of people who sue back. Belson got cleaned out, and couldn't meet the payments. We took back the ranch last Thursday.

"We have the ranch back to sell again, plus Belson's down payment. But Sarah, I don't think we're going to sell. George and I have been talking it over. We sure do miss Montana. We got the money from Belson invested; I think we'll just winter in Arizona and summer on the Bar A, and hire a ranch manager. Don't I sound fancy though. Who would of thunk it—something like this happening to George and me. Ha! Ha!—and thank you Mr. Belson."

Sarah got the letter on a Tuesday, and on Wednesday afternoon Doc was alone on the oxbow bends of the East Fork, fishing the middle fields, and all was right with the world.

From The Journals of Traver C. Clark

March 11, 1910—

Just came back from the cattle drive. Helena is far enough away by wagon but when you add three hundred head in front of you it takes forever. It's the same hot, dusty trail year in and year out. Sometimes Carrie and I wish we could go someplace exotic. Hawaii. White beaches and fruit. The clear blue waters catching fish taller than a man. The places pictured in the Geographic. *That would be something.*

Carrie said we were getting too old for that kind of holiday. I told her that if we can put our butts in the saddle and trail a herd for five days we could survive the rigors of ocean travel.

But it's all a dream. We will never go.

*Hotel bill—Two nights and meals for the
    hands and us -35.50
Sale of three hundred head at five cents
    a pound -13,500.00*

No Fishing Aloud

JUNIOR MCCRACKEN HAD been beside himself all afternoon. In fact, Junior had been beside himself for the better part of three weeks. Hyper enough normally, Junior was really wound up today. But he was justifiably excited because tomorrow his longtime, all-time favorite fishing hero, Conrad Sandolaré, was coming to Travers Corners.

Junior's was a hero worship not unlike the reverence paid other sport legends. A childlike envy that inhabits all men, envious of those few men who were fortunate enough to make play their life's work. There isn't an armchair quarterback out there who wouldn't give damn near everything to have led the life of Broadway Joe Namath. That would be on and off the field. Just as there isn't a duffer anywhere who wouldn't have traded his everyday life for the chance to play the greens as often and as well as Arnold Palmer played them. And there isn't an angler alive who wouldn't rather be fishing, day in, day out, than doing whatever it is he or she is doing for a living. But to be the very best fisherman, to be Conrad Sandolaré, what a sweet life that would be.

Fishing for a living—the very thought of it made Junior's mouth water. As he packaged up Joan Pierson's prescriptions, he pictured a life with no pharmacy, no hardware or groceries. He envisioned the life of a fly-fishing celebrity. To awaken each and every morning in some far-off and exotic place where the only decisions facing you were whether you should cast for tarpon, or cast for bonefish, or maybe give a cast or two for a twenty-pound sea-run brown. One day salmon fishing in Norway. The next day winging your way to Quebec for brook trout. That would be a far cry from his daily cast, which was to cast his lot, body and soul, into the American work ethic. Six days a week, and more often than not seven, and all of them the same.

As he rubbed the prescription label to the plastic container, he wondered, as he had wondered a thousand times, what it would be like to be in Belize sipping a rum drink in one hand and fighting a permit rocketing away with his line in the other, to be in Ireland fishing for Atlantic salmon, to be in Patagonia trying for world-class rainbows, to be Conrad Sandolaré. Junior had read all his books, watched all his videos, clipped and saved every article he had ever written. Tomorrow night he would be having dinner with him.

Adding to Junior's anxiety level: the dozens of prescriptions yet to fill, a shipment of baling twine waiting to be put away, thirty-five cartons of groceries just arrived, and twenty-two boxes of hardware still sitting on the loading dock from yesterday. On top of everything else, he had a meeting with the banker at four-thirty. He was going to need an extension on his loan. With two boys in college and his sales down, he would be asking for the lo-o-ong extension.

No doubt about it, business was off—way off. But that was no fault of Junior's. The Elkheart Valley, like all of Montana, like the entire West, was in its third year of drought. Cattle prices were down. The hay crops were minimal. And when the ranchers tightened their belts, McCracken's General Store felt the squeeze. He even had to cut back Patty Cole's hours. She had worked for him full time for six years, and without her help it seemed he was forever behind.

But even though he was feeling the pressure of work and feeling the guilt of laying Patty off, he had tomorrow night to hang on to. It was going to be grand and memorable. Dinner up at Jud's place. Dinner with Conrad Sandolaré.

Up at the Boat Works, later in the same day, Jud was busy readying everything for the arrival of Sandolaré. Jud dreaded the thought of being a host. A few close friends coming over for dinner, that was one thing, but this thing had gotten out of hand. There were going to be at least sixty people coming for dinner, fishermen friends from up and down the Elkheart. Thankfully, Doc Higgins and Junior had donated the beer, and the side dishes were being brought potluck. But Jud was supplying the beef, and it was costing him more than two hundred dollars at a time when two hundred dollars had higher purposes. Things like his electric bill and the daily groceries came to mind. Drought years are not the best years to be a builder of riverboats. Like everywhere else, things were tight around the Boat Works.

Helping Jud set up the tables, which they borrowed from the school, was Sal. Sal wasn't a fisherman, nor did he understand fishing or people who fished. "So dis guy dat's comin', dis Salderoney, or Santorada, how's dat guy's name go again?"

"San-do-lar-yaa," Jud answered phonetically.

"Okay. Sandolaré. What is he, some kind of a big deal or somethin'?"

"He would be the fly-fishing equivalent of . . ." Jud paused, struggling for the right analogy, ". . . of say, Joe DiMaggio."

Sal gave a comical, incredulous look to Jud. He smirked, gave his shoulders a shrug, and in a motion said without saying, *Who're you kidding? DiMaggio has no equal.* "Hey. Where do ya want me to stack these glasses?"

"Right over there, Sal." Jud pointed to a piece of plywood straddling a pair of saw horses. "Thought we'd put the keg over there out of the sun. Sarah's bringing a tablecloth to dress it up a little. Getting pretty fancy around here."

Jud then looked past Sal carrying two trays of glasses, past the saw horse table, to the reason Conrad Sandolaré was coming to Travers in the first place: his brand-new driftboat, which was now parked and waiting for him in the shade of the aspens and cottonwoods lining the drive. Sitting on padded braces, because Sandolaré was bringing his own trailer to pick her up, she was easily the most beautiful dory he had ever built. Hand-tooled, every inch of her. She was all specialty woods, imported and hand-rubbed to perfection. Her sides, handpicked cedar and mahogany, were low and sleek. Teak gunwales finished with rich brass trimmings made her elegant. The padded braces beneath her, hidden now in the shadow she cast, made the dory appear to be floating already. She was a beauty. She would handle like a dream.

He was prideful all right, on the verge of boasting, and he would have boasted, right then and out loud to Sal, but there would be no point in boasting to Sal. Sal knew nothing about tools, zero about woods, and even less about riverboats. Sal had a major-league fear of the water. Bathtubs were his limit. And though he could sit and watch a river for hours, there was no chance of him physically getting into a boat and floating down one.

Jud took one more look at the dory, so good looking he almost hated to sell her. But, he thought as he returned to setting up the last of the folding chairs, she should be good looking, for she was a driftboat who had her privileges and special treatments. She was coming in at nearly two thousand dollars higher than his usual boats. So Sandolaré's arrival was being anticipated, and not so much because of his fishing status. Jud was looking forward to Sandolaré paying off his rather substantial balance.

Slipping on his usual Yankees warm-up jacket as Jud unfolded the last three chairs, Sal said, "Hey, I don't wanna be nosy, but unfortunately I was born nosy, so I gotta ask. I mean, okay, dis guy has DiMaggio status, but sixty people for dinner? I mean, weren't you just complainin' about havin' no dough just a couple of days ago?"

"Well, the whole thing just got out of hand. For one thing, when I thought of having Sandolaré over for dinner, I thought of it in front of Junior. Sal, never have an idea in front of other people. They somehow end up thinking because they were there when the idea happened, that the idea is as much theirs as it was yours. So Junior got all excited. He invited Doc and Henry and Lee Wright and Red Peterson . . . and . . . you name 'em. Then the word leaked out and from out of nowhere about a week ago, Judge Rinehart called me. Wanted to be invited down. Wanted to bring Senator Mills with him. People are coming from Missoula and Helena. I've got fifty steaks, because there are fifty people coming to eat, and I know of at least ten more folks who said they were going to just try to stop by.

"And another reason I'm going through with this party idea is that Conrad Sandolaré is responsible for a great deal of my business."

"How's that?" Sal asked.

"Well, about ten years ago, Sandolaré was hosting one of those travel fly-fishing video shows. You know where the host takes a celebrity fly fishing to some exotic fly-fishing destination, right?" Sal nodded. "Anyway, this one time he was doing the show from the Big Horn River. A guide over there, a fellow named Reggie Lee, was guiding him and Michael Keaton, the actor, down the river. Reggie rows one of my boats. So, during the show, Sandolaré takes the oars and lets Reggie fish for a while. Well, Sandolaré starts raving about the boat. Then Keaton tries rowing. The Batman at the oars. He thinks it's great.

"Anyway, at the end of the show he thanks Reggie and Keaton for joining him. Then he adds, and this is like a prime-time, coast-to-coast show, if you want to own one of these dories, contact Jud Clark, the Boat Works, Travers Corners, and so forth. Well, that one plug turned the Boat Works from a barely-scraping-by kind of business to a three-year-waiting-list kind of business. And that's why I'm doing all of this—I owe him. Going to take him fishing tomorrow as well."

"Does dis guy know that there's gonna be a mob waitin' for him?"

"Yeah, I've talked to his secretary. He's all clued up. She says he's looking forward to meeting everyone. She also warned me that he has a tendency to show up late."

"Well, I'm late and I'm leavin'," Sal said, walking to his van. "Oh, Sarah said that she's made you about five gallons of chili for your party. Said she'd bring it tomorrow afternoon."

"Hey, thanks for your help, Sal. You're not coming, are you?"

"DiMaggio, sure. Dis guy, I don't think so."

Jud laughed and started walking back to the workshop, thinking about how hot it was and how it was supposed to be even warmer tomorrow. He couldn't stand the thought of it. The beginning of another scorching summer, after another rainless spring. The Elkheart was heading into another hard year. Another summer of drought and Montana would catch fire and burn to the ground.

Consciously he forced himself toward more pleasant thoughts, and he laughed again thinking about Sal, who was right, he considered, when he dismissed Jud's comparison between DiMaggio and Sandolaré. That, he conceded, was a bit of a stretch. But there was a similarity.

Like Joltin' Joe once was, Conrad Sandolaré was now at the top of his sport. However, only fly fishermen knew about him. When DiMaggio took the field and punched one over the centerfield fence in the '47 Series, fifty thousand fans watched it. Millions more heard it over their radios. All across the nation baseball fans were either frozen or frenzied by the moment, and DiMaggio became legend.

Legends, more than not, are usually born at the center of some kind of roar and pandemonium.

When Sandolaré caught a ten-pound rainbow, perhaps the angling equivalent to a Series-winning home run, hardly anyone outside the guide and a few mallards would know about it. Certainly, those fly fishermen who read his articles and books would eventually learn about his rainbow through photographs and prose. But the moment was secondhand, and not exactly the *now* of a Series game.

The angling audience is probably the farthest thing from a ninth-inning, seventh-game, World Series crowd that you could find. They're usually half asleep in an easy chair, recovering after a hard day at the office while intermittently reading and dozing through one of San-dolaré's articles. Dreaming themselves into Sandolaré's shoes. Stalking a salt flat, or tiptoeing up to a trout from the comfort of their den.

Legends are seldom born from the sleepy imaginings of armchair anglers. In their loosened ties and old slippers they quietly muse in front of their fires, Old Shep curled up at their feet.

But Jud, having read Sandolaré's articles and a few of his books, and even struggled halfway through one his videos, sensed that while perhaps 99.9 percent of the world had no idea who Sandolaré was, and wouldn't care if they did, the man still thought of himself as legend. A dry-fly DiMaggio. His ego came across clearly on both page and screen.

But Jud would give credit where credit was due. Like DiMaggio and his bat, Sandolaré with a fly rod was something to see. He was a master fisherman. There was no denying it. On the grand scale of the truly famous, though, Sandolaré was merely a small-time celebrity.

At five o'clock the next afternoon the Boat Works was a hub of activity. The barbecues were being tended, tables being set, and beer being tapped and sampled by some of the men who'd come early. By five-thirty there were clusters of men scattered about under the shade. Doc, Junior, Red Peterson, Lee Wright, Gary Brown, Doug Gillespie, and other local fishermen were gathered near the keg talking about the local fishing. Some of their wives were helping Sarah line up all the potluck additions: salads, potato dishes, casseroles, desserts. Dolores was helping Sarah with the portable propane stove and a five-gallon pot of chili.

Henry would be purposely late, and no doubt he'd be leaving early. He'd never bothered to read but one or two of Sandolaré's fishing articles. He'd never read one of his books, though he had flipped through a few. And never would he bring himself to watch a video. In fact, the very thought of fishing videos made Henry gag. Jud always remembered what Henry had said one night after an evening of fishing some years before: "Videos, fishin' celebrities, books, 'n magazine articles. Most all of it is hype, and what's left is jest another man's bullshit.

"All of it runs contrary to the pleasurable pastime of fly fishin'. It should be outlawed, all of it. If a man wants to learn about fishin' then his father like his father before him should teach him. It's a craft, meant to be practiced alone in the quiet of the woods, and not a goddamn media event." And Jud knew that much of what Henry was saying was true. He also knew that Henry was the best fly fisherman he'd ever seen and would stack his streamside skills against Sandolaré's or anyone else's.

By six o'clock there wasn't a soul coming who wasn't already there. Jud made a rough head count, and the toll was forty-eight. The steaks were covered.

By seven o'clock people were shooting suspicious glances to one another, wondering if Sandolaré was going to be a no-show. A truck was heard coming up the hill. All turned in anticipation, but it was only Henry and Dolores. Jud was getting a little nervous, and Dolores, sensing his uneasiness, gave him a wink. The same wink she'd been giving him since the were in grade school. Now, there isn't a man living, Jud imagined, who wouldn't derive some form of pleasure from one of Dolores's winks. Not being able to help himself, as he hadn't been able to help himself since he was sixteen, he gave her anatomy an almost involuntary once-over. He tried not to stare at her breasts, but failed. Dolores, for a woman in her forties, was still stunning. She was one of those Lena Horne, ageless women with a much younger woman's figure. She didn't care about fishing. She just came to be with Henry.

The whine of low gears was heard. A Land Rover pulling an empty trailer crested the drive. It was Sandolaré.

A shorter-than-expected man bounced spryly out of the Rover. His hat came off with one hand, while his other was extended, and headed for the closest angler. "I'm Conrad Sandolaré. Which one of you is Jud Clark?"

"That would be me," Jud answered, weaving his way through the guests to shake his hand.

~

"So, where's my dory?"

"Sitting right over there." Jud pointed.

"Ah, it looks fine." Then he turned back to the guests. "Hello, every-one." Sandolaré waved. "Quite a gathering." He was noticeably gra-cious and charming, and a lot older looking in real life. "I am so sorry I am late. I was detained, really. But I know"—he spoke in an easy, clear, and slightly louder voice for those still standing back by the keg— "that my excuse for this tardiness will be well accepted, especially in a crowd such as this. You see, late this afternoon, I had an appointment with a five-pound, four-ounce rainbow." A murmur of recognition and under-standing passed through the attending fishermen.

"Where were you fishing?" Jud asked, put off by the fact that San-dolaré had just given nothing more than a cursory glance to the best-looking river dory in the West. The boat was two months in the building. Jud already didn't like this guy.

"I was over on the Big Hole River with my camera and my crew. My fishing was fabulous all day. Despite the heat. I could stand a drink."

"That's a keg of beer over there," Jud said.

"I was hoping for an open bar. More of an adult beverage. Do you have a bottle of Scotch anywhere?"

"Nope."

"Then beer will have to do, won't it?" Conrad was visibly displeased, and only so Jud would know it, then was back to flashing his smile.

"Evidently," Jud grinned. The Great Sandolaré had been at the Boat Works for less than a minute and had rubbed Jud the wrong way twice. The first wave of excuses for not taking him fishing tomorrow began for-mulating in his mind.

"Hey, Junior, do me a favor, will ya?" Jud asked, motioning the man over. "Get Conrad a glass, and would you introduce him around? I'm gonna get these barbecues going. Conrad, this is Junior McCracken, Tra-vers Corners' most ardent angler and easily one of your biggest fans." Jud then turned and walked away, muttering something under his breath.

"Well, it would be a pleasure," Junior responded and started for the fishermen gathered around the keg, Sandolaré right behind him. Junior didn't make it two steps before he walked straight into a folding chair. He went down in a tangle. Conrad looked at him curiously and then continued on toward the beer. Though fifty feet apart, Jud and Henry both caught the fall. They shook their heads and smiled at one another. They'd been watching Junior fall down all their lives.

Junior McCracken was beside himself once more. Any more beside himself and he would have been twins. The comparison made earlier between DiMaggio and Sandolaré would have been more than fair to Junior. In fact, through Junior's eyes, compared to Sandolaré, DiMaggio held a minor-league, second-string, bench-material sort of status. Although Junior was never a sports fanatic, he had always loved fly fishing. It was his main passion, coming in second behind breathing.

Love as he might the art of the angle, Junior's coordination level eventually came into play, and an observer watching him fish would more than likely wonder why he bothered to do it at all. Angling and all its nuances—casting, presenting the fly, mending, wading, tying knots, handling line, scrambling up streambanks, getting in and out of the car—all presented problems to Junior. In those rarest of moments when Junior actually managed to have a fish on, his excitement ran headlong into his diminished agility. It usually resulted in some sort of fumble, mishap, or collision. A betting man could comfortably give away odds in favor of the fish.

Readying the coals, Jud looked over to see Junior over by the keg talking with Sandolaré. He was pacing in place, bouncing up and down on his toes. He was talking fishing with his fishing hero. The crowd gathered around them. Soon Jud could see, though out of earshot, Sandolaré holding center stage and recounting fishing adventures with great animation and style. Junior, standing to Sandolaré's immediate left, was slack-jawed with awe, two feet from his hero, and unconsciously spilling the beer from his glass onto his shoes.

"It's a wonder to me and always has been, jest how he manages to git all those pills into them tiny little bottles," Henry said, opening another bag of coals.

"Now don't you two pick on Junior," Sarah added, joining them briefly—long enough to find a grater. She then went back by her chili and began shredding cheddar.

"Yeah, Junior has always been a caution," Jud said, lighting a match and tossing it on the coals. "But right now he's in hog heaven. I've heard him say many times, too many times, that he's learned more about fishing and casting from Conrad Sandolaré than anyone else. Making either Sandolaré the world's worst teacher or Junior the world's worst pupil."

"Well, it's kinda the monkey and the football situation, ain't it? I mean what's a monkey gonna do with a football? About the same thing as Junior is gonna do with a fly rod. I mean, them videos might jest work for some folks, but this here is Junior that we are talkin' about, and fer Junior walkin' and chewin' gum are scheduled as separate activities." They both laughed then looked over to Sarah, who shot them a mock dirty look as she knew they were still teasing Junior. Just like they always did.

Junior, in Sarah's estimation, was one of the more amazing characters she'd met in Travers Corners, or anywhere else. Sure, he was a klutz, but he was a brilliant klutz. His hobbies for life, in addition to fly fishing, had been math and the sciences: physics, calculus, astronomy, chemistry, biology. He understood why the sugars, amino acids, and carbons of the world did what they did. Sure, he couldn't walk and chew gum, but he could do chemical breakdowns and work algebraic theorems at the same time. And to Sarah, a schoolteacher for fifteen years, this was far more impressive than someone who could masticate and perambulate simultaneously.

On their fishing outings he never ceased to amaze Jud and Henry with all the stuff he knew. They envied his brain, but they never envied his fishing. With Jud, as it was for Henry, fishing was just being out on the stream, aloof momentarily from any responsibility or duty. Just a guy flinging his fly and hoping to fool a few fish.

But with Junior, fishing was always viewed through the sciences. He was never out there casting a fly. He was casting a duplication of one of the macro-invertebrates living in a biomass capable of supporting healthy populations of salmonids. He thought like that. He talked like that. Not all the time, but certainly after a few beers when he tended to get carried away.

At this very moment Junior was getting carried away. He had Sandolaré almost pinned in against the keg. He was pacing back and forth. His back was turned, his hand was raised, as he worked an imaginary chalkboard. He was explaining his theory concerning chemical imbalances in trout streams and their effects on feeding. "You see, if the stream is slightly deoxygenated, then the lateral line is less efficient in its assimilations, and what becomes almost logarithmic at this point is . . ."

But just as Junior was about to reach the biochemical proof of his ideas, he turned from his invisible chalkboard and noticed that Sandolaré was gone. Embarrassed by talking to thin air, Junior picked up his cup and refilled it at the keg. Then he saw Sandolaré moving smoothly through the crowd. He was homing in on Dolores.

Spotting Dolores from the moment he'd arrived at the Boat Works, Sandolaré had kept the gorgeous redhead in the corner of his eye for nearly an hour. Not one man was paying attention to her, although not one man could pass, he'd noticed, without paying Dolores some attention. He bided his time, and when the moment arrived for the guests to stand in line for their chili and steaks, Sandolaré made sure he was standing in that line right beside her. He quickly engaged her in conversation. As the owner of a beauty parlor, Dolores was no stranger to conversation. Conrad naturally mistook the easiness of her small talk, as one with his ego might, for flirtation. When she headed for the table where Junior, Red, Doc, Lee Wright, along with Judge Rinehart with Senator Mills and their wives, were already seated, he followed. And when she sat down, it was Sandolaré sitting down beside her—close beside her.

Henry and Jud joined them after all the steaks were served. Henry sat at the far end of the table next to Junior in a chair Junior had been saving in the hope that Sandolaré would sit next to him. Jud squeezed in next to Doc. Sandolaré was just finishing a story about Atlantic salmon in Russia. He was a good storyteller. While his voice carried easily as far as Junior who was craning after his every word, his eyes, and libido, seldom left Dolores.

". . . and so that was quite a day. I landed twenty-two salmon averaging twelve pounds, and all on a dry fly. The outskirts of Siberia. Wilderness all around me." As a nonfisherman, Dolores took it all in politely. Doc was enjoying himself, along with all the other men, and Junior was nearly caved in from envy.

Sandolaré had the floor and was in no danger of relinquishing it. He raised his glass of beer to those at his table, "They have a toast in Russia, and translated it goes, 'May your days and your fish be long.'"

Henry leaned back in his chair and Dolores did as well. From the opposite end of the table Henry communicated through a tired look that he was bored and about fed up from listening to this guy. He wrinkled his brow and tossed his head toward the road home. Dolores expressed a helpless look by arching her eyebrows and crossing her eyes. She had a silly smile that read, *Get me out of here*. Henry laughed.

"So, Mr. Judson C. Clark, where will we be fishing tomorrow on my new river dory's maiden voyage?" Conrad suddenly asked.

Taken slightly back, as it was the first sentence Sandolaré had uttered all evening that hadn't started with *I* or ended with *me*, Jud answered, "There's about only one place I can take you that has enough water, and that's down the Elkheart. Normally we would be floating the lower East Fork, but it's already too low to float. In fact, another week of this heat and the fork is going to dry up and blow away."

"Good, then the Elkheart it is. This drought of yours is terrible. The nastiest drought I remember was when I was fishing along the Great Barrier Reef in Australia, hopping along the coast from one town to the next. No water for days. Livestock dying everywhere. I was fishing for the rare leaping tiger fish, so named because of the coloration of their tarponlike scales, which, when they are hooked, flare into a burst of orange. And when they jump from the sea they look like a Bengal tiger and fight like one as well. I remember this one fish . . ."

Jud tuned out. He decided to sit back and just watch Conrad's next few sentences. Then it came to him, what it was that was making him so edgy about Sandolaré. Everything about the guy was a contrivance. Starting with his famous fishing hat—a colorful, woolish, Irish-looking thing festooned with fishing pins from around the world. He was never seen without it. Kind of his trademark. A wool hat on the hottest day of the year. He was wearing saltwater fishing attire. While cool, it looked a little silly a thousand miles from the nearest reef. His hair hung straight down: long, wispy, and fine. His leathery face was drawn taut, the kind of unnatural tightness that might have come from a face-lift, but it was hard to tell. His smile was capped and flashy. Only small wrinkles appeared at the corners of his eyes . . . eyes that had a certain madness and a curious manner about them. They were blue and bordering on manic. They almost buzzed. They nearly vibrated from their sockets when he looked at Dolores.

It was like there was a younger man trapped within him and looking for a way out. Jud hoped, for Dolores's sake, that a younger Sandolaré never got out. Conrad, a man solidly in his sixties, would play second lecher to no man. A younger Sandolaré would probably have to be kept on a leash.

His manner of speaking was troubling Jud. It had a European tone but was somehow strangely devoid of any accent. It was clipped, precise, and affected, much like the rest of him. He talked as though scripted.

"... yes, that was the worst dry spell, and the best tiger fishing in the history of Western Australia."

From the far end of the table Junior wanted to shout, *I remember the article you did about the tiger fish,* but he would have felt dumb.

"Well, I'm gonna have a little more of Sarah's chili," Jud said, pushing back his folding chair. "She makes the best." A compliment lost on Sarah, who had left right after she helped serve up the dinners. She had the same basic outlook on fishing as her Uncle Sal. Whenever men gather to talk of nothing but fishing, a little bit goes a long way. In her house hung a sign, one she made after a particularly tedious evening with Doc, Junior, Henry, and Jud. She kept it in her broom closet, only taking it out to post whenever there was more than one fisherman in her kitchen. It read NO FISHING ALOUD.

Joining Jud by the chili, Junior said excitedly, "I remember that article he wrote about the tiger fish. Those fish are huge. Man, on a ten-weight I would have a field day. Those fish ... those fish are like tarpon and ..."

Smiling and meaning full well to interrupt—with Junior, Jud had learned, one needed to nip the fishing story in the bud, or there was no stopping him—Jud asked, "Junior, what are you doing tomorrow?"

"I've got six days' worth of work ahead of me tomorrow."

"Why don't you call in sick? Why don't you come fishing with Sandolaré and me?"

"Oh, jeez. Oh, man. You're kidding? Oh, that would be great. But I can't." Junior's answer caused his face to agonize. His eyes, even behind his thick glasses, were unmistakably pained. His stomach, cramped from the want of going, pitched him slightly forward until chili spilled from his bowl and down his pants. "Oops."

"Call that guy up in Reynolds who substitutes at the pharmacy for you and take the day off."

"Oh, gosh, I don't know ... I ... we ... er ... I couldn't leave Pam all alone?"

"Pam would want you to go. Run the idea by her once."

"Oh, I don't know . . ."

"Go and ask her."

"All right, I will."

When the dinner was finished fans from the other tables started to gather around so they could better hear Sandolaré's stories. Soon everyone was standing around him. Jud stood by the beer where he could hear Conrad entertaining everyone. Right now he was off to South America to be the first man ever to take Uruguay's famous ring-tailed bass on a deer-hair popper.

Jud watched Junior asking Pam about tomorrow. She not only gave him the go-ahead, but gave him a big kiss and a sock on the arm as well. Junior flashed a thumbs-up to Jud. Then he hurried back to hear about the ring-tailed bass, even though he had the video.

Of all the marriages around Travers, Jud was thinking, Junior had the best. They lived and worked side by side. Married for twenty-five years, they could still be seen walking home hand in hand from the general store every evening. Hand in hand. Most married couples, if forced to work and live together, would be coming home hand to hand.

Having heard about enough from this guy, Henry stood and threaded himself between Red Peterson and Lee Wright and some other people he had never seen before. He tapped Dolores on the shoulder and quizzically asked, with a toss of his head and a furrowing of his brow, if it wasn't time for them to go. She motioned back by nodding in agreement, but then wrinkled up her nose signifying that he would have to wait a minute or two. He nodded back and unwillingly joined the crowd.

"I delivered the fly and the bass struck. That last ringtail must have jumped ten times. A world record on five-pound tippet."

A jealous murmur passed through the crowd, and it seemed to be a good time for Dolores to make her move. "Well, it was sure nice to meet you, Mr. Conrad Sandolaré," she said, pushing back her chair, "and I sure hope you have good fishin' tomorrow."

Sandolaré grabbed her arm and gently brought her back into her chair. "But you can't go. The evening is young."

"Well, it's not that I don't want to stay and listen to some more of your wonderful adventures, but I'm tired and we still have some chores." Dolores began to stand up once more.

"We?"

"Henry and me." Sandolaré shot upright and helped Dolores from her seat. Henry was standing behind her. "This here is Henry."

Sandolaré reached to shake his hand, and begrudgingly, but not so reticent that anyone would notice, Henry shook it. "I'm Conrad Sandolaré."

"I've heard," Henry said with his usual deadpan, reacting as though he'd just been introduced to any other man. Most fishermen went calf-eyed in front of Sandolaré, openly coveting his life and reputation. Envy. It's the look celebrities thrive on. Look at them the same way you'd look at anyone else, and it unnerved them.

Henry's look had just unnerved Sandolaré, and he quickly turned his attention back to Dolores. "Henry looks like a capable cowboy," he said pronouncing *cowboy* with an inflection insulting to Henry's ear. "Certainly, he can do the chores alone."

"No, we really do gotta go, Conrad," Dolores said sweetly. She'd had older men flirt with her before, and she was very good at handling them. "You sure have led one incredible life—goin' all those places. You come back to Montana and real soon." Sandolaré took her hand and kissed it. Henry rolled his eyes.

Henry and Dolores said the rest of their good-byes as they moved through the crowd. Sandolaré leered after her. Jud wasn't sure but he thought he saw spittle forming at the corners of his mouth. The gathering then turned its attention back to Sandolaré, who was quickly on to another story, to everyone's delight. Jud sensed a certain despair about him. He told stories and answered questions for more than an hour, but without the same flair.

As the crowd started to thin out, Sandolaré pulled Jud to one side. "Is there any chance of giving Dolores a call and see if she would like to join us fishing tomorrow?" he asked.

"Well, in a word—no. She and Henry have been together for years."

"Those are the kind of women I find the most irresistible. What does a woman of her obvious qualifications find in a *cowboy* like that? He couldn't put more than a few words together."

By this time Jud, like Henry, was closing in on having just enough of this little man. He had reached the Sandolaré saturation point. Purposely choosing the tone in his voice, he answered with a polite sarcasm, "Well, some folks say more in two words than others can say even if they talked all night. As far as what Dolores sees in him, well, that would probably be what everybody else around Travers sees in him. You see, Henry just happens to be a really great guy. But, him being my best friend and all, I might be a little biased. Maybe, just maybe, she likes him for his reputation."

"Reputation?"

"Yeah, old Henry just happens to be, and you can ask any fisherman around here, maybe the best fly fisherman around. Better than anyone I've ever seen, live *or* on video." He could see that all of what he'd said had registered in Sandolaré's eyes, so he quickly changed tack. "Anyway, there won't be any room for Dolores tomorrow because I've asked Junior McCracken to join us."

"You *what?* You should have checked with me! I hate fishing with amateurs," Sandolaré snapped. His upper lip tightened as his voice hissed. His eyes were full of resentment. His face twisted in anger. He closed his eyes, took two very deep breaths, and, just as easily as he might have slipped on a mask, was smiling again. "It's time for me to leave. I will be here at eight, and I will be ready to fish." He went quickly to his Land Rover. Then standing by the door, he reached in and gave the horn a honk to the assemblage (more than half the anglers still remained) and shouted, "It was a pleasure to meet you all. I want to thank you for having me. I had a wonderful time." He then added, with a wave of his famous hat, his signature closing from his articles and films, "Good-bye, and I hope to see you on the next bend of the river."

Jud felt a little nauseous.

The Rover turned full circle, empty trailer behind, and headed back down the hill to his room at the Take 'er Easy Motel. Junior hurried over, looking happier than Jud had seen him in weeks. But then it was Junior's kind of evening, everyone talking about fishing. Usually it was just him talking about fishing whether there was anyone listening or not. "Did you ask him if it was all right if I came along tomorrow?"

"You bet, and he was happy to have you aboard."

"Oh, boy," Junior responded. Jud laughed, as it was strange to hear a grown man say *Oh, boy.*

On the drive home Henry said, smiling, "Old Conrad sure was bird-doggin' you all evenin'."

"That old pervert was more than bird-doggin," Dolores laughed. "He was playing kneesies under the table with me all evenin' long."

"You're kiddin'?"

"Nope."

"Why didn't ya do somethin'?"

"It was a nice party and I didn't wanna make any kinda scene, him bein' Jud's famous guest and all. Anyway, he's just a dirty ol' man and he ain't no kind of threat. It ain't the first time some ol' fart played kneesies with me. Harmless ol' coot."

"I'm thinking that old coot is about as harmless as a sack full of rattlers."

"Well, put the pedal to the metal, son. Git me on home. I want to show you my own special variation on kneesies." Dolores leaned in so she could bite Henry's ear.

The next morning the three men met at the Boat Works. By eight o'clock they were at the river: Junior, Jud, and Sandolaré with his brand-new drift boat, just unloaded, and floating for the first time. Rocking gently in the shallows, the dory's cedar and brass trimmings caught the morning light. Her smooth curves, duplicated and shimmering, reflected in the quiet of the eddy.

Quick as a cat Sandolaré was over the side of her gunwale and taking the oarsman's seat. He cut off Jud, who was aiming for that seat by habit; he knew that if the fishing was going to be any good today, it would be in the morning, and he wanted Junior—far more in need of a little fishing than himself—to have the best chances. So he went to the seat in the stern.

Junior, bursting with anticipation, untied the boat and shoved it into slightly deeper water. He did this so his added weight, soon to be on board, wouldn't cause the dory to hit bottom. Satisfied with the depth, Junior then climbed on board.

Navigating over a gunwale of a rocking boat in full chest waders can be a little awkward even for the coordinated. Junior made it over fine, bringing the bowline with him. But somehow the rope tangled in his feet, and when Junior tried to get it free, he pitched forward and landed head-first on Sandolaré's fly rod. The heart-rendering snap and crush of graphite was heard. The rod was shattered.

Junior felt terrible. Anger flashed in Sandolaré's eyes, but with a few deep breaths he controlled it. "Think nothing of it," he said most graciously, "I've got others." He nimbly leapt out of the dory, went back to the pickup, and was back with another fly rod. "The company I endorse gives me these things free."

It was only eight-thirty but already warm, the sky cloudless. And the only wind blowing was the breeze created by the river, barely strong enough to bend the grasses.

The morning progressed pretty much as Jud had envisioned. Junior had taken one fish; Jud had taken five fish from the stern. Sandolaré never wet a fly. Staying on the oars into the afternoon, he talked about his adventures in New Guinea, Patagonia, Africa: basically a running narrative on Conrad Sandolaré.

Junior was in heaven. He was fishing, talking about fishing, and learning more about fishing from the best angler, in his estimation, in the world. Junior missed another rainbow.

Jud was amazed at how easily the old man rowed the boat, and he did it with a strength that Jud could well measure. For a man of his age and size Sandolaré was powerful, and he handled the boat well. He was dodging all the rocks, usually well underwater this time of the year. It was June but the river looked like August. If they didn't get some rain, and soon, the river wouldn't be there.

"Are you sure you don't want to fish?" Junior asked, turning to Sandolaré. "I'll be glad to row."

"If anyone else rows, it'll be me," Jud answered. "You needed this day off, Junior. I went fishing only last Tuesday, and I've been out, luckily, quite a few times this year. So you go ahead." That wasn't exactly the whole reason why Jud was being so magnanimous—volunteering to row. He knew from many days of fishing with Junior that rowing a boat wasn't one of his best points. He was all right at the oars—unless, of course, anybody in the boat actually wanted to catch any fish. Also, Jud didn't wish to see Sandolaré's new dory hit any boulders. Plus Jud was dying to row her. After all, she was the best-looking boat he'd ever built.

"You're a good friend, Jud Clark." Junior returned to fishing, but not immediately, as his fly had somehow stuck itself into the butt of his waders.

"So, you want to fish a while, Conrad?" Jud asked.

"Yes, I would, but I was wondering if there is anywhere that we can get out to fish."

Junior, anxious to tell his mentor something that he didn't know about fishing, answered, "Sure. The Channels. And that isn't any more than a mile from here."

"Fine, I'll row down to there. Then we'll branch out and do a little fishing."

He turned to Jud and said with a glare, "I like to do my fishing with as few people as possible." The comment crushed Junior.

They drifted down into the Channels, a place where the Elkheart unravels for a couple of miles, each strand lacing one into the other, flowing as one, then two, then three, then two again, the river intertwining across the broad shallows. Separated by gravel bars, deadfall, and small stands of birch, the Channels was a place where a fisherman could choose from three or four trout streams. Jud and Junior knew the water well. They'd fished it all their lives.

Anchoring the dory in an eddy, they had lunch. It was a perfect time, or so Junior thought, to run his theory on deoxygenated water and feeding patterns past Sandolaré once again. "Remember back at the barbecue when I was talking about oxygen levels in trout and their chemical interdependencies? Well, I just wanted to fin—"

"That was just what I needed," Sandolaré said patting his stomach, but his lunch was barely touched. Abruptly he stood up and grabbed his fly rod. "Which way should I go?"

"Err . . . mmmmm . . ."Junior stumbled for his words, disappointed that Sandolaré had cut him off again. "Well, walk on over to that big dead cottonwood you see over there. The best channel is just on the other side of it." Junior knew that for a fact. He'd missed more fish in that channel than all of the others combined. Jud nodded in agreement.

"Fine. Then we'll meet back here at the boat around? . . ."

"Oh, about three would be good," Jud said.

Junior and Jud watched him walk over to the channel they'd suggested and looked on. He started fishing. No doubt about it, the man could cast. He was just like his videos. "Isn't he about the best? Look at the loop. And he knows so much about fishing. I'd give anything to lead his life, boy."

"Well, I gotta tell you, Junior, I really don't share in your keenness for the man."

"You're kidding. All those great stories."

"Yeah, yeah, I know. But there are some pieces to his puzzle that just don't fit."

~

"What do you mean?"

"I don't know really. Just a feeling."

"Naw, you have him all wrong. Nobody could be that good a fisherman—get to do nothing in life but fish, have nothing but fun, get paid for it—and be a jerk. If I had his life I'd wake up in the morning laughing."

"Hitler played a pretty fair fiddle, but it didn't make him a nice guy . . . Now, I don't mean to say Sandolaré is evil. I'm just reminding you about books and their covers."

"Well, I don't know. I do know this. Today is a day I'll never forget. You want to fish the main channel?"

"No, you go ahead. I'll fool around on the small water." By the small water he meant the little streams branching in and out of the larger channels. He knew the main channel would be the best and this was Junior's day.

The fishing was slow. It was worse than slow. It was at full stop. It was hot and getting hotter. For Jud and Junior fishing would be an exercise in futility. Jud was resigned to that fact. Junior wouldn't know the difference.

After an hour or more, Jud had caught nothing. He imagined Junior would be doing the same. Even Junior could do no worse. But he was very curious about how Sandolaré was doing. He wanted to know what a world record holder did when it was slow. What the star of video, the author of books, and the self-proclaimed authority on everything piscatorial did when the fishing was nonexistent.

In fact Sandolaré's fly rod was leaning up against the tree. From out of his fishing vest came all that he needed. A flask of Scotch.

Meanwhile Jud purposely veered off following a small braid of the Elkheart, fishing his way toward the channel they had given to Sandolaré. It wasn't like he was spying exactly. He'd just be fishing along and bump into him. Of course, it *was* spying and exactly, but he couldn't help himself. He fished quickly along, not paying any attention to his fly until he finally stepped from the willows into a wide-open space in the graveled flat. From there he could see a long stretch of the channel, upstream and down.

He stood and watched the summer day; not a cloud, not a whisper of wind. The gravel bars shimmered in the heat. He worried, although he had promised himself not to do so while he was out fishing, about another year of drought facing him and the Boat Works. When suddenly and remarkably close by, Sandolaré emerged from a willow thicket. Fishing rod in hand. Smiling. Jud's presence gave him a start. He asked as to the fishing, "How are you doing?"

"Haven't seen a fish. How about you?" Jud asked.

"I haven't fished yet, but I *will* catch fish."

"Now that's confidence. And just how can you be so sure?"

"Let's just say I feel it in my bo-o-ones." Then he cackled a silly, little laugh. His eyes were wired, vibrating, certainly crazed, looking as if they wanted to break free and fly from their sockets. He was sweating profusely, not just from-the-heat type of sweating, but as if he'd been running.

As they walked along to the next pool, Jud wanted to ask, but didn't, *Well if you haven't fished yet, just what* have *you been doing?*

"Sh-h-h-h," Sandolaré shushed him, and motioned him to stop. "Wait here."

The rush of wind from Sandolaré's hushing was twelve years old. Single malt. Jud shook his head and smiled. Sandolaré was swacked. Jud stopped as instructed and watched Sandolaré quickly and nimbly zigzag his way from bush to willow, willow to deadfall, deadfall to birch tree, finally to creep on bended knee to the edge of the channel. He was still facing a very long cast to the pool.

Gauging by the weight of his breath, Jud knew the man had to be quite drunk, yet he moved with the agility of an old cat. Having never seen anything like it before, Jud was highly entertained. It was difficult to keep from laughing at the absurdity of this eccentric old man and the preposterous folly of anyone thinking he would catch any fish in this heat. Sandolaré turned back to him and held up two fingers. He began his cast.

There were no fish rising, but he acted like a man with a trout in mind. In a few false casts his line was slicing through the air in loops so tight they were almost touching. Casting nearly the whole line, he made one last false cast as a measure and then let go with an improbable cast to land his fly in the smallest possible pocket of branches.

He was much too far away to see the fly, but Jud didn't miss the take, "Well I'll be a . . ." Jud mumbled.

It was a small trout and was quickly in and released. Sandolaré then sent off another rocket of a cast. This time setting his fly down, like the feather it was, along the rocky shallows and in fast water. He caught another small trout.

Sandolaré came back smirking, blowing the water from his fly like a gunfighter might blow the smoke from the smoldering barrel of his trusty six-gun. He looked around and sniffed the air. He looked at the sun. "It's time we get back to the boat," he said, flashing his store-bought smile. "How much do I still owe you for that boat?"

"Forty-two hundred and twenty-seven dollars," Jud answered.

"Fine. I'll send you a check."

"Well, it's always been my policy that the balance is cleared before any dory leaves the Boat Works," Jud said.

"Oh, but I can't. I won't be able to transfer funds until Monday. Then I'll have my secretary send you a check for forty-two hundred and twenty-seven dollars." He had a way of saying the amount as if it was a paltry sum, petty cash, pocket change, and beneath his concern. While Jud had all but the twenty-seven dollars already spent.

"Well, could you see she gets it to me right away? Four years of drought has made it pretty tight in the boat business."

"I can well imagine," he said, distracted.

Jud walked beside Sandolaré, who struck a surprisingly quick pace. Jud was angry. Sandolaré had known the balance on that boat for four months and yet he couldn't show up with a check, like every other customer. He also didn't say anything because, as usual, Sandolaré was talking. "I remember one time I was fishing for razor fish of the coast of Madagascar. I . . ."

Sloshing up the channel, Junior was only slightly put out about the fishing. He hadn't seen a trout all afternoon, but for the most part he was in good spirits. He was smiling and whistling. After all, he was fishing, and not just any fishing, but fishing with a lifelong friend, not to mention his fishing hero.

He was also cool and refreshed, but that was unintentional, as he had just moments before misjudged the stability of a log crossing the stream and fallen in. It wasn't the complete head-to-toe kind of dunking that he was used to taking. This time he fell backward into shallow water, and while the back of his vest was soaked, his fly boxes remained dry. He did, however, invite a few gallons of river water into his waders, which was why he was cool, refreshed, and sloshing.

Finding a comfortable place to sit down, he removed his waders and drained them. He wrung out his shirttails, shorts, and socks, then dressed, and was again walking and whistling. Walking with his rod held behind him, heading for a familiar bend, he hadn't noticed that his fly, a heavily hackled Humpy hand-tied by Junior himself, had freed itself from its keeper and was tumbling along behind him; tumbling twenty-one feet behind him, given nine feet of fly rod and twelve feet of leader; tumbling over the white-gray boulders of the riverbank.

He decided to recross the channel, remembering the fishing was better on this bend from the right side. He went down a steep bank, nearly falling again. The current was fast here but shallow, no more than eighteen inches deep. The rush of swift water over rocks and around waders muted all other sounds and easily drowned out the clicks off his drag—a drag accidentally set nearly to OFF in his most recent fall. His line was spooling out behind him, since his fly had finally hooked itself into a wil-

~

low branch high on the bank above him. Successfully across the channel Junior, daydreaming and his drag set light, walked another hundred feet before realizing what had happened. Looking up his line to his fly high in the willows, like a boy looking up his kite string to his kite high in the tree, he could only laugh at himself, shake his head, set his drag, and begin to reel his way back to his Humpy.

Then he heard the sound of voices, Jud's and Sandolaré's. After breaking Sandolaré's rod, after landing zero trout all day, and still wet from falling in, Junior did not want Sandolaré to see him now with his fly stuck in a bush. He panicked as the voices grew louder. He'd be caught if he tried to reel all the way back to his fly and decided just to break it off. He tugged once on his line, but the fly didn't come, nor did his leader break. He pulled again harder, but neither would give. Hearing them both and clearly now, Junior looked over his shoulder to see them coming through the brush.

Holding his rod tip high, he leaned back, tugging at his line with his left hand. Normally his light tippet would have broken at first pull, but Junior had somehow managed to get his Humpy stuck at the top of a very long and thin willow limb. He'd tug, and the limb would only bend farther. So with rod tip and willow bending, straining against each other until they were bent, and his line stretched tight, a certain energy was building. But the second before his knots met their breaking point, the fly lost its bite in the bark and came sailing high above him. The energy had been released and was showing itself in velocity and motion. The line, sent as if from a sling, like an arrow taking flight, caught a little breeze aloft and kept right on flying.

Stepping into view, Conrad and Jud looked up just as the Humpy had left the willow and line, leader, and fly were sailing toward them aboard a most preposterous cast. The sight stopped them in their tracks. Amazement set in on them both; Jud's came as he'd never seen Junior throw a line more than twenty feet without something going wrong; Sandolaré's from the fact that he hadn't seen a cast like it since the 1984 World Championships in Munich.

The line just kept rolling and rolling; straight toward them; rolling like a sequence filmed in slow motion; rolling like a one-dimensional wave; rolling for the quiet water by which they stood; rolling until the fly finally landed one inch from a fallen log at the top of a pool. It alighted close enough for them both to see the fly was a Humpy. They wouldn't see it for long.

The nose of a tremendous trout broke the water. A mouth about the size of a manhole cover leisurely took the fly. Jud's heart nearly stopped. But Junior, a hundred feet and more away, was so blown away by the physics involved in making such a cast that he missed the take. He would have missed the take even if he had been paying attention—he was that far away. His thoughts instead involved theorems, which in turn involved vectors, velocities, and gravitational pull.

Jud shouted, "Set the hook! Set the hook!"

Still preoccupied, Junior was slow to grasp Jud's directions, but finally he stripped in some line, and by some miracle the fly was still in the trout's face. The giant trout was on. Her first jump took her high in the air, twisting and fighting the hook, and right in front of Sandolaré.

The rainbow headed downstream. Swimming from the pool in a silvered bolt, the trout flashed by Junior heading for the fast water he had just crossed. Reeling like a madman, half numb with the shock of it all, Junior took off in pursuit.

"Uh-oh," Jud mumbled, as he grabbed his boat net from the dory and went running to help. Jud's concerns were obvious: Junior running over uneven ground, crossing swift water, and fighting a trout all at the same time. And not just any trout, but a rainbow as long as your arm; a trout that was more than a match for the most talented of anglers. But this was Junior, and nothing looked promising.

As Jud ran following Junior downriver, he was amazed at Junior's sudden coordination. He ran the cobbled banks, he bounded through the fast water, he jumped deadfalls with the agility of a deer, his legs whirling like a pinwheel. He was gaining on the rainbow. Junior, of course, had no realization he was performing any of these feats. He'd forgotten about his limbs and their positions. His mind was as blank as a piece of paper. It was awash with the white rush of adrenaline. Some kind of providence guided his feet over the rough terrain, for if Junior had stopped to think about what he was doing he would have fallen on his very next stride. He had never in his entire career of fishing seen a trout such as this. Oblivious to all obstacles, and oblivious to his own limited motor skills, he was following his fish.

By the time Jud finally started to catch up to him, Junior was at the top of the next pool. His rod held high above his head, Junior was fighting the fish two-handed just as he should have done, a fine tactical angler ploy. But if Jud had been closer he would have seen that Junior had somehow gotten his rod butt stuck down in his sleeve, and his left hand was frantically trying to free it. Jud was also impressed by the way he kept the steady hard pressure on the trout, playing her tough after that long run. That's the time to tire a trout. No slack. But Junior couldn't have given her slack if he'd wanted to, because a very impressive knot had formed in one of the guides—the line was going nowhere. He could only reel himself to the fish, not the other way around. Jud viewed this as aggressive and smart fishing.

The rainbow jumped three times and tugged her way around the pool. Junior followed her up and down the banks. He had no choice. The knot blocking his guide saw to that. The trout tired quickly after that, and soon Jud was scooping her to the net.

"What a fish! What a fish!" Junior was shouting, and whooping, and hopping around, as he should have done, since this was "the biggest fish I've ever caught!"

They both said nothing for a few moments as they both just marveled at her size. A slash of red the width of a man's wrist marked her sides. She twisted slightly against her webbed cage, so bright a silver she shined, so marvelously wild.

"She's the better part of seven pounds, Junior. She's a beauty and you played her so darn well, and *that* cast. Where did *that* come from?"

Junior explained, nearly out of breath, about his fly getting snagged in the willow limb, and the sciences involved in the resulting cast, "You see," he puffed, "when two opposing vectors of equal energies . . ." Then Junior paused as he realized that Sandolaré hadn't joined them. He looked up the channel to see him sitting in the boat and waiting with his back turned. "Gee, you would think he'd be more interested in my fish than that."

"Sandolaré is only interested in the fish *he* catches, Junior." Then rubbing his hand over his eyes, an incredulous smile slowly spreading across his face, Jud asked, "You mean the cast, the fish, the *whole* thing was a fluke?"

"Yep. Biggest fluke ever."

Easing the trout from the net, Junior cradled the fish in his hands and began reviving her. He couldn't get over how Sandolaré was just sitting in the boat. Fish like this one didn't swim along every day, and even though it was an accident, he did land her. The glory of this moment was somehow tainted by his disappointment in his fishing hero. The trout shook free of his grasp and slipped away. Junior felt thankful. She was a whale of a trout—flukes or no flukes.

"Junior, do me a favor, will ya?" Jud asked, watching the rainbow disappear into the deep water.

"Sure."

"Don't tell Sandolaré about any of this. I mean, all he and I saw was the cast."

"But that wouldn't be right, I couldn't lie about—"

Putting his hand on Junior's shoulder, Jud was grinning ear to ear, and larceny was in his eye. "You know, Junior, there comes a time in every man's life where he is called on to tell a lie, for whatever reason—to protect someone, to help someone, or on those all-too-rare occasions to get even with someone. And this, my friend, is the best of all possible lies, for this was a lie that everyone saw happen—an irrefutable, swear-on-a-stack-of-Bibles, a God's-own-truth, certified fishing lie. In fact, it becomes a lie only if we talk about those things that make it a lie."

"Well, I don't know. I—"

"I mean, all day long we've had to listen to that blowhard, the worldwide braggart, Mister Conrad San-dull-aré, talk incessantly about his exploits and conquests. And now, with an eyewitness, he's just been outfished by one of the locals. Oh, I am loving this. Stick with me. Follow the lead. Neither one of us will have to lie."

Junior nodded. "What a fish, huh?"

"What a fish."

They walked slowly to the dory, Junior slightly delighted at the prospect of telling a fishing lie. He never told them. His mind was much too scientific to digress from the facts, that and the fact that he was very Catholic.

In the bow seat of the dory, with his back turned to them, Sandolaré sat watching the river. He didn't say a word. He'd just been outfished by this nerd, an amateur of questionable skills, and the knife of it all was deep in his ribs. He sipped from his flask. An uncomfortable quiet filled the boat as they rowed away from shore. But Jud, who was at the oars for the short float to the takeout, knew just how to handle the silence. "Conrad, that fish was a beauty. You should have come down and seen it. Twenty-five inches long. Best fish I've seen or even heard of for a long time.

"But Junior, you ought to see Conrad here fish. The guy's unbelievable. He threw two casts and he took two browns. Of course, nothing can top that fish of yours. I guess you could take Conrad's two fish, lay them end to end, and still fall short of your fish. And that cast! I thought *Conrad* could throw it a long way. Whoa, nothing compared to that toss. One hundred plus feet. And you did it with a Humpy, only the most air-resistant fly tied. I've never seen anything quite like it. I really haven't. Have you, Conrad?"

The normally ebullient Sandolaré could only grumble. He took another swig of the single malt. Though Jud couldn't see his face, he could see the sides of his jaws were clenched and grinding. But Jud wasn't done with him.

"I mean, I didn't see a fish all afternoon, and Junior lands a trophy. An absolute monster. Hey, Junior," Jud said, turning around and winking at him, "maybe you should star in your *own* videos?" The hair stood on Sandolaré's neck.

Saying all of this with a natural joy and enthusiasm befitting the moment, there was nothing in Jud's voice to indicate sarcasm, unless of course you'd known him all your life, as Junior had. Then you knew that the sarcasm was there as well as a little contempt. Jud was pissed off. Conrad Sandolaré, the big fishing star, couldn't deal with the fact that he'd been outfished for one day. So sour were his grapes, he couldn't even talk, let alone congratulate Junior on his trout.

Sandolaré's shoulders rose up and down from purposeful deep breaths and then fell silent and motionless in the front of the boat. He took one long pull on the flask. Then in a flash he turned around with his game-show-host smile and said, "I remember I was fishing in Patagonia. It was the day I took seventeen rainbows. The smallest one was only slightly larger than the one Junior just caught. It was cold the morning I arrived and I . . ."

Feeling slightly guilty, knowing that his fish came accidentally, while Sandolaré's came as a result of consummate skill, Junior was about to blurt out the truth. But when Conrad didn't acknowledge his fish, accidental or otherwise, and dismissed it as no big deal by topping it with his Patagonia story, Junior couldn't believe it. Junior never really thought in these terms, but he knew that was bullshit.

At this point Jud wanted to throw Sandolaré overboard. But he smiled politely and tried hard not to listen to anything the man was saying as he rowed to the takeout where Sandolaré's Land Rover and trailer, as well as Jud's old Willys, were waiting.

Jud couldn't remember a faster takeout. In the time it took Jud to winch the new dory onto the trailer, Sandolaré was out of his waders and into fresh clothes. With his Land Rover packed and his driftboat loaded and cinched down, Sandolaré said a very gratuitous good-bye: "Thank you both for the fishing, the party, and so forth." He climbed into the Rover, and with a patented wave of his well-known hat, he began to say his patented television good-bye, but didn't. Instead he pulled onto the highway and was gone.

A giant cloud began forming over Mount D. Downey. "A thunderstorm would be good," Jud said. "You know Junior, that guy was supposed to give me forty-two hundred and twenty-seven dollars today, and he didn't."

Junior added sympathetic to his look of disillusionment, and he felt a little empty. He had one less fishing hero. A gust of wind blew his hat into the river. Jud gave him a mock sock in the arm. "What a fish, huh?"

Junior talked about nothing other than his fish all week. He told the events as they happened, the truth, over and over again. He finally took it to the point where Pam finally had to threaten him. "If you tell that trout story again, I am packing and moving to a desert where the nearest fish is five thousand miles away."

By a strange series of coincidences, Sarah heard of the fish first from Junior, then Henry, and then Doc. She heard fishermen around the café tell the story, and she also heard nonfishermen tell the story, as in a town the size of Travers, any news is big news. She heard the story from breakfast until her lunchtime shift was over. Even her Uncle Sal told her the tale, and he hated fishing stories.

That evening Jud, who had a habit of stopping by around suppertime, came to tell her his version of yesterday's fishing and yesterday's fish. Sarah was at home and in her kitchen, enjoying the silence, after an afternoon in her garden, when Jud came through the kitchen door.

"You won't believe what happened while we were fishing. We—" he started, but wouldn't be able to finish as Sarah went to her broom closet and pulled out her NO FISHING ALOUD sign and posted it firmly. Jud deftly changed the subject, "Gee, whatever it is that's cooking sure smells good." Sarah laughed.

Junior tells the story of that day only when coaxed. It takes the smallest amount of coaxing. And when he tells it, he recounts the day accurately, including how his fly accidentally stuck into a branch. He then usually gets sidetracked by vectors, velocities, gravity, and stored power ratios of willow and rod before he gleefully gets back to the landing of the fish.

Sandolaré never told anyone the story about what happened that day—he didn't feature as the lead. And a story in which he was outfished could never cross his lips.

His boat payment finally arrived. It came in an envelope postmarked six weeks before with South African stamps. Inside Jud found a check for $3,927 and a note. It read:

Balance on driftboat - 4,227.00
Less personal appearance fee -300.00
Balance due - 3,927.00

Conrad's signature was stamped.

Jud, of course, told the story whenever the chance presented itself. The appearance fee probably prompted him to tell it even more often. The story about the Great Sandolaré who was outfished by the town pharmacist. Outangled by a local amateur whose fishing skills were sadly lacking. In fact, if the truth be known (and Jud, Henry, Doc as well, did everything in their power to keep this truth from Junior), Junior might be, pound for pound, one of the most unsuccessful fishermen in the Elkheart barring those who don't fish at all.

But Junior has one dog-eared entry in his fishing journal that no one could take from him: the day he bested the best. An entry recorded for all time. The best kind of entry, a faithful account with witnesses, logging the biggest fish in his angling career. A completely honest entry based entirely on a lie.

Everything about his day is mentioned in his stream diary: the temperatures, air and water; the hatches; the river levels. The fact that Jud let him fish the best water even garners a note. Very little is written about Sandolaré.

Certainly the rainbow was brought to net through a most preposterous chain of unwitting, serendipitous events, and these events are committed to writing with veracity, from the accidental cast to the miraculous landing. Jud's lie to Conrad, a lie based solely on the truth, receives its own page.

But it matters not at all how the fish was fooled and then taken. For in angling, there is no greater truth than the netted trout.

From The Journals of Traver C. Clark

August 9, 1903—
I snuck out for an afternoon of fishing. Carrie packed me a lunch. It was a good day—eighteen trout averaging better than a pound and a half. Later in the day while in town I unfortunately ran into John Rossiter, who also had spent the day fishing.

It has been my observation that every time I have met him on stream-side his catch has more than doubled mine both in number and in size. I told him about my eighteen fish and he told me about his forty fish over three pounds. The man is an obvious liar. Never looks you in the eye.

His lies don't really bother me; lying about your catch doesn't really hurt anyone. But now John Rossiter, wealthy by deceptive methods and as low a character as I have ever met, is entertaining thoughts about running for the state legislature, a place where his lying could do great harm.

Two dozen flies plus shipping - 4.50

~

Woodrow Dickey

IT HAD ALWAYS been one of Jud's primary beliefs that the best are seldom recognized, and the brightest go unseen. Following this line of reasoning, he believed that—because of opportunity, circumstance, and luck—the fairest minds never sat in judgment; the most gifted healers never attended medical school; the finest anglers remained unknown.

Dr. T. Nathaniel Wellsley would have had to disagree. He was honor bound to disagree as he was a graduate of both Harvard Law and Harvard Medical. Given his dual doctorates, it was natural for him to argue against Jud's tenet, just as it was inherent in him to offer a second opinion. T. Nathaniel came from a long line of doctors and lawyers, but he was the first Wellsley to achieve both. Those would be the Pinehurst Wellsleys.

T. Nathaniel, "Nate" to his friends, was brought up to believe that perseverance alone was all that any man needed to achieve greatness. Jud's tenet of circumstance and luck had nothing at all to do with it. If a man wanted to become a doctor or a lawyer or whatever profession, he need only put his mind to it. Hard work was the key. As for the third part of Jud's above conviction, about the finest anglers remaining unknown, T. Nathaniel wasn't sure. There was no way of knowing. But he did know that the very finest of the finest, the fishermen's fishermen such as himself, were known. And if you didn't know, he would be glad to tell you.

It was generally held around Travers Corners, where he spent his summers and falls, that when in residence there was not a smarter man to be found in the Elkheart than T. Nathaniel. It was agreed on by most of the locals that a man just couldn't be any smarter than being both a doctor and a lawyer. That would be *most* of the locals. Henry and Jud, and a few others around town, didn't view T. Nathaniel in the same light, and it was the subject of light, to be more specific the light of the October sunsets, that kept Jud from holding any regard for Dr. Wellsley.

From the Boat Works he'd watched these favored sunsets of fall for years, the pale bands of peach-colored clouds one evening, a cloudless dusk fading to starlight and indigo the next. Tonight's sunset would be his personal favorite, the sky following a rain. When the lightning, thunder, and wind slowly give way to the sun just as it hits the horizon. When the only light is golden. But with sunset still more than an hour away and promising to be spectacular, it could never be the same. It could never be as good.

In the old days, the days before T. Nathaniel came to Travers, Jud would watch autumn unobstructed. He would watch the rains soak the benchlands and the wind bend the aspen groves on the McCarthy Mountains. Why they were called the McCarthy *Mountains* no one could recall since they were no more than a small band of hills that climbed to about three hundred feet above town, then tapered off into cliffs east of the Elkheart Channels.

Around seven-thirty, during the middle weeks of October, for most of his life, Jud had enjoyed that brief moment when the forested hills of the McCarthys split the sunlight into a thousand streams as it filtered its way through the pines and the aspens.

But nowadays, around seven-thirty, the sun no longer set over the wooded knoll. It set over the great log-and-rock catastrophe. It set over the multilayered, multiwinged, multiwindowed blight on the land-scape—the nine-thousand-square-foot architectural nightmare that T. Nathaniel called home. Actually, T. Nathaniel called it "Vision House" possibly induced by some sort of "Tara" Syndrome that evidently still inflicted some of the southern aristocracy. "Vision House" covered the knoll like a deformed crab. T. Nathaniel called it Vision House because of its 360-degree view. Of course, he needed to level the knoll and cut down about one hundred acres of aspens and evergreens to get the full circle.

The construction of this monster was what had torn it between T. Nathaniel and Judson C. Clark. But nothing could be done about it. There it was, sprawling out over the McCarthy summit, high above the river, in all of its contorted nine-thousand-square-foot glory, marring the landscape by its absurdity, and it would be there forever. One man's vision is another man's eyesore.

Vision House wasn't much of a concern for most of the people in Travers, as nearly everyone in town was spared the view of it. The ranches and homes south of town could see it, and it angered some people while others didn't seem to care. But it brought the Heyduke out in Jud.

The raindrops started tapping on the workshop's tin roof. Soon it was a clatter of rain and rattling with the wind. Then as soon as it started it was over. There was a sudden and definite chilling in the air, and while it wasn't cool enough to warrant building a fire, it was cool enough to remind him that life would be revolving around the woodstove in a few weeks' time.

A heavy gust shook the doors and windows, and it jostled him free from his thoughts. Thoughts that he could now recognize as, "Ridiculous. The whole thing is ridiculous. T. Nathaniel is ridiculous. His house is ridiculous. But what's even more ridiculous," Jud said aloud to himself as he looked at his pocket watch, "is that here it is four-thirty and I'm all ready getting upset about the sunset. How does one get upset about a sunset? There is something wrong with this picture."

He went back to the work of milling a pair of oarlocks and mumbling something derogatory about Vision House, which Jud referred to as Division House because it reduced an aspen grove by more than half, a hilltop by at least 20 percent, and the damage done to dusk was incalculable.

At the same time in town down at the general store, Junior was in his element. Unlike his lifelong counterparts, Junior loved it when Nate came into town, more specifically into McCracken's, because it got him out of the pharmacy and into his tackle department. There he could talk fly fishing (something Junior could only do forever) and make a buck at the same time. T. Nathaniel was Junior's best customer. He was standing next to the waders and fly-tying materials and talking to Nate who, in Junior's estimation, was without a doubt one of the best anglers in the world. The luck the man had on the Elkheart was astonishing.

"Hey, Nate, I got the new FX5-T3. It's a nine-foot for a five, three-piece. Boy, she casts like a dream," Junior said as he lifted the fly rod from the rack and placed it in Nate's hands.

Nate gave it a trial swish or two. "Feels re-e-eal good. Well, Junior, if you say she casts like a dream she must. Why don't you put one of these on my tab. I must have half a dozen five weights already up at Vision House. But hell, a man just can't have enough five-weights.

"Lately I've been using my little seven-and-a-half-foot bamboo down in the Channels with fa-a-abulous success. Caught two fish over five pounds last night and one over six. On dr-y-y-y flies," T. Nathaniel explained. He was fitted out in his usual fashion, pretty much the same as you always saw him dressed, more for a safari than a day in town, in his bush pants, bush shirt, and bush jacket. But he westernized his image with a white Stetson and a pair of cowboy boots. Of course, it wasn't bad enough that T. Nathaniel had a double doctorate, but he was good looking as well. Tall and handsome. Salt-and-pepper hair. A man of fifty. Ostensibly, the complete package.

It had been years since Junior had landed a five-pounder. Of course, Junior never doubted T. Nathaniel's stories, gullibility being one of

Junior's leading traits. It would never occur to Junior to lie about his fishing, and if ever there was a fisherman whose angling was in need of a little fiction, it would be Junior's.

Even though he couldn't fish, Junior could talk about it forever. When fishing customers from out of town came into McCracken's he became the resident expert, and as resident expert he could and would prattle on about fishing for hours, or until the line at the pharmacy grew uncomfortably long. But he was at his happiest when the rare customer would come in and talk about adventures in the exotic world of travel fishing: the Bahamas, Patagonia, New Zealand. Of these, Nate was his absolute favorite. He told a good story, and he'd fished all over the world. He'd caught every fish swimming and looked good doing it.

"Yes, I believe I'll fish First Channel tonight," T. Nathaniel said as he picked out a few new flies from the display. "Saw a fish feeding in there the other evening and, my, she was a dandy. Oh, and that reminds me there, Junior"—he dug around in his bush jacket's fifty or so pockets until he pulled out a packet of photographs—"I brought these along to share with you.

"Last spring, the little lady and myself had the good fortune of fishing on the Mandillon Islands north of Guam." He began handing Junior the pictures, the first one being of Jasmine and himself and a beautiful home surrounded by tropical plants. "This one here is one of Jasmine and myself out in front of our friend's house, where we stayed. They own several of the islands. He bought them mainly for the bonefishing, but they also raise mango-o-es. You can only get to these islands by boat, and it's two days and a night in getting there." The picture made Junior long for a vacation such as this, but the next picture made him gasp. "That there is a seventeen-po-o-und bone fish. This one here is a thirty-six-pound skipjack, and this is a . . ."

Both he and Junior were suddenly aware of a man standing at one corner of the tackle department. The stranger was standing in a way that was relaxed and comfortable. His stance—arms folded, legs crossed at the ankles, and leaning against a post—said without complaint that he had been standing there for a while.

"Oh, sorry there, I didn't see you come in. Is there something I can help you with?" Junior asked.

"Well, I hate to bother y'all, but all I need is a fishin' license," the man said with an apologetic smile and in a drawl so protracted that it made T. Nathaniel sound like a northerner.

Junior smiled reluctantly and said, "Sure." But inside he was angry. Now he had to go through the folderol of filling out all the forms and stamps. He quickly went to the counter. Snapping a drawer open, he pulled out the cigar box that held the licenses and tossed open its lid. Junior looked up and asked, "How many days do you want to fish?"

"I'd like to start now and do it till I die," the man said back, smiling.

T. Nathaniel laughed at his answer. Junior just grew slightly more agitated. "I mean, we have season licenses, or you can buy them two days at a time."

"I'm gonna fish for five days, please," the man answered.

Junior took out the needed forms and handed one to the man. "Okay, fill out this here."

"Er, would you mind fillin' it out for me? I left my readin' glasses back at camp."

"Okay," Junior said grabbing a pen. Twisting the form around he asked, "What's your name?"

"My name is Woodrow Dickey. My address is Rural Route One, Frog Level, North Carolina. I'm six foot even and I weigh one hundred forty-two pounds. Born July twelve, 1944. Blue eyes. Brown hair."

Normally a name like Frog Level would have garnered several questions from Junior, but he was in a hurry to get back to Nate's pictures. Junior also thought he might be able to sell him a new reel to go with that rod. "Okay, sign there. That'll be fourteen dollars."

"Well, I'm glad to see another southerner up here in the Far North, and a fellow Carolinian at that. I sometimes feel all alo-o-one with these Yankees."

Woodrow Dickey just looked up smiling, but then he hadn't stopped smiling since he came into McCracken's. He dug into the front pockets of what looked to be either homemade or borrowed pants that were well worn where they weren't patched. The legs were short and they hung on him at the waist. He was also wearing combat-style boots, a bulky camouflage jacket, and a dark green cap. His license read 6'0", 142 pounds, but within the almost clownlike pants and oversized jacket he looked taller and quite a bit thinner. He had a childlike face, a baby face, and he looked ten years younger than someone born in 1944. It was a kind face, and Woodrow's smile continued, where there were teeth and where there weren't.

Pulling a twenty reverently from his wallet, he handed it to Junior as T. Nathaniel flipped another photo onto the counter. Not being the center of attention, even for the brief time it took Junior to sell the license, was more than T. Nathaniel could stand. "Well now, I don't know how this photo got mixed in with the others, because it's from a trip we took last fall. But at any rate, that there is a thirty-six-pound Atlantic salmon from a privately owned river in Iceland. Seven thousand air miles and two hundred helicopter miles from downtown Pinehurst."

Junior fumbled with Woodrow's change. "That'll be six dollars back at you," he counted and handed him the bills. Junior picked up the photo and admired, no, *coveted*, the catch. Then, in accordance with tackle shop etiquette, he handed the photograph to Woodrow.

"I have fished for Atlantic salmon in Ireland, Scotland, Russia, Norway, Sweden, and No-o-va Sco-o-tia, but nothing can compare to the fish of Iceland. Have you ever sampled any of these fisheries, sir?" Woodrow just shook his head. "If you ever get the chance you should go. Have you ever tried for Atlantic salmon?" T. Nathaniel asked.

"They don't usually come up as far as Frog Level," Woodrow replied, still smiling. Then he looked at the print of T. Nathaniel holding his fish, dressed, not surprisingly, in his bush jacket and cowboy hat. "That sure enough is a big fish, and think of it, only nine thousand miles away," Woodrow said in an understated manner. "I can fish for tin-inch speckled trout not twenty feet out my front door back home, and I don't even have to get dressed up for it."

(Author's note: I've given T. Nathaniel's accent some Confederate attention by extending some of the vowel sounds as Foghorn Leghorn might. But I've decided to leave Woodrow's accent alone, other than a contraction or two. Here's why: If written as it was spoken, Woodrow's last piece of dialogue would have read as follows: "I kin phash fir tin-anch spakelt traut not twanty faet owout my frownt dowor bayek haume, 'n I down't neveen havta gaat drasset up firit." I just wouldn't do that to you.)

Woodrow's barb, although it was masked well behind his country smile and a humble backwoods accent, wasn't lost on T. Nathaniel. Being one-half lawyer he asked in his most condescending tone, "Well, then what is a little ol' hillbilly such as yourself with all those 'spakelt traut bayek haume' comin' all the way to Montana for?"

"Well sir, I've always wanted to catch myself a brown trout, and I don't think I'd have missed you for the world." Woodrow grinned and handed Junior back the photo.

Junior was distracted and missed all of what was being said since Julie Tucker was at the counter and waiting for her prescription. "Hold on Nate, I just gotta hand Julie her pills, and I'll be right back. Man, I would have given anything to catch a fish like this one. Thirty-six pounds!" He quickly went over to the pharmacy, and Woodrow disappeared out the door. Just as quickly Junior was back. "So what kind of fly were you using?"

"That was a mi-i-ighty peculiar little fellow," said T. Nathaniel as he watched Woodrow through the front window climbing into a very old pickup.

⌒

"Yeah," Junior agreed. "Were you using a Jock Scott? A Black Panel? Silver Doctor? Do you have any more pictures?"

He looked on as Woodrow's truck pulled away from McCracken's. Then T. Nathaniel was once again his marvelous self. "Oh, here I am back in the Tropics." He handed Junior another photo. "This here is me with a forty-two-pound . . ."

Purring its way up to speed but listing slightly to one side, Woodrow's old Dodge headed out of town. His license plate dangled from the back bumper by one screw and a piece of wire. He was Woodrow Johnson Dickey, of the Frog Level Dickeys. A jack of all trades and a master of quite a few. Back in the hollows he was the man to call if anything needed building or repairing. He could figure out anything mechanical by just looking at it. He was considered by many the most gifted of all the Dickeys.

His coon hound, Nothin', was curled up on the passenger side just as Woodrow had left him. Nothin' lived up to his name, and most of his time was spent curled up or sprawled out. Unless, of course, there was the smell of coon around. Then Nothin' turned into a howling, sniffing, barking, salivating maniac. Four long legs and a nose.

"Nothin', I just met me a real jerk. Look at me, Nothin', do I look like a man who's traveled the world?" Nothin' looked up at him only long enough to show a pair of bloodshot eyes under folds of tan fur. Then he went back to sleep. "Asked me if I've ever gone to Norway or Russia to fish, and if I ever get the chance I should go. Hell, it took me four years of savin' just for this here trip. Have I ever been to Scotland or Ireland? I ain't been out of Frog Level but twice in my life." Woodrow wasn't much for society, and Frog Level, no more than a market with a gas pump, made Travers look like a real town. So a trip to Montana was more than a vacation. It was a lifetime adventure.

"I got pretty uppity back there I know, and it sure didn't sound like me none. My daddy raised me better than that. I should try and be more

~

respectful in another man's town. He always told me to represent the South in a prideful manner and a respectable way. But there was just somethin' about that silver spooner from Pinehurst that set my blood to boil. Pompous carpetbagger posin' around in his safari suit. Makes you sorrowful to be a southerner, don't it, Nothin'?"

But Nothin' was dreaming about being sprawled out somewhere as he had been curled up for three days and two nights: travel time on the road from the Blue Ridge Mountains. The Dodge had a top speed of sixty and any degree of incline slowed her proportionately. Coming into the Elkheart over Albie Pass brought her to an overheated and complete stop.

Soon the thought of T. Nathaniel was nearly gone. There were more pleasant things for Woodrow to think about. He was heading for the Jackson Ranch and the Channels. Doug Jackson, being an old Tarheeler transplant, loved visitations from kin (in the Blue Ridge if your family tree goes back into the 1800s, it's twenty-to-one you were kin), and anybody from North Carolina was welcome to fish. This kind of news even travels as far as the hollows of Frog Level.

Woodrow Dickey with Nothin' at his side was about to angle for and tangle with the brown trout of the Elkheart Channels. All his life he'd heard his cousin Ladson talk about it. Using his brother Ethan's phone (Woodrow had little use for a phone of his own) he'd called the Jacksons months before coming and asked for permission to fish and camp on their ranch. The Jacksons had sent him directions along with their welcoming response, and he held their map above the steering wheel for better light. "As far as I can tell from these here circles and arrows, we got ourselves another mile or two to go." The sun was nearing the western edges of the storm, and the clouds above him were being shaped by the light. "Gonna have a red sky tonight, Nothin'. Red sky at night—dry flier's delight."

Following a ranch road from the highway, Woodrow drove into the Jacksons' yard. A very old and half-lame blue heeler, toothless, his bark gone, sort of rasped at his arrival. Nothin' raised his eyebrows once more but elected to stay curled up. On the front door of the ranch house, he found a note that read,

> Woodrow—Welcome to Montana. Drive through the red metal gate in the side yard. That'll take you right down to the river. You'll see where to camp.
>
> We had to go to Helena to a bull sale and we'll be home late. We'll see you tomorrow. I hear the fishing's been good—Doug.

The road behind the red gate was a rough one and slick after the rain. The Dodge, slightly top-heavy from Woodrow's homemade camper, twisted and swayed over the potholes and rocks. The track ended on a high grassy bank at the river's edge. There, nestled into a grove of birch trees, stood a lodgepole hut, open on all sides but with a new tin roof. A stone barbecue was built beside the shed; under the roof was a picnic table, and beneath it dry ground.

Woodrow and Nothin' climbed down from the truck and walked around a fire ring. Woodrow took a long and well-deserved stretch, while Nothin', who hadn't peed since Bozeman, quickly marked half a dozen cottonwoods and several willows. Sniffing the air for coon but smelling none, he went to dry ground and sprawled underneath the table. The rain washed away any hope of catching a scent. He'd give it another sniff tomorrow.

"This here is a camp a feller could settle into," Woodrow said, turning downstream. The sun was now in and out of a broken sky, the tailings of the storm. Clouds, stretched on the wind, flew into the opening colors of sunset, and the river's currents carried the reflection. "We're only five minutes here, Nothin', and that ain't half bad for a welcomin' sight." In the quiet water above camp a fish jumped. "That's mighty temptin', but I think we better make camp first, and I could stand an early supper and an early to bed. But tomorrow, and every day after, I am gonna fish from can't see to can't see."

The following morning the Tin Cup Cafe was all but empty. Sarah was behind the grill and cleaning up after a slow breakfast. Henry and Jud were in for a midmorning cup. "You know, we haven't gone fishing together one day this year and we're coming up on the end of the season," Jud said, blowing on his coffee.

"What about Friday?" Henry asked.

"Friday sounds good. Let's float the Channels."

Henry nodded as Sarah stepped out from behind the counter. In one hand she held a cup of tea and in the other a fresh pot of coffee. She topped off their cups and sat down next to Henry. "I see that T. Nathaniel is back in town," she said. "Saw the Land Rover roll through town yesterday."

"That T. Nathaniel, what a guy," Jud moaned. "All those five-pound trout up and down the Elkheart are in serious trouble now."

Henry laughed and shook his head, "You know that guy jest can't seem to go fishing without catchin' himself a five-pounder or two. I've fished that river all my life, and the catchin' of five-pounders jest don't work that way.

"God, I can't stand that guy, nor his wife either. They got a high-and-mighty attitude about who they are—treat the world like it was their own personal bellhop. But ol' Junior thinks the sun sets on that guy." Then realizing what he'd just said and winking at Sarah, Henry added with a smirk, "Come to think of it, for some of us, I guess the sun really does set on that guy." He waited for Jud to rise to the bait, which didn't take long.

"I can't—" Jud tried to speak but was interrupted.

"Did you guys *see* last night's sunset?" Sarah asked, winking back at Henry, instantly picking up on his lead. "It was so beautiful. One of the best I can ever remember."

"Oh yeah . . . it might be nice for some. Let me—" Jud tried again.

But Henry butted in, "Man, wasn't that *something* though. I was just finishin' up some fencin' and I looked up and there was nothin' but colors and blue sky."

Jud, though recognizing the humor of the situation, was unable to see anything funny about it. He started again. He'd had enough false starts to be good and wound up. He had a slow way of speaking with a natural stammer, but when excited his speech didn't accelerate; just the stammer. "Oh, sure. Blue skies an . . . and colors. I . . . I . . . mean the guy took a perfectly good forest and a very old knoll, an . . . an . . . ."

Sarah and Henry had heard it all before and they were about to hear it all again.

But from T. Nathaniel's point of view—one shared by Jasmine—Vision House was just another one of the perfections in their lives. Seeing themselves as perfection, they could hardly settle on anything else. They were oblivious to any impact their home would have on the surroundings. T. Nathaniel thought of Vision House as he did of himself, a welcome addition to the landscape, if not an improvement. The Wellsleys never saw any farther than their own personal world and were oblivious to all else. T. Nathaniel was oblivious since his mind was busying itself with more important things than other people, and Jasmine was just plain oblivious because that was her proclivity.

They were a striking couple standing in their domed, three-level octagon of a living room. He was handsome and tall. She was a southern belle, a willowy brunette, and completely gorgeous—flawless, in fact. She was layered in high fashion, an airbrushed beauty in high heels, black pearls, and sapphires. They stood amid their artifacts, their collectibles, their fine art. Everything elegant and costly. Behind them the bronze statue of a life-sized eagle flew in front of an enormous window overlooking the town. There wasn't an artistic bone between them, and the paintings and sculptures weren't displayed for their appreciation. They were there as pretentious tributes to themselves. The house was immaculate; fresh flowers were arranged in every vase. All was perfect for their guests from out of town, the Honorable Senator John Colbourn, his wife, Betty, and the senator's staff.

"I met the strangest little man yesterday while I was down at McCracken's," T. Nathaniel said, popping a grape into his mouth. "I was sharing our pictures of the Mandillon Islands with Junior when this funny little man came in. I tri-i-ied to be polite by including him in my conversation, and he got positively surly with me. It was an embarrassment in front of Junior and all. For this man was from the South. In fact, he was from North Carolina."

"Pinehurst?" Jasmine asked in a quick and disinterested tone. For her there were no other towns in North Carolina.

"Frog Level."

She looked at him quizzically as if she hadn't heard him correctly, then dismissed the little man from Toad Flats, or wherever, with a toss of her head. Taking T. Nathaniel by his sleeve, she led him down the hallway to a full-length mirror. "Now, Nate honey, how many times must I tell you? People are just naturally jealous." Her hand waved to her perceived perfections—their reflections on the wall. "You are a brilliant doctor and a marvelous lawyer, and a very handsome man. I am your wife, and some say I am beautiful," she added batting her eyes. Jasmine's voice was at once girlish and flirtatious, and it demanded affection as she curled around him. He put his arm around her and hugged her like a friend, but never stopped looking at himself.

"Now, you just get that little fool down at McCracken's out of your mind," she said, running her fingers along his cheek and down his neck, "and when Senator John gets here, you two just go on down to the river and catch a few big ones. Betty and I will talk girl talk. I do hope she has done something with her hair. I'll have supper ready for us at seven. I'm making that smoked ham dish you love so much. So you boys need to be back and ready for juleps at five."

"Yes, dear," he said, uneasy at her affections.

It had been more than two years since he was last aroused, a fact that Jasmine would later share with Betty while the boys were out fishing. "Oh, darling, it is so awful. It's been two years since my man has had a straight pecker branch, but even when it was interested it wasn't too much." Betty was one of her closest confidantes, and after a few juleps, she could always achieve a certain level of intimacy with her.

Woodrow and Nothin' spent the morning chatting with Doug Jackson, who had paid his camp a call. Over coffee they talked about the Blue Ridge and home and discovered some common friends. But Doug wasn't around long, for he was trucking some cattle to market.

Woodrow went on to explore the Channels where the Elkheart unravels into shallow braids; four, and sometimes five, branches weaving their way through the gravel bar bottoms and cottonwoods. He was fishing some, but looking around mostly: Learning a little about these different braids, learning about the water and the lay of the land. He'd fished his way upstream to where the river was, but one channel and a two-lane bridge crossed it.

Later in the day he walked downstream along the main channel until he found a safe place for him and Nothin' to cross, a crossing made more difficult by Nothin' being in tow at the end of a long rope leash. Woodrow knew from too many experiences that one smell of raccoon and Nothin' would be gone, and he could be gone for days. Here the current was swifter, the water at times waist-deep, and the rocks in the shallows were slick with moss. But he waded it safely and was now fishing the westernmost braid of the river where the river bottom abruptly ended against the chalk-colored bluffs. Where the Elkheart turned and the white cliffs followed above the long sweeping bend. He'd just fished up the very small channel that had led him here. Fishing it was reminiscent of the creeks around home, the small speckled trout streams of Frog Level. It was rocky, mostly pocket water, and heavily wooded, making pinpoint casting a necessity.

By late afternoon he had fished the full length of the bend and was retracing his steps back to camp. He'd done quite well, he thought, for a first day. He'd learned a little about the waters, and he'd landed five trout, four small rainbows and an even smaller brown. But Woodrow was thrilled with his catch. It was his first brown trout. "Not bad for my first day on a new river," he said with some pride to Nothin'. Nothing' paid him no heed. He was picking up periodic whiffs of raccoon. But there would be no hounding, chasing, or treeing of these creatures. Not as long as he was on the leash.

On the way downstream he walked under the heat of the day, which came suddenly; after such a cool morning and mild afternoon, the sun's intensity surprised him. He'd covered a lot of uneven ground since morning and now entertained thoughts of an early supper, after which he would fish the hatches near camp. "Sleep will come easy tonight, Nothin', and it'll come when it wants to. My eyes won't have nothin' to say about it. Dark-thirty will be my guess. I think this altitude and a lot of walkin' have taken their toll," he said, deciding to take a breather in the welcome shade of a birch grove.

Sitting on a log, Nothin' sprawled at his feet, Woodrow stared at the river, here a long wide quiet pool. Small mayflies were beginning to take their flight, and within minutes thousands appeared. Seemingly suspended above the slow-moving water, the sun flashed from their wings, myriad tiny white lights rising and falling. He'd seen the occasional mayfly all afternoon but nothing that could be called a hatch. But now these tiny mayflies were flying in countless numbers, blue-winged olive mayflies to be more exact. Trout began to rise. Having tied dozens of Blue-Winged Olives before making the trip from Frog Level, Woodrow was prepared for this moment. This moment being the sole purpose of his two-thousand-mile trip. The moment when the big browns came to the small dry flies. Revitalized by the sighting, he dug into his homemade vest for his hand-tied flies and a store-bought leader, and he watched the river closely.

Rings were forming wherever he looked. But they were the light and quick rings made by the smaller fish. There was, however, one heavy ring appearing, and it wasn't an easy riseform to spot. It was showing itself in the middle of the river where the only current streamed softly from the edges of a logjam, and where a branch bobbed slowly in the water. Normally, especially at this distance, a disturbance to the surface like the bobbing of a limb, along with all the natural currents curling off the logs, would be enough to mask the rise even for a good fisherman. But Woodrow wasn't a good fisherman. He was a great fisherman. He was also a true woodsman. He had lived in the back hollows all his life, and very few things about the wilds slipped his notice.

Tying on his Olive, he was watching the big brown working the hatch when suddenly he heard voices. Nothin' perked up his ears. One of the voices, though still at a distance, was recognizable. Woodrow rubbed his eyes and shook his head and moaned lowly, "I don't believe it. I gotta see that guy again." He thought it best to stay hidden down in the willows in the hope that T. Nathaniel and whoever would pass him by. It was a narrow hope at best, as there wasn't a fly fisherman in the world who would pass up a chance at this run. A hope that became totally dashed as the voices became clear.

"You see, Senator? Now what did I tell yo-o-u? Look at all those fish."

"That is something."

The sound of them crunching over the river rock made their sudden appearance more aggravating. Woodrow quieted Nothin' by holding his muzzle. "In the whole great state of Montana. Ten thousand miles of trout streams and we have to fish the same hole," he whispered. Woodrow could now clearly see the transgressors.

"Now sir, I have an appointment with a five-pounder," T. Nathaniel announced as the two men stopped not fifty feet from where Woodrow hid. "I saw him feeding last night as I was heading back to Vision House, and this evening I want to fool him. You should go up to that next bend there. Right above it there's another stretch of water that looks like this one, and the fish should be coming up there as well. Don't worry about trespassing. I o-o-wn it all."

"All right, then I'll see you back here in an hour."

"Sounds fine, and John, I hope you will give some more thought to another medical center in the western part of our state. Some of my people are looking for possible land parcels now around the Asheville area. If we play our cards right we could get ourselves in on the ground floor just like last time. Buy ourselves an old farm at five hundred dollars an acre. Then sell it to the state at five thousand an acre. Oh, that worked so sweet. And there are certain to be more of those handsome behind-the-scenes consulting fees for the both of us—those invisible, untraceable, now-you-see-it, now-you-don't kind of consulting fees. But don't think about too much. I don't want you missing any five-pounders."

The other man turned and laughed, and when he did so, Woodrow recognized him to be Senator Colbourn. He might live deep in the hollows, but even Woodrow knew that face from the magazines, and he'd heard him over the radio enough times. But he had no opinion about him, other than the opinion he held on all politicians. An opinion that wasn't very high and wouldn't even have made it up to the curb back in Frog Level, if Frog Level had a curb.

There he was in the middle of nowhere, and by a happenstance no more clandestine than trying to hide from a blowhard while fly fishing, he was privy to a secret conversation involving a U.S. senator. Six sentences might have been completed, and half of them were about lining Colbourn's pockets. Politicians seldom, if ever, ventured back into the hollows of the Blue Ridge. The folks there would know exactly what should be done with them, and without a trace.

Watching the senator heading for the bend, Woodrow decided to wait until T. Nathaniel was fishing and then he and Nothin' would slip away. But instead of fishing where he should have been fishing, T. Nathaniel chose to walk downstream and then out into the river. He went splashing past the deadfall, spooking with certainty the large feeding brown, and then he turned upstream and began casting for the smaller fish. Woodrow was trapped. Right behind him lay the exposed cliffs. There was no escape, without detection, other than downstream. He wouldn't be able to sneak off until T. Nathaniel's back was to him. With Nothin' asleep at his feet, Woodrow made himself comfortable against the log. He could do nothing other than watch the man fish his way upriver.

T. Nathaniel had a robotic casting style. It was a perfected and effective presentation that was crisp and accurate, not unlike his freshly starched bush jacket. He picked off fish quickly and within no time at all had three small trout. Mechanically he moved upriver, and just about the time Woodrow and Nothin' were about to make their break through the willows, he heard the senator calling. He was back from around the bend and shouting, "Hey, Nate do you have any extra flotant?"

"I sure do," he shouted back, and the two started walking toward one another across the shallows. Woodrow and Nothin' were forced back into their hiding spot.

"Did you see that one I landed back there on the bend?" T. Nathaniel yelled.

"No."

"Got that five-pounder I was tellin' you about. Got him on my first cast, and on a small Olive . . ."

"Well, I'll be damned. Good on you, Nate."

"Yeah, I took him on the first cast. I . . ."

Their voices trailed off as the two men came closer. Woodrow, sitting on his log, leaning back, his hands holding his knee, just laughed. "The only five-pounder that spooner came near was the one he near about stepped on."

The flotant was loaned, and the senator headed back to his bend. When the coast was clear Woodrow and Nothin' snuck from the willows and angled downstream, disappearing into trees and brush, back to camp and evening. Woodrow went to sleep picturing where he'd be tomorrow.

~

Late in the afternoon the following day, a day warmer than the one before, Woodrow was sitting on a high bank above the long quiet stretch where the intruders had spoiled his play. Once again he watched the flights of the blue-winged olives. The fishing, like yesterday, had been slow in the morning and improved as the day warmed. Working the pools in the last three hours he had hooked and released four beautiful fish of around two pounds and two smaller ones. Both angler and fish were in position and awaiting the hatch.

Woodrow had arrived earlier than he had the day before. He didn't want any hope of hooking the large brown to be dashed again by other anglers. Though he had been fishing for almost two days without seeing another fisherman, other than the senator and his pal, he didn't want to take any chances. But surely they wouldn't be here again, and when that trout began rising, he would be the only one to greet them. What Woodrow had no way of knowing was that perched above the gray cliffs, directly above him, where a mountaintop used to be, stood Vision House, and despite its name it couldn't be seen from the river.

The smaller trout had been rising for quite some time before the large brown moved out from beneath the logjam to feed. When he did so, Woodrow tethered Nothin' to the base of the willows and then moved carefully downstream. Wading into position well behind the brown and slightly left of center so his presentation could ride the currents more credibly, he watched the fish proposing to feed. His back was broad and black. Though Woodrow had no experience with this kind of fish, having caught nothing but small speckled trout all his life, he thought the fish could well *exceed* four pounds.

Woodrow's style and riverside demeanor was of another dimension. The river and woods were his domain, and though the terrain differed greatly from the hardwood forest of the Blue Ridge, the element remained the same. He moved into position well behind the trout with the patient moves of a man easy and at one with his surroundings.

His casts were as fluid as the river itself; soft and gentle casts, even over the distance he was standing behind the brown. The distance he judged to be safe. If he settled the fly tied by his hands on the current line, his Blue-Wing would parade past with the rest of the olives only to be ignored. The fish kept feeding. It would be all a matter of timing.

Woodrow's approach was more to the art of the angle, the soul of the matter. He was a man lost in the art, and joyously lost. He stood fishing in a place up to now only imagined, and life was grand. In tune and in control, he had the sure balance of one who belongs. Woodrow had a grace about him, despite his homemade vest, multipatched waders, frayed shirt, and ragged old cap. He was a far cry from his fellow Carolinian, T. Nathaniel, in his bush jacket and white Stetson, with his soulless approach to the pastime of angling. Woodrow cherished river and wood and was pure poetry with a fly rod.

The sound of a motor broke his concentration. From the corner of his eye he could see a bush jacket with Stetson coming through the willows in an open jeep. The disruption caused his presentation to land well to one side of the brown, and another trout came sailing from the water to take it. It was his first rainbow, and a fair-sized one. The leap took the rainbow upstream and the disturbance, in turn, caused the brown trout to rocket downstream, only to pause for a few seconds not six feet from where Woodrow was standing. Then he swam quickly back into his lair beneath the logs.

Woodrow's hands were full with a rainbow that was trying to take him into the logjam, but he still had a good look at the brown—bigger than he'd imagined. He let the rainbow go for one run then another. Then he turned the fish and brought her to net. She was a beauty, shiny and fourteen inches. Releasing the fish slowly and carefully, he looked back to the current line. There were no more rises. The brown would surely be gone for the day.

Behind him traveled T. Nathaniel's voice, and even though it carried over peaceful waters it sounded angry. "Sir, I mean to have a word with you."

Woodrow shook his head and mumbled. "Three days runnin' of this guy might just be my limit. Three days runnin' he's spoilt part of my day. And now he wants to have a few words with me."

While Woodrow waded from midstream, T. Nathaniel paced back and forth. He was badly hung over from last night and very angry with Jasmine who had carried her flirtations with the senator too far. At an orchestrated moment alone, she'd made it perfectly clear to the senator, that while T. Nathaniel might have a dead pecker branch, she was a woman who was willing to swing from a new limb. Things might not be so strained if the senator and his wife weren't scheduled to stay again tonight.

"You, sir, is this your dog?" T. Nathaniel questioned then recognized Woodrow as he climbed the bank. "Oh, it's you. The little man from Toad Flat."

"Frog Level, And, yes sir, that is my dog."

"Then you are guilty of trespass."

"Don't you mean my dog is guilty of trespass? I'm the guy down in the river and mindin' my own business."

"In order for your dog to be tied up here, you had to have climbed this bank, and when you did so, you committed trespass. Montana law clearly stipulates," T. Nathaniel explained in a slow and threatening manner while pulling a pamphlet from his bush jacket, "that once you cross the high-water mark you have committed trespass. I own this land and I would be within my legal rights, and being an attorney I kno-o-ow my legal rights, to have you arrested. The law is specific and I have a copy of it here. I insist that you read it." He snapped the brochure.

"Well, I left my glasses back at camp."

T. Nathaniel might have been a preposterous sight, and a megalomani-acal bore, but he wasn't stupid. No one gets two doctorates by being stupid. The second doctorate, the doctorate of jurisprudence, had taken over. "Well sir, if you can't read this print, then how do you tie on your flies?"

T. Nathaniel had him.

"Well, if'n the truth be told, I can't read." He could weld, build houses, plumb, work on cars, do electrical work, do anything that needed doing if it involved savvy and know-how. But he never learned to read. It was a fact that had shamed him all his life.

Now the legal mind was activated, "You can't read? Yet didn't I see you driving a motorized vehicle? If you cannot read, by law you cannot drive. And if you are driving without a license you can have no insurance. Driving from North Carolina to Montana without insurance. Oh, I think my friend the sheriff will have a fie-e-eld day with this one."

"Yep, that's a good idea." Woodrow smiled and walked over to untie Nothin'. "Give the high sheriff a call. I got a story about you and that land-scammin' Senator Colbourn he might like to hear."

"I beg your pardon." T. Nathaniel stepped back.

"Listen, you miserable, lying son-of-a-bitch. I came here to do a little fishin' and enjoy myself. I was doin' no harm. Nothin' wasn't doin' no harm. I just tied him up there to put him in the shade. We woulda come and gone without botherin' a thing. But me and Nothin' gotta run into you. Ya know I would've had myself a near-perfect vacation if it wasn't fer you."

Woodrow took a step toward T. Nathaniel, and though T. Nathaniel stood on higher ground, he was looking him right in the eye. "You stand there all outraged 'cause me and my dog walked across your land. All swelled up by you bein' the lawyer upholdin' the law, while you and the good senator grease your palms with the citizens' money. So you go on ahead and call the high sheriff and you tell him your story about me and Nothin' trespassin' and me drivin' without a license, and I'll tell him mine about the Asheville Medical Center, your land grabs, and the invisible consultin' fees." Woodrow started down the bank. "Invisible consultin' fees. I was wonderin' what they were callin' low-down thievery these days."

T. Nathaniel turned an ashen color despite his Florida tan, and looked as though all the air had been sucked out of him.

Woodrow stopped suddenly and turned. "*And* you lie about yer fishin'. Five-pounders. I saw you land one of your 'five-pounders' yesterday. It was a pound, maybe. And you all dressed up for big game then catchin' the smallest fish in the creek. Must be a big disappointment for ya."

T. Nathaniel was fuming, "Now, you listen here. I—"

"I've listened to you all I'm gonna. Me and Nothin' are comin' back here tomorrow and I'm goin' to fish this pool and maybe the one above. And I don't want to see you or your buddy, the senator."

Wanting to say something, but unsure as to what it would be, was a strange sensation for the normally ebullient, the usually smooth, and the painfully confident T. Nathaniel. He stammered, then blurted out, "What you think you heard was out of context. The senator and I were having a joke between us." Woodrow just continued to walk away. T. Nathaniel shouted after him, "Let me tell you this, little man, you wouldn't want to get on the bad side of a U.S. senator."

Woodrow, with Nothin' swimming at his side, crossed the channel never looking back. He was angry, but at the same time quite pleased with himself for the way he had just handled everything. It was the most curious sensation, and one he'd never experienced before—to have a sense of power over the more powerful.

Crossing the next channel, he stopped and tried to force the incident from his mind. But he couldn't. He wanted to be thinking about fishing and all he could think about was T. Nathaniel, the senator, and their scam. When those two weren't occupying his thoughts, he had the day after tomorrow to think about and the drive back to Frog Level. He didn't want to leave this place despite his run-ins with T. Nathaniel.

He noticed several fish rising in slick water, and his thoughts of leaving

⁓

and other aggravations slipped Woodrow's mind just as easily as the water flowed at his feet, just as easily as the evening came.

Once again there was heavy drinking up at Vision House. The cocktails started at five and would be ending at seven. At a chosen moment T. Nathaniel took the senator to show him his walk-in gun room, a room-sized safe filled with vintage and present-day armaments, revolvers mostly. Here he explained what had happened on the river. "This little shit from Frog Level heard everything we had to say yesterday. What are we going to do? If word of this leaks, we're through." T. Nathaniel was nervous and had sweated through his bush jacket. Gone was his confident behavior, for no mixture of doctor and lawyer could save him from the media wolves.

Standing beside an amazing array of army Colts, which were displayed under glass and yet another lock and key, the senator showed some concern, but he was used to these situations. "Don't worry about it, Nate, old boy. I'll have one of my staff make a few calls and see what kind of man we're up against. I mean, how many people from Frog Level could be up here fishing? We'll have an answer on him within the hour. Always best to know your enemies before you meet them.

"Could I look at this one here?" the senator continued, pointing to the Colt displayed in the center against red velvet.

"Well, yeah, sure you can, John." T. Nathaniel fished a key out from beneath a cabinet and, fumbling it twice, he finally stuck it into the ornate lock, an American eagle whose wings of hand-crafted silver spanned the display case.

"Ah, there's nothing better than the feel of a good piece." The senator sighed as he fondled the Colt, but he was thinking about Jasmine.

Throughout a five-course meal, more wines were sampled, but the level of last night's debauchery was never achieved. Much to T. Nathaniel's relief, Jasmine kept her flirtations and innuendoes in check at the dinner table—that was, above the dinner table. Beneath the dinner

~

table her foot never stopped stroking the senator's thigh and higher. As the after-dinner drinks were being served, one of the senator's staff came in to hand the senator a note. It was a short note and it was read quickly. The senator smiled and laughed, then leaned over to say something to T. Nathaniel, who was sitting to his right. The unexpected move caused Jasmine, sitting to his left, to lose her toehold on the senator's member, and her foot slipped from his chair to land with an awkward thud.

"My foot's gone to sleep," Jasmine explained as everyone turned. The senator's wife knew where Jasmine's foot had been—the same place she and countless other women had had their own feet while trying to gain the senator's favor. But she didn't care anymore about that, or anything else for that matter, and tossed back her fifth glass of wine. T. Nathaniel was so preoccupied with the events of the day that he didn't notice a thing.

The senator then whispered to T. Nathaniel, "You know that matter we discussed about the man from Frog Level?" T. Nathaniel eagerly nodded. "It's all taken care of. His name is Woodrow Dickey. Seems he's never registered with the Selective Service, or with Social Security. The IRS has never heard of him. Nate, this is a man who can cause us no trouble."

After cigars and brandy, coffee and a late dessert, the two couples had decided to call it a night when there was a rattling at the kitchen door. "What the hell is that?" the senator asked.

T. Nathaniel rolled his eyes. "That would be Jasmine's raccoons. She's made pets out of I don't know ho-o-w many. Every night we have a regular coon-vention around here." T. Nathaniel was breathing easier now that the senator had gotten the goods on Woodrow and laughed at his own joke.

Jasmine winked at the senator. "Would you like to come out and see my little darlin's?"

"Why, sure I would." The senator, though rather drunk, was quick to his feet. There was nothing that could have interested the senator any more than seeing her little darlings, even if he had to go look at a bunch of damn raccoons first. Jasmine grabbed his hand and took him through the kitchen, where she picked up a large bag of scraps from a day of overindulgence. The senator's staff members were eating well, too.

On a glassed-in back porch, they all gathered together: the senator with Jasmine, T. Nathaniel, and a very wobbly Betty. Jasmine flipped a switch and outside lights flooded the lawn and garden. Raccoons were everywhere. Lots of raccoons. Three or four families. There were raccoons hanging from the garden's latticework, hanging on screen doors, hanging from lights, and those that weren't hanging on something had their hands and noses pressed against the windows.

"Aren't my little darlin's precious?" Jasmine cooed to the senator and rubbed her darlings against his arm. "They climb all that way from the river just to see little ol' me." Behind T. Nathaniel's back and the oblivious Betty, she gave the senator a little of her bump and grind. She whispered something in his ear to which the senator smiled and nodded.

Jasmine then opened the screen door and threw out the scraps. A dozen or more raccoons descended. Snapping and snarling, twenty-four manlike hands began snatching and grabbing at the leftover pheasant, the leftover pâté de foie gras, the leftover hors d'oeuvres. Jasmine could never tolerate the thought of leftovers under her roof. The scraps were mixed in with potato peelings, lettuce, and eggshells. The feeding was gluttonous in nature, and several raccoons, finding goose liver amid the melon rinds, began rolling in the food. They were bandits invited to a charity banquet, and their beady eyes flashed through their masks.

Betty first leaned against the wall then slid down it, face-first, to the floor. There she lay quietly and nearly unconscious. T. Nathaniel had taken his eyes off her for a second to watch the raccoons. It was agreed that perhaps it was time for bed.

But the raccoons were far from finished. They were nocturnal. They were just starting. It was the first full moon of the mating season. Orgiastic raccoons gorged themselves on rich food. The females were in season

~

and redolent in their heat. The males, every gland swollen and oozing scent. Soon the males that weren't fighting over the females were having their way with them, and all of this was heightening the smell of coon.

Prevailing winds were gentle, and they lifted the odor of this raccoon bacchanal from the gardens at Vision House and floated it along the cliffs, above the river, through the cottonwoods, and into Woodrow's camp. Had he been awake, Woodrow might have smelled raccoon himself. But it wasn't wasted on Nothin'. Nothin' was born into the business of sniffing out and treeing coons. A coonnoisseur. And though he tried to fight it, there was no way he could suppress what was inherent, and the smell of orgiastic raccoons brought his bloodline to a boil. It took several hours for Nothin' to chew through his leash.

Once free, he was off and howling, causing Woodrow to bolt upright only to see Nothin' going down the road. Woodrow threw on his shoes, grabbed his flashlight, jumped into the Dodge, and drove after the baying hound. He'd seen him do this back in Frog Level, catch the scent of coon, and he knew Nothin' could not be stopped until the critter was treed.

The smell of raccoon lay on the river bottom like a mist, and everywhere Nothin' turned he caught the scent. He zigzagged through the woods, nose to the ground, then nose in the air. Woodrow stopped the truck and killed the engine and heard Nothin's yowling in the distance grow steadily fainter. "He's headin' for the other side of the river," Woodrow reckoned. He followed a ranch road down to the two-lane bridge, crossed the Elkheart, and was soon speeding uphill on a private driveway. The cliffs along the river were nearly white in the moonlight. Nothin's howling was growing louder.

As he crested the McCarthys, Vision House came into view just as Nothin' appeared in his headlights. He was dead on the scent, his bloodhound legs windmilling up the road. A locked gate, which Nothin' leapt in stride, brought Woodrow to a stop. He jumped from the truck and followed on foot, running for the only lights on with trepidation in his heart. The contorted outlines of Vision House fell into perspective. "This place could only belong to one guy."

Nothin' was running for the same lights, the outdoor lights illuminating a narrow corridor of manicured gardens between two wings of Vision House. The dreadful sound of a hound reached the raccoons. Startled, all of them turned at once to see one hundred pounds of crazed coondog coming straight for them. Some of them managed to scale things, while five more tried climbing the screen door. Nothin', coming full speed, left the ground flying and slammed into that family of coons with enough force to break the door nearly in two. The collision sent raccoons and Nothin' tumbling into the kitchen. Raccoons took off in every direction. Nothin' was slightly dazed from the impact, but soon up and running down the dark halls after them.

Woodrow was now running into the garden, flashing his light and shouting Nothin's name. He frightened four more raccoons and sent them scurrying into the kitchen. He paused for a moment at the broken door. A man just doesn't go running into another man's home. The sound of fragile things breaking and no one coming to stop them forced Woodrow into the house.

There were crashes coming from all directions. Woodrow stood at the end of the kitchen. Hallways branched off other hallways. Stairs led everywhere. Hearing a large thud, a howl, then the sound of tinkling glass, he turned to see a raccoon scrambling between his legs and Nothin' coming straight at him. He tried to contain the dog with a tackle, but Nothin' escaped his grasp and ricocheted off a wall and into a lamp, which came crashing to the floor. Raccoons screeching, Nothin' howling, and everything in their path being trashed.

With the immensity of Vision House, and everyone sleeping at the end of a separate wing, upstairs and downstairs, the bedlam at the center of the home hadn't awakened a soul. Betty was out cold. T. Nathaniel was dead to the world, exhausted from the day's worry. The senator's staff were all at the farthest end of the most distant wing, and while some were still awake, no one could hear a thing. The senator and Jasmine, although very much awake, couldn't hear the mayhem, either. They were well insulated inside T. Nathaniel's gun room; a safe with two-foot walls.

The senator, much shorter than Jasmine, was a passionate and lusty little man. Jasmine was a very attractive woman with a beautiful body that hadn't been touched by her husband for years. However, she had been touched, with scheduled regularity, by the pool man, two construction workers, and the teenage boy who lived next door. Spirited in his lovemaking, the senator had her naked and leaning back on the glass housing the rare Colts. She was spread-eagle, not unlike the gold and silver eagle adorning the lock beneath her. Laughing and loving it, Jasmine was feeling the depths of his full senatorial power.

Woodrow grabbed a Navajo rug and with it trapped and released two raccoons, for there was no stopping Nothin'. The only thing he could do was try to stop the slower-moving coons. But how many were there? Nothin' had them treed up curtains, treed up lamps, and treed up tapestries. Three of them were treed up the great bronze statuary of the spiraling eagle. A raccoon was balanced on each wing of the raptor, while a third dangled precariously from its beak. The eagle was exhibited in front of the largest window in Vision House. In fact—and T. Nathaniel prided himself on this—it was the largest single pane of glass in Montana.

Perhaps it was the challenge. Perhaps it was the fact that there were three of them. Perhaps it was the sight of the eagle already wobbling under the added weight, but Nothin' couldn't resist. He drew back and then came bounding. Over a table and off the back of a couch he flew, but Nothin' fell just short of the winged bronze and crashed headlong into the wooden base that held the bird in flight.

The eagle shook violently to one side. It teetered at first, then began to sway. The raccoons were sent tumbling in all directions with Nothin' up and after them. Woodrow stood motionless. There wasn't anything he could do but stand by and watch. The eagle took one more giant swing and then for the first time that great statuary flew. It soared free of its pedestal. It soared free of Vision House. It soared out the largest plate-glass window in Montana. But the eagle, being life-sized and made of bronze, didn't soar far.

The noise was thunderous. An explosion in glass. Lights flipped on. Woodrow heard the sound of voices. Everyone in Vision House was coming on the run from one wing or another, with the exception of Betty, who hadn't heard a sound. The staff gathered around T. Nathaniel, who stood paralyzed and dumbfounded by the damage. He also wondered where the hell Jasmine was.

The eagle had landed. It lay broken on the ground. Shards of glass were everywhere. Everyone stood gaping at the destruction. Everyone but the senator and Jasmine, who were oblivious and sealed away to everything but their own lust.

T. Nathaniel glared at Woodrow and shouted, "You again! What have you done to my house? To my beautiful eagle? I'm calling the sheriff. I'll see that you are sent to prison for this!"

Woodrow tried to explain about the raccoons and Nothin', who were no longer in sight, but was interrupted by a suddenly concerned staff member asking, "Hey, where's the senator?"

Another crash occurred. Nothin' had just treed a raccoon in the kitchen and was now after another in the hall leading to the gun room. "That would be my dog chasin' your coons," Woodrow shouted as he ran following the commotion. The senator's staff and T. Nathaniel joined in after him. They came into the kitchen to find a raccoon hanging from the pots and pans. Then all heads turned to the sounds of screeches and howls coming from down the hallway.

The gun room was at the end of a dead-end passage. Nothin' had the coon cornered in front of its door and was about to pounce when Woodrow finally managed to get him collared.

"So that's it! You were after my guns!" T. Nathaniel exclaimed, seeing that the alarm light was off and that the gun room's door, worthy of any bank vault, was closed but not locked. "Attempted robbery. I'm calling the sheriff."

Realizing that he still held the trump card, Woodrow smiled, "Go ahead. And I'll tell him what I know about you and senator. The medical center scam and the invisible consultin' fees." The senatorial staff stepped back.

"I don't know what you are talking about," T. Nathaniel coughed, then quickly changed the subject. "Perhaps you might have already stolen something." He swung the gun room's door open to make sure.

The senator and Jasmine were now entwined on the floor. One of the staff members gasped. Jasmine shrieked. The two scrambled for their clothes. T. Nathaniel, speechless, could only stare at his wife. The senatorial staff found themselves staring at the senatorial staff. Woodrow could have averted his eyes but chose not to for two reasons. One, Jasmine was truly beautiful, and two, it might have been the funniest thing he'd ever seen. Woodrow was the only one to laugh.

The senator robed himself, smoothed back his hair, and walked down the hall looking at no one as if nothing had happened. Jasmine in the meantime was having trouble covering herself. All she had brought for the rendezvous was a black negligee, and though it was long and flowing, it was paper thin. Thinking she was covered, Jasmine walked out of the safe. But the filmy negligee had caught on itself in such a way that her bottom was perfectly revealed, and there, flying gallantly, unlike its life-sized cousin down the hall, was the American eagle. A wing was passionately imprinted on either cheek. Woodrow couldn't help himself. Saluting the national bird as it wiggled passed, he said, "Kinda brings a whole new meaning to the word *safecracker*, don't it?" Two of the staff laughed.

T. Nathaniel stood frozen in rage. For a long time he just stared at the Colts and the silver eagle that had taken his wife to new heights. Then he reached for one of the handguns and slowly turned to Woodrow with murder in his eye. But Woodrow and Nothin' were gone. They were on a dead run and already over the fence and nearly to the truck. He could have easily shot one of three people and a dog at that moment, but most of all he wanted Woodrow. Fortunately, he was wrestled to the ground by several staff members and held there until he calmed down.

Back in the truck, and driving fast for the bridges, Woodrow was screaming at Nothin', "Of all the coons up and down this river you have to go and chase that guy's."

Once he reached camp, he started packing. He was hopping mad and talking to himself. "All I wanted to do was to come and fish Montana. All I've ever wanted to do was to come out and fish Montana. Then all I wanted was to catch me some big old brown trout. Now all I wanna do is to catch me that fish in the far channel. But no," Woodrow said, changing the direction of his lament. It was now aimed, in scolding tones, at Nothin', who was cowering beneath the truck. "You gotta break a jillion-dollar window and a zillion-dollar eagle." He threw his ax in the back of the Dodge. Then started taking down his tent. "They're goin' to be comin' for me for sure. Ol' T. Nathaniel will have the high sheriff and police down on me like I was some kind of low and sorry criminal. The only wrong thing I've ever done in my whole life was dri-vin' without a license. Just 'cause I can't read.

"That son-of-a-bitch lawyer up on the hill and his senator friend. Oh, they can read all right. And look at what they do with all their brains and learnin'—they steal from the public and get paid for it.

"What am I doin' here?" Woodrow threw the tent rope to the ground. "I can't run and hide from those guys. They know I'm from Frog Level. It ain't gonna be hard for them to catch me there. If I get out on the open road—North Carolina plates, old pickup—they'll get me." He sat on a tree stump, held his spinning head in his hands, and gave the matter some long and serious thought. "I guess, weighin' all things, it would be better to be arrested while fishin' than to be pulled over on some ol' highway." Woodrow retied his tent to the tree.

He hadn't forgotten his trump card. He knew he had the "medical center" goods on T. Nathaniel. But he also knew that he was up against a U.S. senator, and a trump card might be useless when played against such powerful hand.

"How did I get into such a mess?" He grabbed his waders, fly rod, and vest. Then with his sleeping bag rolled and slung over his shoulder, and Nothin' on his leash, Woodrow waded into the Channels. If they came for him they would have to find him, and Woodrow knew how to lose himself in the woods. He knew how to blend in. All he needed to do was to elude the sheriff until around four tomorrow afternoon—when the blue-winged olives appeared. He'd try to land the brown trout, and if he could, he would go to jail smiling. Nothin' skulked along by his side. Not since he was a pup had he seen Woodrow so mad.

Woodrow awoke to another perfect morning. What the day would hold for him, a big brown trout or a year in the pen, he didn't know.

Up at Vision House things were far from perfect. Senator Colbourn, Betty, and the staff left for the airport in the middle of the night. Jasmine had yet to make her appearance. T. Nathaniel was at an all-time low as he stood in the wreckage of his home. But it wasn't the broken window or the fallen eagle, nor was it the adulterous behavior of his wife that precipitated his despair. It was this morning's phone call from one of the senator's staff. The medical center scam had been discovered by none other than the senator's upcoming opponent in next year's election. The senator's advice—"Get home quick and start burying your tracks."

T. Nathaniel and Jasmine, though they never spoke, had to hire a plane and were gone by noon. They left for the airport in separate Land Rovers.

Late that afternoon Woodrow was staked out on the far channel, hidden and watching for the mayflies to appear. He looked for his brown trout to make the first rise. Much to his disbelief, he hadn't seen a soul all day. He'd hiked back to camp twice, but there was no evidence of any visitors. He had even managed to get in a little fishing, with one eye over his shoulder. Then he heard voices. Looking up river he saw a driftboat float around the bend.

Just as they had planned earlier in the week, Henry and Jud had gone fishing. Though she had been included in the original plans for the day, Sarah hadn't been able to join them. "You know," Jud said as he pulled on the oars, "this used to be my favorite water on the Elkheart. But now I can't, well, I just can't get comfortable knowing that fool in his horrible house is looking down on me."

Henry shook his head. "I think we're gonna have to git you exorcised or somethin'. I mean for the last couple o' years you been positively possessed by that house. It gets you worked up just thinkin' about it. Forget about ol' T. Nathaniel. Jest go on out and catch yerself a trout or two and you'll be fine." Henry wasn't mad at Jud, but there was just enough exhaustion in his voice to tell Jud that he had grown tired of his complaint. It wouldn't have been noticed by a casual acquaintance or even a close friend, but only by a best friend.

Jud began rowing to the bank as expected. They'd floated and fished the Channels since they were boys. It was a known fact that they would pull out here and fish this water on foot. Just as it was a known fact that Henry would fish the bend upstream, while Jud, favoring the long slow pool below them, would fish downstream.

From his concealment, Woodrow watched as the two fishermen rowed ashore. One of them tied the boat to a tree. Then they split up. One headed off to fish the water the senator had fished the day before. The other angler was now walking straight for him, coming for the water and the brown trout he'd been waiting on for three days. The brown made his first rise, and then another.

"I don't believe it."

Because of last night, this had to be Woodrow's last day in Montana, unless the sheriff caught up with him, and his last chance to try for the trout of his lifetime. He could see Jud walking right toward his water. With Nothin' at his side, Woodrow stepped from the underbrush, giving Jud a start. "Excuse me, but if you wouldn't mind, I been kinda tryin' to catch a certain trout here for the past couple o' days, and this here is my last shot 'cause I'm headin' home tonight. I mean I just want to fish around them logs there, then I'll be gone. I would be mighty beholden to ya."

Jud smiled. "Yeah, that's a good spot. Well, heck, sure. You go ahead." Because of his homemade vest, his weathered bamboo rod, and the wear on his reel, Jud knew this man to be a fisherman. "Where are you from?"

"Frog Level, North Carolina."

Jud laughed, "Frog Level?" Rings appeared along an edge of the log-jam. "Oooo, I think I just saw the fish you're talking about."

"That was him."

"That's a very large trout. Here, let me hold your dog for you, if you don't mind my watching?"

"No, not a bit."

"What's his name?"

"Nothin'."

"Nothin'?"

"Yep. Named for what he does best, nothin'. Unless, of course, there's coons around, then he can really can be *somethin'*," Woodrow added, staring at Nothin', who hid himself as well as he could behind Jud's leg.

"My name's Jud Clark."

"Woodrow Dickey." The two shook hands. "Well, I better go down and give him a try while he's up and in the mood. Sure do wanna thank ya for lettin' me fish."

"You bet."

Woodrow worked his way across the shallow and well behind the feeding brown. He went about it slowly, evenly, like he belonged on the river and with the river. Hesitating after every step, he positioned himself. Then, working his line out, he made his first cast. Then he made another and another. Woodrow had a natural and easy way of casting, and his line sailed effortlessly, not through the air, but on the air, with the fluidity and grace that is seen only with bamboo. His cast appeared slow, yet it was powerful enough to send his blue-winged offering with phenomenal accuracy to the brown trout time and again. Refusals time and again. Laying his cast gently on the water, he kept his intentions a secret, and the great brown trout continued to feed.

The long pool's serenity was broken only by the movements of its reflections, the shimmer of leaves, the swallows darting above. Trout disturbed the surface now and then with their rises. But Woodrow was only interested in one rise. Standing in the cool mirrored stillness of the river, autumn all around, he was casting to, after years of dreaming about it, the October brown trout he had only heard about. Jud sat on the bank, rubbing Nothin' behind the ears, and though Woodrow was standing halfway across the Elkheart, Jud could easily see that he was grinning.

The rings continued to appear and Woodrow continued to cast. He was in love with the moment, in love with the art of the angle, and in love with the Elkheart. Woodrow's joy was spilling over into the river, and the river issued acceptance.

The harmonics of fly fishing are filled with intricacies. It's the blending of thought and physics, instinct and practice, and Woodrow had distilled it all into one flowing motion. He let his line go once again for its measured target. And for that long instant, when his mind and his fly were in flight, he was worry-free. Gone for that few seconds were any thoughts of broken windows, or broken eagles, of T. Nathaniel, raccoons, senators, and possible prison terms.

The fish, up to this cast, had seemingly picked off every blue-wing on the river but his. But with this last cast timing had come into play, and from the second the fly hit Woodrow had a feeling about it. That feeling down in the gut, the tightening spasm that comes when all things are suddenly in order, and perfection is about to be yours. When something intangible tells you that you're in the groove. The trout took.

Breaching half out of the water, the brown arched, lunging for new water. The fish was larger than Woodrow had first suspected, and the weight and the fight of him was more than he had ever imagined. At first the brown tried to get back to his lair, but Woodrow had the angle on him and, leaning the rod far to one side, bamboo bent double, he made the brown follow his lead. Leaving his hole with a wake behind him, the brown flashed across the shallows, taking his fight to the thin water. But Woodrow was nimble of foot and was moving into the shallows as well. The brown then performed his one and only jump, twisting, showing the length and width of him, showing his black back and the bright orange of his underbelly.

This was the moment he had come for, the moment he had dreamed of, and the moment was now dancing at the end of his line. The fish pulled and tugged, then tried another run for the logjam. Woodrow, though he had never before played such a trout, knew when to let him have the line and when to hold it back. He knew when to take it away. Jud, from his place on the bank, knew he was watching a fisherman.

Slowly Woodrow began to gain the advantage and backed toward the shore. The brown turned and thrashed in the shallows. October's low light and the last of the day pierced the shoals, and the trout's true scale came as a shadow against the bright yellow mosaic of river bottom. This was Woodrow's first long look as he reeled in against the trout and his size took his breath away. He was larger than he had ever imagined, now, or in his dreams.

Finally the fish, after a few desperate rolls, was beaten. Woodrow carefully brought him to the net and into hand. Jud and Nothin' joined him. "Ain't he somethin', though?" Woodrow asked, cradling his catch and freeing the fly from his jaw.

Jud leaned down for a closer look. "You know, Woodrow, I'm pretty fair at guessing a trout's weight, and I would think this fish would go just a shade over seven pounds. I've guided on this river for some twenty years. I grew up fishing it, and I can tell you with certainty that a seven-pound brown trout on a dry fly on the Elkheart doesn't happen very often."

"All my life I been wantin' to come out to Montana and fish. All my life I been dreamin' about catchin' a trout like this one. And I don't mind tellin' you, it feels pretty good."

"Well, you played him well and you deserve him."

Woodrow continued to cradle his fish, while moving it gently and slowly back and forth, until the trout regained his strength. Once he began to swim against his grasp, Woodrow released him. Swimming slowly until he disappeared, vanishing within the river like a lost soul returning home.

The moment was broken as thoughts of T. Nathaniel, shattered windows, fallen eagles, once again flooded his mind. All the images were being chased by the sheriff. "Well, I guess I had better get goin'. Want to make it as far as I can tonight." Then he added in his mind, *Which probably won't be any farther than the city limits of Travers Corners*. He saw himself being cuffed and led away. But he had no other chance than to run for it. He was banking heavily on his hole card. "Thanks again for lettin' me fish that piece of the river. I know you were aimin' for it for your ownself."

"I live here, and I'm lucky enough to fish the Elkheart when I want to. But I have to tell you, over a lifetime of fishing and guiding on this river, I've seen few fish to rival yours. He was something. I mean every once in a while a four-pounder is taken. But a *seven*-pounder—once in a coon's age." Nothin' cocked his head and picked up his ears.

"Well, not if you talk to the guy who lives up there in that house on the hill," Woodrow volunteered.

"Oh, you managed to have the T. Nathaniel experience?"

"Once in town and twice out here on the river," Woodrow answered, deciding it best not to tell a stranger about the their fourth meeting. "Yesterday, I sat right over there and watched him. He'd beat me to the pool, so all I could do was watch. He waded right over the top of that brown. Anyways, I watched him catch a couple o' fish—both of them no longer than a foot. Then I hear him tell his fishin' buddy, who jest happens to be Senator Colbourn, that he caught a five-pounder. He didn't know I was watchin' him.

"So, I come back the follerin' day and he kicks me off his land for trespassin'. All I did was to put Nothin' in the shade of that there tree. The tree jest happens to be on his property. He got real nasty about it. Made me a might testy, too."

"That would be T. Nathaniel, all right."

"Well, I gotta git. Thanks again, and good luck to ya."

"So long," Jud said.

With Nothin' on his lead they headed downriver, back to camp, where who knew what might be waiting for them.

Jud fished for a while along the far bank, looking now and again at Woodrow and Nothin' walking downstream. They grew smaller then were gone.

Jud thought what a contrast at streamside those two must have been. He would have liked to have been there when Woodrow, a man of apparently little means, little education, dressed in a patchwork fishing vest, with his missing teeth, talked trespass laws with T. Nathaniel. "T. Nathaniel," Jud snorted. A man of double-doctorate means, dressed as if he were expecting wildebeest, posturing around from his perfect life with his perfect smile.

There was a ingenuousness and a kindness about Woodrow that made itself immediately evident by the courteous, almost childlike way he had asked if he could fish for that brown.

A small rainbow took Jud's fly and snapped him from his thoughts. He missed it. Looking upstream he could see Henry climbing into the drift-boat. He then turned his thoughts back to angling and away from T. Nathaniel. Fishing for another minute or so, he waded into the shallows to meet Henry.

"How'd you do?" Henry greeted, holding back at the oars.

"Missed one is all," Jud answered as he stepped over the gunwale and aboard the SS *Lucky Me*. "But you should have seen the fish Woodrow Dickey from Frog Level caught."

"Who?" Henry asked, rowing for the deeper water.

"I just watched Woodrow Dickey of Frog Level, North Carolina, catch a brown trout that was easily seven pounds."

Surprised, Henry asked, "Where?"

"Right on the end of his line." Jud smiled. Then he laughed and added, "Over next to the logs. One of the most beautiful browns I've seen in a long time." The crack of gunfire gave Jud a start.

"Ran into Larry Eslinger and his two boys up there," Henry explained. "They were about to sight in their rifles. Gettin' all accurate for elk season. That's why I didn't fish for too long." Another shot was heard. "Gunfire and fly fishin' are two sounds that don't mix very good."

"That reminds me, I heard the damnedest noise last night. Woke me up from a dead sleep. Did you hear anything?"

"Nope."

"It was loud like a sonic boom, but it sounded like breaking glass."

"Didn't hear a thing," Henry answered. Another practice shot was heard as Henry pulled a lazy half circle at the oar. The bow caught the current and the *Lucky Me* picked up speed. They floated beneath Vision House, then away from the cliffs, and back into the heart of the Channels, where the sun was touching the tips of the trees. Everything in its path, save the shadows, was lit in a brilliant yellow, and the Elkheart flowed like blue velvet.

At day's end Jud and Henry came back to a town where the talk was of nothing but the flight of the bronze eagle. The flight, though very short, was most historic. Statuary flying through the largest pane of glass west of the Mississippi was more than newsworthy. The word up and down Main Street was that a family of raccoons had finagled their way into Vision House and somehow climbed the eagle, which sent the bird off balance, then into flight, out the window.

So that was the news in Travers for weeks, and the story will surely be talked about for years to come.

Now, if word of T. Nathaniel and the good senator's medical center scam had ever leaked, the town would probably never tire of talking about it. *But,* if the gossips down at Dolores's Beauty Parlor had ever gotten their hands on the senator-in-the-safe-with-Jasmine story, the whole salon might have suffered spontaneous combustion from the sheer joy of it.

Weeks, then months, passed, but nothing ever became of what surely would have been a prime-time scandal. It so happened that one of the senator's staff managed to dig up an even juicier piece of dirt on the senator's opponent, so it became a political wash. His opponent, in fact, dropped from politics, and the senator won his reelection bid in a landslide. Colbourn's platform centered on additional health care throughout the state.

T. Nathaniel went back to become the CEO and chief financial officer for one of the largest HMOs in America. Dr. Wellsley and his loverly wife, Jasmine, still spend their summers and their falls in Travers. Their giant window was replaced. The eagle was recast and once again flies in place at Vision House.

Jud was only too glad to share Woodrow's story about T. Nathaniel's "five-pounder" with Junior. Junior felt betrayed and never called him Nate again. T. Nathaniel, Nate to his friends, so Nate to damn few.

Woodrow crept out of town safely, to his surprise. He then stayed on the blue highways as much as possible all the way back to Frog Level. He never left Frog Level again. Being a southern gentleman, the only southern gentleman in this story, he almost never said a word about the Vision

House incident. Except at Christmas dinner, when he is begged by all at the Dickey family gathering to tell the story about his fishing trip to Travers Corners, to tell about the raccoons, Nothin', the senator, the safe, the flight of the eagle, its crackup (that would be both the bronze's and Jasmine's), and the seven-pound brown.

From The Journals of Traver C. Clark

June 9, 1897—

Carrie and I are heading for Missoula tomorrow. I have never seen her so excited. We have tickets to see Lilly Langtry on Saturday. Lilly Langtry, the Jersey Lilly, playing at the Opera House—it's hard to imagine. It's such an event.

Your Name in Lights

B Y EVENING THE storm had moved on, and lingering clouds were stretched out and traveling slowly across a three-quarter moon low on the horizon. On the hill above town, the Carrie Creek Boat Works was nothing more than dark shapes lost in the surrounding aspens, lost save for two faint lights coming from the old carriage house. There were no lights on in the workshop, as the work had ended at five. There was one light on in the kitchen, made fainter by the steamed windows—a stew had been simmering on the cookstove since early morning. The second lamp came from the third-floor observatory where Jud sat reading. When the clouds parted and it was moon-bright on a new snow, Jud could nearly read by the light. The only other signs of recent movement around the Boat Works were two sets of deer tracks and the footprints that Jud and Annie the Wonderlab, the world's smartest Labrador, had left leading from the workshop to the house.

The moonlight lit the log rounds of the carriage house, and even in the darkness you could appreciate the size and age of its timbers. Wood smoke drifted over the blue snow, and Jud turned the page. The sound of Carrie Creek gurgling beneath the ice came softly through a cracked window.

He'd been in the observatory since sundown, and he'd looked on as his home town of Travers settled in for the evening. He'd watched the Elkheart River turn silver then darken into a rolling shadow whose currents could only be seen in the reflections made by the homes along its banks. He'd watched as the lamps of Travers began clicking on, first as a few, then as a wave. Side-street lights, porch lights, lights in the living rooms, headlights moving slowly down Main.

Lee Wright was home. Bonnie Cotton was just pulling into her drive. Julie Peterson turned the light on in her kitchen. The lights of Ed's Garage were still on but Ed would be heading home soon.

The lights of McCracken's General Store, always the brightest in town, were made brighter this time of year by the added Christmas lights which used to edge only the store's name and its founding date—SINCE 1947— but now edged the store's name, the entrance, front windows, and nearly every other edge the old general store had to offer. No doubt about it, Jud observed, McCracken's was getting brighter every year. But that was just his old friend Junior McCracken getting carried away again, as with just about everything else he did. The same obsessive behavior that manifested itself through his model train collections, his computers, the ham radio, his beehives, astronomy, his Boy Scout troop, his butterfly, coin, and stamp collections, and his family. All of these things coming in a distinct second to his passion for fly fishing.

Though he couldn't see the front of the Tin Cup Bar and Cafe he could tell by the parking lot that it was filling in for Saturday night.

The lights tripped on at the McQuades'. They were in Arizona for the summer and had their lights on a timer.

The medical clinic was dark and had been all day. Doc Higgins and his wife, Kim, would be taking a well-deserved day off. He'd be at home this evening, having his nightly highball, puffing on his pipe, and tying dry flies while Kim made supper. Such was their usual routine.

Two snow removal trucks with their great blades scraping came down Main and their sound traveled as far as the Boat Works. They were heading for Albie Pass. Swiveling his chair, Jud looked to the Elkhearts, but the mountains were hidden in the storm and showed only the white skirting of their benchlands to the tree line. The peak of Mount D. Downey showed itself above the cloud for a moment, a great bald summit silvered in the moonlight, then it disappeared.

The lights were still on at Dolores's Beauty Parlor, but that was to be expected at this time of the year. This was the last Saturday before Christmas, and all the parties, church socials, plus the Elks Club annual do would be happening tonight. Every woman in Travers would have been in Dolores's today to have her hair twisted or tormented into some fashion or another. But she'd be closing as soon as she could. Then it would be home to change and meet Henry down at the Tin Cup for dinner. After which she'd settle in at Henry's for the weekend. Those two were pretty predictable on a Saturday night and had been for years.

The yard lights from the outlying ranches had made their way through the darkness, first flickering against the twilight then as fixed beacons dotting the bottomland and benches. Jud knew most of the ranches by their lights. Just as he knew that if he wanted to see Henry's ranch light, he would need to tilt his chair back a little; so he could look north, upriver; so he could see past the Baptists' steeple and over the school's gym. He did so and saw the yard light burning. Henry would be heading this way or maybe already at the Tin Cup waiting for Dolores.

Downstairs, Annie was growing restless for her supper, and he could hear her pacing back and forth, toenails clicking, across the kitchen floor. He came down the narrow staircase, which spiraled past the second floor, and into the kitchen. The doorway at the bottom of the stairs was the original and obviously built at the time by a rather short stable hand, causing Jud to bend his long thin frame nearly in two to make it through. He first fed Annie then went to the stove and heaped the stew into a bowl and settled in at his usual chair at the table. From there he could continue his vigil on Main, though any possible views of

McCracken's and the Tin Cup were now blocked by the woods. He could still see South Main and Dolores's.

Annie nuzzled his elbow as he took another bite of his stew and looked back down on town. The activity level on Main was pretty impressive, he thought, considering Travers was a town of three hundred and that a foot of fresh snow on the ground was sure to deter shoppers and celebrants alike. But even with the streets crowded for the holidays, it was a small town, and Christmas gridlock was still no more than two pickups trying to pull away from McCracken's at the same time.

The lights switched on at the Roxy. The neon flooded South Main and the maples lining the streets. The snow was balanced in their branches and the rose-colored lights of the marquee tuned them surrealistic, and surrealism is an odd commodity around Travers Corners. The flash of the neon transported him back to a night from six years ago, six years ago this next April 20. A night he recalled clearly and a night he recalled often. But the night it all happened Travers was still at the eye of the storm. That incredible night when the town's adage about how not much had happened in Travers since Herbert Hoover stopped for gas was not erased, or even replaced, but clearly surpassed. He remembered it was a Wednesday night . . .

Jud was in the observatory enjoying the spring storm. The thought of more snowfall in the mountains brought a smile to his face, as the valley had been in drought for two years and snow was a welcome sight. He was pulling himself from his easy chair and about to head downstairs when the pulse of flashing lights caught his eye and he watched the ambulance speed away from the medical clinic, heading north out of town. The road over Albie Pass and all the way to Helena was sure to be a treacherous one. Perhaps there had been an accident.

The sign at Ed's Garage came on and in moments Ed had his tow truck, hazard lights flashing, heading out onto Main and following the ambulance's lead. He looked over to the medical clinic and saw Doc

~

Higgins getting out of his jeep and going into his office. A few minutes later Leroy's patrol car, siren and lights, sped through town.

Though he couldn't see the Roxy's marquee, he knew it to be on by its reflection on the street, and by the flood of its lights, which lit the snowfall; a seemingly endless lacework, the large wet flakes of early spring. Travers was lost in a sudden whiteout, and with no outlines to support them, the lights of town were held suspended like lanterns in the storm.

The snow was mesmerizing and had held Jud at the window for some time when, once again, he was aware of flashing red lights. The ambulance was back already. It couldn't have gone any more than a mile or two out of town to be back this soon, Jud thought, as he followed it until he could clearly see the ambulance pass beneath the marquee's light. Right on its heels came Henry Albie's pickup truck.

After a notable double take Jud was down the stairs. He grabbed his coat and hat, and ran the downhill path toward the medical clinic. It's an eerie feeling seeing your best friend's pickup follow an ambulance into town.

Jud came through the clinic's back door to see Phil wheeling a woman from his ambulance. Doc was there to help with the gurney, and they quickly steered her into the surgery. He only glimpsed the woman, whose arm was wrapped and bleeding, and though Jud couldn't see her face, something about her seemed familiar. Henry came back out.

"What's going on? You all right?" Jud asked. But Henry just motioned for Jud to follow him. Covered in mud, Henry headed for the rest room down the hall.

"You know who we got in there?" Henry asked as he turned on the water in the basin and grabbed for a handful of paper towels. Jud shook his head, but his response was lost on Henry who had his head in the sink. He stood up with the mud still thick in his hair, and the water sprayed from his lips as he spoke. "We got Angellica Phillips in there! That's *the* Angellica Phillips! Now, I ain't a wiffin' with you, pee wee, it's the real magilla." Henry's face read more of amazement than anything else.

"Unbelievable." Jud was almost staggered by the news of it, for Angellica Phillips had always been his all-time favorite. "What happened?"

"I'm at home and the door busts open, and standin' there, near frozen, is Angellica Phillips. Her arm is bleedin'. She yells for me to call 911. I call Doc Higgins. She screams at me for not callin' 911. I tell 'er 911 is a service we don't own here in Travers. She tells me her dog is still trapped in the car. I mean Angellica is really shook, I mean stricken with panic, and stinking of gin.

"So I grab my tools and we jump in my truck," Henry continued as he reached for more paper towels, "and we head back to the highway.

"What happened was that they hit that icy patch right there on Miller's Bend. They lost it and rolled into the barrow pit. She tried to get her dog out, but the door was jimmied. She could see my yard light and she aimed for it.

"Anyhow, we get there and Phil is there not more than two minutes later. The car was upside down and the door was sprung. I got a crowbar on it and got 'er open, and grabbed this small dog. The dog's out cold. Phil and I git the stretcher and git Angelica and her dog into the ambulance. *And then* Angellica starts tellin' us that if we don't handle this thing right she is gonna sue us. I mean we were working fast. Up to our butts in mud, snow, and ice, trying to save her mutt, and she's threatenin' lawsuits. Movie stars." Henry, so far, had not been impressed by Angellica Phillips.

But Jud and the rest of the world were.

Angellica's fans had rewarded her with the highest of all film honors: They made her a legend. Her screen legacy has perhaps never been matched—Hepburn, maybe. Jud had seen her films hundreds of times. For years, as a young man, when he would try and conjure up his ideal woman, he would see her face framed in the long close-up at the end of *Shadows*. Cinemascope. And now she sat down the hall.

"What's the situation here?"

Even though they were down the hall and behind a closed door, Henry and Jud knew the voice to be Leroy's. Leroy was walking in from the waiting room with his on-duty attitude in place. He was the man of authority and he was looking for a few answers. He was the night cop for four thousand square miles of ranch land, and for one town, population three hundred and change, most all of whom were law-abiding citizens, so not much went on for Leroy other than coffee and doughnuts.

Jud always thought of Leroy as a kind of well-armed Maytag repairman. But he also knew Leroy to have his flip side, and on those rare occasions when he was called into action, Leroy could have delusions of being Dirty Harry. Tonight he was in full swagger, and the swagger suffered because of his fifty-inch waist. He was all code and regulation, and he had swelled to twice his importance. This investigation was going by the book, because at this 11–27 (single-car accident) Leroy had found a 22–14 (possible drug-related activity: a handbag filled with pills and a large amount of money). He'd also stumbled upon a near empty bottle of gin: a 3–15 (driving under the influence). Now, ordinarily this would be excitement enough for one small-town deputy sheriff, but in that same pill-laden purse Leroy had discovered identification belonging to Angellica Phillips, plus five other I.D.'s describing the same woman. He'd also found a briefcase.

Kim came out of the office leaving the door slightly open, and Jud could see Angellica standing in the corner smoking a cigarette.

"She's doing fine," Kim said to him, "just a couple of scratches. One cut on her arm Doc might want to do a stitch or two. But I don't think her little dog came away quite so lucky."

Down the hall came Doc, motioning for Kim. They conferred briefly, then she went on to check on the dog, and Doc went in to talk to Angellica. Once in the room he helped her through another side door and into the privacy of his office.

Half listening in while Leroy questioned Henry and Phil, Jud wondered what a legend in her own time was doing in Travers. The consummate actress and three-time Oscar winner who, some twenty years ago, had surprised the filmgoing world by announcing her retirement. Now she was dogged by the paparazzi, her privacy shattered, like a Brando, a Jackie, or a Liz. He wondered how Doc would be handling the distraught superstar.

"What's your dog's name?" Doc asked as he checked Angellica's bandages and the cut on her arm. His round fatherly face was not clean shaven, since Wednesdays were his day off. Doc was tying flies when the call came in and had a long dry-fly hackle hanging from his sweater, pieces of thread stuck to his lap. He was not the comforting sight for Angellica that he was for everyone else in Travers.

"Jimmy. Is he all right?" Angellica asked. Her hand shook as she brought a cigarette to her lips.

Doc's diagnosis of Angellica was easy. She was going to be fine even though she was half in shock, not to mention half in the bag. She wasn't going to need any stitches. Bandages would do. Shaken and frightened, she was having adrenaline shakes, the ones everyone has after a close call. His prognosis for Jimmy was not so easy. "He's received a very bad blow to his head. The next few hours are going to be quite critical. Normally we would take him to the vet in Reynolds, but the pass is sure to be closed. Even if it were open the going would be slow—and Jimmy doesn't have that much time.

"Unless I miss my guess and without getting too technical, Miss Phillips, Jimmy may be bleeding between his skull and his brain. Kim is taking an X ray right now and I hope I'll know more here in a minute or so."

"Well, guesses, hopes, and maybes aren't good enough, Doctor, Doctor . . ." she said nearly screaming. Angellica's sudden rage turned to fear and confusion. She was lost, disoriented by the whole ordeal. She didn't know if she had ever learned Doc's name, or if she had already forgotten it.

~

"Dr. Thomas Higgins, ma'am."

Angellica could have answered in any one of a hundred voices but she decided upon an incredulous intonation, and she could have chosen from a thousand faces, but she used an expression showing at once disbelief, contempt, and just a hint of disdain. It was the face she used against Burt Lancaster in *Stratton Place*.

Doc was not a regular moviegoer, hardly ever watched TV. However, in a world fascinated by stardom, it was impossible to escape the many veneers of Angellica Phillips. But Doc had never been impressed by celebrity, and her look was lost on him. "I'm not going to sugarcoat this for you, Miss Phillips, Jimmy is badly hurt, but he looks strong. Is he a Jack Russell?" Angellica nodded. Doc smiled. "Good, that just might give him the edge. I know I'm not a vet and my surgery is set up for people, but anatomy is anatomy and if the X rays show that I'm right, I think I can save Jimmy for you." Doc put his hand on her shoulder.

He wasn't a man of a thousand faces and he had but one voice, but he put them together with a manner that had provided comfort to an entire town. On the world's stage Doc had never had so much as a walk-on. His name was never up in lights. But around Travers Corners, which is about as far away from Broadway as you can get without actually leaving the planet, Doc was star status. He'd brought life into the world, he'd held life in the balance, he'd seen life fade away. Around Travers he had but one role and he'd played that role for thirty-two years: He was Doc.

He started to leave, then turned at the door and asked, "Miss Phillips, where were you going?"

"I was on my way to Whitefish. I was going to stay for several days at a home belonging to friends. I wanted a remote drive so I chose this route to Whitefish. Seemed like a good idea at the time."

"I'm pretty sure that the roads in and out of Whitefish will be closed. Heard on the news tonight that they've already had two feet of snow up there."

Doc left and Angellica picked up the phone and then realized she would need her briefcase for the phone numbers. Her secretary, Margie, was at her ailing mother's house in Arizona. Her longtime agent, Sid, was in Miami. She didn't know the numbers. She then tried to phone her friends in Whitefish, but all the lines were down. She wasn't used to thinking about phone numbers or briefcases. Margie was always there to do that. In fact this trip from the Missoula airport was the longest Angellica could remember being alone in a long time. She then remembered— and it came to her quite slowly through a gin haze that was giving way to nausea—that the briefcase must still be in the car.

Hearing voices outside, Angellica went to a crack in the door, thinking perhaps the man who had helped her might have seen it. She looked out and saw Leroy questioning Henry and Phil. With his back to her, gun on his hip, the pear-shaped Leroy was taking notes and reconstructing the situation. Her briefcase and her purse were on the floor next to him. She swore through clenched teeth.

Another man was sitting on the corner of a desk, his long legs crossed out in front of him, his arms folded across his chest. He had an intelligent look about him, wire-rim glasses, a kind face. Angellica knew faces. She went out on a flier. She needed the briefcase. She didn't need the cops.

Listening in, but keeping his distance, Jud became aware of the door to Doc's office opening slightly, and there was Angellica Phillips motioning him over. She also put her finger to her lips to see that he did it without attracting any attention.

Once Jud was through the door, and doing so without Leroy's knowing, Angellica turned on the charm. "Would you ple-e-ase help me?"

She was wrapped in nothing but blankets. Her hair was matted, her makeup was gone, and her face was thirty years older than most of her films, but she was still beautiful.

The circumstances called for her to be fearful and concerned. She summoned all of her forces. She parted her lips to show a certain helplessness while her eyes, those eyes, those unbelievable eyes, beseeched him for a quick answer. It was the same face that had seduced Marlon, Paul, and

Charlton. Jud didn't have a chance. I mean it was *the face* asking for a favor.

"Sure I will, Miss Phillips." Jud said it with instant sincerity; it was the look Angellica had seen a million times. It was that look that told her that she could now ask this total stranger for his last cigarette, his last dollar, his undying devotion, his right arm, his firstborn, his very soul.

"I need a blue address book. It's small. It's either in my purse or in my briefcase. The officer has them. I have to make some phone calls. I need that book. Please get it. It's an emergency."

Interrupting Leroy, Jud knew, as did the town of Travers, was going to be risky business. Leroy was sure to be lost in the moment. This was a situation, and Leroy knew it. He also recognized it to be a *real* situation, the first one he'd had in his eighteen years as deputy sheriff. He was going slow. He was being methodical. He wasn't going to miss a thing. Everything was evidence, everyone a possible witness, everywhere hid the possible clue.

"Eh, Leroy, Miss Phillips needs her purse and her briefcase."

"I'll just bet Miss Phillips *needs* her purse. Hey, how do you know what Miss Phillips needs?" He was angered by the fact that this bystander had somehow managed to talk to the suspect before he had.

"Leroy, she just needs an address book. She has to make some phone calls. She has to have that book. It's a small blue book."

Leroy needed to think about all of this for a moment. The address book might just end up being Exhibit A. "All right," he finally agreed, "but I'll be the one takin' it into her. I have a few questions for *Miss Phillips*. I haven't phoned this situation into the station yet, 'ceptin' about the wreck. I am gittin' the ducks in a row around here. This has drug traffickin' written all over it. I ain't gonna let an obvious drug bust slip through my fingers 'cause I slipped up on procedure. Anyway, how do we know she really is Angellica Phillips? She might be some kind of Angellica Phillips look-alike. There's people make a livin' impersonating famous folks. I saw it on Geraldo."

"Leroy, would you hurry up!" Jud said, exasperated.

Leroy placed both briefcase and purse on the receptionist's desk. He turned Angellica's large handbag upside down, the contents spilling over Kim's appointment calendar. Pills, bottle after bottle, shook free; maybe twenty unmarked vials filled with different-colored capsules. Unsealed envelopes fell as well, envelopes filled with money, and crumpled hundred-dollar bills littered her purse as casually as empty gum wrappers. Amid all this was the usual handbag equipment: hairbrush, mirror, lipstick, et cetera, but no little blue book.

Drug trafficking was a ludicrous assumption, but if Jud had seen those same contents tumble from someone other than Angellica Phillips's purse, he would have to be reaching the same kinds of conclusions as Leroy. The thought of it made him edgy. No way did he want his mind to have anything in common with Leroy's.

Leroy went to the briefcase. In it he found papers, files, notebooks, and he set them on the counter as he went. Finally he found the blue address book. He reached for it, but his sleeve caught the edge of the briefcase and it dropped to the floor. A tape recorder and a small automatic pistol went skidding across the tiles. Leroy bent down and almost grabbed it with his bare fingers, but then remembered procedure and picked it up with a pencil instead. "Fingerprints," he explained to Jud.

Adjusting his gun belt, Leroy mustered his bluster. He headed for the room holding the suspect. Despite his outward bravado, he felt the weight of eighteen years in law enforcement hanging in the balance. He was nervous. He thought about calling for some backup, but decided he would handle this one on his own. Angellica Phillips. Big deal. He didn't care what kind of a star she was.

Kim had finished developing the X rays, and Doc had read them. His worst fears were confirmed. He had no choice if the dog was going to make it. Doc came down the hall and quickly went to Phil. Doc whispered something to him, then Phil was out of the office on the run.

Carrying Angellica's handbag and the blue book, Leroy was almost to the door. He walked past Henry, and with the purse he was almost too easy a target, but Henry shot anyway. "New uniforms this year, Leroy?"

Leroy bristled. Phil had left without asking him his permission. He might have had a few more questions about the accident. Now Henry was taking shots at him like he always did. But he was going ahead. He'd be getting plenty of respect when he got to the bottom of this whole thing.

Doc called Jud over as well. "I'll be needing a third pair of hands on this one, Jud. Get a gown from Kim."

Surprised, Jud nodded a reluctant yes. He'd never been in a operating room, not even as a patient.

Sensing his uneasiness, Doc added, "Don't worry, all I need you to do is . . ." he then became aware of Leroy going into Angellica's room, and knowing Leroy to be Leroy, Doc acted quickly, "Eh, not just yet, Leroy, I need to see Miss Phillips again."

"I'm sorry, Doc, but we have ourselves a situation here. I have to ques—"

Doc was instantly impatient with him. "Leroy, you will have a chance to talk with her when I say you can, and not until." Then he directed Jud, "Go to the surgery and Kim will help you get ready."

"But, Doc," Leroy whined, "she's at the bottom of this situation and I'm going to get to the middle of it," then, realizing his mistake, "er, I mean . . ." But he didn't get a chance to explain; Doc was on to the important matters at hand.

"She's got to have that blue book, Doc," Jud called out, "it's got all the phone numbers she needs."

Doc passed by Leroy, plucking the address book from the deputy's hands as he went.

So there stood Leroy with a purse. His authority ignored, his presence diminished, his bravado deflated, not much left but beer belly. Henry wanted to take another shot, but he left it alone, while thinking, *Every time Leroy gets to the middle of a situation there isn't much room for anything else.* Henry didn't care for Leroy. Henry didn't care for authority in general, small town or otherwise.

She tried to reach her agent but he was gone for the day. At Margie's mother's no one was home. Angellica was angry at the delays, crying, impatient, and shaken. Doc reached out and put his hand on her shoulder. It was at once comforting and strange to have anyone reach out and touch her. Strange because she had become a recluse for that very reason, for no matter where she was thousands would show up to touch her. But a touch was somehow comforting from Doc. He'd never treated anyone like Angellica Phillips, but over his long career he had learned people are their most essential selves in a crisis, and he knew that at these moments people are more in need of solace than long medical explanations. So he wouldn't talk about a spreading subdural hematoma.

"Miss Phillips, Jimmy is hurt seriously. A very small, but somewhat tricky operation is going to have to be done. I have the surgical tools required and I am going to do it right now. We have no choice. We have very little time. Without it Jimmy could lose his vision, his hearing, and if something isn't done he will die."

The door swung open from the hall. "Everything's ready, Doc. Jud's getting scrubbed," Kim said, trying not to stare at the movie star, but it was hard. "And Phil's back."

"Good," Doc said, following Kim. Then he turned to Angellica. "This won't take very long."

Jud was toweling off his hands and Kim was helping him with a surgical gown when Doc came in to scrub, asking, "What's going on out there? What is Leroy all fired up about?"

"Leroy has gone ballistic, Doc. He's got it in his head that Miss Phillips might be an impostor, a celebrity impersonator trafficking in drugs." Doc shot Jud a look of complete disbelief, and as he patted his hands dry, Jud explained, "At the accident he found her purse and it was filled with pills, and wads of money, and phony I.D.'s. And it was. I saw them. A minute ago he found a handgun in her briefcase. If Leroy isn't stopped he's going to turn this whole thing into a carnival. Every tabloid and sleazy TV reporter will be coming here. He hasn't radioed any of this in yet, Doc, except for the accident. Nobody but the people at this clinic know she's here. Perhaps we can somehow stop all this from leaking out."

"How?"

"Maybe you could call Judge Mills."

Doc quickly backed up to the swinging doors of the surgery and shouted down the hall to Henry, Phil, and Leroy, "I want no one to use the phones. We are expecting a very important call from Miss Phillips's doctor," he lied. "And Leroy, I don't want you going anywhere. I might need you." The surgery's doors closed.

Doc, pulling on his rubber gloves, confided to Jud and Kim, "Maybe that'll hold Leroy for a little while. When we're done here I'll give the judge a call. Now here we go." Doc led them to the operating table. From the surgical tray beside Jimmy, Doc picked up an electric drill, not some kind of fancy surgical stainless-steel drill, but Phil's own Black & Decker. He draped the power tool in a sterile cloth and chose a drill bit from those Kim had washed and set in alcohol.

"This isn't going to take long, but once we start we have to work fast. Jud, you hold that light steady. Get a little closer, that's right. Kim, as the blood begins to flow I want antiseptic on the site."

The hum of the operating room lights, the click of Leroy's heels up and down the hallway, all muffled beneath the howl of the north wind: these, plus the brief whine of a Black and Decker, were the sounds of the medical clinic for the next half hour.

Phil stayed. Henry left after telling Leroy he was leaving; he didn't ask. Leroy could feel this investigation slipping away from him. He thought of going out to the squad car and radioing the situation in, but then thought better of it because Doc might be needing him and because he wasn't about to take an eye off this Angellica Phillips character. Something was going down. He'd find out. Angellica, or whatever her name was, would give him the answers. He was practicing his questioning over and over in his mind. Nothing was going to escape him.

First out of the operating room was Jud, looking a little peaked. Then came Doc, who was looking pleased. He patted Jud on the back. "You did great in there, Jud. Now get Harry Mills on the phone. Use the phone back in the surgery. When you get him, hit the intercom button and I'll pick it up in my office."

At the end of the hall, in the posture of a man waiting for some answers, stood Leroy. Doc was coming right for him, and now he would begin to get things in hand. Then, much to Leroy's dismay, Doc suddenly veered into his office to tell Miss Phillips the news. It was the kind of news Doc didn't get to tell as often as he liked. It was good news. He found her waiting by the phone. Doc was practically beaming. "Well the biggest hurdle is over. His breathing is stabilizing. His pulse is stronger. Jimmy's still unconscious, but now he has a much better chance. All we can do now is wait, but I think he's going to be fine."

The intercom buzzed and startled Angellica. The good news from Doc had some calming effect, but she was still very much on edge. And even though she was in blankets and had been inside for some time, she still had sporadic shakes. But the tremors weren't from the cold. Doc knew what she needed. He could stand a whiskey himself.

Doc pushed a button and answered. Jud's voice crackled over the speaker, "Got Judge Mills on the phone, Doc."

"Good," Doc said and picked up the phone. "Harry? Tom. Listen, we have a problem over here and I need your help . . . Well, believe it or not, I have Miss Angellica Phillips in my office . . . Yes. *The* Angellica Phillips . . . No . . . That's right . . . I know . . . I know . . . She's been in an accident . . . No, she's doing fine. A few scratches. Her dog was injured but I think he's going to be fine. No, I can't get her out, not until this storm slows down . . . It's too complicated to explain.

"Anyway, Leroy is here . . . That's right . . . Yes, I know how Leroy can be. He's out in my waiting room right now and being quite the Leroy.

~

Well, at the accident . . . down on Miller's Bend . . . Yeah, it can get real icy down there . . . Leroy found a significant amount of pills, a lot of different identifications, large sums of money, and a handgun . . . Yes . . . I know . . . Well, Leroy hasn't radioed any of this into the sheriff's office, and as of right now only a handful of people know that she's here. What I was hoping is if you could kind of slow Leroy down a little, we might just keep it that way . . . Because, Harry, as soon as word leaks out, Travers will be a nightmare of reporters and the like . . . I know, Harry, but this is Angellica Phillips I'm talking about here, and I'm sure there has to be an explanation for all of this . . . Sure . . . Yes . . . Right here."

Doc handed the phone to Angellica, explaining, "It's Judge Mills. He's the district judge for Elkheart County."

Angellica knew how to handle judges. Didn't she handle Orson Welles in *The Case against Justice*? But for the voice she would use something far short of the drawl that swayed Orson. It had a southernness about it but without the accent. "Judge Mills? Yes, I am fine, thank you . . . Oh, thank you. That is very kind . . . Well, yes, I most certainly can. To begin with, Your Honor, the pills? Well, they are all vitamins, herbs, oils; it's all part of this new diet I'm trying. It's a monthlong program and you take a handful of pills every hour on the hour. Believe me, the strongest drug you will find on me is aspirin. And the money, well, imagine, and I can assure you, Judge, that you cannot, what it's like for someone like me to do something as simple as writing a check or cashing one. It can't be done. And this might explain why I have the necessity for all my different identifications. I simply cannot go anywhere as Angellica Phillips. But if you wish you can call the Beverly Hills Police Department, and you will find that they are all registered aliases. You must understand . . . Yes . . . It' the only way I can travel . . . Oh, yes, the pistol belongs to me. I'm licensed to carry it.

"Yes, yes. That's very kind of you. Yes. Well, I was planning on staying for a week up in Whitefish. But now, Jimmy . . . I hope so too . . . Yes, it's all been horrible . . . Yes . . . Yes . . . Thank you so much, Judge Mills . . . Yes, he's still right here."

She handed the phone back to Doc, who then answered, "Right, he's out in the waiting room. Thanks, Harry." He then went back out into the hall and called, "Leroy, Judge Mills is on the line"—pointing to a phone at the reception desk—"he'd like to speak to you."

Swelling slightly, his esteem instantly intact—for the judge wished to speak to *him*. Now things were going to get straightened out around here. He'd give Judge Mills an eye-opener. But when Leroy lifted the phone, he was only at the receiving end. "Yessir . . . Ye-Ye-yessir . . . but . . . but . . . Yessir . . . Nossir . . . Yessir . . . But the 11-27 . . . Yessir . . . But Judge, I found . . . Yessir. Yessir." The conversation ended. In a matter of seconds Leroy had been stripped of his authority. He went to the phone with visions of commendations and hung up with a near reprimand. He had been taken off the case. Angellica had been placed in Doc Higgins's care.

Back in his patrol car and pulling away Leroy groused, "Tryin' to do my job. Eighteen goddamn years in the department. I think I know a little bit more about police work than Judge *Harold Mills*. He just sets up there behind his bench, while I'm out on the streets. I woulda had Miss Angellica Phillips, or whatever her name is, downtown and booked."

Judge Mills had made it clear, and his words mumbled from Leroy's lips. Leroy had been ordered to " 'stay clear of that woman' " . . . The judge " 'would be handling things from here on out' " . . . The judge would be " 'reporting this to Sheriff Johnson at his home' " . . . He didn't want " 'any news of this to leak out' " . . . and if it did, " 'there would be hell to pay.' " He decided to head back to the scene of the accident and have a little snoop around; might find some little piece of evidence that would put the case back on the burner.

Eighteen years on the force and he would have " 'hell to pay' " for doing his job. Leroy's head bobbed back and forth as he drove down Main, clearly a man talking to himself. After reconnoitering the scene at Miller's Bend, he would go to Ed's Garage and go over Angellica's car with a fine-tooth comb. Might even take a few prints. Judge Mills, Doc

Higgins, Jud, and Henry had no idea what kind of fugitives they might be harboring. He had a feeling about all of this, a hunch that only a man with eighteen years on duty could have.

Slipping into his coat, Jud stopped by Doc's office to see Doc leading an exhausted Angellica out into the hallway. The question was where would she spend the night? The Take 'er Easy? No way. Out of the question. If Wendy Smith had Angellica Phillips staying at her motel, you would have to tie her to a stake to keep her from telling someone. She'd only need to tell but a few, then the word would travel like a wind.

She needed a place to stay. Sarah's was the obvious choice. As of that moment only a handful knew of Angellica. Phil knew how to keep his mouth shut. Doc, Kim, himself, and the judge knew. Her secret was certainly safe within that group. Henry didn't know about trying to keep Angellica a secret so Jud gave him a quick phone call. Henry had gone straight home and hadn't told a soul. The secret remained so. But Leroy was questionable.

"Listen, Doc, if it's all right with you and Miss Phillips, I'm going to go over and have Sarah get her guest room in order. I think it would be the best and most private place for you to stay," Jud said to Angellica.

On the big screen she was the gathering of a million reflections brought to us in the dark down a stream of projected light. On the marquee she needed but one name, Angellica. But now, standing in Doc's office, wrapped in her brown blanket, Angellica Phillips looked like anyone else in her situation would look: dazed and confused; but certainly more vulnerable because of who she was.

"Good idea," Doc agreed. "That's where you'll stay tonight."

"Certainly, there is a motel in town." Angellica's hackles were up slightly, for others were again making decisions for her—nobody did that. Then, once more she realized her predicament, and that these people, strangers, rural as they were, were trying to help her.

"I really think I should stay with Jimmy. I—"

"Nothing to do but wait," Doc said. "No, Miss Phillips I think it would be best if you went over to Sarah's. Hypothermia and shock, not to mention injury, take their toll on a body. I want Sarah to fix you something warm. I want you to rest. And Sarah would love to have you stay, and it's not just because of who you are, either. She would help you out, because you're a person in need of help. That's just how she is. Plus it's a thrill for her just because you *are* so famous. I mean, until you showed up, Miss Phillips, our town's motto has always been: 'Travers Corners, where nothing much has happened since Herbert Hoover stopped for gas.'" Angellica laughed. Kim, who had grown up with the old saying, laughed as well.

"I'm taking Miss Phillips in to see Jimmy," Doc said to Jud, "then I'll have Kim drive her over to Sarah's." He turned to Angellica. "I'll take Jimmy home with me tonight. Now, his vital signs are good, very good. I really believe Jimmy is going to be all right, but head injuries are difficult to predict; there's hardly ever been two alike. But one thing is certain, sitting in an uncomfortable waiting room isn't going to speed things up any. It's all up to Jimmy now."

Jud mucked his way through the snow that was still falling, but now it was a watery and melting snow. Up the alley, over to Second Street and up the hill, the shortcut to Sarah's, the evening played over and over again in his mind. Thinking about Doc. The accident. Henry. The operation. And Angellica Phillips. On any given night word of an accident is newsworthy in Travers Corners. The still-unknown fact that it was Angellica Phillips in the accident was far above newsworthy. It was beyond historic. It was unbelievable, and unbelievable is a rare sensation.

He came through Sarah's back gate thinking about Henry and he laughed. Henry would be heading for bed soon. It was always an early up for Henry. He would have already categorized the night's occurrences into the "just another day" file, for Henry had the amazing ability of never dwelling on anything. He'd been like that since they were kids. Nothing life had sent him so far had caused Henry to stop and worry about all the inner meanings of why things happen. Henry tried to look out for what was coming, and not back on what was gone. His was a simple and straightforward approach to life: "Never git crossways to it, ride with the flow, and never try to go back upstream—it can cripple ya." Cowboy logic.

So while Jud's mind was filled with the night and all that had happened, Henry would be thinking about tomorrow. He certainly wouldn't be giving much more thought to Miss Angellica Phillips. But Angellica's being in Travers Corners had a different effect on Jud. Of course he hadn't seen Angellica in the same light as Henry had, and Jud had to admit to being star-struck.

The lights in the second story window of Sarah's old Victorian were on, as were the lights in the kitchen. Jud knocked while entering and called out her name, "Sarah? Sarah?"

But there was no answer. There was bread cooling on the racks, classical music coming from the living room. His calling her name brought Useless, Sarah's cat, down the stairs, and she greeted Jud with a rub on his leg. Jud reached up and scratched behind her ears, which drew an immediate purr.

The bread, still steaming, was irresistible, but then everything Sarah cooked was irresistible. He cut himself a slice, buttered it, then grabbed a beer from her fridge and headed for the living room. Warm bread, butter, and beer wasn't much of a meal, he thought, but then it was Sarah's bread, which was infinitely better than anything he would have cooked for supper—which, as his stomach reminded him, had been skipped.

Though Sarah wasn't home, he knew where she would be. It was almost certain she would be across the street at the Tutthills'. Since Dorothy broke her hip last month, Sarah had been helping Elmer, who wasn't getting any younger, in the evenings with a few of the chores. Jud knew she would be back soon, surely before Kim would be here with Angellica. This would give him the time needed to explain to Sarah what was going on. He was wrong.

Before he had finished the bread, there was Kim, along with Angellica,

~

already parked on the street and coming up the front walk. He felt uneasy, that awkward feeling you get from greeting people in someone else's home. He quickly tried to make Angellica comfortable by offering her tea or coffee, maybe a slice of Sarah's bread. But she just wished to be taken to her room. "I'll be heading back to the clinic," Kim said. "Now you just holler if there's anything we can do to help."

"Oh, your coat," Angellica reminded her.

"Nah, you just go ahead and keep it. I can get it from Sarah later." Kim went out the door slightly embarrassed for loaning the great actress such an old and tattered coat.

"Sarah's just next door giving her neighbor a hand. She'll be right back," Jud explained. "Ummm, well, your room is right down here, Miss Phillips," he said, picking up her briefcase.

Angellica followed him down the hall. "After what we've been through tonight, Jud, I think you better just call me Angie."

Jud struggled for a moment with the door to the guest room, then stepped into the room, switched on the light, and pointed to a door half closed. "That's the bath through there."

"Listen"—she put her hand on his shoulder—"I just want to thank you, for all you did tonight."

"Anybody would have tried to help your dog, I just happened to be the one, that's all."

"Yes, it goes without saying to thank you for Jimmy, but what I was referring to was your help in trying to keep secret my being here in . . . in . . . what was the name of this town again?

"Travers Corners."

"Travers Corners, of course. The doctor told me after you had left that it was your idea to call the local judge."

"Well, it just seems like every time I see you, you're being caught unawares by some photographer, or hurriedly ducking in and out of limos to avoid some reporter. Somebody's always pointing a camera or a tape recorder in your face. I would hate that. I mean, I've always wondered what kind of a person it is who makes his living off other people's lives?"

She could have answered him a hundred different ways, but thought the financial motive might clear up his question the quickest. "Do you know what it would be worth to one of the paparazzi if he had the exclusive, the photographs and story, on Angellica Phillips being caught drunk, with drugs, and in a serious accident?"

Jud shook his head.

"Fifty thousand dollars. It's worth ten thousand, sometimes even more, to the person who just phones the tip in." She began to pull off a coat, forgetting for a moment about her cuts, and the sudden pain shot her arm back down into its sleeve. Jud reached over and helped to ease her out of a wool coat, an old ranch coat borrowed from Kim; underneath she had on one of Kim's nursing uniforms. He felt embarrassed about being so slow to help her with her coat. He was used to being the same person no matter who he was around, but he was totally off balance around her; constantly wondering just how to act; as awkward as if he were around royalty.

"You wouldn't know if your friend Sarah might have a little brandy around, would you?" she asked.

"There's some beer in the fridge, but Sarah usually never has anything stronger than that."

"No, never mind. I'm all right. Guess I'm still just a little chilled from the accident. I'll just get into a warm tub. Then I will go straight to bed."

The sound of the back door opening echoed down the hall. The sliced bread was the first thing Sarah noticed. "Jud, you bozo. That bread was for the school's bake sale. You can just get your sorry butt in here and help me make another one. Where are you?"

"That'll be Sarah," Jud explained. "I'll go and tell her that you're here."

But before Jud was back into the kitchen, Sarah was already to the heart of the matter. "What's going on around this town tonight? About twenty minutes ago Leroy comes by with luggage, not just any luggage, five pieces of matching Gucci luggage. It's stacked up in the pantry. He says Judge Mills had told him to bring it here. I ask him who it belongs to, and Leroy says he can't tell me." Sarah was excited. Not mad, just excited. Jud could tell because when that happened she became more animated. The New York City in her boiled to the surface, and the Italian side usually bubbled up right along with it.

"Then Elmer calls. Dorothy has fallen down again. So I go over and help Elmer put her back into her bed. She didn't hurt herself, but when I'm walking back, I slip on the ice. I am going to have a major-league bruise," she said rubbing the side of her leg. "Then I come home and you're in the bread."

"Well, Sarah you have a guest—"

"The Guccis have sort of already told me that," Sarah cracked as she slipped off her parka to reveal her cooking ensemble—the same thing she wore cooking at the Tin Cup: Levis and an unusually loud Hawaiian shirt. The only thing missing was her New York Yankees baseball cap, which hung in the hallway. It was her trademark behind the grill.

"In the *middle* of a storm . . ." Sarah realized her voice was carrying, and whoever it was down in her guest room, the one who was running the tub, the tub *she* had planned on for hours, would be able to hear her. She lowered her voice to a raspy whisper. "In the middle of a storm, me baking bread, the house a mess, me a mess, you just show up with a surprise guest. This better be good, Judson."

"We'll, it's like this. There's been an accident . . ."

Back in her room, the words *Gucci* and *luggage* had come to Angellica loud and clear. The luggage held just what she needed. She hurriedly ran a brush through her hair, added lipstick, wrapped a shawl that Sarah had draped at the back of a chair around her shoulders, and was down the hall and into the kitchen more gorgeous than heaven should allow. "Excuse me, but I couldn't help but hear that you have my luggage. You must be Sarah. I'm Angellica Phillips."

~

It was fortuitous Sarah had a nearby wall to fall against and lucky that she was close to the table for something to hold on to, because when she turned to see Angellica Phillips standing in her kitchen, she went legless. All the New York animation was paralyzed. All her fast-paced street Italian collapsed into a wheeze and a gasp. *Stunned* would be the word.

"I thought I'd better come and introduce myself. I know this is an imposition for you, and I apologize. I wanted to find lodging, but Jud thought it would be better if I came here. Know that I will surely pay you for the inconvenience."

"Doc thought it would be best if Miss Phillips could get something warm into her system. She still has a touch of hypothermia."

"No. No. Please. If I could just get to my luggage." Jud opened the pantry door. Looking over to Sarah, asking her with a glance if what he had done was all right. She smiled her wonderful Sarah smile. He had always thought of Sarah as beautiful, and she was, with her smile and green eyes, but he couldn't stop staring at Angellica. This was classic beauty.

"It's the small one on top. That's all I'll need tonight." He handed it to her good arm.

"Making up a little soup would be no trouble, Miss Phillips, no trouble at all," Sarah offered as she began to regain her balance, but she was still dazed.

"No, really, I'm much too exhausted to eat anything. But if I could just trouble you for a glass . . . a glass of water?" Sarah poured a glass from the tap and handed it to her.

"I'll want to be awakened at all costs if there's any change in Jimmy," Angellica instructed. "If not, I'll want to get up when you do, Sarah."

"I get up at four-thirty," Sarah said apologetically, knowing it was a time most people found appalling. Normally Sarah would want to put a consoling arm around someone in pain. It was the Italian in her, her mother's side. But the Welsh from her father told her that you just don't go over and hug someone like Angellica Phillips.

~

"That'll be fine." Angellica was used to getting up early—the camera's best light.

"Again, thank you both, so very much. Jud, it was sweet of you to try to protect me. You were my knight in shining armor."

"Well, you bet, Miss Phillips. If there's anything I can do, I'm easy to find."

"Good night, Sarah, you are most gracious," Angellica said, and walked down to her room with her water and overnight case.

When they heard the door of the guest room close Sarah hollered in a whisper, "Are you kiddin' me? I mean are you *kiddin'* me?" She was - bug-eyed, hoarse, and animated. "Howdidja . . . wheredidja . . ." While Jud explained the night, the accident, Henry, Doc, Phil, the pills, Leroy, the handgun, through Judge Mills, the drill, and Jimmy's operation, Sarah mixed up another batch of dough and tried to get a hold on the fact that all of this was *really* happening. Angellica Phillips was asleep in the next room, and although all the events leading up to this incredible moment were unfortunate, she and Jud couldn't help but feel slightly giddy about the whole thing.

Back in her room, Angellica had put the water to good use—a geranium by the window. The glass had held two generous portions of gin while she had her bath, and now that she was out of the tub, it was holding a third. Doc had given her a pill to take if she did have trouble sleeping, but the booze would put her to sleep. It always had. She cried silently alone, sitting upright in her bed.

At six-fourteen all the characters involved in the incredible incident from the night before were to be found in the following degrees of consciousness. Doc was conscious but tired and had already gone down to the clinic. Henry was vertical and dressed but wouldn't really be conscious until he had his second cup of coffee. Jud was in that state of blissful unconsciousness—the controlled dream world where you float just before you wake. Leroy was conscious but as always he was doing his best to keep it a secret. Sarah was hyperconscious. She was making omelets, flipping flapjacks, frying potatoes, and her mind was whirling from a dozen orders with more coming but no more than a minute could pass without her thinking about her houseguest.

And Angellica, though a little fuzzy, was dressed and drinking coffee with a splash in Sarah's kitchen. Doodling on the note Sarah had left her, which read, "Doc called after you went to sleep. He instructed me not to wake you. You would need your sleep. If you need me call 5552." She was emotional and alone in a stranger's home, and aware, as well as frightened, that at any second the press would be at the door.

But at six-fourteen, it was Jimmy who was traveling the farthest to reach consciousness. It had been the familiar ring of the phone that had jangled him somewhere down deep in his circuitry. There was fire in the synapses. Jimmy was on his way back. He still had a way to go, but he was coming.

Doc hadn't heard the first moan from Jimmy. But when Jimmy rolled over and stood up and began to wag his tail, his prognosis from the night before was realized.

Sitting at Sarah's kitchen table, Angellica listened to the sounds of the neighborhood awakening. Families starting their everyday lives. All the people who knew her and whom she would never know. The phone rang, and Doc told her the news.

She knew how to get to the clinic. It was next to the Roxy. She could see the Roxy from the kitchen window. Getting there unrecognized puzzled her for only a moment. She went to the rack of Sarah's winter clothes hanging near the back door. She selected what she would need as if from wardrobe: a big wool hat, a bulky overcoat, and a muffler. No one could recognize her like that.

It was early, yet it was almost too warm for a coat. She was elated. She was amazed—just last night, she and Jimmy had almost perished in a storm. She stepped around the puddles, almost skipping. The snow was melting quickly and small streams were flowing down Main Street. At the corner, despite the muffler covering her face, she was recognized, not as Angellica Phillips, but as Sarah. An elderly woman nodded and said, " 'Morning, Sarah."

" 'Morning."

"Do you have the morning off today?" the old woman asked.

"Yeah, ah . . . that's right. I took the day off," Angellica answered. The old lady had stopped, expecting that the woman she thought to be Sarah might like to have a chat, but Angellica just hurried past. Although she had only heard Sarah talk briefly, she thought she had matched her pitch quite well. The New York accent was a snap. She used one opposite Kirk Douglas in *The City at Night*. She might have been a little nasal for Sarah, but through the muffler who was to know? Walking up the steps to the clinic she thought how strange and, at the same time, wonderful— to be recognized on the street by your coat.

Other than a shaved place above his eye and some stitches, Jimmy was doing fine and was instantly aware of his master's voice coming down the hall. "Dr. Higgins?" she called out from the door to the waiting room. Jimmy was gone in a shot, barking, sliding sideways, all legs going and trying to gain purchase on a polished floor.

Picking Jimmy up was difficult, first because he was wiggling so much and whining from the sheer happiness of this canine moment. Second, because Angellica had forgotten about her arm, and the lifting of a squirming Jack Russell hurt. "We're a fine pair, you and I," Angellica laughed, while joyful tears rolled down the famous cheekbones to be caught on the corners of her legendary smile. "I mean, to get hurt like this, in the wilds of Montana, and when they brought you here to this small clinic and to a man everyone just calls Doc—I was petrified. But I think this man they call Doc just might have saved your life."

Getting praise for helping was not an uncommon occurrence for Doc. It happened daily, it was part of the profession. But getting praise from Angellica Phillips had a special dimension, and for the first time in many years, Doc felt himself blushing.

The telephone rang and Kim picked it up. It was a short conversation that Kim explained to the others: "That was Sarah. She just tried calling you at her house, Miss Phillips, and when there was no answer she called here. She was just calling to see if you were all right and if there was anything you needed. And that someone named Sid had called." Then the phone rang again. It was Sid.

"Are you all right?" he asked.

Angellica detailed the events from the night before to Sid. She explained about the pills, the I.D.'s, the money, Leroy (if indeed there is any explanation for Leroy), the handgun, and Judge Mills.

"All right, where are they?" Sid asked. *They,* meaning the press. Then Angellica told him about Jud and how much he had helped her last night and how it was his idea to try to keep her presence under wraps.

"Angie, you have never been and you'll never be a secret. I was raised in a small town, and there is no way you're going to remain a secret."

"I've been in this town for fifteen hours and there's no signs of the tabloids yet," Angellica countered. Which was true. Impossible, but true, and Angellica's point was not wasted on Sid.

"Well, we still need to get you out of there. If the press picks this up . . . oh, man. Okay, then you just stay put. I'll hire a jet and I'll be up to get you. I'll call you back when I know more."

"Okay, Sid. But believe me, I'm being well taken care of. Talk to you soon. Oh, and call Margie and have her handle the car. I'm afraid it's pretty badly wrecked. 'Bye."

The only word out on the streets of Travers was there had been an accident last night. Someone from out of town. The secret was holding.

Henry and Jud had bumped into each other at McCracken's while getting their mail, and they walked into the Tin Cup together. Things were quieting down in the café. Almost everyone who went to work had done so, and at the counter sat the usual lineup of retirees. There were a few people in the corner finishing up, and Sarah was at the far end of the counter enjoying her coffee and her first break since daylight. There was nothing on the grill.

Looking at each other, Jud rolled his eyes, and Sarah sort of put her hand over her mouth to conceal her cat-and-canary smile. They were still boggled by the impossibility of it all. That Angellica Phillips would have been anywhere in Montana would have been news, but that she was here in Travers and staying in Sarah's guest room—well, that was historic. Henry wasn't thinking much about last night—he was more interested in breakfast. He'd been up for three hours and had shoed two horses.

"I'm telling you it's hard not to tell anyone. I've been biting my lip all morning. I mean, not to tell my uncle Sal. He would give anything to meet her. He saw her once back in the early fifties on the stage in New York. He still talks about it."

Everyone, down to the last person in Travers, would liked to have known about Angellica Phillips being in town, but right now it was eight. Three of them were sitting at the counter and a fourth was coming in through the door. Leroy was in for his morning coffee and sweet rolls. He gave the three of them a quick and indifferent glance, then sat down on the other side of the retirees.

"Where is she now?" Jud asked.

"Kim just called right before you guys came in and told me that Angellica was back at my house—her dog is doing fine, by the way—and that I wasn't to worry about her, that she would be spending the day on the phone. I still have all that bread to make today for the school's bake sale. I hope that will be all right with her."

Henry was getting a little perturbed at the fuss the two of them were making over this woman. "Hey, you're the one doin' Angellica a favor here. Now, tell me if I'm wrong, but shouldn't she, she bein' the unannounced imposition and all, be a little accommodatin' to yer schedule? And if yer runnin' out of time to git this bread baked, then tell her to git off her rich butt and flour down on a loaf or two. I'll have two eggs sunny-side up and a side of spuds."

Sarah returned to the grill. A few customers came and left and the retirees thinned out. Just as Henry was finishing his breakfast, Leroy walked over to them. "I just thought you might like to know, I got Judge Mills coming over here this afternoon. There's a bottom to this situation, boys, and I'm gonna find it." Then he turned and walked out of the café. He was going to have one more look at Angellica's wrecked rental car. A good look in the light of day.

"The only way Leroy would ever get to the bottom of a situation is if he tripped and fell into it," said Henry.

After the lunch rush at the Tin Cup Sarah came home tired from cooking and facing hours of baking. Angellica was on the phone, a drink by her side. "All right, Sid. Love you, too. Oh, Sid."

The transformation from last night was unbelievable. She'd arrived dressed in a borrowed uniform and an old coat. She was dirty and frightened, and she was still beautiful. Now she was dressed in designer clothing, her hair and makeup perfect. She was gorgeous. She might have been sitting in Sarah's kitchen but Angellica looked ready for a night at the Oscars.

"Sarah," Angellica greeted, "I have a favor to ask and it's a very large one. The Beattys, the people I was to meet in Whitefish yesterday, are still in Los Angeles. They looked at the weather and wisely said no thank you. But they will fly into Reynolds tomorrow—the weather is supposed to change—and pick me up. The favor, and this comes from Sid more than me: Would it be all right if I stayed here with you one more night? It's a dreadful thing to ask, a terrible imposition, but I am rather alone out here."

"I don't look at that as an imposition, I look at that as wonderful news," Sarah said, feeling somehow awkward in her own home and incredibly ugly in her Hawaiian shirt and Yankees cap.

"Could I make you a small drink? I know it's early, but I very much feel the need to celebrate."

"Oh, I better not, Miss Phillips. I hope you don't mind, but I have about three hours of baking ahead of me and it's gotta be done this afternoon."

"Mind? Girl, how could I mind? Nothing could make me mind this afternoon. And this is *your* home that you are so graciously sharing with *me*. And please call me Angie. I'll tell you what, if you have a drink with me, I'll help you make the bread."

Maybe it was because of the way she was dressed, perhaps it was just because of who she was, but there was something so alluring about her happiness. "Well, maybe a short one," Sarah agreed. Sarah, whose six-pack lasted her the week, had just said yes to gin on the rocks at three in the afternoon.

Sarah began gathering the ingredients for making bread, while Angellica made her a drink and freshened her own. "Sarah, I want you to know how much I appreciate all you are doing for me, and I want to pay you something for your inconvenience. Oh, is there someone you know I could hire to take me to the airport?"

"There isn't a person in this town who wouldn't take you there for free. But I think Uncle Sal is the man for this job."

"How far away is the airport?"

"Twenty-nine miles," Sarah answered. "And listen, I couldn't take any money for your staying here. It's thrill enough just to have you. I just wish I could tell more people about you being here. I wish I could tell Dolores. I had to bite my lip a dozen times at work this morning. And not to tell my uncle Sal, well, that was torture. Sal tends the bar side of our café. I saw him all day, and not to tell him was almost impossible. He saw you on the stage in New York. He waited for you outside, and you signed his program, and that program hangs behind the bar next to his autographed picture of Joe DiMaggio. Definitely Sal's two most favorite possessions."

Handing Sarah her drink, Angellica replied, "It's best if we can keep the number of people who know of my being here to a minimum. I pray that those who do know can keep it a secret—until tomorrow afternoon anyway. Sid couldn't believe I had been in an accident, that the accident had occurred in a small town, and that I have been here nearly twenty-four hours and the press still hasn't gotten wind of it. 'It's a goddamn miracle,' those were his exact words.

"But I'll make you a deal." She grabbed an apron from a hook by the stove and tied it around her waist. "It would be fun to meet your uncle, and we'll have to arrange it just before I leave town. Would that be all right?"

"That would be really great."

"Now give me direction, girl, I haven't done any baking since I was a child. I made a cake once for Robert Redford in *The Short Run*. But then I really didn't bake it. I just pretended."

Certainly the ease in which the next three hours passed could be attributed to the drink: Sarah had one more, Angellica had three. Sarah was surprisingly relaxed around her. She was amazingly real.

The only interruption came an hour after they started. The first four loaves were just going into the oven when Judge Mills, along with Leroy, paid them an official visit. Angellica handled it all very easily. Remembering to fall back into her southern-tinged voice, which had worked so well over the phone, she handily seduced the judge. She ignored Leroy as if he weren't in the room. Without hesitation she gracefully produced the supposed evidence against her: the pills, the I.D.'s, the money, the handgun and its license.

Sarah had never seen Harry Mills so effusive. He was absolutely star-smitten. The judge apologized over and over again for all the inconvenience and extended all the services at his disposal. He promised that her being here would remain a secret, in his office and all the departments under him, until Angellica was safely on her way tomorrow afternoon. All allegations were dropped and Judge Mills left satisfied that justice had been served. He also left slightly in love.

Leroy left suspicious. There was more here than met the eye. He knew that Angellica had been drinking behind the wheel last night. And all those pills. How did the judge know they weren't drugs? It had to be a strong hunch, this gut feeling of Leroy's, given the distance a gut feeling would need to travel to be felt by Leroy. He had twenty-four hours before Angellica left. There was time. He was still on the case.

There was one other interruption: a phone call, which came in as they started in on the next four loaves. Angellica took the call, as Sarah's hands were covered in flour. "Hello . . . Yes . . . Yes . . . Oh, that's wonderful . . . Okay . . . That will work out perfectly . . . Sure you can tell them. Tell them I will see them all soon . . . I'm fine . . . Yes, in good hands, very good hands . . . Absolutely . . . Sarah . . . We're baking bread for the school's bake sale . . . Seriously . . . We're having a great time . . . She is *very* pretty . . . She's single . . . Okay . . . Okay . . . All right . . . Yes . . . Thanks, Sid . . . Bye-bye.

"That was Sid again," Angellica explained, "just calling to reconfirm tomorrow's flight. Card party tonight, Sid wanted to know if it was all right to tell the gang. I said sure. I travel in a circle of friends I've been with for thirty years. We call our group the Survivors. If ever there was a group who knew how to keep a secret!

"Sid's a treasure, seventy-one years old, wanted to know if you were single, wanted to know if you were pretty, wanted to know if you would be interested in fifty percent of everything he owns. Sid's been my agent since I came to Hollywood. He's been through it all with me. Betty Ford. Two very messy divorces. But I'm sure you've read, seen, or heard something about my life. It's been an open book, or should I say an open tabloid."

The conversation could have easily centered on Angellica's celebrated life, yet she wanted to talk about Sarah's. Everyone in Travers knew Sarah's story and it surprised her, as she told it, how long it had been since she had told it last: growing up in New York City, college, marriage, teaching school. "My husband and I taught school in the city. One afternoon Bill took our son, Jeremy, to the playground. A fight broke out between some teenagers. One of the boys had an automatic weapon. Shots were fired. Bill fell on Jeremy, but bullets found them and killed them both."

"I am so sorry." Tears instantly formed in her eyes.

"That was fifteen years ago. After it happened, all I wanted was out. I wanted out of the city, I wanted out of its absurdity, its insanity, the senseless bump-and-go; and Sal felt the same way. Sal doted on my little boy. We packed it all up and headed for the Rockies with no particular place in mind. We just wanted to be someplace quiet, someplace small and easy."

"A place where nothing much has happened since Herbert Hoover stooped for gas," Angellica offered.

"Exactly," laughed Sarah as she refloured the breadboard. "Travers Corners was a much harder adjustment for Sal. He'd never been west of Atlantic City. He missed his friends and he desperately missed the Yankees and Yankee Stadium. About ten years ago he started up a Little League team. Now he spends his summers coaching, and the town is really behind him and the team. The T.C. Yankees. Sal fits in around here because he doesn't fit in at all. He's the greatest. You're going to love him.

"Me, on the other hand, I knew this place was the one I had been looking for from the moment Sal and I drove into town."

They talked and baked, Sarah only leaving the room now and then to slap her stereo, which had a short. "I have to have music to bake by," she explained. They laughed a lot and cried a little. They talked about their failures and successes. They talked about men—where most successes and failures are born. The openness and the candor with which the star talked about her life Sarah found to be astonishing, and though she was still very much in awe, she was at the same time comfortable. Angellica, whose life was at the very least incredible, whose career was centered on make-believe and illusions, was turning out to be genuine—and funny.

"Well, in reality the men in my life are few. I know I've been married three times, but primarily those *are* the men in my life. Oh, I've had a few flings, but nothing like the boys in the tabloids would have you believe. If you did, then I've dated aliens, Elvis's ghost, every leading man and every supporting actor from every movie I've ever made, young men, old men, married men, mobsters and ministers, men who used to be women, women who used to be men, serial killers, service station attendants, Jimmy Hoffa, and, of course, let's not forget about the two presidents."

They talked about the heroes from the night before: Doc Higgins, Henry, and now they had moved on to Jud.

"Well, Jud is my best friend in town. He has been from the time I got here."

Angellica raised her eyebrows and rolled her eyes, with a suspicious smile that asked without saying, *Any romantic possibilities?*

"Jud? No, not Jud," Sarah laughed. "When I first came to Travers, well, it was right after John's death, and I had no desire, whatsoever, to fall in love again. So Jud and I became really close friends. The love-sexual-tension thing never really materialized. Now I think if either of us ever made a pass at the other, we would just burst out laughing."

> " '*From quiet homes and first beginning,*
> *Out to the undiscovered ends,*
> *There is nothing worth the wear of winning,*
> *But laughter and the love of friends.*' "

"Hilaire Belloc," Angellica explained, and then asked, "What does Jud do?"

"He builds boats, and he still does a little guiding for fly fishermen in the summer."

"He takes the fishermen down the river in boats?"

"Uh-huh," Sarah answered as she took the last of the loaves from the oven. "He floats the fishermen down the Elkheart—that's the river that runs through town."

"Oh, that's something I've always wanted to do. I've never floated down a river in a boat. The studio wouldn't allow it. It was in my contract that I was never to do anything dangerous around water because I can't swim.

~

"Do you think he could take me down the river tomorrow? Would we have time? Would it be a bother for him?"

Motioning for Angellica to follow her, Sarah led her out of the kitchen, down the hall into the living room, and then to the front window overlooking town. The light from the Roxy's marquee dominated Main Street. "You can see Jud's life from here. Do you see that house across the street from the theater? The old white two-story with the streetlight out front? That was where Jud was raised. His room was on the second floor, and from his window he looked out on the marquee. His mother taught school, and she worked evenings at the theater and so did Jud as soon as he was old enough. He loves the movies. He practically grew up in the Roxy. Now, you want to know if it would be a *bother* for him to row *Angellica Phillips* down the river? He would crawl through cut glass to do it."

"But would we have enough time?"

"Sure. Jud will know where to go," Sarah said, staring out the window at Travers Corners, all lit up for the night—streetlights, starlight, moonlight, and the marquee. "It's going to be a beautiful day tomorrow. It's going to be warm, maybe a cloud or two, and still."

So after a call to Jud—who, as predicted, would certainly take Angellica Phillips down the river—the day was planned. Angellica and Jud would float from the North Fork Bridge to town—an easy three-hour float. Then Angellica would stroll into the Tin Cup, sit down at the bar, and order a beer from Sal. The surprise of it all would be wonderful. She would have one of Sarah's famous taco salads, then Sal would drive her to Reynolds and the waiting plane. Letting herself be known to the general public like that was one of her favorite tricks. She did love her fans, but she could never stay long before the media would come along and ruin everything. Travers wasn't going to be like that. Once she revealed herself here it would take at least an hour for the nearest media man to get to town, and at the end of that hour she would be gone. Angellica was trying to coax Sarah into joining her and Jud on their float, but she was getting nowhere, as the Tin Cup without Sarah might as well lock the doors. "C'mon, have a small nightcap and I'll talk you into it."

"No, I'd love to. I could spend days talking with you, and if I have one more of *those* drinks I'm sure anybody could talk me into anything. But the truth is, I'd better be getting to bed. Four-thirty comes around early." Sarah was astonished that Angellica was having one more. It must have been her fifth or sixth. Sarah had two and quit—one more and she would have been facedown in the dough. She couldn't believe how much Angellica had drunk, and yet nothing about her really changed from her first martini to the last. If anything she just became even more charming. How could any woman drink like this and still look so beautiful?

"Oh, what will I do with Jimmy while I go down the river?" Angellica asked.

"I've got a little room upstairs at the restaurant. He can come with me."

"And that will work out perfectly. I'll pick him up when I see your uncle Sal."

Giggling after saying good night, Sarah headed up the stairs thinking about tomorrow and the look on Sal's face when Angellica Phillips came into the Tin Cup and ordered a beer. She would remember to get some film for the camera.

The morning, as Sarah had promised, was perfect. The snow had receded to the tree line on the hills. The mountains, even on their steepest faces, were draped in snow. Everything would be coming out today, sandhills, herons, geese—all the birds would be flying. The grasses would color the long gray benchlands, and the leaves would twist free from the winter-dead branches. Yes, everything and everybody would be out today in this strong spring light.

There was one thing more that was out and into light and had been for twelve hours: Angellica's secret. It happened like this: When Sidney told the Survivors of Angellica's mishaps, it was overheard by the maid. The maid told her sister. The sister told a friend. The friend sold the tip to the *L.A. Times*.

So as Jud slowly pulled up out front of Sarah's, his old Willys and dory freshly washed and still dripping, there were chartered planes winging their way toward Travers. The lead team for the *Times* was already touching down in Reynolds just as their home paper was hitting the streets. The headline on page one: ANGELLICA CAUGHT WITH DRUGS AND GUNS IN SMALL MONTANA TOWN.

Angellica met him on the steps. "Is that one of the boats you build?"

"Yeah, it is."

"It's lovely."

"Well, thanks."

She climbed into the front seat of the Willys. Two people drove past and Jud waved while Angellica pulled her hat down over her face. "I can't believe I'm still here unnoticed, that my being here is still unknown. It's so wonderful. I wish all towns could keep a confidence like this one."

"Folks from small towns are really no different than the people living in the big cities," Jud explained, driving away from Sarah's. "We have everyone you have, model citizens to wife beaters, but we see it all played out on a much more intimate scale. In a town of three hundred, it doesn't take long to know the people who can keep a secret from those who can't."

A sudden loud clanking noise caused Jud to pull over. He hopped out and Angellica could hear him banging on something. Then he was back in the truck. "I'm afraid this is the year I break down and buy a new trailer. But," he added as he ground the Willys back into gear, "she'll make this trip for sure. Hope Lee doesn't have any trouble with it."

"Lee?"

"Lee's a friend of mine," Jud explained. "He's going to come out and pick up the boat and trailer and have it waiting for us at Town Bridge."

"Curb service," Angellica laughed.

"Without the curbs. It's going to be a fine morning, Miss Phillips."

"Angie."

As Jud loaded the last of the gear into the boat, now tied to the bank and rocking slowly at the edge of the current, he mentioned, "I brought my fishing gear along in case you might like to try your hand at it. Fishing might be pretty good, warm day and all. Have you ever tried fly fishing?"

"No, no, I haven't. But I made a film called *Evening and Afternoon,* a period piece shot on location in Maine, and in it there was a scene where Tony Curtis and Natalie Wood bump into each other on a country road near a river. He's on horseback and she in her carriage. I appear way down the road as a speck and I slowly bicycle my way up and into the action. William Wyler, who was directing, wanted the feeling of a very lazy afternoon, where there were few cares. So he hired a local fly fisherman and stationed him in the river, where he stood casting through the entire scene. 'The fisherman's line,' Wyler always said later, was always one of his favorites. He said he 'liked the way the long line caught the light, how the line set the tempo' he wanted for the scene. Watching that line, he said, was 'like watching a tired man swatting at flies.' " Then she laughed. "I guess the reason I remember it all so well was that Tony and Natalie kept blowing their lines and I had to pedal in the heat for five takes."

"Well," Jud said, sliding his fly rod into its usual place, "we'll just bring it along in case you might like to give it a try."

"But I don't have a license. I need one, don't I?"

"Yeah, but after drug running, money laundering, and gun smuggling, what's fishing without a license?"

Angellica laughed and climbed into the boat.

Jud pushed off from the shallows and hopped over the gunwale, causing the SS *Lucky Me* to rock awkwardly for a moment until Jud was in his seat with his hands at the oars—a place he'd been a thousand times. He eased the boat into the current, the swifter water caught the bow turning Angellica downstream, and the dory was lazily one with the river.

The day was windless except from the breeze brought on by drifting. The cottonwoods were tinged in new green leaves. The sky was cloudless. The river was slightly colored from the melting snow, but very fishable. Though Jud had seen many days such as these at the oars, he knew he had never had, and never would again, a day like this one. In the bow of the boat sat Angellica Phillips, who was instantly in love with it all. "This is wonderful!"

For the first hour Angellica was mostly silent. She asked a few questions about the river and the wildlife, but mostly she just sat there smiling, her hands crossed in her lap, her eyes wandering over the river and the hills. She consciously filled her lungs and enjoyed the river's sound—the rolling motion and the healing powers of the river. Jud tended the oars and left the silence pretty much alone.

"Would you like to stop, stretch your legs a bit?" Jud finally asked, *stretch of the legs* being his euphemism for the call of nature. Jud had two cups of Tin Cup coffee calling.

"Sounds good. Do you have anything to drink in your cooler?"

"Water and sodas. Got a thermos full of coffee and a couple of Sarah's sweet rolls, too."

After each of them visited their respective bushes, they sat on a log enjoying the coffee and rolls. "It is so lovely here. No wonder you call your boat the *Lucky Me*. Thanks so much for taking me, and I want you to know that I mean to pay for all this."

"Well, you know, Miss Phillips, er Angie"—correcting himself before she had the chance—"I was pretty much raised in a movie theater. My mother worked at the Roxy. I did, too. One of the perks of the job was free movies. Most movies I would watch once, some movies I would watch a couple of times. But your movies I watched seven days a week, double feature and matinee, then hoped old man Parrish would hold your movie over another week." Pouring her another cup of coffee, he thought about her and the long close-up in *Shadows*. He remembered perfectly the week it showed at the Roxy because it was that same week he started growing whiskers and looking at women in a completely different light.

"So it's nothing short of an honor to have you in my boat, and I would hope that you would accept this morning as a gift, 'cause that's sure the way it feels to me."

" 'Charmingly said, gallantly put, handsomely done,' " Angellica said with a British accent.

Which made Jud laugh, as he knew the line to be one from her famous portrayal of Queen Elizabeth in *Castle Keep.*

"Oh, look a fish just jumped out of the water!" Angellica said.

"Yeah, I saw him. There's five or six fish in that pool coming up and taking dry flies. Have been since we stopped. Would you care to try and catch one?"

"No, I don't think so, but it would give me great pleasure to watch you." Then in keeping with her character, the queen, she commanded, "Go, kind sir, and battle bravely."

Jud stood, walked to the boat, picked up his rod, and bowed. "For queen and country, Your Majesty, by your leave." He mocked a quick sword fight, parry and thrust, with his fly rod as his foil. Then he walked to the river and stripped off line; the fish were on the other side of a deep glide and it would take a long cast.

Sitting comfortably on the bank, her back against a log, Angellica tilted her face into the warm April sun and watched through barely open and dreamy eyes as Jud cast his line slowly over the river, back and forth "like a tired man swatting at flies." Closing her eyes, she was easily back on her bicycle and in her scene with the fisherman in *Evening and Afternoon,* back to that time in her life when she was a rising young actress and helplessly in love for the first time. How wonderful that summer in Maine had been.

It suddenly dawned on her that she was feeling good. No, it was better than good. She felt genuinely happy: a strange sensation after months of depression. Certainly, and most of all, it was because Jimmy was going to be fine. But this sense of joy was coming from the warmth of the sun and the beauty of the river as well; and the remembrance of that long-ago love affair—a simpler time before stardom and legend. Tears welled up in her eyes, but didn't fall. She was laughing and at the same time crying, two emotions not possible for what seemed to be forever without the catalyst of drink. Her flask was on board the dory, but she braced herself against the log and poured herself another cup of coffee.

She watched as the morning light caught Jud's line, a pendulum now to this timeless art of the angle, tethered not to the rod but to the soul of the fisherman and that, if ever it were to break and cast free, would surely float, like a child's kite, as far as the winds of chance might take it. How peaceful this world, the fisherman's world, and silent, she thought, save the sounds of water and birds and leaves in the wind.

Time and again Jud presented the fly. Not only was it a lengthy cast, but the desired drift of the fly was hampered by whirling currents and boils. Through mends and slack-line casts he was lucky to have his presentation sit on the surface for more than a second or two, before the swifter water would belly his line and drag his fly under. All of this difficulty was compounded by the fact there was quite a hatch of mayflies coming off this morning, and hundreds of naturals danced above the water, with hundreds more floating on the current. So in addition to the skill needed to make *the* cast needed, he would also need a great deal of luck—for it was going to be pure chance, the kind of odds found in lotteries, for the trout to select his offering, an artificial, over the real thing.

He did have one thing going for him: He was fishing with one of Doc's flies. They were, each and every one, tied to perfection, tied by a surgeon's hands. Again he thought of Doc and the night before last. He'd always admired Doc, everyone did, but after watching him in surgery, saving a dog's life with a Black and Decker, well, his respect for Doc just grew that much more.

Glancing over his shoulder he saw Angellica walking slowly toward him, slowly because she was taking her time to be watchful of the nature seemingly strolling along with her: A deer crossed upstream, a heron flew past, ducks, geese, and a pair of hawks circling against a white-blue sky.

He really wanted to catch a fish for her, but not just any fish. He felt some kind of strange obligation: the chance to repay her for all the marvelous hours she had given him as a young man at the Roxy. Only a truly glorious fish would do.

Jud sent Doc's fly into flight once more. While his chances were diminished by the distance and short drifts, he did have one specific fish in mind. At the center of the seven or eight feeding fish rose one very large trout. The trout rolled at the surface, large, broad-backed rolls, and while those trout rising around him made slight ripples as they fed, his rolls made waves.

The fly skipped along the surface. He'd made a long enough cast, and the fly was skating now along the seam of water that would carry it to the trout he hoped for—Doc's fly stuttering, darting along the edges of one current, then playing on another. The large back continued to roll, feeding steadily, dining on every mayfly on line. His mayfly floated the last ten feet, dancing as perfectly as a natural. The back was up. His great mouth opened, only to take the fly not two inches from Jud's own. He felt a slight frustration; it would be many more casts before he would land another cast as sweet, a cast to give his fly as pretty a ride as that one.

Stripping his line slowly in, as to avoid spooking any of the fish, he was just about to lift it from the water when a smaller trout took his fly. The rainbow was up and in the air, once and then again, and before Jud could recover the slack line that had slipped through his hand—he, like the rainbow, had been taken by surprise—the trout was in the air for a third show.

Angellica was up beside him for this last jump and was thrilled. "Oh, you did it! You have one! Oh, that's marvelous!"

Jud was about to tell her that the whole thing had been accidental, but decided to skip it. Being wonderful in Angellica Phillips's eyes was a place he didn't mind being, so he left it alone.

The rainbow was a scrappy one, and though he was no longer than twelve inches, he fought as if he were larger. He jumped once more, then made a run across the current. The line sliced through the water, sending his reel spinning.

"Well, I have to confess, he wasn't the one I was trying for. There was a dandy out there but I couldn't fool him," Jud explained. He was thinking of the large brown he had missed, and he was looking at the rainbow as something decidedly less. He bent down to revive and release the fish.

Angellica bent down with him. She was looking at the rainbow, not for his size but for his colors, symmetry, and design. "He's so beautiful."

Holding the trout in his hands, Jud removed the hook then gently cradled the trout. The light, the piercing spring light, the light made in the mornings, spangled across the shallows, a crackling mosaic of light, a quaking lacework of reflections, fractured and jumbled. The light danced on the faces of Jud and Angellica. It jitterbugged over the river rock. And the trout's colors were lit like his namesake: a prismatic separation, through water, of sunbeams; a rainbow lit by a rainbow.

"Will he be all right?" Angellica asked.

"He'll be fine, just a little winded."

"So lovely."

The trout slowly finned himself free from Jud's grasp, hesitated for a moment at the edge of the current, then shot back to the pool from whence he was fooled.

Taking a quick check at his pocket watch, Jud said, "You know, I think we'd better get back on the river if we're going to get you back into town at noon."

Back on board the *Lucky Me* and floating, Angellica told wonderful stories of her life and of the people she knew: Jack Lemmon, Walter Matthau, Sophia Loren. Of all his days on the river this would stand clearly above the rest. She was enchanting, that was the word, *enchanting*. She also mentioned the rainbow trout and his beauty several times. "That was so wonderful to watch you catch that fish. Well done," she said in her role of queen, and lifted his fly rod from its rack. It became Excalibur in her hands as she dubbed him, shoulders and head, with its tip, "I knight thee, Sir Fishwell of Trout."

They were just one bend out of Travers Corners and Town Bridge where the river ran swiftly. Suddenly, from out of the cottonwoods and along the shore, came two men running. They were shouting, but you couldn't understand them over the sound of the river. Jud began to pull over, thinking there must be an emergency. But Angellica shouted, "No! Don't stop!"

"But they might need help."

"They're reporters." Her eyes went slate-colored with hatred.

The men's voices came clear as they ran to the river's edge, "Miss Phillips. Ed Green from the *L.A. Times*. Do you have anything to say on these allegations of drug smuggling, and running guns?"

"Must you ruin every day?" Angellica shouted angrily and tears filled her eyes.

Jud turned the boat and was back in the current. "It's all right. They can't keep up with us on foot for long 'cause the river splits right here—not unless they want to swim." One of the reporters had stopped and was taking pictures with a long lens. The other kept chasing, shouting questions, but Jud moved the dory to the other side of the river, and quickly they were again out of earshot.

The *Lucky Me* slipped easily down the narrow side channel and was moving fast in the chop. "We lost them, Angie," Jud said, trying to comfort her.

"There'll be more."

Town Bridge came into view and she was right. There at the boat ramp were a dozen or more cars. A pack of journalists stood waiting, their cameras trained on the driftboat. A small crowd of townspeople had gathered behind them. The mobile TV unit from KMTS out of Missoula was just pulling up.

And in the middle of all this stood Leroy, arms crossed, inflated, swollen with importance, and sanctimonious; gloating because somehow word of Angellica had leaked out, but it hadn't been by him (he hadn't told a soul except for his wife). Now, because of all this attention,

~

the truth, more correctly what he thought to be the truth, would finally win out.

"Oh, God," Angellica cried and her anger turned to fear; almost a terror. She was trapped. "Jud, is there anything we can do? I hate them. I hate them."

"The plane can wait a while?" he asked.

"The plane can wait."

"Then hang on." Pivoting the driftboat sharply, Jud took a firm grip on the oars. He moved himself forward in his seat and centered his feet firmly. The *Lucky Me* was now rigged for serious rowing. He then sent his oars spinning. He was heading for the opposite shore, which put Leroy, the reporters, and part of the crowd on a dead run over the bridge. As the mob neared the end of their crossing, Jud spun the dory once more and began rowing furiously back to the boat ramp.

Leroy had made the first crossing of the bridge in good time, but as the reporters recrossed the bridge, again at a dead run, they left Leroy midspan and breathless. Just as they began gathering at the ramp, Jud turned the boat again, but this time heading her straight downriver.

The river was slow and deep through town, but Jud was giving it his all on the oars, so the *Lucky Me* was moving right along despite the lack of current. Some of the reporters who were quick enough to get back on the bridge began shouting questions as the dory passed beneath, but twenty guys asking fifty questions just turns into a din.

Staring off downriver, with her hat pulled down over her face, Angellica handled the press in her normal manner—by simply pretending that they were not there. But Jud, well, he just couldn't help himself, and standing at the oars he shouted, "Miss Phillips would like to make a statement." Suddenly there wasn't a sound but the gurgle of the river and the wind from Angellica's hat as her head snapped around from utter surprise. Then the whir and click of cameras heightened as her famous and secretive face looked up at Jud, who continued, "Miss Phillips would like you to know that she really enjoyed watching all of you run back and forth across the bridge." Jud smiled and tipped his hat, then sat back down to the oars and began rowing away.

Angellica began laughing. Her face, usually covered, dour, or angry for the cameras, was now in full view for all, and she was laughing and laughing hard. The sight of Leroy's beet-red face appearing at the side of the bridge, the face of too many doughnuts, made her laugh harder. Leroy wanted to shout. He wanted to order Jud to pull ashore, but he didn't have the wind for shouting, he could only gasp. Then when a media man, hanging over the bridge for an even closer camera shot, fell into the river, she got nearly hysterical.

Spotting Junior McCracken on the bridge, Jud yelled, "Junior!"

"Yeah!"

"Get somebody to move my rig down to Birch Creek, will ya?"

"You got it, Jud!"

Sarah appeared at the edge of the railing. She shouted something but couldn't be heard over the press. Jud waved, motioning her to go back to the Tin Cup.

The reporters were still hollering questions as Jud oared the dory downriver, until he and Angellica were once again out of earshot and nearly around the bend. Then Angellica asked, "Jud, what are we going to do?"

"Well, the boys back on the bridge have no choice. The next place the road crosses the river is at Birch Creek, which is about four miles from here. They'll be waiting for us there. Only we aren't going to Birch Creek. We're pulling over at Owen Griffith's. His farm's on the river."

For the next hour they floated and formulated their plans. They would walk to Owen's farm. They would call Sarah from there, have her gather all of Angellica's belongings and meet her in the alley behind the café. Then they would head to the airport.

"We have to move pretty quickly," Jud explained as he rowed the drift-boat ashore, " 'cause it's quite a walk to Owen's and we'll probably get there around the same time as we should be showing up at Birch Creek. And when we don't show up, they're bound to come looking for us."

The thought of the press prompted Angellica to add one more thing to their plans. "Tell Sarah to have her uncle Sal make a double for me. In fact, have Sal at the ready. I'm going to need a full-time bartender, and very soon." She smiled but it wasn't because of her joke; it was the twisted and pathetic smile of resignation. "Anyway, I promised Sarah that I would meet her uncle, and I plan to keep that promise, press or no press."

Jud docked the *Lucky Me* in a back eddy, and the two began their hike. The day once so lovely and carefree for Angellica had once again turned back into her everyday nightmare of avoiding the press. She was on edge. She grew silent. She needed a drink.

Owen and his wife, Nancy, were in their backyard having lunch when they saw two figures walking up from the fields, and once Nancy made one of them out to be Jud she went to the kitchen and came back with two more glasses of cider.

"Owen," Jud greeted, and looked at his watch. "I'm going to need some favors. Oh, sorry, Owen and Nancy Griffith, this is Angellica Phillips."

Nancy collapsed in her chair as the introduction and the recognition hit her at the same time. Owen stood with his mouth unhinged.

"Listen, Owen, I need to borrow your phone and your stock truck. It's kind of an emergency and we're in a hurry."

"You bet, Jud," Nancy answered for her husband. Owen wanted to answer but couldn't. He was star-struck and speechless and far from forming sentences. Being very short he just stood frozen in place, staring up at the statuesque Angellica.

"Thanks," Jud said and headed into the kitchen. Through the screen door, the others could hear Jud's side of the conversation ". . . Sarah . . . Yeah . . . Yeah . . . Get over to your house and gather up Angellica's stuff and have it waiting in the alley behind the café . . . Right . . . Right . . . The back door . . . Right . . . And tell Sal to have a martini waiting for her . . . What? . . . Damn . . . I don't know . . . Okay . . . Okay . . . Well, go get him . . . Ten minutes . . . Right."

"What's wrong?" Angellica asked as Jud reappeared on the porch.

"Sal is down at the Birch Creek Bridge with the rest of the town. He closed the bar. Sarah was just about to close the restaurant, as everybody in Travers is down at Birch Creek. She's going to go down and get him. We're giving her ten minutes. Then were meeting her behind the Tin Cup."

If pig farms have a certain air about them, pig trucks share in that certain air but even more so. As Jud helped Angellica into the front seat, she grimaced against the smell but said nothing. Nancy brought them two more ciders for the road. Owen looked on.

Driving the truck from the yard, Jud reached out and grabbed the hat from Owen's head and yelled back at him, "I'll have your truck and your hat back in a couple hours, Owen, and thanks." Owen nodded.

The smell was causing Angellica to gag a bit. "Jud, couldn't you just as easily have borrowed the family car?"

"Well, they won't be looking for you in a stock truck, and this *is* the family car." He took off his hat and put Owen's hat on, then he stuck his hat on Angellica's head as the truck neared the highway. Two rental cars filled with reporter types whizzed past heading toward town. There were more cars coming.

"Looks like they've figured out that we aren't on the river," Jud said as he wheeled the truck out onto the blacktop. "You better duck down out of sight." He slid down into the seat as well. "Owen is so short that when you see him driving into town all you can see is the top of his straw hat. And he has a strange way of waving, waves like there's something stuck on his hand, waves like this." He showed her and she laughed. Making her laugh was his purpose.

Crunching his tall frame down low in the seat, Owen's hat pulled down on his head far enough to bend his ears over double, Jud threw his hand up in Owen's silly wave as the cars passed him by—Leroy, the reporters, and most of the crowd. Jud looked so ridiculous that every time he waved he and Angellica would both laugh, even though the sound of every passing car gave her the chills.

They drove the truck into Travers by way of the back road, then turned onto First Street and down the alley to the back door of the Tin Cup Cafe. Sarah and Sal, with Jimmy under his arm, were waiting. The town was crawling with media, but the alley was deserted. Jud, however, was taking no chances. He came to a rolling stop and Sal, with his cooler, his porkpie hat, wearing a Yankees jacket, and looking more like a man dressed for the bleachers, climbed into the cab. He sat down not two inches from Angellica Phillips. Sarah loaded the luggage into the back of the truck, then ran and jumped on the running board. She reached her hand through the window for Angellica's. "You take care now, Angellica, and if you ever need a place to hide, well, you can help me bake bread anytime." She was surprised to feel tears in her eyes.

"I will never forget your kindness," Angellica replied.

The truck was coming close to Second Street and Sarah hopped off and ran back to the café. She had things burning on the grill. The Tin Cup was packed. People were driving down from Reynolds in the hope of catching a glimpse of Angellica.

Angellica tossed down the first martini, and Sal, whose hands were trembling from disbelief and excitement, had no trouble shaking her up another one. He shook one for himself as well. He found himself wanting to speak, but was unable to form any words. His dark round eyes were soft and gentle by nature. But now, in Angellica's presence, they were one minute melting with love and admiration, and almost bursting the next, from the joy of the moment.

Jud elected to take the old road to Reynolds. It was dirt and a lot slower than the highway, but there would be no traffic, except for the occasional rancher. A couple of miles out of town they were safe—there were no cars in their rearview mirror and none ahead. "I think we're in the clear," Jud explained while straightening himself up behind the wheel, "and we'll have you at the airport in about an hour."

A few sips into her second martini Angellica breathed a great sigh of relief, then, incredibly, in the wave of a hand, in the slap of a clapboard, she was suddenly charming and elegant, a combination rare to the front seat of a pig truck.

She and Sal relived the glory of old New York, the Palace Theater, Forty-second Street, and Sal retold his story, the story behind the program hanging on the back bar down at the Tin Cup. "Well, now, I'm tellin ya and I'm telling the bot-a-yahs," Brooklyn still thick in his voice, "it was 1953. It was da trill of my life—standin' outside the stage door of the Palace. Opening night for *Mr. and Mrs. Jones*. I was twenty-two years old. I was dressed in a new suit. It wasn't my suit, it was my uncle Luigi's. You came out with Hume Cronin and Jessica Tandy. It took every ounce of courage, but I stepped up to you and I says, 'Miss Phillips, you are da greatest in the world, and I would very much appreciate it if you would sign my program.'

"You stopped and smiled and you held out your hand and took my program. You asked me to turn around, and you asked me what my name was, and then you signed it against my back. It said, 'Sal, I hope the critics tonight will be as kind as you are.' I still have it hang—"

"Hanging next to your picture of Joe DiMaggio?"

"That's right," Sal said, surprised.

"Sarah told me. The 1953 Yankees, now there was a baseball team. Mantle. Berra. Phil Rizzuto." She knew the Yankees. Sal fell in love in 1953 with Angellica Phillips, and he was in love again . . . no, he was in love, still.

A plume of dust billowed out behind them as Jud wheeled the pig truck down the bench road. They looked out on the snowcapped Elkhearts, the river winding below, the cottonwoods and the valley greening before their eyes. The windows were down, which made them doubly grateful for the warm day, for windows up in a pig truck is not recommended. The rooftops of Reynolds came into view.

Pulling into the airport, Angellica spotted her jet. "That's the one over there," she said, pointing. Usually there were no more than a couple of planes on the ground at the Reynolds airport, but with the media (still back in Travers and searching for clues) converging on the valley there must have been more than a dozen. There, next to the plane, stood Sid, who looked up at the oncoming stock truck, but didn't look twice, as he was expecting Angellica to arrive with the driver they had sent. But when Angellica leaned on the truck's horn and began waving, he recognized her and waved her on.

After a happy reunion, which was mostly Angellica reassuring Sid that she was all right, Sid carried Jimmy back to the plane and urged Angellica to say her good-byes quickly. Sal and Jud helped the crew load the woman's luggage, then the jets began to whine and Angellica came over to them. "Sal, I want to thank you for the best damn martini I've had in years, and please give Sarah my love. Tell her she'll be hearing from me." Then she turned to Jud. "You'll give my thanks to Doc and Henry for me?"

"You bet."

"And as for you, my dear Jud, my Sir Fishwell of Trout, there are no words to express my gratitude."

"For queen and country, Your Majesty." Jud smiled and gave a deep bow.

She kissed them both quickly. "I'll be in touch. I promise you." Then walked quickly to the plane, waving to them once again at the door. In a few moments the jet taxied; then came a roar and it was gone.

The next couple of days Travers Corners was abuzz with talk of Angellica. The reporters stayed around hoping for a story, but soon learned that the people who weren't involved knew nothing but what they had seen from Town Bridge. However, they would learn even less from the handful of people who were involved . . .

Judge Mills answered the press's questions by simply stating that he had "No comment."

Doc's response to the media was quick and irrevocable. "Privileged doctor–patient information." Kim and Phil answered by quoting Doc.

Sal said, "Didn't know from nuttin'," but he was glad to tell his story about meeting Angellica in 1953 to anyone who would listen.

Sarah wouldn't say a word; she only smiled back at the reporters and went about her work.

Leroy's rejoinder was, "That's classified." It made him sound official. He wanted to tell it all but Judge Mills promised him that if any of the details of the case were ever to slip out, Leroy would lose his job.

Jud, who was besieged the hardest by the media, packed up the *Lucky Me* and spent the next three days fishing and camping along the Elkheart.

And Henry, well, Henry handled the press just as you might expect Henry to handle the press: The first reporter who got pushy was grabbed by the lapels and slammed up against a wall and told, through a certain series of expletives, that his existence was in immediate danger. Henry wasn't bothered by the reporters again.

A few weeks passed and Travers eventually settled back into normality. Then two months went by and nothing was heard from Angellica. Though none of the people involved would admit it, they were surprised and a little disappointed because she'd seemed so genuine when she promised to stay in touch. Henry wasn't surprised: "Movie stars. Them Gollywood types are nothin' but a handful of gimme and a mouth full of much-obliged."

Another month passed. Then another.

Angellica's letter came to the Tin Cup on a Friday in September and all it said was, "Dear Doc, Sarah, Jud, Sal, and Henry. I want you all to be at the café tomorrow morning at 9:30. Love, Angie."

There was hardly time to speculate about what it all could be about before tomorrow and half past nine arrived. All five, even Henry, who had to be badgered before he agreed to coming, were sitting now at the

Tin Cup's counter, drinking coffee and watching the clock. They were pretty sure they knew what this was all about—Angellica was coming back for a visit.

But at the appointed half hour, it was not Angellica pulling up in front of the Tin Cup, but a Mountain Freightways truck. The driver read his bill of lading. "I've got eleven boxes and a Jud Clark is supposed to sign for 'em. Also, I got these two letters he has to sign for."

Signing, Jud looked at the letters: One was written to him with instructions on the envelope, which read "Jud—Open this first and read it aloud—Angie." The other one was addressed to the "The Ambulance Driver."

They moved the boxes, all of them gift-wrapped, into the bar of the Tin Cup. Opening the letter as instructed, Jud began reading it to the others.

" 'I will start by apologizing for not having written and thanked you for your kindnesses earlier, but I have been back at the Betty Ford Center. I am dried out once more—and forever. But most of all, I am happy, and in a very large part I have you all and your lovely Elkheart Valley to thank. But I'll explain all that later. Let us get to these presents. I love giving presents.

" 'Doc—How does one repay the gift of Jimmy's life? I wanted to do something very special for you so I did a little research and decided that only a very special gift concerning fly fishing would do. My old friend Jack Lemmon told me where to go and what to buy.' " In a large box that Doc began to open at the urging of the others he found a new bamboo rod in a leather case; written above the grip was THANKS, DOC.

"Well, that is fine, very fine." Doc was visibly moved.

" 'Kim—I hope it fits,' " Jud read on as Kim pulled a long winter's coat from the same box. " 'If not, you can return it to Bloomingdale's for a different size or for anything else you want.

" 'I am so sorry, but I have forgotten the name of the ambulance driver. Will you see that he gets the envelope?

" 'Sal—,' " Jud continued with the letter, " 'your package is a small one, compared to the others, but two tickets to next season's opening day at Yankee Stadium and reservations for three nights at the Plaza just don't take up a lot of room. I understand DiMaggio is already scheduled to throw out the opening ball. I also understand that you and your guest will be seated right behind him—sometimes it's fun being me.'"

Sal, who never was a man to be short on words, couldn't say a thing.

"'Sarah—A woman needs music to bake bread by; shipped to you this day—a new sound system. I think of you often.'"

Everyone listening to the letter looked over to see Sarah smiling. "Well, I never . . . I . . . didn't expect . . . Oh, go on, Jud, read the letter."

"'Henry—Jud told me while we were on the river that your opinion of me was less than favorable. You were right, of course. You saw me at my absolute worst: drunk, frightened, and angry. There is no telling what might have happened that night without your heroics. The only thing I know about you is that you shoe horses. What do you get for a man who shoes horses? A new forge? A better anvil? No. So, I hope you like it. It's not very good but it's from the heart. Thank you.'"

Out of the crate came a painting, a watercolor of horses running and signed by Angellica. "Oh, my, it's beautiful," Sarah said before the others had a chance.

"Well I'll be dipped." Henry, who was standing, had to sit down.

"'Jud—The SS *Lucky Me* has a new trailer. It was built in Maine and reputed to be the best and if all has gone according to plan it should be being delivered while you read this letter.

"'While I know that a trailer is what you needed, I have to tell you that shopping for a trailer wasn't much fun—a very uninspired gift. So also please find included the original sword from *Castle Keep*. I don't mind telling you that took a great deal of doing but it was the perfect gift and perfect gifts cannot be compromised.'"

Jud paused, opened the long cylinder to find the saber, admiring it for a minute and incredulous. Then, handing it to Sarah to see, he read on.

"'Jimmy and I send these gifts knowing that they are given merely as things that one can buy or one can sell, and they pale when presented to friends who cannot be bought or sold. They are one way of saying thank you: thanking you for all you did for us in Travers Corners. May they thank you for all that you did for me *after* I left the Elkheart Valley. Let me explain . . .

" 'When I arrived home from Montana, my life was nearing rock bottom. My constant search for privacy had become a living hell. Some years ago I turned to alcohol. I wasn't the kind of drunk who drank every day, I'm the kind of drunk who stays sober for three months and then goes on a one-month bender. You all caught me at the tail end of one of those benders. Being a legend isn't all it's cracked up to be.

" 'Even though I was only part of your lives for two short days, I learned a great deal; things that were far more beneficial than anything Betty Ford had to offer . . .

" 'From Sarah I learned about real courage. What you went through when you lost your son and husband—well, it made signing up for another stay at Betty's seem ridiculously easy. Any sadness I have ever had in my lifetime is nothing compared to your losses.

" 'And Sal. What an honor for me, to have you as a fan of mine. You brought back memories of all that I once was, and that was an actress. You made me once again proud of my career. Being a celebrity takes no talent at all.

" 'Henry, you didn't care if I was Angellica Phillips or the man in the moon. To your credit, you are obviously one not very impressed by stardom, which is precisely the way celebrities should be treated. You reminded me that movie stars are no more than anyone else, and we need that.

" 'Doc, I wish more people could be exposed to your warm and caring manner. L.A. doctors could take a lesson. I know I did.

" 'Jud, I play the sights and the sounds of your beautiful river over and over in my mind. That was a remarkable morning. The light. Your wonderful trout. I had only seen a morning such as that once, and as I sat on the bank watching you fish, it took me back to a time in my life I hadn't thought of for years; to a time when I was a young and unknown actress. I was genuinely happy at the beginning. Perhaps, somehow, it was the emotions I felt reliving those images. Maybe it was the warmth of the sun and knowing that Jimmy was going to be fine. Most probably it was a combination of all three, I don't know, but something very strange came over me. I didn't know what it was for a moment, such a foreign feeling. Then it dawned on me. I was happy. It was an emotion I hadn't visited for years without alcohol. It was a feeling of strength, the strength to try to be happy again.

" 'I have arrived at airports by limousine, helicopter, and police escort, but I had never arrived in a pig truck. That less-than-redolent ride somehow put a lot of things into perspective: riding in a farm truck, sandwiched between a bartender and a boatbuilder; rolling down that dirt road. It was life and it was adventure. It was as real as I had been in years. If ever I write a book, the ride to Reynolds will surely be a page or two. Travers will be a chapter.

" 'Someday I hope to come back to Travers Corners and see all you wonderful people again. Thank you now and forever.

" 'Love to all and the best from Jimmy,
Angie' "

Saturday afternoon was an unusually warm one for the middle of September. Fishing had been good all week on Carrie Creek, and Doc could be found knee-deep and loving his new rod.

Henry spent the afternoon coming in and out of the house between chores to look at his watercolor now hanging over the fireplace. His opinion of Angellica Phillips had certainly changed, and not because of the painting but because he liked the way she chose her words. His opinions about anyone else from L.A., however, remained resolute.

～

Sarah and Sal spent the day connecting all the wires from CD and tape machines to preamps, amps, and equalizers, and to speakers in nearly every room. That evening from one end of Travers to the other, you could hear anything from Debussy to Jerry Garcia. One note from Aretha was thought to have been heard as far away as Reynolds when Sal grabbed hold of the volume control and gave it a twist, "just to see what it'll do."

And Jud, well, he followed the directions found on the brass placard welded to the tongue of his new trailer: SIR FISHWELL OF TROUT, TAKE THYSELF FISHING. THANK YOU, ANGIE. He, along with Annie the Wonderlab, were now aboard the SS *Lucky Me,* the day nearly over. Town Bridge was coming into view. The fishing and the day had been grand, and he'd fished until dusk. The lights from the homes along the Elkheart shimmered on the currents, and the sight triggered the story. It all played over again in his mind, not start to finish, but rather as images dissolving into one another, flowing through him as the river flows—the red lights of the ambulance, the lights on the marquee, the light in his hand during the surgery, the light on her face from the long close-up in *Shadows,* the light on the river that day with Angie.

Light was the central theme. But then he realized that light always was. When you remember a moment, the first thing you remember is how it was lit. Lights. Where would we be without them? In the dark, that's where.

Jud rowed the dory into the shallows near the landing. His new trailer was waiting, shining in the twilight.

Light again, he thought, bringing in the oars. It figured into everything. If Henry's light hadn't been on the night of the accident, Jimmy might have died and in that weather, hypothermic, Angellica could have died as well. If he hadn't seen the red lights, he wouldn't have seen the headlights of Henry's truck. He wouldn't have been there to guide the light for Doc's hands, the only hands for a hundred miles that could bring back the light within Jimmy. Angie's day on the river could have

just as easily been clouded over. Then there would have been very little light on the rainbow trout, if there would have been a rainbow at all. No light—no heat—no hatch of the mayfly.

Light. Other than artificial, Jud knew of only two kinds of light. There was God's own natural light, and the light from another gender, the one only Lady Luck can make shine. Now, God's light comes every sunrise and it's there for everybody. Has to be—it's in the Genesis clause of His contract. But the Lady's light, being female, is at once random and selective, fickle but determined. You just never know when Her light is about to shine. But one thing was for certain—it occurred to Jud while he winched his old dory onto a new trailer behind his new pickup—and that was, the Lady had surely shined her light on him lately and She hadn't spared a watt.

That's what it all boils down to, it being the absurdity and glory of being alive. It's nothing but light and luck. Light plus Chance, divided by Luck, equals Life. Jud's mind went to work on his theory.

Afterword

THERE YOU HAVE it, a few more tales from Travers Corners.

It's early fall in the Elkheart as this book draws to a close. Not even a week into September, and Travers has already suffered its first few frosts. The edges of autumn are beginning to appear on the maple trees lining Main Street.

And out on the Elkheart River, Henry and Jud were fishing. Jud was daydreaming at the oars, and put the bow of the SS *Lucky Me* right into the hole which Henry was trying to fish. "All right, you wanna pay attention there? That sloppy piece of rowin' probably cost me a three-pounder."

"You know I've been at these oars for what seems like most of my life, just waiting for you to land a fish," Jud said, smiling and pulling lazily against the oars.

"That's the damndest thing. Just as ya said that, I thought I saw a little gray come into yer beard. But if you think you can land one any quicker, I'll be happy to switch. I don't know why you had to go and pick this day, anyways. Hotter than blue blazes, and us tryin' to catch trout. If them trout were down any deeper in this river, they wouldn't be lunkers anymore, they'd be *spe*lunkers."

"Well, I was in need of a day on the river," Jud said, switching places with Henry. The boat rocked back and forth from their movements until Henry was settled into the oars. "I knew the fishing wasn't going to be spectacular. But you never can tell for sure. I mean, remember that day on Miller's Bend when we were kids? That huge rainbow? It was a day a lot hotter than this one."

Jud picked up his line and looked downstream to where a likely looking rivulet suddenly spilled into a dark hole. "I'll bet there's a fish down there." He made his cast.

"Not a chance. Fer a guy to catch a trout in this heat would take more than luck. It'd be more like some kind of feat, flat-out magic."

A rainbow took Jud's fly. Two sandhill cranes crossed the river. Though still a bend away, they could hear the waters of Carrie Creek joining the Elkheart, where all the beauty ever dreamed of tumbles into the reasons for it all.

Jules Archer
History for Young Readers

WINNER AND LOSERS

HOW ELECTIONS WORK IN AMERICA

JULES ARCHER

Foreword by Kathleen Krull

Sky Pony Press
NEW YORK

Historical texts often reflect the time period in which they were written, and new information is constantly being discovered. This book was originally published in 1984, and much has changed since then. While every effort has been made to bring this book up to date, it is important to consult multiple sources when doing research.

Fondly, for my delightful companions Barbara Edell, Caroline Coffey, Marilyn Steck, and Carla Wolfe

CONTENTS

FOREWORD   ix

1 Teenage Voting Rights   1

2 Your Right to Participate at Any Age—and How   11

3 Why Elections Are Important to You—Now and
Tomorrow   21

4 How the System Works   29

5 How We Got That Way   39

6 What It Takes to Be a Candidate   57

7 What the Democrats Are All About   73

8 What the Republicans Are All About   87

9 What Third Parties Are All About   103

10 What Goes On at Political Conventions   122

11 Hot Air and Cold Turkey on the Campaign Trail   134

12 The Man Who Clowned His Way to the State Capitol—A
True Story   158

13 Should You Vote for the Candidate—
   or the Party?   167

14 How Lobbyists Influence Elections   174

15 Stealing Votes   183

16 "What Difference Does My Vote Make?"   194

17 Is Your Job Done When Your Candidates Win?   201

18 How Other Countries Choose Their Leaders   208

19 What's Good and What's Bad About Our System   224

ACKNOWLEDGMENTS   236

APPENDIX—PRESIDENTIAL WINNERS
   AND LOSERS   237

BIBLIOGRAPHY AND RECOMMENDED
   READING   240

INDEX   246

FOREWORD

In this election year and the ones to come, *Winners and Losers* is a must-have for young readers who want to know what all the fuss is about.

How *do* American elections work? In many mysterious ways, reveals our wise author Jules Archer. His handsome book, for ages twelve and up, originally came out in another election year, 1984. It was edited by yours truly while I was Senior Editor at Harcourt, and Ronald Reagan was being challenged by Walter Mondale.

Archer and I had a lot in common, and to work on this book was not work. I agree with him that you can't start getting interested in politics too young. He dates his political interest to age thirteen, when he wrote letters to newspapers expressing his enthusiasm for Herbert Hoover. The thrill of seeing his name in print not only fanned his lifelong political fervor—it inspired him in his career as a full-time, prolific, and successful author.

I've been drawn to the political scene ever since watching the Kennedy/Nixon debates at the tender age of eight. This strange spectacle on TV distracted me from the bleakness of a stomach virus. In my heavily Republican neighborhood, a neighbor girl threatened to beat me up unless I made my parents vote for Nixon (like I could do this). I've been keenly interested in politics ever since, though not always well-informed. For example, not until college did I cotton to the differences between Democrats and Republicans. I for one would have benefitted hugely from a book like this.

And so will today's readers—well into high school, I believe. This is a timeless exploration of a subject all citizens need to know about, a thorough treatment of the American political system. Archer includes even-handed chapters on what the Democrats are all about and what the Republicans are all about, and another on third parties. He addresses what it takes to be a candidate, what goes on at conventions and during campaigns, how we came to have the system we do. Along the way, readers will painlessly absorb a lot of information about our presidents and our history.

As always with his books, Archer seeks to inspire readers to get involved and make a difference. Even young people can do their part in elections, he insists, and he describes the many ways how, providing the tools necessary to be active participants. Being apolitical or apathetic is not an option. It just takes a bit of prodding to expand every kid's cry of "That's not fair!" to an interest in events around school, around community, around America.

He doesn't hesitate to point out the weaknesses of our system: "All too frequently each party nominates a presidential candidate who is such a compromise of conflicting interests within the party that he [sic] is a mediocre, uninspiring choice." In the chapter "How Lobbyists Influence Elections" he addresses the role of money in campaigns, pointing out that lobbyists were a cause for concern as early as 1852: "The problem may never be solved until the amount of money that can be spent on election campaigns is strictly curbed by law." He notes the unfortunate length of our election cycle and the many successful attempts at disenfranchising voters. He even tackles the question: What the heck is the Electoral College?

But he also includes a whole chapter on how other countries choose their leaders. At long length, he concludes that a flexible, democratic electoral system such as ours is the only antidote to a dictatorship. Immigrants from other countries without such a system may especially gain insight from this book.

Archer focuses almost exclusively on national presidential elections. So his one attempt at humor, about a man who "clowned his way" to five terms as lieutenant governor of Washington state, sticks out.

The book, enhanced with carefully chosen photos and a strikingly elegant design, did well at publication. In a starred review, *School Library Journal* called it an "entertaining account . . . Archer's most important success is in motivating teenagers to get involved in politics, showing that individuals can make a difference." The magazine named it a "Best Book of 1984," and it also made the list of "Notable Children's Trade Books in the Field of Social Studies."

The major drawback here is, of course, that the book was originally published in 1984 and therefore a little dated. It would be a pleasure to know what Archer thought of it all—especially what's going on this year.

Savvy teachers, however, can turn this drawback into a strength by inspiring classroom activities to research exactly what has changed. This will apply to many statistics throughout the book, as well as many thoughtful questions: Whatever happened to the Equal Rights Amendment, prominent then? What groups are there now for teen Democrats and teen Republicans?

This is important stuff, and few were as successful as Jules Archer at rendering it accessible. It was a great privilege to work on this book, and it is a great joy to see it having a second life.

—Kathleen Krull, 2016

I

Teenage Voting Rights

Mouths fell open when fifteen-year-old Eric Salem of Lincoln, Nebraska, announced his intention to run for election as a board member of his county's Noxious Weed Control Authority. His reason: The mother of his best friend had been killed in an auto accident because her view of traffic at a corner had been obstructed by a large stand of weeds.

Two rivals for the post—one 37, the other 67—objected to letting a "kid" run against them. Finding nothing in the county's laws to stop him, they asked the state attorney general for a ruling. The answer came back: "It's legal—let him alone." The unusual spectacle of a fifteen-year-old running for public office against two adults fascinated the media.

News stories brought Eric $67 in campaign contributions, to which he added $300 of his own savings. Invited to speak to many local organizations, he also trudged from door to door, day after day, seeking people's support. On Election Day in Lincoln he received 20,000 votes, beating out both of his adult rivals to become probably the youngest person ever elected to public office in the United States.

Ironically, Eric couldn't even vote for himself. According to the Twenty-sixth Amendment to the Constitution, he had to wait three more years before he could cast a ballot in any general election. In fact, until 1971 you had to be at least 21. Congress then reduced the voting age to 18 because of protests by American youths being drafted for the Vietnam War. TOO YOUNG TO VOTE FOR OUR LEADERS, read one demonstration banner, BUT NOT TOO YOUNG TO DIE FOR THEM.

The Twenty-sixth Amendment increased the size of the voting electorate by some 12 million young citizens. That was more than enough to play the decisive role in any election if the teenagers of America ever decided to vote as a solid bloc. Significantly, in the first year that eighteen-year-olds were able to vote, two American towns elected nineteen-year-old college students as mayors.

The potentially huge youth vote emphasizes the importance of citizenship training in junior high and high school. An impartial political course can equip you to vote intelligently when you reach 18, in the best interests of your community, your nation, and yourself. This book represents a modest step in that direction.

Casting a vote is not the only way you can participate in elections. Even before you turn 18, you can help elect candidates you think deserve to be in office by joining their campaigns and working to win victory for them. Every political campaign has a welcome mat out for young volunteers.

Most of us believe that our precious right to vote was guaranteed by the Constitution and the Bill of Rights drafted by our Founding Fathers. Not so. Most of them were aristocrats who found it unthinkable to grant universal suffrage to the "common people." They considered the right to vote something to be granted only to "responsible" white males, especially those with property. Neither women nor African Americans were to be taken seriously, of course.

Elitists like Alexander Hamilton had nightmares that universal suffrage would elect a rabble-rousing demagogue who would use the presidency to destroy the wealthy. The question of exactly who should be permitted to vote was left largely up to each state to determine as it chose.

States' rights were a sensitive issue. While the House of Representatives gave representation in Congress according to each state's population, the Senate was another story. The Founding Fathers were sensitive to the protests of smaller states that they would always be outvoted by states with bigger populations unless they had equality in the Senate. So each state was awarded only two senators, whether the state population was over 20 million, as in California today, or only 302,000, as in Alaska. Without this concession, the smaller of the original 13 colonies would never have agreed to give up their sovereignty to join the United States of America.

Our electoral system is remarkably elastic, able to accommodate the demands of drastically different interests. Candidates have to appeal to such diverse elements as Chicano farm workers, New York bankers, Denver police, Michigan farmers, Eskimo hunters, Texas oil rig workers, Pennsylvania coal miners, naturalized Cuban American exiles in Miami, Mississippi River barge workers, San Francisco teachers, and Montana ranchers.

Voting patterns are changing as a result of the movement of millions of American families from cities and suburbs to small towns and rural areas, mainly in the South and West. When some localities tried to prevent newcomers from voting, the U.S. Supreme Court held in 1972 that one month was long enough to establish residency.

The swelling number of immigrants in the 1970s alarmed Congress into passing a new law requiring would-be voters to be able to read, write, and understand the English language. But when new elections liberalized Congress, the use of English literacy tests was suspended on grounds that immigrants could still understand the issues in elections through their own language newspapers.

Despite laws liberalizing voting rights, huge numbers of Americans don't bother going to the polls. In 1976 Jimmy Carter was elected President by only 27 percent of all Americans qualified to cast ballots. "Two-thirds of our people do not even vote," he observed sadly. In 1977 the new governor of New Jersey was elected by only 15 percent of that state's qualified voters, while only 12 percent of qualified New Yorkers elected the mayor of their city. And in 1980 only 28 percent of qualified Americans elected Ronald Reagan as president.

By contrast, up to 95 percent of qualified voters in Western Europe go to the polls to choose their representatives. Are Europeans more public spirited? More aware of the benefits of voting one's choices?

Qualifications for voting are largely left to each state to determine, provided they do not conflict with federal law. Thus in most states convicted felons are denied the vote even after they have paid for their offense. Many states have on their books dusty, obsolete laws curbing voting rights, which are not enforced. In California you can legally be barred from the polls for fighting a duel; in Florida for betting; in Vermont for disorderly conduct; in South Carolina for being a pauper; in Idaho for not owning property; and in Connecticut for not possessing a "good character."

In addition to voting in general elections, Americans 18 and over also have the right to vote in a *primary*—the contest within a political party to decide who will be its candidates in the general election. When you register to vote, most states require you to indicate in which political party's next primary you wish to participate. You can do so without being bound to vote for either the party or its candidates in the next general election. If you prefer, you can register with no party at all, abstaining from voting in any primary.

When you become a college student, a special voting problem may arise. Some towns in which colleges are located resent students voting there, influencing local issues, instead of voting in their home communities by absentee ballots. If you claim the college town as your true residence, you may be required to prove it by a local bank account, car registration, or tax return.

No youth 18 or older may be prevented from voting because of race or color (Fifteenth Amendment), sex (Nineteenth Amendment), or requirement to pay a poll tax of any kind (Twenty-fourth Amendment).

From our earliest beginnings the right to vote did not come easily to all Americans. In the Massachusetts Bay Colony, no colonist could vote unless he supported the Puritan Congregational Church and attended services regularly. Minister-teacher Roger Williams, banned from the colony as a dangerous radical, established the new colony of Rhode Island, where every man was granted the right to vote.

In the Virginia Colony of 1668, poor farmers were banned from the polls. They finally stormed the Virginia Assembly with muskets, forcing the terrified legislators to grant them suffrage on pain of death if the demand was rejected.

George Washington urged Congress to support public education throughout the country so that when the ballot was given to all men it would prove "a blessing and not a curse."

But John Adams was firmly opposed to extension of the voting privilege. "There will be no end of it . . ." he warned. "Women will demand a vote; lads from twelve to twenty-one will think their rights not enough attended to; and every man who has not a farthing will demand an equal voice. . . . It tends to . . . prostrate all ranks to one common level."

When he succeeded Washington as president, Adams moved swiftly to disenfranchise voters who supported his rival, Vice-President Thomas Jefferson. Aware that French- and Irish-Catholic refugees would vote for Jefferson's Democratic-Republican Party, Adams branded them "treasonous aliens." He ramrodded the Alien and Sedition Acts through Congress, making immigrants wait 14 years instead of five to become voting citizens.

The three groups of Americans who had to wait longest for the right to vote were ethnic minorities, teens, and women.

Before the Civil War, only five states in the whole country had allowed nonwhites to vote. The Fifteenth Amendment, ratified in 1870, finally prohibited states from denying the vote to anyone "on account of race, color, or previous condition of servitude."

But discrimination persisted in many Southern states, which found other pretexts for barring blacks from the polls. They were refused ballots because they didn't have grandfathers who had voted; hadn't paid a poll tax they couldn't afford; couldn't pass a special literacy test forced on blacks alone; or hadn't voted in a primary election open only to whites. And there was always the threat of lynching by the Ku Klux Klan to deter any blacks brave enough to insist upon their voting rights.

In 1867 when federal troops were posted in Mississippi to enforce black suffrage, almost 67 percent of that state's blacks registered to vote. But when the troops were withdrawn in 1892, less than 6 percent of the blacks dared to register.

In 1904 Northern liberals in Congress sought to punish states that blocked blacks from voting by slashing their representation in Washington. But President Theodore Roosevelt crushed the move. If blacks were given an unqualified ballot, he declared, parts of the South would become "another Haiti," which at that time had a black ruler. In his view most Southern blacks were unfit for suffrage.

Not until the Civil Rights Act of 1957, passed over bitter Southern opposition, was a civil rights division established in the Department of Justice. The Civil Rights Act of 1960 set fines and prison terms for anyone using threats or force to prevent blacks from voting.

Black leaders themselves began to take steps to translate American laws into reality. They led sit-in demonstrations, "freedom rides" to the South, protest marches, and voting registration campaigns, often at the risk of their lives.

In 1964 a new Civil Rights Act forbade the use of different voting requirements for blacks and whites, while the Twenty-fourth Amendment forbade the imposition of poll taxes. The following year a Voting Rights Bill authorized federal election officials to take control of any election district found to be using discriminatory tactics against blacks seeking to vote.

Signing that bill, President Lyndon B. Johnson declared, "If any county anywhere in this nation does not want federal intervention, it need only open its polling places to all of its

President Richard M. Nixon signs the Twenty-sixth Amendment to the Constitution, lowering the voting age from 21 to 18. WHITE HOUSE PHOTO.

President John Adams feared that extending the voting privilege would "prostrate all ranks to one common level." LITHOGRAPHY BY PENDLETON.

U.S. Constitution
AMENDMENT 26
Administrator of General Services

Certification of Amendment to Constitution of the United States Extending the Right to Vote to Citizens Eighteen Years of Age or Older

To All to Whom These Presents Shall Come, Greeting:

KNOW YE, That the Congress of the United States, at the first session, Ninety-second Congress begun at the City of Washington on Thursday, the twenty-first day of January, in the year one thousand nine hundred and seventy-one, passed a Joint Resolution in the words and figures as follows: to wit—

JOINT RESOLUTION

Proposing an amendment to the Constitution of the United States extending the right to vote to citizens eighteen years of age or older.

Resolved by the Senate and House of Representatives of the United States of America in Congress assembled (two-thirds of each House concurring therein), That the following article is proposed as an amendment to the Constitution of the United States, which shall be valid to all intents and purposes as part of the Constitution when ratified by the legislatures of three-fourths of the several States within seven years from the date of its submission by the Congress:

"Article—

"SECTION 1. The right of citizens of the United States, who are eighteen years of age or older, to vote shall not be denied or abridged by the United States or by any State on account of age.

"SEC. 2. The Congress shall have power to enforce this article by appropriate legislation."

And, further, that it appears from official documents on file in the General Services Administration that the Amendment to the Constitution of the United States proposed as aforesaid has been ratified by the Legislatures of the States of Alabama, Alaska, Arizona, Arkansas, California, Colorado, Connecticut, Delaware, Hawaii, Idaho, Illinois, Indiana, Iowa, Kansas, Louisiana, Maine, Maryland, Massachusetts, Michigan, Minnesota, Missouri, Montana, Nebraska, New Hampshire, New Jersey, New York, North Carolina, Ohio, Oklahoma, Oregon, Pennsylvania, Rhode Island, South Carolina, Tennessee, Texas, Vermont, Washington, West Virginia, and Wisconsin.

And, further, that the States whose Legislatures have so ratified the said proposed Amendment constitute the requisite three-fourths of the whole number of States in the United States.

Now, therefore, be it known that I, Robert L. Kunzig, Administrator of General Services, by virtue and in pursuance of Section 106b, Title 1 of the United States Code, do hereby certify that the Amendment aforesaid has become valid, to all intents and purposes, as a part of the Constitution of the United States.

IN TESTIMONY WHEREOF, I have hereunto set my hand and caused the seal of the General Services Administration to be affixed.

DONE at the City of Washington this 5th day of July in the year of our Lord one thousand nine hundred and seventy-one.

Robert L. Kunzig

ROBERT L. KUNZIG.

The foregoing was signed in our presence on this 5th day of July, 1971.

Richard Nixon

Paul T. Sarumey

Joseph H. Layd Jr.

Julianne Jones

The Twenty-sixth Amendment, signed into law on July 5, 1971.

people. Let me say now to every Negro in this country, 'You must register. You must vote. You must learn, so that your choice advances your interest and the interest of our beloved nation.'"

The following year, hundreds of thousands of new black voters registered in Alabama alone. For the first time in that state's history, not a single candidate for governor dared utter a word proclaiming white supremacy. In fact, many candidates shook the hands of black voters, seeking their support.

The right to vote was also won with difficulty by those Americans who had been present to greet the Pilgrims arriving on the *Mayflower*. Not until 1924 were Native Americans awarded a qualified citizenship in the land that once had been all their own. Even then, as their lands were stripped away from them, most Indians were kept from voting by restrictive state laws. Finally, in 1953, Congress ended their "ward" status by making them full-fledged citizens with the right to vote.

Other minorities have also had a long struggle to win that right. In 1970 Genoveva Castro, a native-born U.S. citizen of Mexican descent, was denied the right to register to vote in California because of a discriminatory 1891 clause in the state constitution. It specified, "No person who shall not be able to read the Constitution in English . . . shall ever exercise the privileges of an elector in this State." Tens of thousands of Mexican Americans in California had been barred from voting by that clause.

Ms. Castro happened to be literate in the Spanish language, and she could read a Spanish translation of the California constitution. She also had access to 18 Spanish-language newspapers and magazines, many of which carried discussions of political affairs. So she sued the state on behalf of all Spanish-speaking residents of Los Angeles County, claiming that the law barring them from voting violated their right to "equal protection under the law," as guaranteed by the Fourteenth Amendment.

The California Supreme Court awarded her the verdict, declaring, "It would indeed be ironic that petitioners . . . identified with the birth of California and contributing in no small measure to its growth, should be disenfranchised in their ancestral land, despite their capacity to cast an informed vote."

So today, when you reach the age of 18 you have the right to vote whether you're male, female, poor, a newcomer, black, Indian, Hispanic, Asian, or any other kind of citizen.

2

Your Right to Participate at Any Age—and How

Even if you haven't reached voting age yet, you still have the right to participate in the election process in different ways and at different levels.

The early teens are a good time to begin getting involved in elections. I did myself when I was only 13, after becoming interested in the 1928 presidential race between Republican Herbert Hoover and Democrat Al Smith. At the time I felt strongly that Hoover would make the better president. So I began writing letters urging his support to the editor of the New York *World-Telegram*, then an important newspaper with over a million readers.

To my delight the editor—not realizing that I was only a thirteen-year-old boy—printed my long letters under bold headlines that dominated the editorial page. It was a thrill seeing my name in boldface type as the author; in fact, they gave me the incentive to continue with writing as a lifelong career. I have been an active political participant ever since.

I had no way of knowing how many of the paper's million-plus readers I influenced to vote for Hoover, but I received dozens of letters from people agreeing with me. That was how I—a mere slip of a youth without even a vote of my own—was able to make my voice heard in the 1928 election.

That option still remains open today for young teens. In addition, they will find the welcome mat out for them in youth groups sponsored by various political parties.

Teen Age Republicans (TARS) has some 120,000 teenage members in 50 state clubs. President Ronald Reagan credited them with having a significant impact on his election in 1980. "You walked the precincts," he told them, "you licked stamps, stuffed envelopes, got senior citizens to the polls, and babysat while mothers voted. It may not sound very glamorous, but it's absolutely essential and especially in this era of campaign spending limitations. And often, what you did made the difference between winning and losing!"

TARS are trained for political leadership; over 85,000 have attended workshops dealing with current issues and with the specifics of campaign organization.

The Democrats sponsor a similar program, called Teen Dems, for young people in some 17 states. "The Teen Dem Clubs were utilized . . . to acquaint high school students with the principles of the Democratic Party and to interest them in politics," explained former Indiana Senator Birch Bayh. "They secured members of their own age group to help with . . . campaign chores. These young people, working after school hours, were extremely valuable to our Democratic organization, and I believe will become valuable workers for the senior party in later years."

Teens who get high on politics can wield an amazing amount of clout. When Oregon prepared to hold presidential primary elections in 1964, Sunset High School students in Beaverton decided to stage a mock Republican primary. They invited Governor Nelson Rockefeller of New York, then a presidential candidate, to be their keynote speaker. To their delight he accepted and showed up in Beaverton (pop. 5,937). The Oregon press played up the story, and when Rockefeller won the state primary he credited his victory to the students of Sunset High.

Getting involved in politics as a teenager, you could find yourself occupying a more important position in an election campaign than you ever imagined possible. When Illinois Senator Charles Percy first ran for office, he chose as manager of one of his Chicago campaign centers a bright eighteen-year-old boy who did a superb job for the candidate, who emerged victorious. Edward Bouchet was only 25 when he ran for the Rhode Island Senate. People laughed when he made his seventeen-year-old sister his campaign manager. But she mustered an enthusiastic corps of supporters from her high school. With the aid of 75 of them, she steered her brother to victory.

Over 200 high school political clubs supported the campaign of Senator Howard Baker of Tennessee. "The enthusiastic participation in our campaign by the young people of our state," he declared, "was the single most important factor in our success."

Former Senator George McGovern of South Dakota also credited high school students for his senatorial victories "by doing precinct organizational work, mass mailing preparation, maintaining the campaign headquarters, and the thousand and one other tasks that inevitably come up in any bid for political office."

The AFL-CIO Committee on Political Education (COPE) welcomes teenage volunteers interested in electing pro-labor candidates. They seek youngsters who can spare anything from an hour to a few days a week to telephone, canvass door-to-door, type precinct lists, keep card files up-to-date, check registrations, canvass voters on their choices, distribute handbills, post election notices, and help get voters to the polls.

Even if you don't join a political campaign, you can still get involved in the electoral process that most directly affects you—in your own school. Most schools have student councils. By winning election to one of these, a student gets a voice in the rules and conditions governing the school day.

"Students in school as well as out," the U.S. Supreme Court has ruled, "are 'persons' under our Constitution . . . [and] possessed of fundamental rights which the state must respect."

According to the American Civil Liberties Union, students and student organizations must be allowed to hold meetings in schoolrooms and auditoriums, or on school grounds, to discuss freely and pass resolutions about any matter concerning them. In court cases students have won the right to distribute political campaign literature at high schools and to collect signatures on petitions.

One group of New York high school students formed a City General Organization Council, claiming to represent some 275,000 students who demanded a voice in educational policies. They called for representative student government in each school "free from domination by the administration and faculty adviser." When the Council's president, seventeen-year-old Donald St. George Reeves, protested cuts in the school budget, he was suspended. But he was reinstated the next day when several hundred students demonstrated in his support.

Responding to the youthful Council's pressure, the New York Board of Education issued directives ordering every high school to organize "an elective and truly representative student government," with all students allowed to form political organizations and vote. This government was also given the power to allocate student activity funds and participate in making decisions "in certain areas, including curriculum and disciplinary policies." Many school boards have since followed suit.

Political-science teacher Steven Teel of Berkeley High School in California sought to give his students a better understanding of our political system. He turned his classes into a mock Senate and House of Representatives for a whole term, with each student impersonating a real senator or congressman. Learning how to process bills into law, many students developed a deep interest in politics. Some began to think of running as real candidates in future elections.

You might even consider running for a seat on your local school board. In New York, Susan Spencer, an eighteen-year-old senior at Linton High School, ran for election to a vacancy on the school board. Her name was banned from the voting machines, however, when State Attorney General Louis J. Lefkowitz issued an opinion that no one under 21 could hold elective office. Susan fought the action in court. The State Supreme Court ruled that the election had been illegal because Susan had been excluded, and ordered the local board of education to hold a new election in which she could run. Subsequently the New York legislature passed a new law permitting persons under 21 to run for elective public office.

Students who get involved in school politics and elections are likely to enjoy participating in local, state, and national elections as well. Their experience with the details of campaigning makes them especially welcome in the headquarters of political candidates.

There are special rewards for getting involved in political campaigns. You have the satisfaction of accomplishing an important goal. You enjoy the pleasure of working together with others who feel as you do about the candidate and the issues. You earn respect from them by your participation. You're often invited to hear and meet leading political figures. And you acquire a behind-the-scenes understanding of what goes on in American politics and how elections work.

Teenagers are often more welcome than adults in campaign headquarters because adults are more likely to be bored with routine jobs like phoning prospective voters or addressing envelopes, while teens tend to be cheerfully eager to do whatever is necessary to help their candidate win the election. Working together, they make even the dullest of chores fun.

"The importance of young volunteers cannot be overemphasized," observed former Senator Philip Hart of Michigan. "No one else has their enthusiasm and their tireless energy and their willingness to do anything and everything. No campaign could function without such a devoted band. But on the other hand the volunteers get as much from campaigning as they give, and I hope and believe they find it a rewarding experience."

Participating in a campaign also gives you the chance to meet people who can be helpful in developing a political career of your own. If an influential person becomes impressed with you, he or she can open doors for you that can launch you on your way.

A Texas youngster who arrived in Washington as a congressional aide came to the attention of President Franklin D. Roosevelt. The President selected him to be an official in the National Youth Administration. That was the beginning of a skyrocketing political career that took Lyndon B. Johnson all the way to the White House.

As in any other field of endeavor, when you get your foot inside the door in any capacity, anything can happen.

Mark Hatfield was only ten years old when he passed out handbills asking voters to reelect Hoover in 1932. That was the beginning of a political career that first made Hatfield governor of Oregon, then a United States senator.

"I have been fortunate in having many young people volunteer in my campaigns," declared former Utah Senator Frank Moss, "and my debt to them is great. I have found also that some of the boys and girls who worked for me in past campaigns, and who continued working in politics when they were able to vote, are now candidates in their own right."

Political candidates are often surprisingly successful at very young ages. Early on, Roger Bedford of Alabama participated enthusiastically in many political campaigns. Then, at age 26 he decided to run for the state senate. Winning an upset victory, he became the youngest senator ever to sit in that statehouse.

When law student Paul Soglin was arrested in the late sixties for taking part in a peace demonstration in Madison, Wisconsin, the police force of conservative Mayor William Dyke forcibly shaved off his long hair. Paul never forgot that humiliation. Four years later he organized a coalition of students, anti-war activists, minorities, and labor groups. Running against Dyke for mayor, he won and dumped that chagrined official out of office.

Participating in an election campaign can also open other career doors for you. Suppose, for example, that you aspire to write the speeches that candidates deliver on the campaign trail. If you volunteer to do office work for a candidate, you'll get a chance to meet his or her speech writers. They'll appreciate your offer to do research for them in the library and help them bang out some speeches. If you do a good job, you might end up as a paid writer of campaign speeches.

Working for the election of a successful candidate, you could also possibly win a summer internship in Washington, working in a congressional office or government agency. Thousands of such jobs with pay are available each summer—invaluable training for anyone interested in a political career.

Women today have greater opportunities in the political arena than ever before, and they need not hesitate to get involved.

Before Harriet Keyserling of South Carolina ran for her first office in county government, she was active as an observer for the League of Women Voters. "While observing County Council one day," she recalled, "I thought, I can do that as well as, or better than, some of them.'" Running for a seat on the council, she won. Then she went on to win election to the South Carolina House of Representatives.

Keyserling advises women not to be too self-critical. "Just look around you," she suggests. "Can't you really do as well as, or even better than, at least half the people now in office?"

A 1977 survey showed that nationally some 19 percent of city council members were women, and in California 23 percent of school trustees were women.

During California elections in 1976, 31 women ran for office on major party tickets. Eight were elected to seats in Congress, the State Senate, and the State Assembly.

Representation of the sexes in the nation's governing bodies is still far from equal. Nevertheless, more and more women are winning public office in every election.

President Lyndon B. Johnson began his national political career as a youthful Congressional aide.

Young people can influence the outcome of elections through distributing party literature.

These five young people ran for the Ann Arbor, Michigan City Council in 1972 as members of the Human Rights Party.

The type of government you have is your decision.

Women can also participate in politics by joining such organizations as the National Women's Political Caucus, the League of Women Voters, the National Organization for Women, the Women's Campaign Fund (which provides money and help to female candidates), and special groups campaigning for or against the Equal Rights Amendment (ERA), abortion on demand, and prayer in the public schools.

In the final analysis, what kind of government you have is up to you. If you want change, you won't get it by just complaining to your friends. As an individual you may feel powerless to influence your government. But *collectively* you can have tremendous impact. And the way to begin is to get a small ground swell started in the neighborhood, district, or town where you live.

3

Why Elections Are Important to You—Now and Tomorrow

"I am the law!" boasted Jersey City Mayor Frank Hague, political boss of New Jersey during the 1930s. He controlled the state's corrupt political machine, which rigged elections. His goon squads beat up, jailed, or ran out of town anyone who dared oppose or challenge his iron rule. Excitement ran high when two congressmen declared they were coming to Jersey City to defy his ban on free speech.

As a young New Yorker then, I crossed the Hudson River with a friend to attend their rally. What we saw in Journal Square frightened us. Hague's burly goons had set up roadblocks to keep the congressmen out. They roamed the square snooping into out-of-town cars, eavesdropping on groups waiting to hear the congressmen, and abruptly seizing and running out of town any "undesirables." Police were invisible.

The atmosphere was tense and fraught with violence.

"I've been in Nazi Germany," one man near us suddenly shouted in angry defiance, "and this is ten times worse!" Hague's henchmen promptly pounced on him and dragged him out of sight.

After that my friend and I spoke only in careful whispers.

Word finally spread that the two congressmen had been persuaded to call off their trip because of the danger to their lives. My friend and I left Jersey City quickly. When we reached the New York side of the border, we whooped and hollered in tremendous relief, shouting, "Hooray for New York! Hooray for democracy!"

That was a taste of what can happen even in the United States—and from time to time has happened—when voters lose control of their state to a corrupt, dangerous political boss. As a result of my chilling experience in Hague's New Jersey, I joined the American League Against War and Fascism to work politically against other attempts to sabotage the democratic processes that protect our liberties.

Similarly, it was no coincidence that youth was in the forefront of the widespread protest movements of the 1960s and 1970s. Young people are always the most idealistic and energetic generation, because it is mostly their future that is at stake.

Most of us older Americans tend to blame the government when things go wrong in the country, without reflecting that our own votes—or more often, the lack of them—put incompetents in power. Unfortunately many of us are too busy with our jobs, our families, and our recreation to pay much attention to the news or to analyze the political issues of the day.

As a result, out of Americans eligible to vote, only 25 to 30 percent exercise their right of suffrage with any degree of regularity. Another 30 to 40 percent vote so infrequently as to have negligible influence on the electoral process. Thus only a tiny minority of Americans select the candidates who run for and win the over 500,000 elective offices in the United States.

The ancient Greeks, who invented democracy as a political system, held that political authority must remain in the hands of the people, not in any ruler's. Since there are too many of us to rule ourselves directly, we elect representatives to enact or revoke our laws. But when those representatives are elected by only a third of Americans, do we really have a democracy?

In contrast, a country like Australia insists that voting is a civic duty, not just a privilege. Anyone who, without a good reason, fails to vote is subject to a fine. Australia, consequently, has one of the highest voting turnouts in the world. This guarantees that their elected officials really represent the will of the vast majority. Critics of compulsory voting, however, doubt that it is any guarantee of better government because it drives to the polls many voters who don't really understand the issues.

The question of who "really" understands the issues in an election campaign is a value judgment. Democrats are convinced that Republicans blindly vote for issues that will turn the clock back to 1920. Republicans are convinced that Democrats don't realize their programs will bankrupt the country.

Our system nevertheless urges both to vote their choices. The larger the vote, the more clearly the will of the citizens is manifested.

Election issues can be of supreme importance to every American. The candidates we elect to Congress and the White House can keep us at peace or embroil us in a war overseas, with all the anguish and terror war brings. William Lloyd Garrison, the famous abolitionist, mocked his fellow countrymen for singing the praises of peace while electing military presidents.

Even when voters are not well informed, the ballot in their hands is less dangerous to our society than any attempt to deprive them of it by some kind of qualification test. Whenever citizens are denied the right to vote for who governs them and how, you have a dictatorship, not a democracy. If people are not given the opportunity to get rid of officials by voting them out of office, they may become desperate enough to do it the only other way possible—by violent revolution.

America's young people, who are expected soon to become a majority of the voting population, need to become aware of the crucial issues of our society if they are to vote intelligently.

"The schools, in their fundamental obligation to prepare youth for citizenship, have failed completely," thinks Professor of Education Arthur Pearl, University of California, Santa Cruz. "Schools continue to be places . . . where children go to learn how to become stupid about war, economics, labor, minorities,

Frank Hague, the corrupt, dangerous political boss of New Jersey in the 1930s.

A 1972 poster, picturing a young man who participated in the 1965 Selma, Alabama Voting Rights March. Young people, it is predicted, will soon become a majority of the voting population.

poverty, and communism. . . . Thus it is possible for a candidate to prate about economies leading to savings of *millions* of dollars in cutbacks in welfare benefits, school children's lunches, or excesses in poverty programs, while almost in the same breath he may ask for *billions* of dollars more . . . for military expenditures."

If America is to have a bright future, young people need to understand the whole truth about our past as a nation. When they do, they will know how to recognize and avoid mistakes made in the past, while voting to uphold and advance the best traditions in our history.

Too often, however, our schools have given us a simplistic, dressed-up version of our history in the belief that patriotism requires young people to think of our country as always being in the right. But *all* nations make mistakes, and we are no exception. Unless we learn from our mistakes, we are likely to repeat them.

In 1972 an estimated 25 million new young voters became entitled to the ballot for the first time. The National Association of Student Governments announced the formation of a "National Youth Caucus" to get student activists into power on the local level of every state, where they could influence that year's presidential elections.

This was supposed to be a problem for the Nixon administration, which most high school and college students opposed because of its persistence in prosecuting the Vietnam War. But the Nixon administration did not take the notion of a united "youth vote" very seriously.

"The thinking here is that the young people who vote for the first time in '72 will split more or less along the same old lines as their parents," observed campaign correspondent Hunter S. Thompson. "'How many will even register?' they ask. 'And even then—even assuming a third of the *possibles* might register, how many of those will actually get out and vote?' The implication, every time, is that the 'youth vote' is just a noisy paper tiger." Nixon's reelection seemed to validate that prophecy.

The Vietnam War and the Watergate scandal contributed to making many older Americans, as well, cynical about politics. In a book called *A Tide of Discontent*, Clifton McClesky observed that from 1964 to 1978 the number of people who trusted the government to do what was right plummeted from 76 to 29 percent. The number who felt that a few big-business interests controlled the government rose from 24 to 65 percent.

The growing disinterest of Americans in elections was dramatized sharply in 1980 when, in an election year, President Jimmy Carter bought half an hour of TV time to tell why he felt he ought to be reelected. Only one American in 25 was willing to listen. Two weeks later when his chief rival for the Democratic nomination, Senator Edward Kennedy, took half an hour on TV to discuss vital problems confronting the nation, he talked to just 10 million Americans. Hours later when the Super Bowl football game was broadcast, 105 million tuned in.

Americans who don't bother voting often excuse their apathy by saying, "It doesn't matter who gets elected, because all politicians are just a bunch of crooks."

"When a man says to me that politics is dirty," Woodrow Wilson told a New Jersey audience in 1912, "I ask him if he voted at the last primary. If he says that he didn't, I invite him to shut up!"

Politics is neither automatically clean nor dirty. It is exactly what we, the voters, make it—just as businesses, churches, labor unions, and other American institutions are what their constituents make them. If most of us refuse to get involved in politics, we leave it to a few unscrupulous people eager to control it for their own selfish ends.

Who, then, is really to blame?

The candidates who win election to public office have the power to change your life by the laws they pass. Does it make sense to entrust so much power to persons you don't know anything about? Whom you've had no say in electing?

Political activist Dick Gregory is convinced that youth offers the best hope for solving our national problems. "We can expect to see some real change in the political life of the United States," he believes. "The number-one thing young people in America—indeed, young people around the world—have going for them is their sense of honesty, morality, and ethics. Young people refuse to accept the lies and rationalizations of the established order. They will be looking for candidates who are honest, candidates who have a moral vision, candidates who are concerned more with solving social problems than they are with merely winning an election."

How can you select such candidates to vote or work for?

First, listen to what all the candidates have to say and read the literature distributed by their headquarters. Read about them in newspapers and magazines. Discuss them with friends, family, and other people whose opinions you respect. Check the recommendations of impartial political organizations, such as the League of Women Voters.

When you've made up your mind, it makes sense to get involved in the campaigns of the candidates whose views you support, even if you're not yet of voting age. Laws affecting your future life will be made either by them or by candidates whose ideas may be opposed to yours.

Those laws can decide whether you will be faced with the threat of nuclear war; whether you can be drafted to fight a foreign war; how much tax you will have to pay out of your salary; whether you will have a job, and what kind; how much you will have to pay for imported cars and motorcycles or for food; whether you will be able to afford your own home; whether your savings will be safe in the banks; whether the school system will improve or get worse; whether you can get financial help to go to college; whether prayer will be introduced in your local schools; whether you will be forced to live with polluted air and water; whether there will be a new energy shortage.

These problems won't go away quickly, and they won't solve themselves. You may have to deal with them for the rest of your life. You have every reason, therefore, to get involved in electing the kind of candidates who convince you they have intelligent plans and the ability to help solve those problems.

By participating in the political life of your community, you also forge common bonds of interest with others who have the same concerns. That is your best weapon against feeling powerless in local issues directly affecting you.

In 1970 the town leaders of Trenton, Maine, were ready to license the building of a nuclear power plant and an aluminum factory to bring jobs to the town. Despite the need for those jobs and the tax relief the new industries would provide, the little town's citizens were vehemently opposed to allowing the pollution they knew would poison their environment. Banding together against the town officials, they forced the issue to be put on a ballot, and they defeated it by a vote of 144 to 77.

There's a lot at stake for you in elections—local, state, and national. The earlier in your life that you get involved, the better the chance that you and your generation can create an American future closer to your heart's desire.

And when you have the vote, remember the late Martin Luther King's advice, born of a lifetime of struggle:

"The most important step that a person can take is that short walk to the ballot box."

4

How the System Works

When Ronald Reagan and George H. W. Bush challenged each other for the Republican presidential nomination in 1980, Reagan proclaimed his plans for improving economic conditions. Bush sneered at his program as nonsense—"voodoo economics."

Politics makes strange bedfellows. When Reagan won the nomination, he chose as his running mate none other than his detractor, George H. W. Bush. Bush, in turn, had no qualms about accepting the vice-presidential nomination that pledged him to endorse the very "voodoo economics" he had derided.

"So what?" laughed one Republican delegate. "Nobody takes seriously what one candidate says about another when they're both fighting for the nomination."

President Jimmy Carter, the Democratic opposition candidate, was quick to quote Bush's view of Reagan's "voodoo economics" during the ensuing campaign. Voters nevertheless elected the Republican ticket.

One of the odd ways in which our system works is that a party's rival candidates for an office will often attack each other as harshly as if they were members of different parties. Afterward, however, party loyalty requires them to reconcile, with the loser campaigning for the winner against the candidate of the opposition party.

As established by Congress in 1845, we elect our presidents on the Tuesday after the first Monday in November. On this day Americans also vote for many members of Congress and for state and municipal candidates as well.

Elections held halfway in a president's four-year term are called off-year or mid-term elections. In these we vote for all 435 representatives, about a third of the senators, about half the state governors, and many state and local officeholders. Midterm elections are often viewed as a vote of confidence in, or repudiation of, the president's policies, depending on how well his party does at the polls.

The national candidates for whom you can vote to serve you in Washington are the president, vice-president, two senators, and a congressman. The state candidates for whom you can vote include a governor, lieutenant governor, other state officials, and members of your state legislature. The town and county candidates you vote for may include a mayor, sheriff, city councilpersons, and school-board members.

Each state has the right to decide how to hold its elections, as long as this does not conflict with federal requirements. Thus, one state may hold elections for governor every four years, while another will elect a new governor every two years. Each state is entitled to elect two U.S. senators for six-year terms and members of the House of Representatives every two years, in numbers proportionate to the population.

The Founding Fathers arranged this plan to create a balance between the popular will and states' rights. If all our laws were passed simply by popular vote, the people of New York, with 34 representatives, would have 34 times as much power in Congress as the people of South Dakota, who have only one. But in the Senate, South Dakota has equal power with New York, each state having two senators apiece.

Many people are confused about the difference between primary and general elections. "A good many political-science professors and government teachers never taught people the difference..." observed Louise Lindblom, 1982 Executive Director, Alabama State Democratic Committee. "People do not understand that a primary is a party matter for the purpose of nominating a candidate for the general election ballot in November."

The voting process begins with your registration at a designated place. Election officials and poll watchers are entitled to check your name and address to make sure you are qualified in terms of age, citizenship, and length and place of residence, as well as to make certain you vote only once.

You may register as a Democrat, Republican, Socialist, or member of any other party, or as an independent. No matter how you register, you can vote any way you please in the general election. But if you register as a member of a particular party, you are then entitled to vote in its state primary to select its next candidates for the general election.

A few states hold open primaries in which you can vote without prior registration, provided you don't vote in the primary of more than one party.

State primary results are watched carefully by national party leaders because they indicate the popularity of various party candidates. Thus if John Smarthead emerges as the favorite presidential choice in the first five or six state primaries, he may become the party's "front-runner" candidate, likely to win substantial support at the party's national convention, which will choose the final candidate.

State primaries also test whether or not a candidate has liabilities that may hurt him in a national election. When John F. Kennedy sought the presidency in 1960, many Democratic leaders opposed his nomination because they felt that Americans would never elect a Roman Catholic to the White House. But they were forced to sit up and take notice when he entered the early West Virginia Democratic primary and emerged the victor in that almost entirely Protestant state.

Still, there were reservations about Kennedy's youth. He entered six more state primaries and won them all, making himself the front-runner who deserved—and won—the nomination at the Democratic Party's national convention.

A candidate can win primary after primary and still be denied his party's presidential nomination at the national convention.

In 1952, Senator Estes Kefauver emerged from the primaries as the most popular Democratic candidate. Yet the convention nominated instead Adlai Stevenson, who had entered no primaries at all. This happened again in 1968 when Vice-President Hubert Humphrey, who had avoided all primaries, was chosen over Senator Eugene McCarthy, a winner in the primaries.

A candidate's showing in the primaries is only one factor influencing the choice of convention delegates. A public-opinion poll showing that a candidate is likely to beat the other party's front-runner can help him or her enormously. Some candidates also spend several years before the national convention doing favors for party leaders in many states, counting on their support in return when they lead delegations to the convention.

Little more than one in three states holds a primary. "I hope that people have had a bellyful of these primaries," said former President Harry S. Truman in 1960. "They are outrageously expensive and exhausting." States without primaries use any method they wish to select delegates to the national convention.

Until the 1970s most delegates were chosen at closed party gatherings called *precinct caucuses*. About a third are still chosen in this manner. A 1967 survey by the League of Women Voters revealed that in many states only a handful of party loyalists showed up at the caucuses. When one Arizona party invited 500 members to attend, only a dozen appeared. That two percent of the party's membership then selected national delegates on behalf of the whole party in Arizona.

When all parties select their nominees at their conventions, state candidates as well as national, you may be dissatisfied with all their choices. You always have the option to write in on your ballot the name of any unlisted candidate you prefer. It is rare that a candidate is elected by this method, but it serves as a protest vote. Poll officials are required to show you how to cast a write-in vote, upon your request.

The smallest voting units in a state are called *precincts* or *districts*. In most states these are grouped into wards. But the voting structure differs from state to state. The best way to understand how it works in your state is to join a local political club and take part in an election campaign.

Ward or precinct captains were once powerful figures in our electoral system. Before the introduction of our present-day welfare system, America's poor felt compelled to turn for assistance to city or county political organizations. The ward or precinct captains responded by providing coal, warm clothing, baskets of groceries, and persuasion for landlords to hold off on the rent.

Recipients of this largesse expressed their gratitude by voting into office the choices of the ward politicians, who were frequently repaid by opportunities to plunder city and state treasuries through graft. Loyal party workers were rewarded with government jobs and could be counted on to lead family and friends to the polls to keep the party in power.

In old turn-of-the-century New York, the corrupt Tammany Hall political machine was famous for its skill in mustering votes. A ward boss named Plunkett explained, "I know every man, woman, and child in the Fifteenth District. . . . I know what they like and what they don't like. . . . I hear of a young feller that's proud of his voice . . . I ask him to come around to Washington Hall and join our glee club. . . . Another young feller gains a reputation as a baseball player in a vacant lot. I bring him into our baseball club. . . . I rope them all in by givin' them opportunities to show themselves off. I don't trouble with political arguments. I just study human nature and act accordin'."

As in Plunkett's day, some voters still vote as they do because of favors received or expected from a candidate's political apparatus. But most Americans today cast their ballots for candidates who most closely approximate their own views and whose election they feel will benefit them personally as well as being good for the country.

There is a great deal of bloc voting for candidates because they are of the same race, religion, or ethnic origin. The 1980 census found that one in five Americans belong to some minority group—26.5 million blacks, 14.6 million Hispanics, 3.5 million Asians, 1.4 million Native Americans and Eskimoes.

Black Americans tend to vote as a bloc either for black candidates or for white candidates pledged to remedy black grievances. They usually vote the Democratic ticket in the conviction that this party is more sympathetic to black problems and has done more about them. At the same time, many blacks feel that they are not getting their fair share of elective offices. Constituting about 11 percent of the population, they represent only one percent of elected officials. Pointing out that a solid black vote can tip any election, black leaders have warned both the Democratic and Republican Parties that they must either nominate more black candidates or have black candidates run independently against them.

Not so long ago black leaders who merely tried to get blacks to the voting booths did so at the peril of their lives. In June 1963, Douglas MacArthur Cotton and eight other members of the Student Nonviolent Coordinating Committee (SNCC) attempted to lead 200 black citizens of Greenwood, Mississippi, to the courthouse to register them to vote. Arrested for "disturbing the peace," they were given a five-minute trial without permission to obtain an attorney and were sentenced to $200 fines and four months' hard labor at a county farm.

Mistreated by guards, they went on a work and hunger strike in protest. They were punished by transfer to Parchman State Penitentiary, where they were put in a "hot box"—a windowless, lightless closet—and kept locked there for two scorching days and nights. Several collapsed. Later Cotton was hung by his hands from the cell bars for three hours.

The black students were finally bailed out after 55 days, and Cotton was threatened with being shot if he returned.

All this punishment was for asserting the right to vote for 200 black citizens of Greenwood, Mississippi. The civil rights acts of the Johnson administration ended such blatant miscarriages of justice.

In addition to the black vote, politicians are also sensitive to other voting blocs that play an important election role in certain states. Among these are the strong "Jewish vote" in California, Florida, and New York; the "Irish and Greek vote" in Massachusetts; the "Portuguese vote" in Rhode Island; the "Cajun vote" in Louisiana; and the "French-Canadian vote" in Maine and New Hampshire.

Jewish American voters have their own special interests. For many these include the state of Israel; candidates sympathetic to the Palestinian cause instead may find a heavy Jewish vote cast against them. Jewish constituents also tend to vote solidly for Jewish candidates, so that in 1980 no fewer than 8 out of 100 U.S. Senators were of Jewish heritage. Like the blacks, most Jewish voters vote Democratic, considering it the more liberal of the two major parties. Nevertheless they voted as enthusiastically for Republican Dwight Eisenhower as they did for Democrat John F. Kennedy.

Other minority groups also tend to vote for candidates of their own ethnic origin. In 1982, for example, Italian American voters elected almost 30 Italian American representatives to Congress. Hispanic voters in California made their weight felt by compelling the state's public schools to adopt a policy of bilingual education.

When you vote for national, state, or local candidates in a general election, your vote counts directly—except for two political offices, those of president and vice-president. Although millions of Americans think they are voting directly for candidates for those two offices, in fact they are voting for members of an Electoral College who cast the official vote. This "college" has no building or campus. The victorious electors of each state simply meet in their state capitol.

A drawing depicting the voting process in 1889. WOOD ENGRAVING FROM FRANK LESLIE'S ILLUSTRATED NEWSPAPER.

Two North Dakota farmers read the ballots posted outside a schoolhouse on Election Day in 1940. Politicians must be sensitive to the needs of many voting blocs. PHOTO BY JOHN VACHON.

Adam Clayton Powell and the New York delegation in 1942 on their way to protest the poll tax filibuster. Poll taxes were one method employed to keep blacks from voting. PHOTO BY GORDON PARKS.

They represent only the party receiving the highest presidential vote in that state. They are usually first chosen at their party's state convention from among influential and prominent party members. Each state is guaranteed the same number of electors as it has members in Congress. No state has less than three, but states with the largest populations have the largest number of votes in the Electoral College.

The electors meet on the first Monday after the second Wednesday in December. By long-established custom they vote for their party's nominees, usually the candidates who have won a majority of the popular vote, although the electors are not specifically required to do so by law.

All of a state's electoral votes are awarded to the winners of that state's election race. Then all the states' results are tallied. The presidential team receiving a majority of the Electoral College votes is officially proclaimed the winner of the election. If no team has a clear majority, however, because of third-party votes, the election is then thrown into the House of Representatives. They select a president from among the three candidates with the highest Electoral College vote. In that case, all the congressmen of each state must combine their votes to cast a single ballot.

If the Electoral College fails to give a majority to any of the vice-presidential nominees, then the Senate chooses from the two with the highest votes, each senator casting a single vote.

A presidential candidate can actually receive a majority of the votes cast in the nation and still lose the election if the Electoral College votes for someone else. Three presidents have gone to the White House with fewer votes than their opponents. In 1824 Andrew Jackson received over 43 percent of the popular vote, and John Quincy Adams less than 31 percent, but the Electoral College still elected Adams.

In 1876 Samuel J. Tilden won almost 51 percent of the popular vote, compared to Rutherford B. Hayes's 48 percent, yet by one vote the Electoral College made Hayes president. And in 1888 Grover Cleveland won more of the popular vote than Benjamin Harrison, but the Electoral College put Harrison in the White House instead.

These were isolated instances, however, and today it is taken for granted that the presidential team that wins the largest vote in the popular election will automatically win the Electoral College vote. The presumption is that the College is morally obligated to follow the will of the people. But the election is not official until the Electoral College announces its choices.

It should be noted, too, that a presidential candidate can be elected without winning a majority of the popular vote. This happened to 15 of our presidents. All they needed was the *highest* vote given to any of three or more candidates, even if it was less than 50 percent. Consequently they became presidents with the majority of American voters having voted against them.

With all these flaws, the remarkable thing about our electoral system is that it works as well as it does.

5

How We Got That Way

The first presidential convention and the first campaign hoopla took place in 1828 during the election race between Andrew Jackson and John Quincy Adams. Jackson, a former frontiersman born in a log cabin, was viewed by the poor masses as one of their own, rather than a patrician like former presidents.

To stir up popular enthusiasm for his election, his supporters organized a kind of political carnival at which the man in the street could enjoy himself. High-spirited celebrations similar to the New Orleans Mardi Gras made politics suddenly fun, inducing millions of Americans to participate for the joy of it. Bands played, citizens danced and pranced along with them, banners waved, and elaborate floats rolled by with raised hickory poles to symbolize "Old Hickory" Jackson.

There were by then twice as many eligible voters as when Madison had been elected only 20 years earlier, because of the opening of the West and the elimination of property requirements. This vast increase in the "common man" vote gave Jackson a smashing 68 percent victory in the Electoral College. To dramatize the new spirit of democracy in the White House, Jackson rode to his inauguration on horseback.

All Americans who wanted to were invited to attend. They stormed into Washington by the thousands, crashing the White House reception. Standing on costly damask-covered chairs with muddy boots, they cheered their hero enthusiastically. Many rushed forward to pump his hand, elbowing aside the rich and fashionable. People shoved, scrambled, fought, romped. Women fainted; men got bloody noses; clothing was torn; expensive glass and china went splintering against walls and floors. A dazed Daniel Webster stammered, "I never saw anything like it!"

One Washington society woman, Margaret Bayard Smith, wrote in outrage, "What a pity what a pity! . . . The whole house had been inundated by the rabble mob. . . . The President, after having been *literally* pressed to death and almost suffocated and torn to pieces in their eagerness to shake hands with Old Hickory, had retreated through the back way and had escaped to his lodgings. . . . Those who got in could not get out by the door again, but had to scramble out of windows."

The mobs were finally lured out of the White House by tubs of punch planted on the front lawn for 20,000 people. There has never been an election celebration quite like it since.

Popular prejudice against the rich and powerful became the emotional stock-in-trade of Jackson, around whom a new Democratic party rallied. The Democrats insisted upon the rights of workers to organize, called for a ten-hour limit to the workday, demanded protection for religious minorities, championed total freedom of expression, and pressed for a secret ballot, which was already the practice in far-off Australia.

After Jackson's election, campaign hoopla and political conventions became the established procedure for nominating party candidates.

Only during Jackson's first try for the presidency in 1824, when he lost to Adams, was the popular vote first recorded. We have no idea how many Americans voted for Washington, John Adams, Jefferson, Madison, or Monroe. The only record we have of their elections is the Electoral College vote.

The reason for the Electoral College goes back to the Constitutional Convention in 1787. The states with small populations were suspicious of those with large populations. If a president were to be elected by popular vote, they feared, one big state like New York could outvote three small states like New Jersey, Delaware, and Georgia.

So a compromise was reached—the Electoral College. The aristocrats and the smaller states felt that this system would place the real power in the hands of well-to-do, outstanding citizens who would select the most qualified candidate in the nation for America's top job.

Although the Electoral College system has frequently been attacked as undemocratic, unfair, clumsy, and antiquated, no amendment to give Americans the power to elect the president and vice-president directly has ever succeeded. One reason is that a straight popular vote would reduce the importance of each state in presidential elections, with the smallest states losing the most power.

We began our national existence in 1789 as a flawed democracy. We permitted slavery, and slaves were not allowed to vote. Neither were many of the poor. Only the educated rich were allowed to hold office.

At the first meeting of the Electoral College, Washington was elected president with a 47.2 percent vote, topping the 34 percent vote of John Adams, who became vice-president. Although parties were not indicated on the ballots, both men were Federalists, advocates of strong national government, as opposed to Anti-Federalists, who favored state sovereignty. Both parties were listed for the first time in 1792, when Washington was reelected.

At first they were actually factions rather than organized political parties. The Federalists were mostly merchants, landowners, and bankers who supported the new Constitution. The Anti-Federalists were mostly workers, farmers, and local politicians who distrusted the Constitution, fearing that a rich man's aristocracy might replace the overthrown British crown.

Anti-Federalist Madison wanted a government that gave more power to the people. But Federalist Alexander Hamilton told him contemptuously, "Your people is a great beast."

Led by Jefferson and Madison, the Anti-Federalists became the Democratic-Republican Party, later known simply as the

Democratic Party. The Federalists underwent several transformations, becoming in turn the National Republicans, the Whigs, and finally the Republican Party we know today.

Because no provisions for parties, or election contests between parties, had been made by the Constitution, candidates were chosen at first by congressional caucuses. In 1796 the first real contest between party candidates resulted in a narrow victory by incumbent Federalist John Adams over Democratic-Republican candidate Jefferson.

As originally conceived, the system called for the presidential candidate receiving the most electoral votes to be named president, and the candidate running second to become his vice-president.

The system was changed when passions flamed over the controversial 1800 elections. When Jefferson and Aaron Burr were tied in the Electoral College with 73 votes each, the election was thrown into the Federalist-dominated House of Representatives. Here, too, a deadlock developed. Finally, on the thirty-sixth ballot, Alexander Hamilton broke the deadlock by voting for Jefferson, whom he hated, because he loathed Burr as "a dangerous man who ought not to be trusted with the reins of government." Embittered at Hamilton, Burr subsequently challenged him to a duel and killed him.

To avoid any more messy elections like that, Congress changed the electoral system to have the president and vice-president voted for separately, our present system. It was also now recognized that the election was not just between candidates, but also between parties, so that it didn't make much sense to have a president of one party stuck with a political opponent as his vice-president just because he was the runner-up.

We take it for granted today that the election ballot is cast in secret, to make certain that it remains our own business for whom we vote. But in Jefferson's time there was no secret ballot. Each Electoral College or congressional voter had to get up in public and announce his preference, leaving himself open to reprisals from vindictive, politically powerful candidates. It was because Hamilton had had to vote against Burr openly that Burr was to take revenge by murdering him.

Another bizarre election took place in 1824, when a split developed in the ranks of the Democratic-Republican (Democratic) Party. That year the election process reverted to a contest among three candidates who ran without party designation: Andrew Jackson, John Quincy Adams, and Henry Clay.

This was the first election enumerating the popular vote. Although Jackson led 155,000 to Adams's 105,000, he failed to win an absolute majority of the Electoral College vote because his lead of 99 to 84 was diluted by Clay's 37 electoral votes. So again the election went to the House of Representatives.

To win, Jackson needed the votes of 13 of the 24 states then represented. But he had only 11, while Adams had 12. The crucial vote fell to New York, which was split evenly except for Congressman Steben Van Rennselaer, a rich patroon.

"The election turns on my vote," he reportedly sighed. "One vote will give Adams the majority. This is a responsibility I cannot bear. What shall I do?" He is alleged to have bent his head in silent prayer for guidance, after which, upon opening his eyes, he saw a discarded Adams ballot at his feet. Taking this as a divine sign, he supposedly picked it up and dropped it into the ballot box, making Adams the sixth President of the United States, despite his smaller popular vote.

One suspects, however, that a wealthy land baron who kept 100,000 tenant farmers in feudal serfdom did not really require divine guidance to persuade him to vote against Jackson, the champion of the common man.

Women were beginning to grow irked at being excluded from the electoral process under the pretext that they couldn't understand politics. Suffragettes began to protest against their second-class citizenship. In 1848 Elizabeth Cady Stanton issued a call for a Women's Rights Convention. Held at Seneca Falls, N.Y., it was the first public demand for female suffrage.

When Congress was still turning a deaf ear in 1870, Victoria Claflin Woodhull, publisher of a news weekly, warned that she intended to lead an open revolution. "We mean treason," she threatened. "We mean secession. . . . We will overthrow this bogus Republic!" Jailed, she ran unsuccessfully for president from prison as head of the Equal Rights Party against Ulysses S. Grant.

Not until almost half a century later, in 1920, were women finally granted the same right to cast ballots in American elections that men had enjoyed since the days of the Pilgrims.

By the election year of 1852, issues of slavery and expansionism had begun to divide and weaken both the Democrats and the Whigs. New parties sprang up to challenge both—principally the Republican Party and the American or Know-Nothing Party, so called because members were taught to reply, "I know nothing," when asked about its violent tactics.

The Republicans absorbed and replaced the Whigs in the 1856 elections, and four years later they nominated Abraham Lincoln as their presidential candidate. The Democrats split over the slavery issue, the South and North each fielding its own candidate. The combined Democratic vote of over two million outpolled Lincoln's 1, 865,000. But because it was split between Stephen Douglas and John C. Breckinridge, Lincoln won his rendezvous with history.

Lincoln's conduct of the Civil War split the Republican Party. One wing, called the National Union Party, nominated him for reelection, with the support of War Democrats. The election of 1864 was the first and last in which not all the states participated—the missing eleven being the seceded Southern states, whose 81 electoral college votes were not cast.

After the war a controversy arose over whether freed slaves in the South should be permitted to vote. President Andrew Johnson was firmly opposed, claiming that this would provoke racial conflict and that the right to vote was subject to state laws. Johnson privately feared that politically active Southern blacks might sharply reduce white power.

It was President Ulysses S. Grant who won ratification of the Fifteenth Amendment, giving blacks the vote, and who executed the Enforcement Act of 1870 to empower it.

The election of 1872 developed an issue that has been controversial ever since. Under Grant the Republican Party split badly when its liberal wing, the Radical Republicans, attacked the administration for seeking to grab Santo Domingo. Feeling they could not support Grant for a second term, they ran their own candidate for president.

Party regulars denounced them as traitors, citing Stephen Decatur's famous toast: "My country, right or wrong!"

Senator Carl Schurz replied, "Our country, right or wrong! When right, to be kept right; when wrong, to be put right!"

Those clashing viewpoints were to be echoed all through that century and our own, whenever the United States became enmeshed in wars, hot or cold.

One of our most questionable elections took place in 1876 between Republican Rutherford B. Hayes and Democratic Samuel J. Tilden. When the popular votes were counted, Tilden had some 250,000 more than Hayes, who went to bed resigned to having lost the election. But in the morning the Republicans refused to concede. They charged that Tilden had been unfairly elected in Louisiana, South Carolina, and Florida, because blacks had been prevented from voting in those states.

Republican leaders met in secret with Southern Democrats to strike a deal. The three contested Southern states agreed to switch their electoral votes to Hayes in exchange for a Republican promise to withdraw federal troops from the South and let the Southern states control their own affairs. Hayes was then awarded the presidency by one electoral vote.

Federalist Alexander Hamilton voted in 1800 for the Democratic-Republican candidate and his longtime adversary, Thomas Jefferson, to break the electoral college tie, thus helping to defeat Aaron Burr. ENGRAVING BY A. CHOPPEL, 1861.

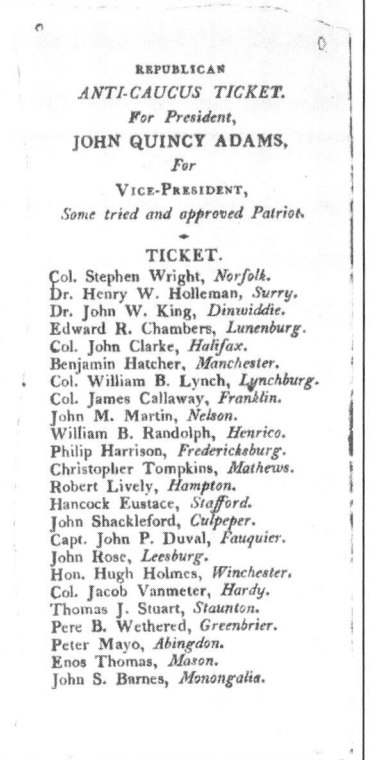

REPUBLICAN
ANTI-CAUCUS TICKET.
For President,
JOHN QUINCY ADAMS,
For
VICE-PRESIDENT,
Some tried and approved Patriot.

TICKET.
Col. Stephen Wright, *Norfolk.*
Dr. Henry W. Holleman, *Surry.*
Dr. John W. King, *Dinwiddie.*
Edward R. Chambers, *Lunenburg.*
Col. John Clarke, *Halifax.*
Benjamin Hatcher, *Manchester.*
Col. William B. Lynch, *Lynchburg.*
Col. James Callaway, *Franklin.*
John M. Martin, *Nelson.*
William B. Randolph, *Henrico.*
Philip Harrison, *Fredericksburg.*
Christopher Tompkins, *Mathews.*
Robert Lively, *Hampton.*
Hancock Eustace, *Stafford.*
John Shackleford, *Culpeper.*
Capt. John P. Duval, *Fauquier.*
John Rose, *Leesburg.*
Hon. Hugh Holmes, *Winchester.*
Col. Jacob Vanmeter, *Hardy.*
Thomas J. Stuart, *Staunton.*
Pere B. Wethered, *Greenbrier.*
Peter Mayo, *Abingdon.*
Enos Thomas, *Mason.*
John S. Barnes, *Monongalia.*

In 1824, John Quincy Adams was elected president despite his trailing in the popular vote, with 105,000 to Andrew Jackson's 155,000. This was Adams's election ballot. WOODCUT.

Elizabeth Cady Stanton initiated the first public demand for women's suffrage in 1848.

The Democrats roared their rage over the stolen election. Some threatened armed violence and a march on Washington to force Tilden's inauguration. Congress hastily set up an electoral commission made up of seven Democrats, seven Republicans, and one ostensibly impartial Supreme Court justice to decide whether the Electoral College vote was valid.

Just 56 hours before Tilden had expected to be inaugurated as the nineteenth president, the commission voted eight to seven to accept the rigged electoral vote that had reversed the popular vote. It later turned out that the "impartial" justice on the commission had secretly been a Republican.

The election that made Benjamin Harrison president in 1888 was equally dubious. Republican politicians bought the votes they needed to win in Harrison's own Indiana, a key state. In New York they bribed the corrupt Democratic politicians of Tammany Hall, the political organization built by Aaron Burr, to fix the vote count in favor of Harrison. Even so, Grover Cleveland, the Democratic incumbent, won 100,000 more popular votes than the Republican contender. The Republicans nevertheless maneuvered to get Harrison 233 electoral votes to Cleveland's 168.

"Providence," Harrison piously told Republican National Committee Chairman Matt Quay, "has given us the victory."

Quay later laughed to a fellow politician, "Think of the man! He ought to know that Providence hadn't a damn thing to do with it!"

The 1896 presidential campaign became famous for a speech made at the Democratic National Convention by Nebraska Senator William Jennings Bryan. He led a Western demand for the free and unlimited coinage of silver, in opposition to Republican William McKinley, who favored the gold standard exclusively. What was at stake were the interests of Eastern creditors—chiefly the banks—against Western and Southern debtors, chiefly farmers. Silver was worth much less than gold. If debtors could pay off what they owed in silver instead of gold-backed currency, they could save themselves huge sums.

At the end of an impassioned speech, Bryan thundered, "You shall not press down upon the brow of labor this crown of thorns, you shall not crucify mankind upon a cross of gold!" His "Cross of Gold" speech took the Democratic convention by storm, and he was nominated its candidate for president.

Bryan traveled 13,000 miles by rail in 14 weeks, making 600 speeches in 29 states. The Republicans portrayed him as an "anarchist" and "revolutionist." McKinley, who disdained campaigning as undignified, stayed home and from his front porch addressed state delegations brought to him by train.

Bryan lost the election. But ever since, "dark-horse" candidates for the presidency have hoped to emulate his example by sweeping convention delegates off their feet with a brilliant speech, winning the nomination by acclaim.

States varied in the methods they preferred for choosing delegates to the national party conventions that would select candidates. In one state, delegates of the victorious party would be pledged to vote for one particular presidential candidate. In another, elected delegates supporting a candidate would still be left free to make up their own minds at the convention. Such delegations were often split in their choices, rather than voting as a solid bloc. This difference is still valid today.

The election campaign of 1928 between Democrat Al Smith and Republican Herbert Hoover was significant for the issues involved. The first Roman Catholic to run for the White House, Smith was subjected to a vicious anti-Catholic campaign that insisted his victory would give the Pope a "pipeline to the White House." Another key issue was Smith's stand that Prohibition, the Eighteenth Amendment which had given rise to "speakeasies" and gangster warfare to control the illicit liquor trade, should be repealed as a failed experiment.

The Democratic platform also pledged collective bargaining for labor and federal relief for hard-pressed farmers. Hoover

Republican Rutherford B. Hayes defeated Democrat Samuel J. Tilden in the controversial "stolen" presidential election in 1876. This was Hayes's campaign song. WOODCUT PUBLISHED BY THE CAMPAIGN SONG COMPANY, COPYRIGHT 1876.

This drawing shows the crowd outside the *New York Herald* office on election night in 1860, reading the returns. WOOD ENGRAVING IN *HARPER'S WEEKLY*, NOVEMBER 1860.

This 1896 *Washington Post* cartoon shows William Jennings Bryan, dark horse of the Democratic convention with his "Cross of Gold" speech. PEN AND INK DRAWING BY G. Y. COFFIN, AUGUST 1896.

branded this program "state socialism," insisting that "rugged individualism" was the traditional American way.

This contest, which Smith lost, sharpened the issues between Democrats and Republicans. It foreshadowed the confrontation between Hoover and Franklin Delano Roosevelt four years later in the depths of the Great Depression.

Roosevelt, confined to a wheelchair because of polio, nevertheless campaigned vigorously, covering 27,000 miles in 41 states. Addressing 14 million unemployed Americans, he promised them a "New Deal." Hoover accused Roosevelt of prescribing communism for the United States, and he warned that a Democratic victory would mean "grass will grow in the streets of a hundred cities." But Roosevelt won by a landslide of over 7 million votes, carrying 42 out of the 48 states.

Then in 1936 he won reelection easily, and in 1940 he broke precedent by running for a third time. The Republicans screamed foul and ran a Republican liberal against him. The Democrats reelected Roosevelt with the slogan: "Better a third termer than a third rater!" Roosevelt was so popular during World War II that he easily won a fourth term as well, but he died less than three months into it. No president before or since was ever elected to more than two terms.

When the Republicans sought to win the White House away from his successor, Harry S. Truman, in 1952, they drafted as their candidate Dwight D. ("Ike") Eisenhower, a popular military hero of World War II. Eisenhower was irked by the Republican National Committee, complaining, "All they talked about was how they should win on my popularity. Nobody said I had a brain in my head!" Personality was the magic ingredient.

The Democratic Convention nominated the witty governor of Illinois, Adlai Stevenson, as their candidate. Eisenhower's friend George Allen assured him, "Stevenson will be easy to beat. He's too accomplished an orator!"

The history of our elections has largely validated Allen's assessment. Intellectuals seldom win the White House, with the notable exceptions of Thomas Jefferson and Woodrow Wilson. Most Americans do not identify with brainy candidates, feeling more comfortable with conventional or ordinary types.

The Eisenhower-Stevenson contest was the first in which TV was an important campaign tool. Actor Robert Montgomery directed Eisenhower's TV appearances. Americans were captivated by the candidate's engaging charm and warmth. They saw him as a candid, modest, "typical American nice guy," a kindly father figure who would keep the nation safe and secure in peace, as he had in war. In contrast, viewers saw the sophisticated Stevenson as a college professor with "more brains than heart."

"I Like Ike" buttons sprouted on millions of coat lapels and dresses. By campaigning as himself, rather than as the Republican candidate, Eisenhower made it possible for millions of Democrats to split their ticket and vote for him personally, while voting for Democrats in all other offices.

"Democrats for Eisenhower" clubs sprang up all over the South. When he spoke at Harvard, his car was mobbed by collegiate souvenir hunters. Police had to make a solid shield of their bodies to keep admirers from tearing off his clothes and "at times," he sighed, "I thought even part of my arm!"

Eisenhower won a stunning victory—the first Republican presidential win in 24 years—with almost 7 million more votes than Stevenson and over 86 percent of the Electoral College vote.

After his second term, Vice-President Richard M. Nixon sought to succeed him. The Democrats' candidate was John F. Kennedy. The contest was basically decided by a series of four TV debates held in September and October of 1960, the first time TV had ever played a decisive role in determining the presidency. Before an audience of up to 70 million Americans, a confident, vigorous Kennedy triumphed over the sallow, nervous Nixon, who blamed his TV image for his defeat.

Seeking a political comeback two years later, Nixon raced Edmund G. Brown for the governorship of California. Losing, he told news reporters bitterly, "Well, you won't have Richard Nixon to kick around any more!" This added to his political handicap the reputation of being a sore loser.

When President Kennedy was assassinated in 1963, he was succeeded by Vice-President Lyndon Johnson, who won a term of his own the following year. Involving the United States deeply in the unpopular Vietnam War, Johnson promised voters that he had no intention of sending "American boys 9,000 or 10,000 miles away from home to do what Asian boys ought to be doing for themselves." But he ended up sending half a million U.S. troops to do just that, angering some supporters who thought he was neglecting his promise to build a "Great Society" at home to help poor and black Americans.

Anti-war and anti-draft demonstrations erupted all across America. Along with ghetto riots, civil disorders, student revolts, and a people's march on Washington, they forced Johnson to realize that he could not be reelected. So in 1968 he threw his weight behind the candidacy of his vice-president, Hubert Humphrey, who promised to persist with the Vietnam War.

Meanwhile Senator Robert Kennedy, brother of the assassinated president, entered state Democratic primaries as a presidential candidate. When Humphrey announced that he would campaign with "the politics of joy," Kennedy told crowds, "If you want to be filled with Pablum and tranquilizers, then don't vote for me. . . . If you see a small black child starving to death in the Mississippi delta, as I have, you know this is not the politics of joy. I'm not going to be like that."

He accused the Johnson administration of spending $300,000 per Vietnamese soldier killed, while millions of poor Americans went to bed hungry every night. His campaign was so successful that it looked as though a second Kennedy would go to the White House. But just as he won the important California primary, he fell to an assassin's bullet, just like his brother. His death cleared the way for the Democratic nomination of Humphrey.

But anti-war Democrats staged stormy street demonstrations against that nomination at the Democratic National Convention in Chicago. They demanded the nomination of Senator Eugene McCarthy of Minnesota, who promised to end the Vietnam War. The Chicago police of Mayor Richard J. Daley, a Johnson/Humphrey loyalist, rushed out in force to break up the demonstrations violently. In bloody clashes, young dissenters were beaten, subjected to tear gas and Mace, and dragged into police vans. TV cameramen filming these scenes were also attacked by police. Indignant delegates inside the convention hall angrily denounced Mayor Daley for using "Gestapo tactics." An impartial presidential commission investigating these election disorders later called them "a police riot." But the Johnson forces were able to ram through Humphrey's nomination.

Meanwhile Richard Nixon, shaking off the "Tricky Dickie" image that had plagued him as a public figure, campaigned for the Republican nomination. He cinched it by a "Southern strategy" that pledged to downplay school integration and civil rights programs, in return for the support of leading Southern Republicans. The program was also designed to win over conservative Southern Democrats, known as "Boll Weevils," in the general election.

His strategy radically changed the electoral picture in the United States. Since the days of the Civil War, white Southerners had punished Abraham Lincoln's Republican Party by persistently voting Democratic. But in 1968 this pattern fragmented. Millions of traditional Democrats either went over to Nixon or voted for Democratic Governor George Wallace of Alabama, who bolted his party to head a new American Independent Party opposed to civil rights.

At the Republican convention, Nixon was nominated over rivals Ronald Reagan and New York Governor Nelson Rockefeller. To reward his Southern supporters, he took Maryland's Governor Spiro T. Agnew as his running mate. He campaigned with promises to end the Vietnam War, negotiate with the communist powers, and restore "law and order" to the turbulent streets of America.

Humphrey's problems were compounded by the disgust of Democratic liberals with the violence at the Chicago convention and with his pledge to continue the Vietnam War. Millions stayed away from the polls or voted a third-party ticket in protest, and Nixon won the election.

He soon infuriated young Americans, especially those on college campuses, by intensifying the Vietnam War instead of ending it as he had promised. Anti-war rallies swept the country as Nixon appealed to America's "silent majority" to support him. When over half a million people marched in a Washington protest, Nixon ordered the Justice Department to make mass arrests. The 13,400 arrests were afterward declared illegal. When six students were killed by National Guardsmen in Kent State, Ohio, and Jackson State, Mississippi, college demonstrations, over 440 campuses shut down in a national protest strike.

Nervous about his chances for reelection, Nixon's aides sent a burglary squad into Democratic offices in the Watergate complex in Washington to steal campaign secrets. The burglars were caught red-handed. When their links to the White House were exposed by two reporters of the *Washington Post,* the president and his top aides tried to conceal their responsibility for this and other election campaign misdeeds.

Their cover-up succeeded well enough to let Nixon win reelection in 1972 over liberal Democratic candidate George McGovern. The Nixon campaign violated many provisions of the Federal Election Campaign Act of 1971, which set limits to the sources and spending of campaign funds. Through their Committee to Reelect the President (CRP), the Nixon forces secretly raised and spent huge sums illegally, in part for a "department of dirty tricks."

When these facts and the president's guilt in the Watergate cover-up were exposed early in his second term, Nixon was faced with impeachment by Congress and was forced to resign. Before doing so, he had forced the resignation of Vice-President Agnew, who was facing prosecution for previous crimes in Maryland. Nixon named Representative Gerald Ford of Michigan as the new vice-president. When Ford replaced Nixon in the White House, he protected Nixon from prosecution for his misdeeds by issuing him a pardon.

The election of 1976 pitted Ford against Democratic Governor Jimmy Carter of Georgia. Carter won the White House by a narrow one percent of the popular vote. He was defeated after only one term, partly because of his failure to obtain the release of 52 American hostages held in Iran after a revolution. Republican Ronald Reagan's landslide victory also gave the Republicans control of the Senate and a working arrangement with conservative Southern Democrats ("Boll Weevils") in the House of Representatives.

The Reagan victory demonstrated the remarkable resilience of the American political system. After the Republicans' Watergate disaster, political experts predicted that they were finished as a party. Yet only six years later they were back in power, even though most registered voters were Democrats.

6

What It Takes to Be a Candidate

The word "candidate" comes from the Latin *candidatus,* meaning "clothed in white." In ancient Rome, candidates for the Roman Senate had to appear in public places draped only in a white "gown of humility," which they had to lift upon request to show their war wounds, proof of their service to Rome.

In Shakespeare's play *Coriolanus,* that proud Roman warrior wants to be elected consul, but he begs the Senators, "I do beseech you, let me o'erleap that custom, for I cannot put on the gown, stand naked, and entreat them, for my wounds' sake, to give their suffrage."

In the United States today, candidates must come before the public and display their qualifications to the voters whose favor they seek. Aspirants for the White House must be at least 35, native-born citizens, and residents of the nation for at least 14 years. Our youngest presidents when they assumed office were Theodore Roosevelt, at 42, and John F. Kennedy, at 43; our oldest, Ronald Reagan, at 69.

Most Americans expect presidential candidates to seek the office actively, but out of a desire to serve the nation rather than out of personal ambition; to be experienced in some high government office; to have a pleasing personality; to have leadership quality and skilled persuasive powers.

Bearing a famous name can help. Franklin D. Roosevelt was no national figure when he ran for the White House in 1932. But the name of his distant cousin, former President Teddy

Roosevelt, didn't hurt. "One of my best political assets," he said, "is that a lot of backcountry folks think I'm Theodore!"

White, Anglo-Saxon, Protestant (WASP), male candidates stand the best chance of nomination and election, because they represent the stereotype of leadership to American voters. Nevertheless we have already had one Catholic president, whose brother Robert Kennedy declared in 1961, "There is no question about it. In the next forty years a Negro can achieve the same position my brother has." In 1983 black leader Jesse Jackson challenged the Democratic Party to nominate a black for president in 1984, and then announced his own candidacy.

Black candidates for mayor had already been elected in seven major American cities—Los Angeles, Detroit, Atlanta, Washington, New Orleans, Newark, and Chicago.

A presidential candidate's personal life must be able to withstand intense scrutiny. Voters prefer family men who have not been divorced, although their divorces did not prevent Adlai Stevenson from becoming the Democratic candidate in 1952 and 1956, nor Reagan from becoming president in 1980.

If a candidate is not well-known, he faces an uphill battle to win media attention. When Jimmy Carter, former governor of Georgia, announced his candidacy, even his hometown newspaper ridiculed him by headlining the story: "Jimmy *Who* Is Running for *What?*" The "Jimmy Who?" tag plagued him through much of his campaign. But Carter plunged doggedly ahead, talking to people in shopping centers and supermarkets and at Democratic dinners, winning state primary after primary until the media were forced to take notice.

The candidate considered the "front-runner" for his party's presidential nomination is usually the one who emerges first in public-opinion polls and state primaries. The front-runner has the advantage of getting the most media attention and of attracting campaign funds. The disadvantage is that in the white-hot glare of publicity, any mistake he makes is magnified, and the loss of any state primary may destroy his image as a winner.

In 1974 Senator Walter Mondale decided not to compete with Jimmy Carter for the 1976 Democratic nomination, stating, "I found that I did not have the overwhelming desire to be president." He did not, he explained, want to spend two years of his life living in Holiday Inns on the campaign trail. But it's the rare politician who resists the temptation of America's top office when opportunity knocks. After serving as Carter's vice-president, Mondale changed his mind and became an active campaigner for the Democratic nomination in 1984.

A candidate needs to be perceived to have good physical and mental health to stand up to the strains of the Oval Office. The remarkable exception to this rule was Franklin D. Roosevelt, elected four times despite being in a wheelchair, disabled by polio. He had spent two years in bed just trying to move his big toe, after which, he said, "anything else seems easy."

Sturdy physical health was actually more important for a president in the old days, when Washington was built on a partially reclaimed marshland infested with mosquitoes, malarial fever, rats, and bad drinking water.

Character is invariably considered more important than intelligence by most voters. Adlai Stevenson was a brilliant candidate; his campaign speeches were witty, original, and brainy. In contrast, Dwight Eisenhower was a dull, uninspired speaker. But Republicans pinned the label of "egghead" on Stevenson, suggesting he was not practical enough to be trusted with the presidency, and Stevenson lost twice to Eisenhower.

Most candidates for the White House, and for Congress, are lawyers—some 60 percent of all presidents, about 67 percent of senators, and 53 percent of representatives. There is some justification for it. Lawyers are familiar with the operations of the law, which is what government is all about. They are also trained to be persuasive public speakers. Familiar with the business world, they often have as clients wealthy men who can provide them with campaign funds.

Through determined personal campaigning, Jimmy Carter fought for attention by the media to become president in 1976.

Ronald Reagan was elected president in 1980, the oldest man elected to that office. He was 69 at the time.

The next most frequent occupation of those who seek public office is that of businessman. In earlier times military heroes like George Washington were sought as presidential candidates, because of the awe in which they were held by unsophisticated Americans. Andrew Jackson and William Harrison, for example, were considered presidential caliber because of their prowess as Indian fighters.

Ulysses S. Grant had little to recommend him except his renown as the general who had won the Civil War. When scandals broke out under his administration, he admitted sadly, "It was my fortune, or misfortune, to be called to the office of the Chief Executive without any previous political training."

Civil War General William Tecumseh Sherman commented acidly on the naivete of Americans in believing that because a man was expert at the science of killing, he therefore possessed the necessary civilian skills to govern the nation. "Any senator," he insisted, "can step from his chair at the Capitol into the White House, and fulfill the office of president with more skill and success than a Grant, Sherman, or Sheridan who . . . were not schooled in the practice by which civil communities are and should be governed."

Confederate General Robert E. Lee also mused on the failure of most Army men in public life: "It is rare that any one of them have achieved success." Even Dwight Eisenhower declared, four years before he gave up his general's stars for the Oval Office, "The necessary and wise subordination of the military to civil power will be best sustained when lifelong professional soldiers abstain from seeking high political office."

When Eisenhower was persuaded to seek the presidency, President Truman grinned. "He'll sit here, and he'll say, 'Do this! Do that!' And nothing will happen. Poor Ike—it won't be a bit like the Army. He'll find it very frustrating."

Today no political party risks nominating a military man as its presidential candidate. Too many voters have become wary of the military mind, especially with the grave risk of precipitating a nuclear war.

Candidates who aspire to the White House have to spend years in advance of their party's nominating convention trying to win support. They have to travel thousands of miles from state to state wooing party leaders. Standing in front of stores and factory gates, they have to shake hands and kiss babies. They have to speak to every group that will listen, attend fairs, give away bumper stickers and buttons, get on radio and TV programs, attend organization dinners, and often end each day on the campaign trail totally exhausted.

Yet when William Henry Harrison addressed a campaign meeting in 1840, he said, "It has ever appeared to me that the office of the President of the United States should not be sought after by any individual, but that the people should spontaneously, and with their own free will, accord the distinguishing honor to the man whom they believed would best perform its important duties."

Similarly, when William McKinley sought the Republican nomination in 1896, he refused to leave home to seek it. "I cannot get the consent of my mind," he declared, "to do anything that places me in the position of seeming to seek an office."

President Harry S. Truman disagreed emphatically. "This draft business is hooey," he scoffed. "There never was a man drafted for president in the history of the country. A draft is created by the fellow who wants it and is willing to fight for it."

The president in office who wants a second term has a distinct advantage over all challengers in his party. He is seldom denied renomination. Even party members dissatisfied with him will vote for him again if it appears that he offers the best chance of defeating the opposition.

Abraham Lincoln's conduct of the Civil War angered many of his own party, who wanted to deny him renomination. Horace Greeley, the influential editor who had originally supported him, wrote: "Mr. Lincoln is already beaten. He cannot be elected.

We must have another ticket to save us from utter overthrow." But many Republicans felt that to deny Lincoln renomination would be an admission that their war policy had been a mistake. "Don't swap horses in midstream!" they urged.

Lincoln won another term to finish the war.

It helps a candidate's chances if he comes from a state with a big population, since he is assumed to have a good chance to command that important bloc of votes.

He is also expected to look "presidential"—dignified, powerful, imposing, tall, assured, photogenic. "I think the American public wants a solemn ass as president," wryly observed President Calvin Coolidge. Perhaps the most presidential-looking president ever to occupy the White House was Warren G. Harding, who turned out to be one of the worst of our chief executives, presiding over a corrupt, inefficient administration riddled with scandal.

Nevertheless there is no denying the impact on voters of a candidate's appearance. This was highlighted in the race between Richard M. Nixon and John F. Kennedy in 1960. When Nixon agreed to a series of TV debates with Kennedy, they were watched by over 120 million Americans. Kennedy projected the image of a handsome, intelligent, well-informed, clean-cut young leader. Nixon seemed unattractive, awkward, and malevolent. These contrasting images, probably more than anything the two candidates said, decided the election.

When California's sixty-eight-year-old Senator Alan Cranston sought the 1984 Democratic presidential nomination, he was criticized for being bald, unglamorous, and too old. One constituent, Elise Beraru of Los Angeles, wrote *Newsweek* angrily, "Our insistence that our presidential candidates be 'pretty' rather than effective will condemn us forever to the Jimmy Carters and Ronald Reagans who populate American politics."

Tact is an important attribute for a candidate; without it he may get himself in hot water with large groups of voters. Jefferson lost urban votes by declaring wryly, "The mobs of the great cities add just as much to the support of pure government as sores do to the support of the human body."

When Theodore Roosevelt castigated anti-war Americans as "undesirable citizens," over a million voters promptly pinned on buttons proclaiming, "I'm an undesirable citizen."

When Wilson ran for president, his rivals circulated earlier writings in which he had expressed contempt for "sordid" Polish, Hungarian, and Italian immigrants as a "coarse crew." Wilson had to apologize to spokesmen for these groups.

Adlai Stevenson once joked that a politician was a statesman who approached every question with an open mouth.

A prime concern of every candidate is how to win time and space from the media. In ancient Rome a candidate's supporter would paint notices about him on walls. Modern campaign managers leave no stone unturned to get their candidates a constant stream of favorable publicity.

How the media portray candidates has tremendous impact on how voters perceive them. Voters are often alienated by candidates represented as racists, radical leftists, extreme right-wingers, lamebrains, warmongers, big business apologists, cronies of labor racketeers, or anti-conservationists.

Candidates who rank high in the public-opinion polls tend to receive more media attention than those who do not. Likewise, those who receive more media attention tend to rank high in the polls. This closed circle makes it difficult for new faces to win serious consideration as candidates. It is also difficult for them to raise adequate funds for their campaigns, since they are considered long shots. Contributors prefer to bet on favorites to win.

"We have put a dollar sign on public service," declared President Eisenhower, "and today many capable men who would like to run for office simply can't afford to do so. Many believe that politics in our country is already a game exclusively for the affluent. This is not strictly true; yet the fact that we may be approaching that state of affairs is a sad reflection on our elective system."

Eisenhower himself had to raise $4 million for his own campaign in 1952. One problem with such fund-raising is that the candidate incurs obligations to the people who help him raise the funds. Eisenhower's finance committee was headed by New York banker Winthrop W. Aldrich. Within weeks after Eisenhower entered the White House, Aldrich was appointed to the choice post of Ambassador to Britain. Democratic presidents have also rewarded their fund-raisers with important appointments.

Often rich men themselves become candidates for public office, spending small fortunes to get elected, primarily to enjoy the prestige and power. Nelson Rockefeller, for example, spent over $5 million in 1966 to get elected to the $50,000-a-year job of governor of New York. The Supreme Court has ruled that wealthy candidates cannot be prevented from spending as much of their own money as they want on their own campaigns, calling this a form of "free expression."

The total amount spent by all candidates in the 1980 national elections broke the billion-dollar mark for the first time, doubling the amount spent in 1976. In his book *Financing the 1980 Election,* Professor Herbert Alexander blames the increasing use of costly high technology—computers, opinion polls, direct mail, and wildly expensive TV advertising.

The Federal Election Commission also reported that candidates running for Congress in the off-year elections of 1982 spent more money than in any past Congressional elections. Senate candidates spent an average of almost $2 million apiece, and House candidates an average of over $200,000 each.

Victory can nevertheless elude the candidate with the biggest campaign fund. In 1982, Mark Dayton of Minnesota spent $7.2 million, much of it his own money, seeking a Senate seat, only to lose to incumbent David Durenberger, who spent less than $4 million.

In 1972 the dairy industry donated $2 million to President Nixon's reelection campaign in return for a promised increase in milk price supports. When this and similar deals surfaced in 1974, a shocked Congress passed amendments to the Federal Election Campaigns Act that limited organizations to a maximum contribution of $5,000 per candidate and individuals to a maximum $1,000 contribution per candidate. Public disclosure had to be made for all large contributions.

To lessen the need for candidates to obligate themselves to private supporters, the major parties were offered $2 million apiece in public funds for their national convention and up to $20 million each during a presidential election, provided they agreed to forego private financing.

Candidates have been able to circumvent all limitations, however, by the use of Political Action Committees (PACs), which ostensibly operate in their behalf but outside their control. These clubs are set up by business, labor unions, and other special-interest groups to further the campaigns of candidates of their choice. The PAC campaigns are in addition to, and independent of, the candidates' official campaigns.

The Republicans, generally favored by big business, have always been able to raise much more money than the Democrats. In the 1980 presidential election, Ronald Reagan's campaign expenditures were six times greater than Jimmy Carter's. Nevertheless, from 1932 through 1980, the Democrats still won 8 of the 13 presidential contests.

Colorado Senator Gary Hart, who managed the presidential campaign of Senator George McGovern in 1972, explained how the nomination of a candidate is achieved: "You start out with small meetings. Then you go on to the next circle using that network to reach several thousand people. You ask them to reach out, hopefully, to tens of thousands of people. This is a long, long process." He estimated that candidates have to spend up to half their time soliciting campaign funds.

Democratic candidate John Glenn sighed in 1983, "I'd rather rassle a gorilla on the floor than ask somebody for 50 cents." But the higher the office to which a candidate aspires, the more money he needs to mount a credible campaign.

A presidential candidate also needs a thick skin. He must be able to take criticism and verbal abuse, much of it unfair, by rivals and the media. Should he win the White House, he must still expect further abuse from segments of the country that remain opposed to him.

When Lincoln was president, even in the North he was vilified as a drunkard, atheist, socialist, and baboon. Harper's *Weekly* described him as "a Filthy Story-Teller, Despot, Liar, Thief, Braggart, Buffoon, Usurper, Monster, Ignoramus Abe, Old Scoundrel, Perjurer, Robber, Swindler, Tyrant, Fiend, Butcher, Land-Pirate."

But as President Truman once suggested, "If you can't stand the heat, stay out of the kitchen."

A sense of humor helps. Representative Morris K. Udall of Arizona tells of campaigning in New Hampshire in 1976 and approaching two men who were whittling. "Mo Udall, running for president," he introduced himself. One replied dryly, "Yep, we know. We were just laughing about it."

Presidential candidates also need to be free of any breath of scandal in their past. In 1969 Senator Edward Kennedy became involved in a tragic accident when a car he was driving on Chappaquiddick Island, Massachusetts, plunged off a bridge and into a tidal pool, drowning a female aide. Kennedy's account of his role in the accident aroused considerable skepticism. Subsequently, whenever the prospect of his presidential candidacy came up, the Democrats hesitated to nominate him, for fear the Republicans and the media would continually remind voters of Chappaquiddick.

A "dark-horse" candidate is one given only an outside chance of winning his party's nomination. He hopes that if the front-runner and other top candidates fail to muster enough votes, the convention might then turn to him as a compromise candidate acceptable to all and opposed by few. This was how Lincoln won the Republican nomination in 1860.

"My name is new in the field," he wrote to a supporter, "and I suppose I am not the first choice of a great many. Our policy, then, is to give no offense to others—leave them in a mood to come to us if they shall be compelled to give up their first love."

Candidates and their campaign managers need to be skillful at wheeling and dealing in political conventions. They often have to persuade delegates in opposition to change camps, while holding onto their own pledged delegates against similar raids by their rivals. They may promise rewards or hint at reprisals in order to round up the votes they need.

It has not escaped women that no major party has ever nominated a woman as its candidate for president or vice-president. Professional politicians insist that the vast majority of American voters aren't ready for that innovation.

Nevertheless in 1972 at the Democratic National Convention, Representative Shirley Chisholm of New York became a candidate for the presidential nomination, and Frances Farenthold of Texas sought the vice-presidential nomination.

"Many women now see that a career and family are not mutually exclusive for them any more than . . . for a man," declares Susanne Paizis in her book *Getting Her Elected*. "Many more women are eager to participate in government. . . . Little girls can grow up wanting to be president just like little boys do. And one day, one of them *will* be president."

Meanwhile, feminists are urging more and more women to run for Congress to demonstrate female ability in seats of power. "A woman's place is in the House," one woman politician rewrote the old bromide, "and also in the Senate!"

The decade of the 1970s seemed to mark an important turning point for women in politics. Many communities voted for their first woman mayor, town councilor, county commissioner,

Democratic candidate Jimmy Carter with incumbent President Gerald R. Ford on the set of their 1976 television debate. Media portrayal of candidates influences voters. PHOTO BY FRED.

Once women were granted the right to vote, they were courted by both political parties, the Democrats and the Republicans (Grand Old Party). POLITICAL CARTOON BY J. F. KNOTT IN THE *DALLAS MORNING NEWS*, AUGUST 29, 1920.

THE TWO ADAMS: "IT WAS MY RIB, EVE"

state representative, lieutenant governor, governor, congressperson, and senator.

"I think one of my major uses," said Shirley Chisholm, "is as an example to the women of our country, to show them that if a woman has ability, stamina, organizational skill, and a knowledge of the issues, she can win public office."

The National Women's Political Caucus, founded in 1971, played an important role in winning greater consideration and participation for women in the political process. The following year fully 40 percent of the delegates at the Democratic National Convention were women. The Republican Convention hastily increased its number of female delegates from the previous 17 percent to 30 percent. And Republican feminists were able to get a women's rights plank inserted in the party platform.

"Talented women are wasted playing supportive roles only," observed an editorial in the Macon, Georgia, *Telegraph*. It added, "Developing leadership among women, both as party workers and as elected officials, is important. . . . We need women in politics."

The nation began to see women governors—Ella Grasso in Connecticut, Dixy Lee Ray in Washington—and as many as six lieutenant governors. The number of women state legislators doubled in the ten years ending in 1979, a period which saw the election of Jane Byrne as mayor of Chicago and Dianne Feinstein as mayor of San Francisco.

When March Fong Eu became California's secretary of state, she declared, "I think none of us can deny the fact that women have traditionally found greater barriers to effective campaigning than men. We're inexperienced, and often not comfortable asking people for money, for example. Nevertheless, none of us can deny that women are entering the political field with increasing success." Dianne Feinstein, for example, became one of the first woman candidates to be considered by the Democratic Party for the office of vice-president.

In the 1980 Congressional races, almost 15 percent of the major party candidates for the Senate were women, while 51 female candidates were nominated for the House.

"There are more activists among women now," noted House Speaker Tip O'Neill. "The ERA [Equal Rights Amendment] is responsible in part. It's activated a lot of women. It's the trend that's coming."

On the other hand, Colorado Congresswoman Pat Schroeder felt that political progress for women was too slow. "We are still a novelty act," she complained in 1979. Asked by skeptics how she could effectively deal with both motherhood and her political career, she replied, "I have a brain and a uterus—and they both work."

To become a candidate for the United States Senate, a man or woman must be at least 30, and have been a citizen for nine years. To run for the House of Representatives, a person must be at least 25, and have been a citizen for seven years. Both must be residents of the state represented. A senator serves for six years, a representative for two.

Because of their longer term of service and their fewer numbers, senators have a better chance than representatives of becoming well-known enough to win consideration as presidential candidates. But it costs a lot more to campaign for the Senate.

Candidates for the office of vice-president are aware that it commands little power. Vice-President John Garner, disgruntled that he was given practically nothing to do by President Franklin D. Roosevelt, groused inelegantly that the office "wa'nt worth a pitcher of warm spit."

Nevertheless, the vice-president may suddenly become president because of the death or assassination of the chief executive, as has happened a number of times. The vice-president also has a good chance to be nominated by his party as successor to the president.

Voters are often disappointed in the candidates they elect to the White House. President Truman warned Americans against regarding any candidate with starry-eyed worship, expecting him to be a superman. When we do, we are fated to be disappointed.

Any president, Mr. Truman reminded us wryly, is only a man like the rest of us, who puts on his pants one leg at a time.

7

What the Democrats Are All About

When President Truman campaigned to remain in the Oval Office in 1948, the Republicans castigated him as a typical Democratic bureaucrat. Truman told reporters with a grin, "You know what a bureaucrat is? A bureaucrat is a Democrat who's got a job a Republican wants!"

In the early 1950s, Republican Party leaders grew annoyed by the implications of the Democratic Party name, which seemed to suggest that it was the party of democracy. Republican National Committee Chairman Leonard Hall began referring to his opponents simply as the "Democrat Party," dropping the "ic." He explained to the media, "I think their claims that they represent the great mass of people, and we don't, is just a lot of bunk!"

Democrats do like to consider themselves the party of the common people, looking out for the interests of ordinary Americans, in contrast to the Republicans, whom Democrats label the party of big business and banks.

The origins of the Democratic Party go back to the Anti-Federalists, who then became Democratic-Republicans. Those who flocked to its banners were chiefly farmers, city workers, small businessmen, and some professional people. During the Jackson administration the name was considered too unwieldy, and it was shortened to simply the Democratic Party.

The party was founded on Jefferson's belief that the government should be close to the people, serving their needs rather than the demands of powerful special interests. The Democratic program, sensitive to public hardships and geared to do for individuals what they are unable to do for themselves, has become known as *liberalism*. In practice this policy has meant unemployment insurance for the jobless, medical care for the poor who are ill, welfare for the poor who cannot work, and Social Security payments for the aged and handicapped—all measures first introduced by the Democrats.

The party tends to be a coalition of many different groups. Traditionally the Democrats have been heavily supported by minorities in the population—Catholics, Jews, blacks, union members, most Hispanics, and immigrants. These groups have tended to view the Republicans as controlling the economic power structure that excluded them, while considering the Democrats their defenders.

The Democratic Party claims credit for almost all the landmark legislation for social and economic reform. They initiated and passed the Adamson (eight-hour workday) Act, women's suffrage, TVA (federal power supplied to Tennessee Valley farms), the Wagner Act (giving union labor bargaining power against big corporations), Social Security, the Rural Electrification Act, federal housing acts, the Full Employment Act, the Low Rent Housing and Slum Clearance Act, civil rights acts (protecting minorities from discrimination and guaranteeing equal education), the Minimum Wage Act, and other important changes in our system.

Because Democratic programs have cost a great deal of money, they are often attacked by Republicans as being wasteful and a heavy burden on taxpayers. The Democratic view is that money is less important than equal opportunity for all Americans.

A basic difference between the parties is that the Democrats, who call themselves "the party of progress," favor the maximum use of the federal government to solve the nation's problems, while the Republicans want a minimum of federal involvement, calling instead upon the states and private organizations to do the job at local levels.

The Democrats' greatest voting strength is in the nation's big cities, where most minorities live and where most people have a liberal outlook. The Republicans rely more on rural and suburban areas, which tend to be conservative.

The father of our country, George Washington, was considered a conservative Federalist, but he refused to call himself one. He opposed the development of separate political parties, fearing they would destroy national unity, much as the Whigs and Tories had been at each other's throats before the Revolution. "If I could not go to heaven but with a party," Washington vowed, "I would not go there at all."

Parties were unnecessary at first because there was general agreement that Washington should be our first president. But as his second term came to an end, there was no agreement on who should succeed him. It was then that the Democratic-Republicans were formed to elect a president sympathetic to farmers and city workers. At that time the Republican part of their name signified that they opposed kings and favored the French Revolution. On the other side of the fence, the Federalists, representing bankers, businessmen, and the middle class, viewed the Democratic-Republicans distastefully as "the party of the mob."

After the Federalist regimes of Washington and John Adams, the Democrats held the White House from Jefferson's election in 1800 for 11 out of 14 presidential terms. The twenty-four-year period of the Jefferson, Madison, and Monroe administrations was known as "the era of good feeling," because there was little serious opposition to the Democratic-Republican Party.

Party platforms—the party's promises to voters—did not become a part of the election process until 1840. The Democrats wrote the first one, deciding it made sense to spell out to voters what the party's candidates stood for. Then as now, however, what parties promised to do if elected often bore little resemblance to what they actually did once having persuaded the electorate to put them in power.

The election of Democratic-Republican Thomas Jefferson in 1800 began the "era of good feeling," when there was little opposition to that party for almost a quarter of a century. WOOD ENGRAVING BY HENRY WOLF, 1901.

Most of the early political machines that developed in the large cities were Democratic and corrupt. Editor Horace Greeley ran exposes of New York's "Bloody Sixth" ward, an almost all-Irish election district whose political bosses organized thugs to terrorize the voting booths, driving off Whig voters. The ward bosses threatened to smash Greeley's presses unless he printed a retraction. Instead he sponsored a bill to register voters as a method of fraud prevention, and armed his employees with muskets from the City Guard to defend the paper.

By 1855 Irish-Catholic immigrants made up 34 percent of New York City's electorate. They voted a solid Democratic ticket in gratitude to the ward bosses who helped them out of trouble and got them city jobs. Anti-Catholic prejudice was held in check by a 100 percent Irish police force, which limited the attacks by extremist Whig, American Republican, and "Known Nothing" Party mobs on the Democrats.

As Irish immigration swelled, so did the power of the Democrats in many big cities of the Northeast. In Boston one year, four Irish ward bosses met privately to dictate the city's Democratic nominations. Three opposed the grabbing of a seat in the House of Representatives by the fourth, John Francis "Honey Fitz" Fitzgerald, known as the Napoleon of the Sixth Ward.

He thwarted them by simply arming a mob of seamen with pistols, paying them to toss out of the polls all but Fitzgerald voters. Subsequently he made himself mayor of Boston. To sell city jobs to those willing to pay him for the appointments, he circumvented civil service requirements by inventing jobs like Tea Warmers, Tree Climbers, and Wipers.

Big-city voters tolerated the corrupt Democratic political machines partly out of fear and partly because of favors and services the ward bosses provided to loyal voters.

In the 1840s the Democrats put themselves in front of an aggressive new movement of expansion. As New York newspaperman John L. O'Sullivan put it, Americans had the "manifest destiny to occupy and to possess the whole of the Continent which Providence has given to us." When the Democrats elected James K. Polk to the White House, he began the Mexican War to grab the New Mexico and California territories from Mexico.

General Lewis Cass of Michigan won the Democratic nomination to succeed Polk, advocating further annexations for the "glory of the nation." Cass now wanted to grab Mexico, Peru, and Cuba as well. This was too much for most Americans, who elected Whig General Zachary Taylor instead.

As conflict grew between the slave and free states, a split developed within Democratic ranks. At their 1860 convention, Southern Democrats, infuriated by abolitionist party members in the North, demanded that the party take a stand for the "divine institution" of slavery. When Northern Democrats balked, delegates from Alabama, Mississippi, Florida, Texas, South Carolina, North Carolina, Louisiana, Georgia, Arkansas, and Delaware walked out.

The Northern Democrats then nominated Stephen A. Douglas as the official party candidate. The Southern Democrats angrily nominated their own candidate, John C. Breckinridge, who actually won 72 Electoral College votes to Douglas's 12. This Democratic split allowed Republican Lincoln to win.

After the Civil War the Democrats benefited from a solid Democratic vote in the South, because of the bitterness of Southern whites against the Republicans for ending slavery and for stationing federal troops down South to protect blacks. But the Democrats rapidly lost ground elsewhere because America entered a phase of great economic expansion, and most voters saw the Republicans as the party best able to achieve the American dream for every citizen.

For 64 years the only president the Democrats were able to elect was Grover Cleveland (twice) until Woodrow Wilson in 1912. And Wilson's election occurred only because of a split in the Republican Party between President William H. Taft and the bolting Bull Moose faction of Theodore Roosevelt.

At the Democratic Convention the corrupt Tammany Hall political organization of New York put forth the nomination of Rep. James Clark of Missouri. Opposition to him was led by William Jennings Bryan, who thundered, "We hereby declare ourselves opposed to the nomination of any candidate for president under obligation to J. Pierpont Morgan . . . or any other member of the privilege-hunting and favor-seeking class!"

A near riot ensued when one furious New York delegate rose to yell, "I offer $25,000 to the man who will kill William Jennings Bryan! Kill him! Hang him!" But only Clark's nomination was killed.

The stormy Democratic Convention took 46 ballots to decide, finally, on a compromise candidate—Governor Woodrow Wilson of New Jersey. His administration produced two important changes in the image of the Democratic Party. The taint of corruption faded because of Wilson's reputation as a thoroughly honest politician. And because of his passionate effort to bring the United States into the League of Nations, the Democrats became identified with international efforts to work for world peace.

The Republicans, endorsing Washington's policy of "no foreign entanglements," attacked the Democrats as the party that pledged peace, then took the country into war. They subsequently pointed out that all our wars from World War I on— World War II, Korea, and Vietnam—had been begun under Democratic administrations.

American disillusionment with World War I and the League of Nations turned the Democrats out of power for the next 12 years. Prosperity during the 1920s gave Republican candidates an easy time of it until the Great Depression suddenly materialized under the administration of Herbert Hoover.

Then frightened Americans turned back to the Democrats for a change in direction. Under Franklin D. Roosevelt, the Democrats once more emerged as the party of the common people. F.D.R.'s "New Deal" promised to provide jobs, unemployment relief, support for a dynamic trade-union movement, aid to small farmers, a moratorium on mortgage foreclosures, Social Security for the aged, and other vital measures to rescue imperiled Americans. They supported him enthusiastically.

The Republicans charged Roosevelt and the Democrats with introducing "communism" into the American system. The Democrats replied that because the nation's economic machinery had broken down, with a threat of revolution developing, the Democrats had saved the capitalist system by reforming it.

The thirteen Roosevelt years in the White House stamped the Democratic Party as indelibly dedicated to government action to solve the economic problems of the nation. The millions who elected Roosevelt four times felt that he had a sympathetic understanding of their difficulties and was determined to use government programs to come to their rescue. Even when some of his programs failed, voters were grateful to him for making the effort.

The Republicans, however, charged that the Democrats had not really been able to solve the unemployment problem until the threat from Nazi Germany had compelled the United States to put its defense industries into high gear.

The Democrats were given high marks by voters for the successful prosecution of World War II. But there was grave doubt after Roosevelt's death in office that the Democrats had another candidate who could fill his shoes. The vice-president who succeeded him, Harry S. Truman, was attacked by the Republicans for being "soft on communism" and tolerating an administration riddled with communists. Demagogues like Senator Joseph McCarthy of Wisconsin stirred national hysteria with unfounded and fraudulent charges, accusing the Democrats of "twenty years of treason." Forced on the defensive after the war, the Democrats had lost control of both houses of Congress.

They ran into further trouble when Southerners grew furious over Truman's determination to press for civil rights legislation. In 1948 the Southern Democrats formed a third party called the Dixiecrats, with Governor Strom Thurmond of South Carolina as their presidential candidate. Truman's hopes of staying in the Oval Office were further dampened when he angered former Vice-President Henry Wallace, who felt that

Truman had betrayed the Democratic Party's liberal traditions. Wallace formed the Progressive Party to oppose him for the liberal vote.

Running against Republican opponent Governor Thomas E. Dewey of New York, as well as Democratic rivals on the right and left, Truman made a 60,000-mile whistle-stop train tour of the country. Supporters delighted by his blunt campaign oratory cried, "Give 'em hell, Harry!" The underdog in the election, he was given no chance by the opinion polls to win. "The President's influence," observed the *New York Times*, "is weaker than any President's has been in modern history."

Truman later recalled the events of election night:

"At six o'clock I was defeated," he said. "At ten o'clock I was defeated. Twelve o'clock I was defeated. Four o'clock I had won the election. And the next morning . . . in St. Louis, I was handed this paper which said, DEWEY DEFEATS TRUMAN!"

Grinning, he held up the mistaken newspaper for photographers to record the historic journalistic blunder.

But the Democrats swiftly became aware that, despite holding the White House, they had a permanent, serious problem in Congress with the conservative Southern wing of their party. Those "Boll Weevil" Democrats did not hesitate to make deals with Republicans against the programs of liberal Northern Democrats. This split persisted even into the Reagan administration thirty years later, when they would often vote against their own party for Republican bills.

In 1952 an Eisenhower landslide swept the Democrats out of the White House, They were not able to return until 1960, when the charisma of John F. Kennedy prevailed. A new wave of idealism swept the Democratic Party. Kennedy—young, handsome, articulate, vigorous—struck sparks among his fellow Democrats by crying, "Ask not what your country can do for you; ask what you can do for your country!" Youth, in particular, was swept up in an idealistic fervor. The Kennedy administration was revered as the "new Camelot."

Although the split between Democrats resulted in Stephen A. Douglas receiving 12 electoral votes to John Breckinridge's 72, Douglas is the more famous man because of the Lincoln-Douglas debates.

William Jennings Bryan, unsuccessful candidate for president in 1896, 1900, and 1908, in the heat of a vigorous speech. PHOTO COPYRIGHT 1908.

Incumbent President Harry Truman was considered a certain loser in the 1948 election as evidenced by the famous banner headline that mistakenly announced his defeat.

But the new President sent confusing signals to his starry-eyed followers, most of whom were dedicated to keeping the nation at peace. He mounted the Bay of Pigs invasion of Castro's Cuba, which proved a disastrous failure. When Cuba reacted by allowing the Soviet Union to base missiles on its soil, Kennedy brought the world to brink of nuclear war by blockading Soviet ships headed for Havana. War was averted only by a last-minute Soviet agreement to remove the missiles, in exchange for a U.S. pledge not to invade Cuba.

Finally, Kennedy intervened in the Vietnam civil war by sending American advisers and aid to South Vietnam.

Democratic intensification of the Cold War did not end with Kennedy's assassination in November, 1963. His successor, Lyndon B. Johnson, escalated American intervention in Vietnam to the extent of committing half a million U.S. troops to fight in that unhappy land. Disclosures of atrocities they committed against Vietnam civilians shocked and revolted the country. American college students, and gradually many Americans of all ages, became so disillusioned with the Democrats that the country was swept by massive anti-war demonstrations.

At the same time, President Johnson's domestic policies favored the poor and minorities, in the tradition of his political idol, Franklin D. Roosevelt. He assured Americans that the nation could afford both guns and butter, but in actuality he ran up an enormous national debt leading to inflation. More and more his "Great Society" program was neglected as he persisted in trying to win the Vietnam War.

Disillusionment with the Johnson administration split the Democratic Party, making it clear he could not be reelected. Senator George McGovern told the *New York Times* reporter Tom Wicker, "I've made up my mind. . . . I'm going to run for president and the coalition I'm going to put together is going to be built around the poor and the minorities and the young people and the anti-war movement."

The McGovern forces shook up the structure of the Democratic Party by forcing the selection of delegates to be more representative. Those who assembled for the 1972 Democratic Convention were far younger and more liberal, with a larger representation of women, than at any previous convention.

Awarded the presidential nomination, McGovern called it "all the more precious in that it is the gift of the most open political process in our national history."

But the party's professional politicians, disgruntled by the "bunch of amateurs" who had taken over, largely abstained from the campaign. McGovern lost every state in the election except Massachusetts. "We opened the doors and windows to the Democratic Party," he joked wryly afterward, "and everybody walked out." With the party in disarray and in the doldrums, Democratic chances for a comeback looked bleak.

The Watergate scandal of the Nixon administration renewed their hopes for 1976. In the Democratic scramble for the nomination, Jimmy Carter bypassed party leaders and made himself the front-runner by campaigning hard in the primaries. Winning over Republican President Gerald Ford, Carter tried to give the new Democratic administration a "common man" flavor by walking instead of riding to his inauguration and by carrying his own clothes on hangers off the presidential plane.

But Carter seemed indecisive and lacking in leadership qualities to many Americans, especially in his handling of the Iranian hostage crisis. So he became a one-term President, and once more the Democrats fell out of power.

Democratic leaders decided that the McGovern reforms had weakened the party too much. Changes were subsequently made in the rules so that almost 600 congressmen, senators, governors, and state party chairmen were granted delegate status.

The Democratic Party has always been the one that kept an ear open to what third parties were saying, in order to co-opt policies that seemed to have great appeal for special voting blocs in American society. Franklin D. Roosevelt's New Deal program was made up in part from ideas advocated by American socialists and progressives. The Democrats can be expected to continue this tradition, whenever there is widespread public dissatisfaction and some third party seems to have a popular answer to the problem.

The party's newest rules, adopted during the Reagan administration, attempted to shorten the campaign season by creating a thirteen-week period during which states could hold primaries or caucuses, with Iowa and New Hampshire compelled to delay theirs to conform. This change was intended to make campaigning less costly and avoid wearying voters. But dark-horse candidates felt this would unfairly favor better-known Democrats, not giving them sufficient time to win national recognition and campaign funding.

Reagan's resounding victory in 1980 made it seem as though the whole country had turned Republican. But the fact was that there were still far more registered Democrats than Republicans. That is why, although voters may elect a popular Republican to the White House, they invariably vote a heavy percentage of Democrats into the House of Representatives. They count on a Democratic House to protect their economic benefits.

The Democrats also enjoy the important support of most black voters, who have become increasingly active politically. The almost 100 percent black voter turnout in Chicago in 1983 for Mayor Harold Washington demonstrated the power of a united black vote. To keep the loyalty of blacks, Democrats generally include planks in their platform that respond to black demands, and they give blacks important roles within the party. In 1982 blacks were shown to hold 5,000 elected offices at the local level, usually through Democratic campaigns.

On the other hand, the white South is no longer solidly Democratic. Many Southerners, antagonized by the Democrats' civil rights policies, have been permanently wooed away by the Republican Party. Also, the migration of many middle-class, conservative Northerners to the South has led to a further decline in the Southern Democratic vote.

The Democrats today suffer somewhat in public opinion from the Republicans' persistent campaign to depict them as the spendthrift "party of bureaucracy." This was the thrust of Ronald Reagan's successful 1980 campaign for the presidency to "get government off the backs of the people."

Democrats today have a wide-open door for young people they hope to involve in their politics. Their Teen Dem program for teenagers operates in a number of states, and they seek to encourage the formation of more such clubs. The party offers an organizational manual that tells how to set one up.

"These young people, working after school hours, were extremely valuable to our Democratic organization," declared former Indiana Senator Birch Bayh, "and I believe will become valuable workers for the senior party in later years."

The Young Democratic Club of America was formed in 1932 to give young people a significant role in the party's councils. President Franklin D. Roosevelt told them at the time, "America will have to be led in the days to come by the youth of today. . . . You will find that your fight against selfishness and injustice, against oppression, and above all, against war, will take you into a man-sized struggle."

Those reasons still appeal to young people today who view the Democratic Party as the instrument for achieving those objectives, and who are willing to get involved.

Further information can be obtained from the Democratic National Committee, 430 South Capitol Street Southeast, Washington, DC 20003.

8

What the Republicans Are All About

Will Rogers, the famous cowboy-comedian of the 1920s, was once asked what made an American citizen become a Republican. "Wa-al," he replied, chewing gum and twirling his lariat, "when a Democrat scrapes together ten bucks, that's when he becomes a Republican."

This wry joke reflected the commonly held concept that Democrats were the party of the poor, while Republicans represented the well-to-do classes. It also suggested that as soon as many Americans at the bottom of the economic ladder saw an improvement in their prospects, they became ambitious to join the ranks of the prosperous Republicans. The Republican vote usually soared in times of prosperity.

According to the Teen Age Republicans (TAR), the Republican Party today stands for six major principles:

1. Decentralization of power and building up local units of government.
2. Protection of private enterprise, freed of all regulations except those absolutely necessary to safeguard the public interest.
3. Curbing inflation.
4. Protection of Constitutional liberties.
5. Rejection of class struggle.
6. Balance of power among the branches of government.

The senior Republican Party adds to those goals:

7. A sound money policy.
8. Opposition to excessive taxation and government waste.
9. Maintaining a strong military.
10. Getting people off welfare rolls by assisting them to become productive and self-supporting.
11. Developing individual responsibility and initiative among Americans.

The Democrats accuse the Republican Party of traditionally siding with business against union labor; favoring the elimination of social welfare programs; seeking the suppression of liberal and left-wing ideas; favoring big business over small business; opposing conservation and pressing for private exploitation of America's resources; giving aid to right-wing military dictatorships while seeking to overthrow left-wing governments; favoring big military expenditures and an aggressive foreign policy, while opposing anti-nuclear and peace movements.

The Republican Party, however, has its liberals as well as right-wingers, and there is often sharp disagreement between them. At the 1964 Republican Convention in San Francisco, liberal Republicans led by New York's Governor Nelson Rockefeller tried to add an anti-extremist plank to the party platform.

The presidential nominee, Arizona Senator Barry Goldwater, objected, declaring, "I would remind you that extremism in the defense of liberty is no vice." The plank was defeated.

Next year, after Goldwater's defeat, liberal Republican Senator Charles Percy of Illinois called upon right-wing extremists to get out of Republican ranks and form their own political party. "The fanatical pseudo-patriotism of these men is misdirected," he charged.

George E. Reedy, former press secretary and special assistant to President Lyndon Johnson, observed, "The Democratic Party has continuing trouble with left-wing crackpots, and the Republican Party has continuing trouble with right-wing crackpots."

Denying that conservatives are reactionary extremists, the Republican Party states, "The conservative ideals of the Republican Party represent true progress. . . . The Republican Party believes that government is the servant and not the master of the people. . . . The constantly growing federal power as espoused by the Democrat Party can come only at the expense of the individual."

The majority of Republicans are Protestants, with above-average educations, above-average incomes, and high-status occupations, living outside the South. Generally they tend to identify the national interest with the interest of the higher socioeconomic classes. Unlike the Democrats, they believe that the federal government should cut business taxes to create jobs by stimulating prosperity, rather than by helping the jobless directly.

As explained by President Ronald Reagan, the corporations would invest tax savings in new plants and equipment, which in turn would put more people to work. The Democratic rebuttal is that this "trickle-down" theory is misleading, because the corporations use their tax savings only to buy up other companies and fatten their profits.

The Republican Party came into being in 1855 because abolitionist lawyer Alvan E. Boray was disillusioned by the failure of both the Whig and Democratic Parties to stop the spread of slavery. He appealed to his old friend Horace Greeley, editor-publisher of the influential New York *Tribune*, to support a new third party he and other abolitionists were forming.

Greeley agreed, telling Bovay, "Call your party Republican. No prefix, no suffix—just plain Republican!"

The new party attracted various splinter groups—abolitionists, Free Soilers, prohibitionists, Know-Nothings (afterward the American Party), dissident Whigs like Lincoln, and anti-slavery Democrats like William Cullen Bryant, the leading Democratic editor in New York.

Greeley joined in organizing the first Republican National Convention in Philadelphia on June 17, 1856. To oppose the Whig nominee, former President Millard Fillmore, and Democratic nominee James Buchanan, the Republicans nominated Colonel John C. Fremont of California. He was the famous "Pathfinder" whose expeditions had helped open the West.

"Enthusiasm tremendous!" Greeley wired his paper. As he viewed the three-cornered election, the chief issue was whether the West would be "blessed with Freedom or cursed with Slavery." Moreover, who better than the Pathfinder could be relied upon to develop the West with rails, roads, and waterways?

Greeley's arguments swelled the ranks of the new Republican Party. But the wealthy conservative interests behind both Buchanan and Fillmore spent ten times as much on each candidate's campaign as the Republicans could raise for Fremont. The Republicans were portrayed as "wild-eyed abolitionists" whose victory would provoke a Southern rebellion.

Buchanan won with 1,838,000 votes, but Fremont received 1,335,000 votes, an impressive showing for a new third party. The Whigs, whose nominee was also supported by the American Party, received only a humiliating 874,000 votes, ending their life as a political party. From this time forward the Democrats and Republicans were America's two major parties.

The Republicans' opportunity came in 1860, when Buchanan's demand that Kansas be admitted to the Union as a slave state tore the Democratic Party in half. The Republicans chose as their presidential nominee Abraham Lincoln, whom Greeley had lifted to national prominence by publicizing his debates with Senator Stephen A. Douglas.

When Lincoln defeated the two feuding Democratic candidates running against him, it was Greeley who rode with him on the presidential train to the first Republican inauguration. But Greeley's support gradually ebbed as he grew convinced that Lincoln was turning a deaf ear to the public outcry against the bloody Civil War, refusing to talk peace with the South. In 1864 Greeley's opposition split the Republican Party into two wings. The Radicals nominated Fremont, while the National Union Party combined with War Democrats to renominate Lincoln in support of the war effort.

Lincoln's aides worked hard to persuade the influential Greeley to change his mind, finally succeeding two months before Election Day. Greeley's defection from the Radicals took Fremont out of the race. The Republicans then reunited behind Lincoln, reelecting him easily.

The Republican Party dominated national politics throughout the last half of the nineteenth century and the first part of the twentieth. Although the party alienated Southern white votes because of the Republicans' enforcement of black voting rights in the South, they more than made up for this loss by turning out a heavy Northern vote for their candidates. They did this by stirring memories of Civil War passions with the slogan: "Vote As You Shot!"

One of the more colorful Republican figures at the close of the nineteenth century was William McKinley's campaign manager, Mark Hanna. In 1896 he plastered the country with billboards advertising McKinley's candidacy, leading Theodore Roosevelt to complain, "Hanna was selling McKinley like a patent medicine." Hanna directed big companies to threaten their employees with closing their plants if McKinley wasn't elected.

Hanna spent $3,500,000 on McKinley's campaign, an unprecedented sum raised by levies on businessmen and corporations.

As President, McKinley presided over the only American war begun under a Republican administration. His secretary of state, John Hay, called the Spanish-American War "a splendid little war." Spain was forced to cede to the American victors the Philippines, Puerto Rico, and Guam and to yield Cuba to the American sphere of influence.

In the election campaign of 1900, William Jennings Bryan led the Democrats in opposing what they termed American imperialism. McKinley and his vice-presidential candidate, Theodore Roosevelt, defended the Spanish-American War and its territorial acquisitions. The Republicans won.

Roosevelt became President the following year when McKinley was assassinated. He committed the Republican Party to an expansionist foreign policy by seeking naval supremacy, making the United States the dominant power in the Pacific and in Central and South America. To give our navy quick passage between the Atlantic and Pacific, he decided to build a canal through a narrow pinch of Colombia's land.

He conspired with a military junta in Colombia, which revolted and seized the land he wanted. Roosevelt then recognized them as the "Republic of Panama," and two hours later he had the grant to build the Panama Canal. When a hot quarrel over his grab broke out in Congress, Roosevelt said, "I took the Canal Zone, and let Congress debate, and while the debate goes on, the Canal does also."

A colorful, dynamic president, he was popular with the people in the street, but surprisingly less so with corporation executives. They saw him as a reformer out to restrict their operations with such bills as the Pure Food and Drug Act and the Hepburn Act controlling rates the railroads could charge. But the muckrakers—reform-minded journalists of that day—charged Roosevelt with only faking a crusade against big-business abuses to fool the public.

Big business, fearing that a Democratic administration would pay more attention to the muckrakers, supported Roosevelt for a term of his own in 1904.

Roosevelt helped elect his friend William Howard Taft as his successor in 1908. But the two men fell out when Taft refused to let Roosevelt be the power behind the throne.

New York Tribune editor Horace Greeley (seated) was instrumental in the formation of the Republican Party in 1855. He, in fact, gave the party its name. PHOTO BY BOGARDUS.

The number of votes Republican John C. Fremont received in the 1856 election heralded the downfall of the Whig Party. Since 1856, the Democrats and the Republicans have been America's two major parties. LITHOGRAPH BY CURRIER AND IVES.

At the Republican Convention in 1912, Roosevelt sought to prevent Taft's renomination, attacking him as a "hopeless" reactionary. When the Republicans chose Taft anyhow, Roosevelt bolted the party angrily. "The fight is on," he snapped, "and I am fit as a bull moose!" He arranged for his own nomination by a third party, the Progressives, which became known as the Bull Moose Party.

Roosevelt's dynamic campaigning beat Taft by almost 632,000 votes. But the split Republican vote gave the election to the Democratic candidate, Woodrow Wilson, who subsequently led the nation into World War I. Had there been no third party to thwart Taft's reelection, the course of world history might have been changed, since Taft deplored war, favoring arbitration to solve international disagreements.

The Republicans were restored to power in 1922 through Senator Warren Harding, who appealed to an electorate weary of World War I and foreign entanglements by promising a "return to normalcy." At that point the Republican Party committed itself to an isolationist policy—staying apart from Europe's incessant quarrels.

Harding had one solid achievement during his administration—a five-power naval-disarmament conference in Washington. But his administration fell into disrepute when he surrounded himself with trusted politicians who proved corrupt, plundering the nation's naval oil reserves for personal profit.

The scandal, however, did not end Republican control of the White House. When Harding died in office, he was succeeded by Vice-President Calvin Coolidge, a taciturn New Englander who rarely said one word more than necessary. In 1924 Coolidge was elected for a term of his own on a platform of "Coolidge prosperity." Business, Coolidge insisted, was "America's chief business."

As president he maintained high tariffs to protect American industries, curbed government regulation of business, eliminated and slashed taxes on corporations and wealthy individuals, and reduced both the national debt and the national budget. Coolidge set a precedent for Republicans who followed him to exercise federal powers as little as possible, allowing the free-enterprise market to regulate itself.

As long as business remained prosperous and jobs were plentiful, Americans kept voting the Republicans back into office. In 1928 Herbert Hoover succeeded Coolidge as President. Unfortunately for him, overheated stock speculation brought on a market crash on "Black Thursday," October 24, 1929, followed by the worst economic depression in American history. Over 15 million Americans found themselves without jobs.

Hoover's dogged belief in "rugged individualism," based on his own career, held that courageous and determined Americans could shape their own fortunes. This outlook did not go down well with desperate Americans thrown out of work.

To make matters worse for the Republicans, Hoover committed a grievous error in judgment. In 1932 over 20,000 jobless veterans and their families joined a Bonus Army march to Washington to demand prompt payment of war bonuses promised them. Hoover ordered out the Army with tanks to chase them out of the capital. Pictures of American troops using bayonets and tear gas against the nation's veterans horrified the public, dooming Republican chances in 1932.

In a desperate attempt to hold onto the White House, Hoover appealed, "This thirty years of incomparable improvement in the scale of living . . . did not arise without right principles animating the American system which produced them. Shall that system be discarded because vote-seeking men appeal to distress and say that the machinery is all wrong and that it must be abandoned or tampered with?"

But American voters, disillusioned with the Hoover administration, swept it out of power by an overwhelming vote. The Democrats were then able to hold power for the next twenty years, during which the thrust of American policy was turned completely away from the Republican emphasis on uncontrolled private enterprise to the Democratic emphasis on government intervention in the American system.

During that period most Republicans favored isolationism, staying clear of the growing war clouds in Europe. The Democrats urged the need to render aid to European democracies facing the threat of Nazi Germany and Fascist Italy. Only after the Japanese attack on Pearl Harbor in 1941 did the Republicans reluctantly support President Franklin Roosevelt's entry into World War II.

When Roosevelt died and was succeeded by Vice-President Harry S. Truman, voters became disaffected by Washington scandals and incompetence exposed by reporters. The Republicans capitalized on public anger by their Congressional campaign slogan in 1946: "Had Enough?" Voters gave them massive gains in both houses of Congress.

The Republicans mounted Congressional investigations that sought to picture Truman's administration as riddled with communist spies and sympathizers. Meanwhile Republican Party leaders split on the choice of a presidential candidate for 1952. Isolationists wanted Senator Robert A. Taft of Ohio, while the party's internationalists backed New York Governor Thomas Dewey.

In an effort to unify the two factions, party leaders persuaded General Dwight D. Eisenhower to run instead. He was the perfect compromise because he spoke in generalities that offended neither side. He was also one of the most popular men in American life, both with ex-G.I.s and the general public. Even Democrats wore "I Like Ike" campaign buttons.

Elected, Eisenhower worked tirelessly to reduce tensions between the United States and the Soviet Union. His rigid secretary of state, John Foster Dulles, took a hard line instead. The two reflected the conflicting views within the Republican Party. In the end Eisenhower took over the direction of foreign policy himself, to keep hotheads from pressing the United States into a war situation.

The Korean War, which had begun under Truman, was stalemated when Eisenhower took office. In just a few months he ended it with an armistice—a peace without victory, but a peace. The Democrats complained that if they had done the same thing, they would have been accused of "appeasing communism." But no one dreamed of bringing such an accusation against a distinguished Republican war hero.

Eisenhower also had the courage to propose universal disarmament, declaring, "Every gun that is made, every warship launched, every rocket fired signifies . . . a theft from those who hunger and are not fed, those who are cold and not clothed. . . . We pay for a single destroyer with new homes that could have housed more than eight thousand people."

He also warned the American people against letting the military-industrial complex acquire unnecessary influence, because this would lead to a shocking waste of the nation's resources and a growth of militarism. "We must never let the weight of this combination," he warned, "endanger our liberties or democratic processes."

Although Eisenhower was easily reelected in 1956, his personal popularity did not carry over to his "coattails"—other Republican candidates on the ticket. Both houses of Congress fell under the control of the Democrats.

The extremist wing of the Republican Party, led by Senator Joseph McCarthy, persisted in trying to portray the Democratic Party as "riddled with communism." McCarthy used unscrupulous methods to smear and damage many innocent people. He was angrily opposed by Eisenhower, especially after McCarthy began to attack U.S. Army generals. When the Senate finally destroyed McCarthy's power by a vote condemning his conduct, Eisenhower warmly congratulated the Senators.

After Eisenhower, the Republicans fell out of power for another eight years. In 1968 Richard M. Nixon was elected

Theodore Roosevelt at the Panama Canal: "I took the Canal Zone, and let Congress debate, and while the debate goes on, the Canal does also." PEN AND INK DRAWING BY CLIFFORD K. BERRYMAN.

October, 1920: Senator Warren Harding arriving in Washington. Later, as president, he surrounded himself with reputable politicians who proved corrupt. PHOTO COPYRIGHT 1920 BY HARRIS & EWING.

Republican Dwight D. Eisenhower, president from 1952 until 1960, was so popular that even Democrats wore his campaign buttons.

president as a result of the split in the Democratic Party over the Vietnam War. Instead of ending it as he had promised, Nixon widened the war for another four years. Angry protest demonstrations kept the country in an uproar. Not until Nixon's second term was a peace finally signed, on virtually the same terms Nixon could have had four years earlier.

On the other hand, Nixon was given high marks for opening a new door to the People's Republic of China. His "journey for peace" to Beijing in 1972 normalized relations with that country, ending 24 years of mutual hostility. Only a Republican president with Nixon's history of rigid anti-communism could have made that move without provoking angry cries of "appeasing communism." This triumph of international diplomacy helped reelect him in 1972.

Republicans became dismayed, however, when the *Washington Post* exposed the notorious Watergate scandal. The Nixon administration was revealed as using dirty tricks and illegal campaign tactics against the Democrats, then committing crimes to cover up their felonies. Nixon sought to spike congressional and court investigations by insisting that "national security" prevented him from supplying subpoenaed evidence.

He also tried to keep aides from being forced to testify on grounds that their conversations with the president were protected by "presidential privilege." But the Watergate scandal grew so great that outraged Republicans as well as Democrats were ready to impeach him. To avoid that disgrace, Nixon resigned and Vice-President Gerald Ford took his place. Many of Nixon's top aides were convicted and jailed.

To soothe shaken Americans, Ford promised a clean and open administration. His conduct in the White House did much to restore public confidence in the government.

When Ford failed to win a term of his own, the Republicans did not return to power until 1980, with the election of Ronald Reagan. Charging that "big government" spending was the cause of inflation, Reagan moved swiftly to reduce taxes and the federal budget, except for military spending. The new thrust of Republican policy sought to dismantle as much federal apparatus as possible, turning its functions over to state and local governments for funding and control.

The Reagan administration produced a dramatic drop in the inflation rate but also a severe business recession that caused widespread unemployment. Reagan blamed that on preceding Democratic administrations. During his first two years in office he proved skillful at manipulating Congress, getting most of the legislation he wanted out of a Republican-controlled Senate and a Democratic House, by winning the votes of the conservative "Boll Weevil" Southerners.

Reagan was also skillful in handling the "New Right," a coalition of ultra-conservative groups that had helped elect him. He needed to keep their support, while at the same time not offending Republican liberals and moderates and independent voters, who viewed the New Right as an extremist pressure group.

Reagan's solution was to appear before New Right convocations to support with resounding oratory their goals of voluntary school prayers, a ban on abortion, a ban on busing for integration, discrimination against homosexuals, opposition to the Equal Rights Amendment, and censorship of TV, films, and magazines that offended their values. Their cheers and applause obscured the fact that Reagan was careful not to try to press such legislation through Congress.

Reagan's policies abroad showed a return to the expansionist military philosophy of Theodore Roosevelt. He gave military aid to right-wing governments like El Salvador, and also to right-wing guerrillas fighting to overthrow the leftist government of Nicaragua, dubbing them "freedom fighters."

Controversy arose when a peace-keeping force of U.S. Marines he sent to strife-torn Lebanon in 1983 was attacked by terrorists, who killed 237. More controversy occurred when he sent Marines to invade the Caribbean island of Grenada to overthrow the Cuban-influenced Communist government there as a threat to U.S. security, claiming it was necessary to rescue American medical students. The U.N. condemned the invasion, but the majority of Americans supported it.

The Republican Party has never lacked for Democratic critics. In 1915 Woodrow Wilson said, "The trouble with the Republican Party is that it has not had a new idea for 30 years. I am not speaking as a politician; I am speaking as an historian."

And in 1955 Lyndon B. Johnson avowed, "The Democratic Party at its worst is better for the country than the Republican Party at its best."

Political cynic Arthur Pearl, professor of education at the University of California, Santa Cruz, observed wryly, "If a man doesn't know anything about a job before he's elected to it, he's probably a Democrat. If he doesn't know anything after holding a job for four years, he's a Republican."

If the Democratic Party can be said to occupy the liberal-to-center side of the political spectrum, the Republicans in general can be found in the center-to-conservative side. But both parties try to give the appearance of being as close to the center as possible, where most votes are usually found.

As the Republicans see themselves today, they are the party of fiscal sanity; of defenders of the people against the excesses of big government; of encouragement for the exponents of free enterprise to create prosperity; of making America so militarily strong that no nation will dare attack us.

Like the Democrats, the Republicans welcome teenagers to join their ranks. "I know nothing more encouraging for the future of our party," Ronald Reagan declared, "than Teen Age Republicans." Over 80,000 TARS are active in almost 2,000 TAR clubs around the country.

Teens interested in joining may write to National TAR Headquarters, 10610-A Crestwood Professional Center, P.O.

Box 2128, Manassas, VA 20108, to learn where their nearest local unit is located. TAR will also provide a manual for any teenager interested in organizing a chapter in his or her own district.

9

What Third Parties Are All About

New Yorkers were upset when scandal after scandal erupted in their city hall under a Democratic mayor in 1933. Angered Republican Congressman Fiorello H. La Guardia, known as "the Little Flower," vowed to clean up his beloved city by returning home to run for mayor. But Republican Party leaders in New York refused to nominate him. La Guardia was too liberal for their taste. So he decided to run on a new third-party ticket. His Fusion Party appealed to New Yorkers to support him and restore the city to good government.

"Isn't it grand?" La Guardia grinned to reporters. "Not a single county leader of either political party is endorsing me. Well, as Al Smith used to say, 'I could run on a laundry ticket and beat those political bums!'"

The third-party candidate was as good as his word. Winning the election easily, he booted corrupt officials out of the city government and delighted New Yorkers by his refreshing honesty and eccentricity, which included a lisping reading of comic strips on the radio to the city's kids during a newspaper strike. He was reelected in 1937 and 1941.

When elections are discussed, usually the only parties mentioned are the Republicans and the Democrats. But there are many more seeking to challenge both at the polls. The nation's principal third parties are the American Independent Party, American Party of the United States, Communist Party U.S.A.,

Conservative Party of the State of New York, Liberal Party of New York State, Libertarian National Committee, National States' Rights Party, Socialist Party, Socialist Labor Party, and Socialist Workers Party.

All have in common a distrust of the two major parties, between which they profess to see no real difference. Many third parties are oriented around a basic issue, such as labor, socialism, communism, states' rights, law and order, etc.

Professional politicians disdain the efforts of third parties to win elections. Nevertheless they sometimes influence the outcome of tight races, denying the margin of votes needed for victory to a major-party candidate. And from time to time they do manage to elect their own candidates both to Congress and to state legislatures, as well as to city halls.

Today's two major parties were originally third parties themselves. By 1803 both the Federalist and Anti-Federalist Parties were dominated by wealthy men. Jefferson broke away from the Anti-Federalists to challenge both with a new third party that spoke for the people—the Democratic-Republican Party. And in 1856 the Republican Party emerged to challenge both the Democrats and the Whigs.

The earliest party to advocate class struggle in America appeared in 1828, following the failure of a Mechanics Union strike. This was the Workingman's Labor Party of Philadelphia, which campaigned for a ten-hour workday. The following year they held a convention in New York, where they denounced "hereditary transmission of wealth on the one hand and poverty on the other" as twin evils. Calling for an end to all privileges and monopolies, they castigated bankers as "the greatest knaves, imposters . . . of the age." They demanded identical education for children of the poor and the rich, up to and through college—"as in a real republic, it should be."

In a campaign song, the "Workies" called upon all American workers to desert the major parties:

Mechanics, cartmen, laborers
Must form a close connection,
And show the rich Aristocrats,
Their powers at this election.

At first, professional politicians scoffed at the Workingman's Party as a bad joke. But when its candidate for mayor of New York polled 30 percent of the vote, it was taken seriously. The United States Bank, through its mouthpiece, the New York Courier and Enquirer, assailed party members as "immoral infidels whose doctrines threaten to topple the very foundations of private property and the American Republic."

The New York state legislature took a more adroit tack. By introducing a few "reform" bills that paid lip service to some of the party's demands, but actually changed little, legislative leaders flattered the party's firebrands into easing their crusade. By 1831 the movement was becalmed, with no more wind in its sails.

The drive of the Workingman's Party for universal education picked up new steam, however, with the emergence in 1831 of another third party, the New England Association of Farmers, Mechanics, and Other Workmen. In addition to agitating for the ten-hour workday, this party pressed hard for free public schools.

The great acceleration of immigration during the 1840s, with many immigrants coming from Catholic countries, provoked a strong anti-immigrant, anti-Catholic movement similar to the kind of hostility we see today directed toward recent immigrants from Mexico, Cuba, Puerto Rico, Vietnam, Haiti, and El Salvador.

Small extremist groups like the Order of the Star-Spangled Banner, the Order of United Americans, the American Protestant Society, and the American and Foreign Christian Union amalgamated into one new party called the Native American Party, derisively branded the Know-Nothings by Horace Greeley.

Their intolerance poisoned the minds of millions of Americans with anti-Catholic suspicion. Every Catholic cardinal, they charged, was really a spy and inquisitor for the pope, sent to America "for the sole purpose of opposing, persecuting, and fighting against the Protestant . . . community."

Know-Nothing candidates showed impressive strength at the polls, almost capturing New York State, winning in Massachusetts, and electing governors in nine other states. In Congress, 8 out of 62 senators and 104 out of 234 representatives, were avowed Know-Nothings. Catholics and immigrants grew dismayed and frightened in the land that had promised religious liberty, justice, and equality for all.

When the Know-Nothings obtained control, declared Abraham Lincoln angrily, the Declaration of Independence would be amended to read, "'All men are created equal except Negroes, foreigners, and Catholics.'"

The Know-Nothings fielded pro-slavery ex-President Millard Fillmore as their presidential candidate in 1856. Their campaign urged factory workers to vote for Fillmore as a vote against "cheap-working foreigners." When he finished a poor third behind the two major-party candidates, the Know-Nothings went into a rapid decline.

The earliest abolitionist party was the Liberty Party, which met at New York in 1843 to nominate James G. Birney for president. In the presidential elections the following year, the race was so close between Democrat James Polk and Whig Henry Clay that if Birney's 62,300 votes had gone to Clay instead, he would have become president instead of Polk, and the Mexican War might never have taken place.

Another early third party was the Barnburners. Opposed to the extension of slavery, they joined with the Liberty Party in 1848 to support a new Free Soil Party, which had as its slogan, "Free soil, free speech, free labor, and free men."

Leading abolitionist William Lloyd Garrison called the Free Soilers "unmistakable proof of the progress we have made, under God, in changing public sentiment." Their candidate in 1848 was former Democratic President Martin Van Buren. Had their vote gone instead to Democratic candidate Lewis Cass, he would have become president instead of Whig Zachary Taylor.

Following the Civil War, many Americans felt that the government was aiding the corporations and special interests but neglecting farmers, workers, and the poor. A new Greenback Party formed in 1875 to demand the issuance of greenbacks—paper money with no gold or silver backing. An inflated currency would cause prices to rise, giving farmers more for their crops and letting them pay off their bank loans in cheap money worth less than the hard currency they had borrowed. the Greenbackers also joined the Labor Party in demanding a shorter workday and other social reforms.

When they ran candidates for Congress in 1878, they polled a million votes and elected 15 representatives. But their appeal gradually diminished, and they felt compelled to merge with a newly formed National Anti-Monopoly Party.

This party developed when big-business monopolies began to gouge the public in the late nineteenth century by charging exorbitant rates for food, clothes, homes, furnishings, transportation, light, fuel, matches, whiskey, and bank loans.

The Democrats were quick to steal the new third party's thunder. In 1884 their presidential nominee, Grover Cleveland, began denouncing the big corporations as "the people's masters." Congress was pressured into passing the Sherman Anti-Trust Act outlawing monopolies.

The Anti-Monopoly Party joined other splinter parties like the farm-oriented Grangers to form a new People's Party. These Populists, as they were called, demanded cheap money through free coinage of silver on an equal par with gold; government loans to farmers; a graduated income tax (the rich went untaxed); government ownership and operation of the railroads, telephones, and telegraph; stripping railroads, banks, and big corporations of their huge Western land holdings; an eight-hour workday; adoption of the secret Australian ballot to end vote fraud; and curbing immigration to end the supply of scab labor used to break strikes.

Populist Mary Ellen Lease, known as "the Kansas Pythoness," traveled around the plains urging farmers to "raise less corn and more hell." She told them, "Wall Street owns the country. It is no longer a government of the people, by the people, for the people, but a government of Wall Street, by Wall Street, and for Wall Street. Our laws are the output of a system that clothes rascals in robes and honesty in rags!"

"Socialism!" roared the Eastern press. But the elections of 1890 swept Populists into power in a dozen Southern and Western states and sent 13 of their candidates to Congress. Within the next generation, as Populists proved the popularity of their demands at the polls, both major parties quickly adopted some of their planks.

In Kansas, Populist Governor L. D. Lewelling spelled out the party's insistence that Washington must protect farmers and workers: "The government must make it possible for the citizen to live by his own labor. . . . The people are greater than the law or the statutes, and when a nation sets its heart on doing a great or good thing, it can find a legal way."

The Populists won almost a million and a half votes in the mid-term elections of 1894. In 1896 when the Democrats pledged to introduce silver coinage, making William Jennings Bryan their presidential candidate, the Populists made him their candidate, too. But Bryan still lost narrowly to the Republican candidate of big business, McKinley. After a carbon copy of the election in 1900, a weakened People's Party dropped from the national scene.

One of the oldest third parties in the country was the Prohibition Party, organized in 1869 after over 70 years of vigorous

In 1904 the Socialist Party was a major third party, with Eugene Debs as its major candidate. LITHOGRAPH, 1904.

Millard Fillmore, pictured here as a candidate for vice-president, was in 1856 the Know-Nothing Party's candidate for president. His loss heralded the party's decline. LITHOGRAPH BY N. CURRIER, COPYRIGHT 1848.

anti-liquor agitation. Although its major aim was to outlaw the manufacture and sale of intoxicating liquors, it also advocated many economic and social reforms that later found their way into major-party platforms.

The Prohibitionists made little headway against the powerful political influence of the brewers for half a century, but they refused to be discouraged. Their action wing, called the Anti-Saloon League of America, was led by a one-woman cyclone named Carrie Nation. She would enter saloons carrying a hatchet and announce, "Men, I have come to save you from a drunkard's fate!" *Wham! Crash!* The bar mirror was shattered, and every glass and bottle on the back bar went next.

Once, when she had smashed a saloon's mirror, a detective rushed in and told her, "Madam, you're under arrest for defacing property!"

"Defacing, nothing!" Carrie shouted. "I am *destroying!*"

Carrie Nation and the zealous Prohibitionists who came after her finally persuaded Congress to pass the Volstead Act of 1919 and subsequently to adopt the Eighteenth Amendment that made Prohibition part of the Constitution. Fourteen years later, however, gangster wars over bootlegging so outraged the public that Prohibition was repealed as a failed experiment.

A new version of the Workingman's Party was formed in 1874, subsequently renaming itself the Socialist Labor Party. It was the first openly socialist party to operate on a national scale. Led by Daniel De Leon, its aim was to overthrow capitalism through a general strike by labor unions.

Another labor party called the Single Tax Party formed in New York in 1886 behind Henry George, who demanded a tax on wealthy landowners based on the increase in the value of their land since its purchase, because they had done nothing to earn or deserve this gain, while farmers and laborers who paid rent for its use grew poorer.

New York labor unions ran George as a reform candidate for mayor in 1886. He was given a good chance of winning against the corrupt Tammany Hall Democratic machine until a bomb exploded in Chicago's Haymarket Square. Blamed on labor radicals, the incident soured public feeling toward labor candidates. George was narrowly defeated, but he still polled more votes than the Republican candidate, Theodore Roosevelt.

In 1894 when oppressed Pullman railroad workers went out on strike, America's railroad tycoons acted quickly to crush the new American Railway Union (ARU) led by Eugene Debs. Federal troops were called out. The power of the press, police, and courts were used to destroy the ARU. Twenty strikers were killed in the ensuing violence, and Debs went to jail for six months. Millions of embittered workers followed him into the Socialist Party of America.

"The issue is socialism versus capitalism," Debs cried. "I am for socialism because I am for humanity!" Running for president, he won 88,000 votes in 1900, almost 900,000 by 1912.

The Socialist Party of America demanded a social-security program; improved labor conditions; housing and welfare legislation; increased educational opportunities; votes for women; and federal control over business practices. They differed from the Socialist Labor Party in that they stood for reform of the capitalist system, whereas the SLP was dedicated to its overthrow.

Both socialist parties fielded candidates in the 1912 presidential election that put Wilson in the White House. Debs rolled up over a seventh of Wilson's vote, while the Socialist Labor candidate only won three percent of Debs's vote. American socialists clearly preferred reform to revolution.

Debs ran for president in 1900, 1904, 1908, 1912, and 1920, but he never made a strong enough showing to receive any Electoral College votes. His best run was in 1920, after being jailed by Wilson, when he won almost a million votes.

World War I, which brought a communist revolution in Russia, also gave rise to the American Communist Party in 1919. Claiming to represent the interests of workers, farmers, and the lower middle class, the CP was originally affiliated with the Communist International, controlled from Moscow. It won its greatest vote—103,000—in the presidential election of 1932, a year of record unemployment. The CP did not sever its ties with the International until 1940.

The loyalty of all Marxist parties, whether pro- or anti-Soviet, came into question when the New York Legislature expelled five legally elected members of the Socialist Party from its Assembly. This action was reversed as unconstitutional by the Supreme Court in an opinion written by Justice Charles Evans Hughes.

A new Progressive Party arose in 1924, endorsed by the Farmer Labor Party, the Socialist Party, and the American Federation of Labor. Its candidate for president was Senator "Fighting Bob" La Follette, who called for government ownership of railroads and water-power resources; a ban on injunctions against strikes; freedom for farmers and workers to organize and bargain collectively; elimination of child labor; and an end to unlimited powers by private monopolies.

La Follette made an impressive showing against the winning candidate, Republican Calvin Coolidge, scoring almost a third as many votes. It was a record for any third party, broken later only by Governor George Wallace.

From 1928, Socialist Party candidate Norman Thomas ran for five consecutive presidential elections, making him the candidate who had run most frequently in our history.

When the Depression and unemployment plagued Hoover's administration, many third parties pressed their programs as the solution to America's problems. Franklin D. Roosevelt shrewdly undercut all of them by borrowing many of their planks for his own Democratic campaign. He won easily, while six members of the Farmer Labor Party also won congressional seats.

Roosevelt's first-term reforms infuriated ultra-conservatives, who organized the Union Party to oppose his reelection in 1936. Headed by Representative William Lemke, it was endorsed by Rev. Charles E. Coughlin, a powerful "radio priest" whose National Union for Social Justice claimed almost 10 million members. Coughlin peddled Nazi Germany's anti-Semitic propaganda. Urging Lemke's election, he cried out on his radio program, "One thing is sure . . . democracy is doomed! This is our last election. It is fascism or communism. We are at the crossroads. . . . I take the road of fascism!"

Roosevelt received almost 28 million votes and Lemke less than 900,000, but still more than any other third party. Thomas now polled less than 200,000 because most socialists preferred to vote for Roosevelt's popular, liberal New Deal.

Two far-out third-party candidates enlivened the elections of 1956. Henry Krajewski, a tavern owner and former New Jersey pig farmer, ran on the Poor Man's ticket, promising free beer and lower income taxes. His pig emblem mocked the Democratic donkey and Republican elephant. Simon Gould of New York promised to turn America into a meatless society and to abolish war.

The 1960 elections saw a fresh explosion of third parties, each with its own answer to the nation's problems. Joining the scramble for votes were the Socialist Workers' Party, the Socialist Labor Party, the Socialist Workers and Farmers Party of Utah, the Conservative Party of Virginia, the Conservative Party of New Jersey, the Constitution Party, the Constitution Party of Texas, the Prohibition Party, the American Vegetarian Party, the Afro-American Unity Party, the Farmer Labor Party of Iowa, the Industrial Government Party, the Tax Cut Party, the National States Rights Party, the American Third Party, the Greenback Party, and the American Beat Consensus.

The latter party nominated a Chicago bookseller on a platform that promised to abolish the working class, give artists a ten-billion-dollar subsidy, make peace with everybody, and legalize everything. Like most of the third parties, they had little real hope of winning, but they viewed the election process as a way to publicize their ideas and win new followers.

A 1939 meeting of the Michigan branch of the American Communist Party, another prominent third party. PHOTO BY ARTHUR SIEGEL.

"Fighting Bob" La Follette, pictured here in 1910, ran for president as the 1924 Progressive Party candidate. PHOTO COPYRIGHT AMERICAN PRESS ASSOCIATION, 1910.

The Prohibition Party persuaded Congress to adopt the Eighteenth Amendment which banned the sale of liquor and spawned gangster wars over bootlegging in the 1920s. LITHOGRAPH, 1888.

The largest third-party vote that year—almost 228,000—went to the National States Rights Party, which opposed the integration of Southern schools and colleges.

In the 1964 election that saw Lyndon Johnson triumph over Barry Goldwater, the best any third party could do was little better than 21,000 votes for the Socialist Labor candidate.

In 1968, however, a strong new third party arose—the American Independent Party (AIP), which nominated Governor George Wallace of Alabama, a defecting Democrat, for president. The AIP was supported by White Citizens Councils that sprang up in the South in an angry backlash against the Democratic desegregation and civil rights movement. The new party pressed for "law and order," code words for cracking down on civil rights and anti-war demonstrators as well as street crime. Wallace also demanded an end to "control from Washington."

"They say I'm only popular 'cause I'm sayin' what the people want to hear," he declared. "Well, what's wrong with that?" Chomping his cigar in satisfaction, he noted that the segregationists weren't being laughed at anymore. He promised to end federal intervention in Southern civil rights cases and to send "those bureaucrats back to Washington with their briefcases and throw them in the Potomac River. . . . We're gonna show 'em in November that the average American is sick and tired of all these over-educated ivory-tower folks with pointy heads lookin' down their noses at you and me!"

In September, public-opinion polls showed that Wallace was being supported by 20 percent of the voters. Republican candidate Richard Nixon appealed to conservatives not to "waste your vote" on Wallace, since that would only help elect the Democrats. Both major-party candidates held their breath as election results started to pour in.

Because of the AIP's "spoiler" third party, the race was extraordinarily close. The outcome remained in doubt until the following morning. Then Americans learned that Nixon had defeated Hubert Humphrey by only eight tenths of one percent. Wallace's AIP vote reached almost ten million, most of whom would otherwise have voted Democratic, electing Humphrey.

The AIP continued to field a presidential slate in subsequent elections. The party insisted that it was needed to give voters a real choice because "it is common knowledge that the Democratic and the Republican Parties are a farce, and are only two parts of the same political machine—their ideology is the same." The party is strongest in California, its hundred and fifty thousand registered voters making it the largest third party in any state.

The AIP's program calls for local control of schools; a halt to school busing; the election, not appointment, of judges; opposition to handgun control; an end to foreign aid; protective tariffs; strict curbs on immigration; slashed government spending; a return to a gold and silver standard; repeal of the income tax; no government interference in labor unions; less bureaucratic control of the environment; a ban on abortions; withdrawal from the United Nations; a strong military; and vigorous opposition to communist countries. At the same time it opposes stationing American troops in trouble spots abroad.

Party officials are bitter about their treatment by the media. "The AIP has gotten a news blackout and what news coverage we got was not the best," complained G. W. Brown. "Many of our people have bad feelings about the media."

Nevertheless the party succeeded in electing a candidate to the state senate of Tennessee and many others to local government offices in various states. At times the AIP has affiliated with other third parties such as the Conservative Party, the Constitutional Party, and the National American Party, which it broke with in an organizational dispute.

Some states sought to make it almost impossible for a third party to get on the ballot. In Ohio, even though Wallace supporters had gathered over 400,000 signatures on his nominating petition for the 1968 election, they were unable to place his name on the ballot. Ohio's major parties had passed special qualifying laws designed to eliminate third-party and independent candidates.

The case was fought up to the U.S. Supreme Court, which invalidated Ohio's restrictive laws as unconstitutional. In most states now, to qualify for the ballot a candidate needs only five percent as many petition signatures supporting him as there were votes for that office in the previous election.

Attempts to harass left-wing third parties were made by the FBI. For 15 years, starting in 1961, the Socialist Workers Party (SWP) and its affiliated Young Socialist Alliance (YSA) were the targets of electronic surveillance, mail interceptions, forged poison-pen letters, interrogations of members and their families, and scores of break-ins of their homes and offices. During 92 FBI burglaries in a six-year period, the agency photocopied some 10,000 SWP and YSA documents.

Yet when a federal judge demanded that the FBI produce any evidence it had uncovered of "violent revolutionary activity or any other illegal activity" by the SWP or YSA, the FBI had to admit that it had found "absolutely nothing."

The SWP finally sued the FBI for $40 million in damages and demanded an end to any further government harassment. The *New York Times* noted that the FBI then had to admit that the SWP was "a nonviolent Marxist organization committed to running candidates for public office."

Once when a bill had been introduced in Congress to ban the Communist Party, Representative Emanuel Celler of New York pointed out, "If we outlaw the Communist Party, there is no reason why if the Republicans are in control they could not outlaw the Democratic Party. . . . You could say that any party that opposes high tariffs or believes in deficit spending is subversive."

Advocates of keeping *all* third parties legal insist that it is wiser for Americans to hear what they have to say, and to discuss the merit or lack of it of their arguments, rather than have those views circulate illegally where they cannot be confronted. "How will we defeat communism," President Eisenhower once asked, "unless we know what it is, and what it teaches, and why does it have such an appeal for men?"

The Socialist Workers Party stems from the Workingman's Party of 1876. Its Marxist goal is still a classless society based on collective ownership and control of industry and social services. The SWP wants a socialist industrial union government composed of democratically elected representatives from all industries and services. Production would be carried on to satisfy human needs, instead of for profit.

"The same corporations and capitalists who have polluted the air, land, water, and food are the ones who dominate the government and own the politicians who run it," reads the SWP platform. "Government regulatory agencies are bureaucratic wastelands where nothing happens. . . . By 1981 almost 30 million people were living below the official poverty level. Millions more were living just barely above it. . . because the workers who built and operate the nation's economy don't own it. Instead it is owned by a small capitalist class. . . . When its markets are filled, it shuts down production, hurling millions into the ranks of the unemployed."

The party calls for "opposition to the government's war against working people at home and abroad . . . support for the revolutions in Cuba, Nicaragua, Grenada, and El Salvador . . . support for affirmative action and abortion rights . . . for school desegregation . . . for unilateral disarmament of the U.S. military machine." Other demands of the SWP include the Equal Rights Amendment, free college educations, a curb on police brutality, shutting down all nuclear power plants, free medical care, and a secure retirement for all.

The SWP's youth branch, the Young Socialist Alliance, is active on college and high-school campuses. YSA national committee member Lisa Collins explained, "We are leaders in the struggles for Black rights, the rights of women, Latinos, and other oppressed minorities. We work for solidarity with the struggles of workers and oppressed all over the world."

The YSA urged young people to join them in a "Help Wanted" ad that read: "Socialist youth organization needs fighters for a better world. No experience necessary. We guarantee on-the-job training. Work will include participating in the fight for jobs, against racist and sexist discrimination, and against war and union-busting. No pay but very rewarding."

Many third parties feel that the election laws today place them at a disadvantage. Under the Federal Election Campaign Reform Act of 1974, each presidential candidate for the nomination of a major party is eligible to receive federal funds up to $5 million for primary campaigns, and then each major-party nominee is eligible to receive $20 million more for election expenses. Both major parties also receive $2 million each to pay for their national conventions.

Minority parties receive nothing under this law, because not one can meet the difficult eligibility requirements. They see this as a violation of the spirit of free elections.

Third parties also protest their lack of access to the media, while the Democrats and Republicans share equal time. A clause in the Federal Communications Act calls for the media to give fair representation to third-party candidates. But in practice neither the press nor TV gives even a fraction of the time and space allotted to major-party candidates.

Realistically, third parties serve more as gadflies than serious opponents to the Democrats and Republicans, although they may influence a tight election race by diverting votes away from one candidate or the other. The only third-party candidate ever to win the White House was Abraham Lincoln, running on the Republican ticket.

But it was from third parties that Americans first heard about the eight-hour workday, worker's compensation, unemployment insurance, safety codes for working women and children, old-age pensions, public education, public housing, tenement inspections, public health programs, regulation of utilities, and other reforms. Third-party pressure forced the major parties to include many of these demands in their own platforms.

Third parties are vital to our electoral system because they introduce fresh, needed ideas into the political arena, keeping the two major parties from becoming too complacent. They also provide an outlet for protest by those dissatisfied with both the Democrats and Republicans. A high third-party vote sends a message to both major parties.

Significantly, by 1983 only 25 percent of American voters claimed strong ties to a major party, and 33 percent claimed no ties at all. These figures give heart to third-party candidates in their struggle to win over independent voters.

In 1929 Senator William E. Borah, who considered himself a "progressive Republican," told the Senate, "We need not take shelter when someone cries 'Radical!' If measures proposed are unsound, debate will reveal this fact better than anything else that has been discovered in the affairs of government. But if the measures are sound, we want them."

Abraham Flexner, the noted American educator, said, "We must not overlook the important role that extremists play. They are the gadflies that keep society from being too complicated or self-satisfied; they are, if sound, the spearhead of progress."

The day that third parties are no longer allowed to function in American elections will be the day that marks the end of our First Amendment right of dissent.

If you are dissatisfied with the two major parties on a national, state, or local level, investigate which third parties will be on the ballot in the next election. Contact the headquarters of those parties for campaign literature, which will give you a broader base for decision. Your local librarian will be able to help you contact third-party national headquarters.

10

What Goes On at Political Conventions

Probably the funniest national political conventions ever held were those that took place in 1948, the first to be televised to tens of millions of Americans.

At the Democratic Convention in Philadelphia, its stagers decided to put on a spectacle with pigeons ("doves of peace") sweeping dramatically past a huge floral Liberty Bell during a speech by a committee woman. At a given signal, her chauffeur tried to stir the pigeons out of their hampers. When they refused to fly, he was forced to throw them into the air.

Delegates roared with laughter as the pigeons roosted on perches from which they began soiling the clothes of the dignitaries seated below, who tried to dodge them. When the upset chairman, Speaker of the House Sam Rayburn, banged his gavel for order, one pigeon tried to land on his bald head. He ducked and it landed on his lectern. As he frantically sought to shove it off, the convention fell into hysterics.

Not to be outdone that year, Republicans supporting the nomination of Senator Robert Taft took a huge inflated rubber elephant to their convention to symbolize "Mr. Republican" for the TV cameras. But before the voting began, the elephant began to collapse and sag into a mess of rubber. Some Taft people accused the Democrats of stealing into the convention and sticking a pin in it. Like the elephant, Taft's no candidacy also quickly collapsed, and his rival, Thomas Dewey, ran away with the Republican nomination.

If you've ever tuned your TV to a national political convention in progress, you could be forgiven for thinking you were witnessing a carnival. People seem to be going crazy, jumping up and down, tooting horns and shouting, with bands marching around a vast auditorium, drum majorettes dancing, jubilant paraders jiggling signs, streamers flying, balloons soaring. Foreigners witnessing this scene are usually baffled by what all this has to do with elections.

Some sociologists have compared conventions to a form of tribal dancing celebration. The traditional hoopla gives delegates a chance to discharge their high spirits, having fun while going about the serious business of president-making.

While conventions have been criticized as absurd spectacles, the show that they put on has value for the electoral process. It causes millions of voters to tune in and watch, thereby participating vicariously. If the proceedings were devoid of fun and bedlam, most Americans wouldn't watch.

Delegates have usually been middle-class citizens prominent in their community. In 1972, however, the Democrats broke with tradition and sought to make their delegates more representative of the total population. Delegations included students, housewives, blacks, and Hispanics.

The Democrats' rules for delegate selection have since been amended to give professional politicians greater representation once more in each state's contingent. Nevertheless Democratic conventions are still markedly more diverse in composition than those of the Republicans.

The size of a state's population determines how many delegates it is entitled to send to a national convention. About two thirds of the states choose their delegates at their own party conventions. The others hold state primary elections in which all party members can vote directly for delegates pledged to the various candidates.

Each state party determines its own rules for how its delegates may cast their votes at the national convention. Some states hold "winner-take-all" primaries, with the whole state party delegation pledged to vote for the winning candidate. Other states send unpledged delegates, each free to vote for a personal choice. A few states expect delegates to vote whichever way the delegation leader directs.

Still other delegates are pledged to vote for a "favorite son" candidate as president—often their state's governor or senator—for one or two ballots. After that they are freed to shift their votes. If no candidate wins the nomination on the first ballot, a favorite-son candidate may swap his state's support for a political advantage.

At the 1932 Democratic Convention in Chicago, for example, Franklin D. Roosevelt fell short of the two-thirds vote then needed to nominate him. The Texas delegation stood firmly behind their favorite-son candidate, "Cactus Jack" Garner, who was also supported by the California delegation. A deal was then struck by which Garner threw his votes to Roosevelt, cinching FDR's nomination, in return for which Garner was named Roosevelt's choice for vice-president.

Each major party's convention is held in the summer of a presidential election year. The city chosen is usually one with a huge convention hall, lots of hotels, good transportation, and enjoyable recreation facilities. For about a week the attention of the whole nation, and much of the world, is centered upon each party's national convention as it goes about the business of choosing the person who will be one of the two candidates for president of the United States.

Each convention has a credentials committee that "seats" the delegations, ironing out any quarrels over entitlement. At the 1968 Democratic Convention the committee denied seats to the entire Mississippi delegation, on grounds that the state party's procedures for choosing delegates had discriminated against blacks. A rival multi-racial Mississippi delegatation was approved and seated in its place.

After a permanent convention chairman is elected, a prominent party member delivers the keynote speech. The delegates then vote on a party platform drawn up by a platform committee. Its planks usually represent a compromise among various factions within the party who have differing views.

Sometimes the platform so angers one faction that its supporters will walk out of the convention. In actual fact, however, the platform is seldom taken too seriously because the candidate, if elected, usually decides how much of it, if any, he will adhere to during his administration.

By the third or fourth day of the convention, nominations for the presidential candidate begin. Each nominating speech usually ends in a boisterous demonstration, as loud, jubilant, and prolonged as the candidate's supporters can make it. They snake-dance up and down the convention aisles as the band blares.

As shorter seconding speeches are heard, supporters of the candidates scurry around on the convention floor, in side rooms, hotel rooms, and candidates' headquarters, trying to make deals to capture blocs of votes from delegations whose candidates clearly have no chance of being nominated. Little by little, minor candidates are eliminated.

Voting is done verbally, with the states reporting in alphabetical order. A simple majority of the total delegates now elects the nominee in both parties. If the vote is split several ways so that no one candidate wins the required majority, ballot after ballot occurs. The tallies begin to change as minority and favorite-son candidates yield their voting blocs to one leading candidate or another after hasty political deals.

By tradition the presidential nominee gets to name his choice for vice-president. He usually selects someone from a populous state in a different part of the country, where the party ticket needs strengthening. If he is a conservative, he is likely to choose a moderate or liberal vice-president to "balance" the ticket, broadening its appeal. If he is a liberal, his running mate is apt to be moderate or conservative.

State conventions took place before national conventions. During the late 1820s and 1830s, state party conventions were being held all over the country.

"In days gone by, particularly in the nineteenth century, the presidential election was an all-consuming interest for the public," observes historian Jules Abel in his book *The Degradation of the American Presidency.* "It was not a spectator interest. . . . It was an event for mass participation in parades, torchlight processions, meetings, and barbecues, not only for adults, but for teenage boys and girls. There was endless speech-making and discussion. Contemporary observers noted that the carnival proceedings provided an emotional outlet and even communal recreation for the masses, at a time when there was little else available that would give the same emotional release or stimulus."

The first national party convention was called by the Anti-Mason Party in Philadelphia in 1830, to defeat a second term for Andrew Jackson. Two years later the Democrats and National Republicans held nominating conventions of their own.

The conventions provided galleries where the public could enjoy the spectacle and join in yelling enthusiastically for their favorite candidates. At the 1860 Republican Convention in Chicago, William H. Seward emerged as the front-runner for the presidential nomination. Reacting swiftly, Abraham Lincoln's campaign manager counterfeited admission tickets and used them to pack the galleries with Lincoln supporters. As they kept yelling his name to stampede the convention, Lincoln aides scooted around the floor making deals for votes. Lincoln won on the third ballot.

The 1896 Democratic Convention, also in Chicago, brought about the first real political class struggle in the nation. The nomination was wide open until the relatively unknown "Boy

National conventions today are considerably more lavish than they were at the time of the 1860 Republican Convention, pictured here. WOOD ENGRAVING FROM HARPER'S WEEKLY, 1860.

The merry-making at national conventions has been compared by sociologists to a tribal dancing celebration of sorts. The scene on the left is of the 1888 Democratic Convention in St. Louis. REPRODUCTION OF ENGRAVING BY WOODWARD & TIERNAN IN NATIONAL DEMOCRATIC CONVENTION.

Despite the bedlam, the delegates at a convention are usually prominent middle-class citizens. Democrats, beginning in 1972, sought to include more diverse representation.

Orator of the River Platte," thirty-six-year-old William Jennings Bryan, made his famous Cross of Gold speech attacking Eastern bankers on behalf of America's poor debtor class.

"The delegates arose and marched for an hour, shouting, weeping, rejoicing," poet-reporter Edgar Lee Masters related. "They lifted this orator upon their shoulders and carried him as if he had been a god. At last a man!" The delegates shouted themselves hoarse crying his name, and he was nominated on the fourth ballot.

Worried, Republican Party boss Mark Hanna wrote to his presidential choice, William McKinley, "The Chicago convention has changed everything. . . . I consider the situation in the West quite alarming as business is going to pieces and idle men will multiply rapidly. With this communistic spirit abroad the cry of 'free silver' will be catching."

When the Republican Convention met, it fascinated a Russian visitor, M. I. Ostrogorski, who witnessed it. "As soon as the aspirant's name is uttered," he reported, "the delegates who support him and the paid applauders jump up on their seats and break into cheers. . . . It is enough for the claque to give the signal for the [crowd] to go into convulsions. . . . [The candidate's] portrait . . . is hoisted aloft and carried about the hall, everyone is on his legs, shouting, screaming, tossing hats and handkerchiefs into the air, waving small flags and open umbrellas. It is a sort of pandemonium or Bedlam. . . . The crowd does not stop until compelled by fatigue, by exhaustion." The popularity of the candidates was judged by how long the demonstrations for them lasted.

Ostrogorski took a dim view of the American way: "You realize what a colossal travesty of popular institutions you have just been witnessing. A greedy crowd of office-holders, or of office-seekers, disguised as delegates of the people . . . indulged in . . . intrigues and maneuvers, the object of which was the chief magistracy of the greatest Republic."

In those unsophisticated days it was easier for state party bosses to handpick delegates and manipulate conventions. Robert White noted in his book *American Government: Democracy at Work* that when the 1896 Cook County Convention was held in Chicago to select delegates to the Democratic National Convention, some 89 percent of those chosen were either ex-convicts, saloonkeepers, persons previously tried for murder, vagrants, ex-prizefighters, gamblers, or political employees.

One of the most colorful years for national conventions was 1912. At the Republican Convention in Chicago, supporters of William Howard Taft and Theodore Roosevelt clashed when the Taft forces stacked the convention with 74 delegates whose credentials were challenged by the Roosevelt forces.

When Taft supporter Elihu Root was named convention chairman, ruling in favor of Taft, Roosevelt supporters jeered this "railroading" by yelling, "Toot! Toot! All aboard! Choo choo!" Sandpaper was rubbed to imitate the noises of a train.

As Senator Warren Harding of Ohio rose to nominate Taft, fistfights broke out. Angry Roosevelt delegates stormed out of the hall when Taft was renominated. One month later they staged a Progressive Party convention to nominate Roosevelt.

The split in Republican ranks assured the election of whichever Democratic candidate was nominated. When the Democrats met in Baltimore, party bosses had decided to nominate House Speaker Champ Clark of Missouri, who held a commanding lead in ballot after ballot. Woodrow Wilson's campaign manager, William McCombs, begged him to make a deal with New York's corrupt Tammany political machine for their 90 votes.

Wilson refused. On the tenth ballot, Clark had a 200-vote lead over Wilson. His managers decided to stampede the convention with a long, noisy Clark demonstration. But while this was going on, Wilson's aides ran around the hall urging his delegates to hold fast. They did. Had Clark's aides not given the Wilson forces time to rally their delegates, Clark might have won on a fast eleventh ballot.

The struggle went on for four days and thirteen ballots. In desperation Clark made a deal with Tammany for their votes. When William Jennings Bryan learned of it, he rose angrily to declare that since "sinister forces" were now supporting Clark, he intended to throw his support to Wilson.

The convention fell into an uproar. In the next three days Wilson's vote mounted steadily until he was finally nominated on the forty-sixth ballot.

A new dimension to the art of manipulating a presidential convention was developed by Senator John F. Kennedy in 1960. He posted spies in every state delegation to relay sentiment there, with hour by hour checks of every change and daily reports on each delegate's voting intentions. Kennedy's brother

Republican platform of 1868. Platforms are seldom taken too seriously, because the candidate decides how much of it he or she will adhere to once elected. WOODCUT PRINTED BY LAND, COPYRIGHT 1868

Robert had 23 phones at Kennedy headquarters, all busy pressuring delegates in opposition camps to switch over.

Perhaps the stormiest convention in history was the 1968 Democratic convention in Chicago, when protests against the Vietnam War resulted in brutal attacks by Chicago police against anti-war demonstrators. When delegates became aware of what was going on in Chicago's streets, Senator Abraham Ribicoff of Connecticut furiously deviated from his speech to the convention to denounce the Chicago police as "gestapo."

TV cameras caught Chicago's enraged Mayor Daley shouting obscenities at Ribicoff. The next day, Daley packed the galleries with his patronage workers, who chanted on cue, "We love Daley, we love Daley!" On signal they whooped it up for him throughout the evening. When the New Hampshire delegation tried to protest the arrest of their chairman by Daley's police, they were drowned out by the roar of Daley's claque.

Jubilant Republicans demanded, "How can the Democrats bring order to the country if they can't even bring order to their own convention?" The riotous Democratic convention doomed the chances of its nominee, Hubert Humphrey.

But it enabled the peace forces of Senator George McGovern to reduce the role of party bosses at the next Democratic convention, in 1972. This convention was probably more representative of rank-and-file Democrats than any other ever held. McGovern easily won the nomination, only to lose every state but one in the national election.

As a rule the weakness of the convention system is that all too frequently each party nominates a presidential candidate who is such a compromise of conflicting interests within the party that he is a mediocre, uninspiring choice. The electorate is then faced with a choice between what they often see as Tweedledum and Tweedledee. Even though third parties offer alternative candidates, when the chips are down most voters play safe, voting for a major-party candidate.

If a major party nominates a candidate who takes a bold stand on controversial issues, like McGovern in 1972, it is likely to suffer a devastating defeat. Political wisdom decrees that most voters are middle-of-the-road. Thus our conventions tend to nominate candidates who appeal largely to moderate voters. Democrats generally nominate a somewhat liberal candidate, like Jimmy Carter, while Republicans choose a somewhat conservative candidate, like Ronald Reagan.

America will have to be faced with a desperate dilemma before voters will be given a major-party choice between extreme left- or right-wing presidential candidates.

11

Hot Air and Cold Turkey on the Campaign Trail

A leather-lunged politician campaigning for the Senate cried out to a crowd in ringing tones, "I want you to know that I hate communism, socialism, atheism, Marxism—and every other ism in the world!"

"What!" shouted a straight-faced heckler. "Do you expect all of us here to vote for a man who comes right out and says he hates capitalism and Americanism?"

When candidates hit the campaign trail, most of them try to give the impression that they are talking cold turkey to their constituents. Often, however, their sentiments come across more like hot air. There is widespread skepticism about the factual content of candidates' assertions and about the validity of the promises they make.

Voters also sprinkle liberally with salt the charges and countercharges candidates fling at each other. Some candidates find it more effective simply to laugh off a rival's accusations. Attacked, one mayoral candidate replied blandly, "There are no depths, apparently, to which my opponent will not rise." The subtle joke brought laughter and applause.

Becoming a political candidate requires a peculiar combination of pride and humility. One must consider oneself eminent enough to be elected to govern others, yet humble enough to plead for votes. As historian Jules Abel noted, "It is certainly undignified for a man who will be President of the United

States to be darting in and out of drugstores, supermarkets, and beauty shops clasping hands."

For that reason, early presidential candidates in our history did not campaign. The election contest that first introduced campaigns, complete with raucous rallies, torchlight parades, campaign songs, and windy speeches, occurred in 1832, when Andrew Jackson ran against Henry Clay. "God help the nation!" wrote one observer. "I am afraid it will run mad."

Windy political speeches became labeled "bunk" as the result of an 1821 session of Congress, which was forced to twiddle its thumbs on an important bill because Representative Felix Walker of North Carolina insisted upon making an endless speech on behalf of his constituents back home in Buncombe County. After pleas and groans failed to shut him up, Congress immortalized him by labeling all such political prattle "buncombe," which soon became shortened to simply "bunk."

If candidates can, on the campaign trail they will duck or straddle controversial issues when endorsing one side means losing votes on the other. When the first Adlai E. Stevenson was campaigning as the Democratic vice-presidential candidate in 1892, he showed a touch of genius in the art of waffling on a ticklish issue. Touring the Northwest in a campaign train, he became aware that a hot battle was raging over whether to name the region's highest mountain Mt. Rainier or Mt. Tacoma. He was pressed at each stop to name his choice.

Speaking from the rear train platform, Stevenson would end each speech by saying, "I pledge myself, here and now, that if elected I will not rest until this glorious mountain is properly named—." At that point he would pull a cord and the engineer would blow his whistle, drowning out Stevenson's choice as the train chuffed out of the station.

President Martin Van Buren was so careful not to take any stand in his political speeches that a story circulated about his being asked if he agreed that the sun rose in the east. Van Buren supposedly replied, "I presume the fact is according to the common impression, but as I sleep until after sunrise, I cannot speak from my own knowledge."

When Van Buren ran for reelection in 1840, it was Horace Greeley who brought campaigning to the height of absurdity. Greeley masterminded the campaign of Van Buren's Whig opponent, William Henry Harrison, a former Indian fighter who had won the obscure battle of Tippecanoe 29 years earlier. Since there were few real issues in the election, Greeley decided to invent a personality issue.

He publicized the Harrison-Tyler ticket with a nonsensical slogan, "Tippecanoe and Tyler, too!" and stirred emotions with rallies, cannon fire, fireworks, torchlight parades, and campaign songs. ("*What has caused this great commotion-motion-motion, Our country through? It is the hall a-rollin on—for Tippecanoe and Tyler, too!*") Parading men pushed huge balls taller than themselves. The nation waved Tippecanoe flags, wore Tippecanoe badges, blew their noses in Tippecanoe handkerchiefs, washed with Tippecanoe soap. Every town had its Tippecanoe club and chorus.

A whisper campaign by Whigs accused Van Buren of being a fop who sprayed his whiskers with French eau de cologne, who slept in a King Louis XV bed, who ate French food from silver plates, and who rode in a British-made gilt coach.

Stung, one Democratic journalist sneered that if old Tippecanoe were given $2,000 and a jug of hard cider, he'd be happier in a log cabin than in the White House. Greeley gleefully seized on this admission that the Whig candidate was a Davy Crockett type. He flooded the country with log-cabin badges, songs, and clubs and even log cabins on wheels where thirsty voters could toast old Tippecanoe with hard cider.

"We could meet the Whigs on the field of argument and beat them without effort," complained an editorial in the Democratic *New York Evening Post*. "But when they lay down the weapons of argument and attack us with musical notes, what can we do?" After old Tippecanoe was elected, politician Philip Hone observed that he'd been "sung into the presidency."

Greeley later expressed regrets for his part in "bamboozling" the American people, and broke with the Whig Party he had helped put in office. But the example he set was not lost on politicians. Ever since, election campaigns have been enlivened by lots of music, parades, souvenirs, stunts, and hoopla to whip up enthusiasm for candidates.

When Greeley himself ran for president in 1872 on the Democratic and Liberal Republican tickets against the corrupt Grant administration, his campaign theme was: "Turn the rascals out!" Grant's forces lampooned Greeley as a wild, inconsistent, impulsive, impractical dreamer who would plunge the nation into chaos. When only six states—all Southern—had given Greeley their electoral votes, his defeat was humiliating.

"I am the worst beaten man that ever ran for high office," he told his daughters gloomily. "And I have been assailed so bitterly that I hardly know now whether I was running for the presidency or the penitentiary!"

Dirty campaigning is marked by last-minute slanders aimed at damaging a candidate just before voters go to the polls, when it is too late for an effective answer. In 1844 James Polk's political enemies waited until the last moment to circulate a false document accusing him of buying and branding a slave.

In 1884 Republicans charged Grover Cleveland with having fathered a child out of wedlock. They paraded up New York's Fifth Avenue taunting, "Ma, Ma, where's my Pa?" The Democrats had time to shape up a quick counter-parade yelling the answer, "Gone to the White House—ha-ha-ha!" And Cleveland did go.

In this century an amusing technique to slur a political opponent was invented in a 1950 Florida senatorial campaign by George Smathers. He thundered that Senator Claude

Pepper's sister was a "thespian," his brother a "practicing Homo sapiens," and that at college Pepper had openly "matriculated."

Uneducated voters who didn't understand these terms assumed that they were shocking disclosures. When Pepper lost the election, he could hardly blame Smathers for accusing him of having a sister who was an actress and a brother who was human, and of having been enrolled in a college.

Professional politicians expect candidates to spout a lot of hot air, but they are sometimes dismayed when a candidate they support turns out to mean what he says. New Jersey's political boss, Democrat "Sugar Jim" Smith, wasn't ruffled in 1910 when he read an article by Woodrow Wilson that declared, "The boss—a man elected by no votes . . . makes himself a veritable tyrant among us, and seems to cheat us of self-government."

Wilson had entered the governor's race and had widespread support. Smith's lieutenant, Bob Davis, was asked whether he thought Wilson would make a good governor. "How the devil do I know?" he growled. "He'll make a good *candidate*, and that's all that interests me!" But before Wilson could get the Democratic machine behind him, he had to promise Smith not to interfere with it if he were elected.

Wilson astonished Smith by refusing to spend a penny more than necessary on his campaign, even returning some contributions as unnecessary. He perplexed the political boss further by making fun of himself in campaign speeches.

When the Republicans opposed him with a handsome candidate who referred to Wilson as ugly, Wilson evoked roars of laughter from crowds with a satire of himself he'd written:

For beauty I am not a star,
There are hundreds more handsome by far,
But my face, I don't mind it,
For I am behind it;
It's the people in front that I jar!

In his campaign Wilson promised voters to end the power of political bosses in New Jersey. Boss Smith merely smiled at such vote-getting rhetoric. But after Wilson's election, when Smith decided to become a state senator, the new governor prevented it. Smith was outraged.

"The governor has given striking evidence," he snarled, "of his aptitude in the art of foul play."

From across the river in New York came indignant agreement from another political boss, Tammany Hall's Richard Croker. "An ingrate is no good in politics!" he thundered.

But Wilson had his own political code of honor. He displayed his integrity when he ran for president against Theodore Roosevelt and William Howard Taft in 1912. Three weeks before Election Day, while Roosevelt was speaking to a crowd in Milwaukee, a fanatic shot him at almost point-blank range. The bullet punctured his rib, but the bloodied candidate insisted upon continuing with his speech. "I do not care a rap about being shot," he growled. "Not a rap!"

Admiring Roosevelt's courage, Wilson showed gentlemanly restraint, unusual in politics, by halting his campaign until his opponent had recovered. The country admired his sportsmanship and ended up putting him in the White House.

But Wilson proved less than generous as president toward a third-party candidate who dared criticize his decision to take the United States into World War I "to save the world for democracy." In 1918 socialist candidate Eugene Debs denounced the war as a capitalist scramble for markets. "I am opposed," he declared, "to every war but one . . . the worldwide war of social revolution." Furious, Wilson saw to it that Debs was arrested and sentenced to ten years in prison.

From behind bars in 1920, Convict 9653 ran for president against Republican Warren Harding and Democrat James Cox. Debs appealed to voters to think deeply about the issues, declaring, "I would rather have a man think and vote against me than give me his vote like a sheep!" Although Harding was elected, almost a million Americans voted for Convict 9653.

There were two ironic aftermaths to Debs's imprisonment. When Wilson toured America pleading for support to U.S. entry into the League of Nations, his argument was an echo of the very one he had jailed Debs for presenting earlier.

"The real reason that the war . . . took place," he then admitted, "was that Germany was afraid her commercial rivals were going to get the better of her, and . . . they thought Germany would get the commercial advantage of them." Yet Wilson still refused to pardon Debs for having told that truth.

The second irony was that Wilson, a professed liberal, was the president who kept Debs behind bars while Harding, a conservative Republican, was the president who issued the socialist firebrand a pardon.

The first time Americans heard campaign speeches over the radio was in 1924, during the election race between Republican Calvin Coolidge and Democrat John W. Davis, with Progressive/Socialist candidate Robert M. La Follette challenging both.

The Republicans won handily with their slogan "Keep Cool with Coolidge," although La Follette won almost 5 million votes, over half as much as the Democratic total.

A notable governor's contest took place in South Dakota in 1926. William J. Bular delighted voters with what has to be the most wonderfully candid campaign in election history.

"There are no issues," he declared bluntly. "My opponent has a job and I want it. That's what this election is about." Such unabashed honesty made him governor of South Dakota.

Another delicious campaign occurred that year in the North Carolina Democratic primary for senator, when Robert Reynolds defeated incumbent Senator Cameron Morrison by holding up a jar of caviar and blaring, "Cam eats fish eggs, and

Red Russian fish eggs at that, and they cost two dollars. Do you want a senator who ain't too high and mighty to eat good old North Carolina hen eggs, or don't you?"

One of the worst hate campaigns was mounted against Democrat Al Smith in the 1928 presidential race with Republican Herbert Hoover, who subsequently promised to put "a chicken in every pot and a car in every garage." Scurrilous campaign literature accused Smith of favoring interracial marriage and seeking to put the White House under control of the Vatican. The six-million vote margin of his defeat was so severe that no other Roman Catholic candidate was nominated for president until Kennedy, 32 years later.

Hoover's election, however, turned out disastrously for the Republican Party. A severe economic depression beginning in 1929 required drastic corrective measures. In 1932 Democrat Franklin D. Roosevelt's campaign insisted that only total federal planning—a New Deal for the "forgotten man"—could provide jobs for 15 million unemployed workers.

Hoover denounced Roosevelt's New Deal as "a promise no government can fulfill . . . a proposal of revolutionary changes that would undermine and destroy the fundamentals of the American system."

This election contest saw the first airplane used in a political campaign, when Roosevelt flew from the governor's mansion in Albany to Chicago to accept the Democratic nomination. From then on, most major presidential candidates used air travel to meet their speaking commitments.

Despite Roosevelt's election, the economic crisis in the 1930s brought out a proliferation of third-party and independent candidates with radical solutions for the nation's ills. Dr. Francis E. Townsend of California won followers with his Townsend Plan to end the Depression by paying every American over 60 the sum of $200 a month to be spent the same month, thus providing a business stimulus. This general idea was co-opted by Roosevelt in his Social Security program.

Senator Huey "Kingfish" Long of Louisiana unveiled his "Share the Wealth" program ("Every man a king!"). He promised every American a $6,000 homestead allowance, a $2,500 income, a car, and a radio. "Of course we can have Fascism in this country," he said, "but we'll have to call it anti-Fascism."

But all third-party candidates were decisively defeated by Roosevelt. Most Americans were suspicious of radical solutions, preferring to trust the programs of the more liberal of the two major political parties.

The heated political climate, however, allowed some far-out candidates to win election with bizarre rhetoric.

In Mississippi, demagogue Theodore Bilbo won a U.S. Senate seat by haranguing crowds with a list of the people and institutions he opposed. These included "farmer murderers, poor-folk haters, shooters of widows and orphans, international well-poisoners, charity hospital destroyers, spitters on our heroic veterans, rich enemies of our public schools, private bankers . . . unemployment makers, pacifists, communists, munition manufacturers, and skunks who steal Gideon Bibles." He was elected again and again.

Most Americans were less gullible. When Roosevelt ran for reelection in 1936, his Republican opponent, Alf Landon, told an Albuquerque audience, "Franklin D. Roosevelt proposes to destroy the right to elect your own representatives, to talk politics on street corners, to march in political parades, to attend the church of your own faith, to be tried by jury, and to own property." New Deal enthusiasts laughed. FDR was voted back into office by every state with the rock-ribbed Republican exceptions of Maine and Vermont.

The Roosevelt thirties saw the rise of some American sympathizers with Adolf Hitler's Nazi Germany. Organized in such groups as the Christian Front, the German-American Bund, and Defenders of the Christian Faith, they denounced Roosevelt as a communist. The Defenders' leader, Rev. Gerald B. Winrod of Wichita, Kansas, claimed 100,000 followers. Seek-

Democrat and Roman Catholic Al Smith was the object of a hate campaign by Republican presidential candidate Herbert Hoover in 1928. Smith was accused of seeking to put the White House under control of the Vatican. PHOTO BY UNDERWOOD & UNDERWOOD.

When Eugene Debs denounced President Woodrow Wilson for entering World War I, Wilson had him sentenced to ten years in prison. Debs was later pardoned by President Warren Harding, against whom he had run for office from prison.

ing the Republican nomination for senator in 1938, he labeled the Catholic Church "the harlot of the Bible" and called the moderate National Association for the Advancement of Colored People (NAACP) "a black nest of Reds."

William Allen White, respected editor of the *Emporia Gazette,* warned fellow Kansans, "To nominate him, we must defend his position as a peddler of racial and religious hatred—a Nazi position." Kansans rebuffed Winrod in the primary.

Popular though he was, Roosevelt was not above some political chicanery when he sought to break presidential tradition by seeking a third term. To give the impression that Roosevelt was only responding to an imperative draft, Chicago's Superintendent of Sewers, Thomas McGary, was hidden in the basement of the convention hall with a microphone connected to the convention loudspeaker. For 22 minutes he kept yelling, "We want Roosevelt!" until all the delegates joined in, touching off a wild demonstration on the floor.

The Republicans were desperate to stop a fourth term for Roosevelt. Seeking an issue to oust him, their candidate, New York Governor Thomas Dewey, accused the president of having ordered a U.S. Navy destroyer to the Aleutians just to pick up his dog Fala, which had been left behind.

Roosevelt shrewdly boomeranged the attack with humor, declaring, "These Republican leaders have not been content with attacks upon me, or my wife or my sons—they now include my little dog Fala. Unlike the members of my family, he resents this. Being a Scottie, as soon as he learned that the Republican fiction writers had concocted a story that I . . . had sent a destroyer back to find him at a cost to the taxpayers of two or three or twenty million dollars, his Scotch soul was furious. He has not been the same dog since!"

Dewey suffered a further setback when a news photographer snapped him from the side of a stage. The photo showed the small, stiff-looking candidate standing on two cardboard cartons in order to have his head reach above the lectern.

Reporters also had a field day when Alice Roosevelt Longworth, Teddy's daughter and a celebrated figure in Washington, expressed her opinion of Dewey. "How can you vote," she asked wryly, "for a man who looks like the bridegroom on a wedding cake?"

Demolished by Roosevelt, Dewey tried again in 1948 against Harry S. Truman. The unlucky candidate made another mistake while campaigning by train through the Midwest. One day the engineer mistook a signal and pulled the train out of the station while Dewey was still speaking from the rear platform.

"That lunatic!" Dewey exclaimed. "He ought to be shot at sunrise! But we'll let him off this time." These remarks, quoted widely in the press, cost him millions of labor votes.

Truman, in turn, antagonized many Southern voters by pledging to ask Congress for a new civil rights act to give voting power to Southern blacks. Some 6,000 Southern delegates bolted the Democratic Party. Reporters pointed out to the Southerners' own presidential candidate, South Carolina Governor J. Strom Thurmond, that Truman was simply pursuing policies advocated by Roosevelt. "I agree," Thurmond replied testily, "but Truman really means it!"

Some presidential candidates have not hesitated to use below-the-belt tactics to achieve their ambition to sit in the White House. Richard M. Nixon manifested this ability from the very beginning of his political career.

When he first ran for Congress in California, his campaign manager, Murray Chotiner, taught him how to use untrue charges to keep his opponent off balance. With Cold War hysteria rampant in America after World War II, Nixon falsely accused his Democratic opponent of "voting the Moscow line in Congress." He won the election.

In 1950 Nixon campaigned for a Senate seat against Democratic Congresswoman Helen Gahagan Douglas. Labeling her "the Pink Lady," he charged, "During five years in Congress,

Helen Douglas voted 353 times exactly as has Vito Marcantonio, the notorious communist party-line Congressman from New York."

Outraged, Douglas replied, "Although Mr. Nixon is a Republican, he voted 112 times the same way Marcantonio did. I voted 85 percent of the time with a majority of either the House or my party. I am not a communist." But just before Election Day, Nixon and Chotiner distributed over half a million bright pink leaflets repeating the same slur. Douglas was defeated, and Richard Nixon went to the Senate.

Years later, seeking to shed the nickname "Tricky Dickie," Nixon apologized for the smear of Helen Douglas. "I'm sorry about that episode," he said plaintively, explaining, "I was a very young man." But in his campaigns he persisted in trying to pin a Red label on Democratic opponents. Eminent journalist Walter Lippmann described him as a "ruthless partisan . . . who divides and embitters people."

During Nixon's 1952 campaign for the vice-presidency on the Republican ticket with Eisenhower, the *New York* Post revealed that wealthy California bankers had provided him with a secret slush fund. Their spokesman explained frankly, "Dick did just what we wanted him to do." Shocked aides of Eisenhower urged him to drop Nixon from the ticket.

Nixon accused communists of trying to smear him, but Eisenhower compelled him to go on TV to convince voters that he was "clean as a hound's tooth." If he failed, he would be dropped, his political career finished. In his famous televised "Checkers" speech, Nixon denied using the slush fund for his personal use or doing favors for his wealthy backers.

Pointing out that his wife, Pat, had no mink coat but only a "respectable Republican cloth coat," he said he had accepted only one personal gift—his cocker spaniel, Checkers. He appealed to millions of dog lovers with a sentimental account of how much his children loved Checkers, so that "regardless of what they say about it, we're going to keep it."

Republican Thomas Dewey was defeated by both FDR and Truman. The media picked up on his physical shortcomings and a belittling comment that he directed at the engineer of his campaign train.

Richard Nixon, here at his 1969 inauguration, consistently tried to portray his Democratic opponents, in various elections, as communists.

Variety, the show-business weekly, called the Nixon telecast a soap opera—"a slick production" aimed at plucking the heartstrings of the unsophisticated. But it worked. Nixon was kept in the campaign, his career saved.

When Eisenhower decided to campaign in the Democratic "solid South," his advisers protested it would just be a waste of time and money. But the South proved to have plenty of "Citizens for Eisenhower" clubs. They turned out enthusiastically at all whistle-stops of his campaign train, even after midnight, when Ike would appear on the rear platform, yawning in his dressing gown, with his wife, Mamie, in robe and curlers.

Campaigning in Wisconsin, home state of then-powerful Senator Joe McCarthy, Eisenhower told him bluntly, "I'm going to make it clear that I oppose your un-American methods of combatting communism."

McCarthy sneered, "If you say that, you'll be booed."

Ike retorted, "I'll gladly be booed for standing for my own conception of justice!" And he did tell crowds that if elected, he would oppose McCarthy's practice of slandering people as Communists.

Eisenhower proved such a popular campaigner that the Republican National Committee kept him traveling and speaking seven days a week, with only five hours of sleep a night. "Are they trying to perform the feat," he moaned, "of electing a dead man?" He admitted he often asked himself, "What the dickens are *you* doing here, Eisenhower?" He once sighed, "If the people don't want me, that doesn't matter. . . . I've got a heck of a lot of fishing I'll be happy to do!"

The Republicans introduced a new campaign tactic, following Democratic candidate Adlai Stevenson wherever he went with a "Truth Squad" that rebutted him in the local media.

After Eisenhower won a landslide victory, the two candidates faced each other again in 1956. When his Republican advisers urged him to indulge in some campaign hyperbole, Ike refused, telling them, "There's no use my making compromises with the truth, supposedly for the party, because if I were caught in one falsehood, and what I stand for in people's eyes got tarnished, then not just me but the whole Republican gang would be finished!"

Poor Stevenson was almost drowned out by cries of "I like Ike!" Smiling bravely, he would concede, "I like Ike, too, but not his policies."

Eisenhower refused to listen to Stevenson's speeches. "It's not going to do me any good to study what that monkey's saying," he snapped, "since I have no intention of answering him anyway!"

Voters gave him a near-record plurality of almost 10 million votes, a tremendous personal triumph. But he could not transfer his personal magic to the entire Republican ticket. The Democrats captured both houses of Congress.

Eisenhower was a sincere candidate, but he was not without a touch of political cynicism. Shown a speech written for him by Emmet John Hughes of his staff, he scowled that he wanted "a few more 'cheer' lines in this speech. 'Cause a mob like this doesn't want to think—they just want to yowl."

John F. Kennedy and his brother Ted, sons of a wealthy father, had to face insinuations that his millions were being poured into their campaigns to "buy them elections." Both brothers chose to reply tongue in cheek.

At a political dinner of New Yorkers supporting John F. Kennedy's presidential candidacy, he read out a pretended telegram from his father: "Dear Jack: Don't buy one vote more than necessary. I'll be damned if I pay for a landslide!"

Campaigning for the Senate in 1962, Ted Kennedy also drew roars of laughter by telling of speaking at a factory where one worker angrily accused him of never having had to work a day in his life. "Afterward," Kennedy joked, "another worker came up to me and said, 'Let me tell you something, son—you ain't missed a thing!'"

In the 1964 election the Democrats sought to portray Republican presidential candidate Barry Goldwater as a right-wing extremist who might unleash a nuclear war with the Soviet Union. They broadcast a TV commercial showing a little girl with a daisy dissolving in a cloud of atomic dust, as President Lyndon Johnson described the consequences of people not loving each other. The allusion to Goldwater was clear.

Republican Senator Thruston Morton of Kentucky raged against "President Johnson's efforts over national television . . . to win the election by scaring the wits out of the children in order to pressure their parents." Many Democrats were equally offended; Vice-President Hubert Humphrey called the controversial commercial "unfortunate." It was withdrawn, but Goldwater's image as a warmonger lingered. Johnson was elected by a huge majority.

One of the most difficult campaigns in American history was waged by Hubert Humphrey in 1968 after the split in Democratic ranks because of his support of the Vietnam War. While Nixon drew 100,000 people to a Chicago rally, a few days later in Philadelphia only 10,000 turned out to listen to Humphrey. And many hecklers booed and jeered, shouting "Sellout!" and "Shame!" at the once respected liberal.

When his running mate, Ed Muskie, was similarly drowned out by a crowd of angry college students, he offered their leader ten minutes at his microphone to air their grievances, if they would then agree to listen to his reply. The students cheered him and accepted the offer.

Late in the campaign, Humphrey desperately broke with the president on his discredited war policy, but by then it was too late. Liberals refused to forgive him. As the campaign grew hot down to the wire, Humphrey taunted Nixon as "Sir Richard the Chicken-Hearted" for refusing to debate him. Nixon scoffed at Humphrey as "an adult delinquent . . . the fastest, loosest tongue in the West."

In his bid to be president, Nixon used Madison Avenue ad experts to sell a "new Nixon" to the public, to erase his old "Tricky Dickie" image. "There certainly is a new Nixon," he stated at a carefully staged TV group interview. ". . . As a man gets older he learns something."

Jim Sage, a member of Nixon's TV staff, revealed confidentially, "We're moving into a period where a man is going to be merchandised on television more and more. . . . When [the public is] fed this pap about Nixon they think they're getting their money's worth. . . . Nixon has not only developed the use of the platitude, he's raised it to an art form. It appeals to the lowest common denominator of American taste. It's a farce. . . ."

Yet the public not only elected Richard Nixon in 1968 but also reelected him in 1972. Then, with something like horror, Americans watched the Watergate scandal unfold. Nixon's resignation to escape impeachment for covering up his administration's felonies made millions of voters cynical about government.

In the 1980 contest between Democratic President Jimmy Carter and Republican challenger Ronald Reagan, Reagan scored heavily with voters by coming off the clear winner in a series of TV debates with Carter. He went to the White House.

Three years later a fresh scandal erupted when it was revealed that before those debates, the Republicans had illegally obtained secret Carter campaign materials. These tipped off Democratic strategy, enabling candidate Reagan to know beforehand exactly what Carter would say in the debates and to prepare effective answers. Top Reagan aides nervously contradicted one another in explaining their roles in having handled the pilfered materials. Seeing the parallel to Watergate, the media dubbed the new scandal "Debategate." Both the FBI and a House committee mounted investigations.

Another political controversy in 1983 involved a seventeen-hour TV "telethon" by Democrats to solicit contributions for

Martin Van Buren, depicted here in an 1848 cartoon, was careful not to take any stand in his political speeches. LITHOGRAPH BY N. CURRIER, 1848.

Ronald Reagan went to the White House in 1980 after besting incumbent Democrat Jimmy Carter. This campaign cartoon portrays what was, for Carter, a disastrous election. The elephant is the traditional symbol of the Republican party; Carter is a former peanut farmer.

their 1984 campaign, through entertainment and appeals by TV and film stars. Democrats were outraged and threatened to sue when the Republican National Committee sent cablegrams to its members urging the phoning of toll-free numbers set up by the Democrats to "tell them what you think of their unfair attacks on our party." Democratic National Committee Chairman Charles Manatt accused the Republicans of trying to tie up the phone lines so that Democratic viewers seeking to pledge campaign contributions would be discouraged by constant busy signals.

Most political campaigns have traditionally begun on the Labor Day weekend in September, with candidates addressing outings, picnics, organization conventions, or other large gatherings. Each candidate is usually backed up by a campaign manager, a staff of paid aides, and as many volunteers as the campaign is able to muster.

Campaign slogans are tested in local areas for their effectiveness; those that prove popular are proliferated in banners, buttons, bumper stickers, and media ads. In 1968 when Nixon Republicans wanted to turn the Democrats out of office, they used the slogan: "Had Enough?" Then in their campaign for Nixon's reelection, they urged: "Four More Years!"

Public-opinion surveys are used to determine the electorate's views on certain issues. Computers break down voters' views according to election districts. These statistics are evaluated to determine the views a candidate should espouse to win the largest vote.

This leads a candidate to reflect the views of constituents democratically. But it also tends to make a candidate a follower instead of a leader. As Professor Art Pearl noted, "We determine by 'scientific' means what people want, and we package our candidate accordingly."

Leonard Hall, former Republican National Committee chairman, admitted, "You sell your candidates and your programs the way a business sells its products."

Polls showing how the public is leaning toward one candidate or another are often criticized as harmful. By spotlighting a leader, they may create a "bandwagon effect"—influencing undecided voters to back a winner. They also make it more difficult for trailing candidates to raise contributions.

Critics also question poll accuracy. In 1936 a poll by a leading magazine, the *Literary Digest,* predicted a landslide victory by Alf Landon over Franklin D. Roosevelt. When instead every state but two voted for FDR, the chagrined *Literary Digest* was laughed out of business.

Aware that the public does not identify with wealthy candidates, rich men running for office do all they can to play down their economic status, while rivals emphasize it. Mississippi Senator Theodore Bilbo once accused his rival of having taken up the "upper-class" game of golf: "Golf! An effete and effeminate game that is the snare of the devil, an insult to Mississippi!"

The dirty campaign tricks in the 1972 Nixon campaign led Congress and many states to pass new laws requiring that campaign literature must reveal the identity of its sponsors as well as that of the candidate on whose behalf it is circulated. These laws now make it riskier to circulate last-minute anonymous false allegations, such as Nixon used in 1962 in his campaign to replace California Governor Pat Brown.

Two weeks before Election Day, the Nixon team conducted a phony poll of voters on behalf of the "Committee for the Preservation of the Democratic Party in California." Almost a million registered Democrats received mailings branding Brown a left-wing radical. A faked photo showed him with his arm around communist longshoreman-leader Harry Bridges.

Donations solicited to "bring the Democratic Party back to the middle of the road" went into the treasury of Nixon's Republican team. Governor Brown sued Nixon for issuing scurrilous and fraudulent mailings and won.

Campaigning today is an exhausting affair, with candidates for both state and national offices expected to "barnstorm" as many communities as possible in a single day. Campaign managers try to plan trips so that a candidate can dash into one town after another to shake hands in factories, on the street, and at social clubs, then dash off quickly to the next town or community. Political belief has it that every voter whose hand a candidate has clasped is a probable vote won.

To plant photos in the press and shots on TV, a candidate's advance man may urge him to cooperate in any kind of stunt from riding a mule at a picnic to going up a girder at a skyscraper under construction.

In modern campaigning, it is considered more important for a candidate to appear on TV as often as possible than to "press the flesh" in person. Just one TV appearance can often reach a thousand times more people than a candidate could with a month of personal appearances. Local and network reruns of news events increase this coverage even further.

An incumbent president seeking a second term has a great advantage over rivals within his party for the nomination. He usually has his party's political machinery at his disposal and can also use the power and trappings of his office to appear before the electorate as often as he wishes. Sometimes his renomination is such a foregone conclusion that the party worries a lack of suspense will keep bored TV viewers from tuning in to the party convention.

A sitting president can also use his office to woo the votes of disaffected minorities opposed to him by actions designed to soften their opposition. Thus in 1983 when the NAACP attacked the Reagan administration as hostile to blacks, Reagan quickly announced he was seeking new powers to enforce fair housing laws, and the Reagan Justice Department announced its first school desegregation suit, against Alabama's colleges.

Racism and prejudice still play a part in election campaigns. This truth became painfully apparent in the 1983 Chicago mayoral race between Democratic black candidate Harold Washington and his Republican opponent, Bernard Epton. Epton's campaign managers used as their campaign song lyrics set to the tune of "Bye Bye Blackbird." Epton supporters wore T-shirts emblazoned "Vote Right, Vote White." Epton slogans warned significantly: "Epton—Before It's Too Late."

Many Democratic ward bosses and voters bolted to campaign for the Republican candidate. "I've been in this business a long time," said Democratic ward committeeman John Geocaris, "and I know people vote along racial and ethnic lines. So what's wrong with that?"

When a white crowd shouted racial epithets at Washington outside St. Pascal's Roman Catholic Church, a parish priest admitted sadly, "We cannot deny that there is prejudice."

The racial issue stirred Chicago blacks to turn out at the polls in record numbers. Together with enough white Democrats who deplored the racist attacks on Washington, they managed to elect him Chicago's first black mayor. Impressed with what a solid black vote could accomplish, black leaders began talking about uniting black voters nationally behind a black presidential candidate.

In view of all the hot air dispensed on the campaign trail, it might seem that campaigning causes more confusion about candidates than it clears up. If it doesn't, it's because a good deal of cold turkey is also talked by candidates. Our country could undoubtedly use fewer politicians and more statesmen. But as a nineteenth century Maine congressman, Thomas Brackett Reed, once observed, "A statesman is a successful politician who is dead."

12

The Man Who Clowned His Way to the State Capitol—A True Story

"My fur-riends!" bawled the tubby little man on the spot-lit platform. "When yew elect me—John F. Dore—the next mayor of our gre-e-at city of Seattle, yew will get a mayor who knows how to eee-conomize on city contracts. The taxpayers' money will not be used for guh-raft or coh-ruption!"

There was a sudden loud, razzing noise behind him. Dore glared around furiously. The other candidate on the platform, innocent-eyed Vic Meyers, was blowing his nose. It was one thing to suspect, but another to prove, that Meyers had a rubber razzer beneath his handkerchief. The audience guffawed.

Red faced, Dore finished his speech abruptly and sat down in a rage. Then Vic Meyers came forward into the spotlight. He blinked blandly at the still-tittering audience.

"Ladies and gentlemen," he began, pointing a melodramatic finger heavenward, "when you elect *me* mayor of Seattle, there's not gonna be any more cheap chiseling on city contracts. You know why?" He paused for emphasis, staring around solemnly. Then he added dryly, "Because I'm gonna take all the loot *myself*—and no cheap chiselers are gonna be cut in!"

The roar of laughter almost swept away John F. Dore's hopes of election. He felt helpless to cope with the most unorthodox political candidate who ever burlesqued an election.

Certainly the funniest and most astonishing story in American politics is the amazing career of Victor Aloysius Meyers, five times lieutenant governor of the state of Washington and once its secretary of state.

That career began in 1932, when a group of Seattle reporters were gloomily discussing the dullness of the mayoralty campaign. There were nine candidates—mostly political hacks—seeking the voters' favor. The reporters were resigned to the election of Dore, an ultra-conservative lawyer who had the backing of most of Seattle's businessmen.

"How boring can a campaign get?" one reporter sighed. "The voters are snoring. Things are so bad that I even heard Vic Meyers wants to get into the act and jazz things up."

The reporters grinned. Everybody in Seattle knew Meyers—the screwball thirty-four-year-old bandleader who would do anything for a laugh or a headline. Once when he fell off a stepladder and broke his arm, and the story made page one, he phoned reporters to hold up their afternoon editions while he climbed back on the ladder to fracture his skull.

A loud bell rang in the mind of Doug Welch of the *Seattle Times*. Racing back to his paper, he told his editor, "Hey, I've got an idea. What if we gave a hotfoot to all those stuffy jerks running for mayor by backing a candidate who'd campaign for laughs? He'd make crazy promises with a straight face. The town would get the best laugh it's had in years. And we'd make voters realize what a bunch of incompetent windbags they keep electing to office!"

The editor grunted thoughtfully. "Who would we run?"

"Vic Meyers. Who else?"

The editor phoned the Club Victor. "Vic? I hear you're thinking of filing for mayor. If you'll go down to city hall and do it right now, I'll give you a top line in the last edition. You won't get another break like it. What do you say?"

Startled, Vic Meyers quickly assented. He was an owlish-looking, stocky man with rimless spectacles and a sparse mustache. His sense of humor had been developed as a matter of self-preservation; he was the youngest of 16 children.

Vic's musical talents were evident at an early age. By the time he was 25 he was leading his own orchestra. He quickly discovered, however, that it was his love of the ridiculous, rather than his brand of jazz, that won him space in the press. He obliged by being as nutty as a fruitcake.

Borrowing $75 from his cornet player, he raced over to the county building to file officially as a candidate. He told reporters, "I figure I better toss my hat in the ring because these other clowns are such ridiculous candidates that they're making me look like a straight man!"

The *Bellingham Herald* observed, "You may think that Seattle's leading troubador is making a laughingstock of himself with his entry into politics. Maybe he is in one sense, but don't forget that this same boy Vic is dumb—just like a fox. He never did and never will receive any less expensive publicity than this he is buying for a paltry $75 filing fee."

Commented the *Bremerton News Searchlight*: "Seattle has had injected into its coming city primary elections a bit of comedy that threatens to steal the thunder from a host of serious-minded gentlemen who are flooding the city with promises of less this and more that. Suave Vic Meyers, the orchestra leader with the elegant mustachio, has filed for the office of mayor, basing his campaign on a promise to 'jazz' things up a bit. To the outsider it's extremely laughable, but we'll bet a wooden nickel that right now some of the optimistic political leaders are wondering how many votes the baton-wielding Victor will poll."

Vic won headlines with his first campaign promise—to make Seattle a tourist mecca by serenading all incoming passengers on transcontinental trains with a jazz band. "I'll get tourists flocking in if I have to dress our traffic cops in hula skirts," he promised solemnly. "Elect me and I'll get publicity for the old town—just as I'm doing now!"

Every day saw a new campaign promise by the syncopated candidate. He intended to choose a new captain of police by his ability to play the piccolo. Daylight savings would be abolished because, as Vic explained, "I don't believe in it. Seattle should have two-four time, allegro."

Vic campaigned on a beer wagon pulled by four horses, preceded by his band playing "Happy Days Are Here Again." At busy street corners, he would make wild speeches burlesquing his rivals' campaign promises. Once a wheel of the wagon came off, precipitating Vic—accompanied by two beer kegs—into the street.

"Drink is my downfall!" yelled Vic. "Vive le downfall!"

One of his rivals accused, "Meyers is just a mushroom politician—a flash in the pan!"

"I resent that implication!" Vic roared. "I'm not a politician at all. But it's nice to know I've got the bums worried!"

Vic's next move stunned his opponents. He announced that Laura La Plante, a top screen star of the day, was flying up from Hollywood to become his campaign manager.

"True to my promise to inject a little color into the campaign," he declared, "I'm bringing a blond into the controversy. I've got the women's vote already. But what I need is more of the men's vote, and Laura will get it for me."

Sure enough, the stunning blond—an old friend of Vic's—flew in at Boeing Field, where he serenaded her with his jazz band. Appearing at all Vic's rallies, she attracted record crowds.

Prohibition was still the law of the land. Members of the Olympic Breakfast Club chuckled when Vic, addressing their meeting, suggested that as mayor he hoped to raise city revenues by opening a small saloon. Reading this, B. N. Hicks, state superintendent of the Anti-Saloon League, declared that he respected Meyers's lack of hypocrisy so much that he was supporting the bandleader's candidacy.

Vic threw his next bombshell at a Shrine Club luncheon. All the candidates were present, scheduled to speak. Vic waited until they were all seated. Then he shuffled in dressed as Mohandas Gandhi, leading a goat on a chain. Taking his seat at the speakers' table, he sipped goat's milk and munched raw carrots. As his dumbstruck opponents floundered through their speeches, Vic peered at them benignly over the tops of gold-rimmed "granny" spectacles.

It was the kiss of death. Vic, sitting in his bedsheet, listening with an idiotic smile, made every speech completely ridiculous. When it was his turn to speak, he grinned toothlessly—his teeth had been blacked out—and handed a card to the toastmaster. It read, "This is my day of silence."

The press agreed with the guffawing guests that Vic's rivals had been hopelessly outclassed.

At first Vic campaigned in shirt sleeves ". . . to prove there's nothing up my sleeve, and that I'm not a stuffed shirt." Then he switched to appearing in tuxedo, silk scarf, velvet-lapeled overcoat, and kid gloves. Indicating his rivals in business suits, he would shake his head sadly and explain, "Somebody's got to give this campaign a little class."

When leading contender John Dore promised government economies, Vic declared, "I'm not very thrifty myself, but you ought to see my wife! As soon as I'm elected, I'll turn the city over to her to run." He promised to put flower boxes all around the city's fire hydrants. "That," he explained, "would utilize any water that dripped out." He also planned to string hammocks at street corners, for the comfort of visiting rustics while count-ing the stories in Seattle's tall buildings.

Vic had a solution for getting the city's decrepit streetcar line out of the red. "We'll put beautiful hostesses on all the cars," he explained blandly. "And we'll employ professional wrestlers to open the windows. It wouldn't hurt, either, if we served certain unmentionable liquids poured over cracked ice."

Describing himself as the nation's first "maybe" candidate, he explained that candidates who said "yes" or "no" on any issue were bound to lose 50 percent of the vote. When any heckler in a crowd tried to pin him down on where he stood on a question, Vic would roll his eyes thoughtfully and then assure his listeners, "Oh, I'm okay on *that!*"

Nothing was too nutty for the unconventional candidate. He went out to an Indian reservation and beat out his platform on tom-toms. Told the Indians didn't have a vote, he declared, "Well, if they elect me, they'll get it!" He went after votes at a lumber camp by wooing the jacks with his saxophone.

Commented the *Tacoma News Tribune,* "Personal platforms are usually verbose and high-sounding, but resolve themselves down to the simple formula of 'I want the job.' Small wonder then that Seattle turns with joy and delight from the worries of a bankrupt municipal street railway to welcome the picturesque primary campaign of Vic Meyers." But some papers attacked Vic's campaign as a "sinister plot of the power trust" to distract public interest while the treasury was looted.

Vic's use of jazz in the campaign led the president of the Chamber of Commerce, I. F. Dix, to comment dryly, "Campaign keynoters often cry for harmony. Now we can try it to music." And a former Superior Court judge, Charles Moriarty, told reporters, "Poland had a pianist—Paderewski—as premier. Why couldn't Seattle have a jazz bandleader for mayor?"

This kind of support made the zany candidate begin to wonder if he might not actually have a real chance to turn a pure farce into a political triumph. A week or so before election, Vic suddenly announced that the comedy was over. From now on he was campaigning for votes, not laughs. Refusing to wear the Gandhi costume, he began dressing in a sober business suit. Eschewing gags, he started talking about real issues.

It was a mistake. Bored, voters gave their attention to the other candidates. When the votes were counted, Vic finished sixth in a field of ten. Vic went back to his dance band at the Club Victor. But not for long. Bitten by the political bug, he decided to run for state office. Broke as usual, he was relieved to find that for only $12 he could file for lieutenant governor.

Candidates for political office, as the sign above this diner indicates, can come from a variety of backgrounds. Wendell Willkie, who ran for president in 1940, was once a dishwasher; Vic Meyers was a jazz musician. PHOTO BY JOHN VACHON.

Vic Meyers as Washington's lieutenant governor, February 22, 1946. WASHINGTON STATE LIBRARY PHOTO.

Despite their name, few political "cartoons" are intended to be humorous, as evidenced by this 1848 cartoon. Vic Meyers, on the other hand, found that humor was key to his popularity. LITHOGRAPH, 1848.

"I can't spell it," he told the clerk, "but I'll take it."

He stumped the state, tootling his saxophone and making weird campaign promises. This time his nuttiness swept him into office with a cool 40,000 majority. A reporter told him he'd have to learn parliamentary law in order to preside over the State Senate. "Phooey on that!" Vic snorted. "We're going to have nothing but good old *American* law!"

He added blandly, "I also hope that somebody tells me how to do whatever a lieutenant governor does." Somebody apparently did, because Vic was reelected four times, twice as the only Democrat surviving a Republican landslide.

As lieutenant governor, Vic horrified the political bosses by pushing bills to sweeten life for the unemployed, the aged, and dependent children. He was supported by the Washington Commonwealth Federation, a radical group.

"Just let the governor leave the state for one day," its secretary, Howard Costigan, vowed, "and Vic will show him how a state *ought* to be run!" One governor was so alarmed at this prospect that he actually didn't dare leave the state once during his entire four years in office.

He explained plaintively, "Meyers might call a special session of the legislature to listen to him play the saxophone, or to vote $100 bonuses for street cleaners." He added reflectively, "I don't know which would be worse."

Vic nevertheless managed to get enacted a lot of legislation helping the underprivileged. When Jim Farley, F.D.R.'s Postmaster General, visited Seattle, he reported in consternation, "There are forty-seven states and the Soviet of Washington!"

Political enemies tried to pin a Red label on Vic. "Who the dickens ever heard of a communist," Vic snorted, "with a middle name of Aloysius?"

He was asked how he felt about serving five consecutive terms in the state's number two spot without getting a chance at the top position. He said wistfully, "I guess with me waiting to move up, all of those governors just never dared to die!"

Vic's enemies finally unseated him in the 1952 landslide for Eisenhower. At liberty for the first time since 1932, he described himself as the best-dressed politician in the breadline.

In 1956 he campaigned for the post of Washington's secretary of state. Voters knew he was still the same old Vic when he was asked why he was a Democrat. He explained, "I don't say that all Republicans are sourpusses, but I never knew a sourpuss who wasn't a Republican!" As he once more unleashed his zany sense of humor, guffaws trailed him up and down the state.

He had sound advice for his fellow campaigners. "Spread your business out," he told them. "Make a lotta stops. Buy a quart of oil here, a gallon of gas there. You know, I once made eighteen stops en route from Seattle to Everett for a political rally. You'd be surprised at the number of votes I picked up at ten cents a glass. I never drank so much Coke in my life!"

The voters happily put Vic back in public office.

The secret of Vic Meyers's oddball political success was simple. He'd just figured out that there were more belly-laughers than sourpusses in the sovereign state of Washington.

13

Should You Vote for the Candidate—or the Party?

In 1960 the Republicans and Democrats agreed to have their presidential candidates confront each other in a series of TV debates. After one round between Kennedy and Nixon, a Chicago woman was asked by a reporter which candidate had persuaded her to vote for his party.

"I'm voting for Kennedy," she replied. Asked why, she explained, "Because of Nixon's eyes. Especially the left eye. Something about his eyes bothers me!"

Marshal McLuhan, authority on TV's impact on audiences, observed, "Without TV, Nixon had it made."

Some Americans vote for candidates principally because of their stand on crucial issues. Others vote largely because of party affiliation. Still others vote because of personality.

A great many voters identify with one political party or the other, often because "everybody in my family has always voted that way." Some vote for a party because it represents the value they believe in. Most Republicans tend to be conservative, high status or middle-class. Most Democrats tend to be liberal, low-income or lower middle-class. Many acquire their party loyalty even before reaching voter age.

Americans unclear about the issues in a political campaign usually play safe and vote the ticket they most trust. Since registered Democrats outnumber registered Republicans three to two, a straight party vote could almost always elect Democratic nominees, however unworthy. Fortunately Democrats refuse to give their party that power, often voting with Independents according to their own judgment of each candidate.

This is the value of a multi-party system. In any country that legalizes only one party, voters are denied a choice. The result is dictatorship instead of democracy.

Many great leaders in our history, however, did not value political parties very highly. George Washington opposed forming them, declaring in 1796, "The spirit of party . . . agitates the community with ill-founded jealousies and false alarms; kindles the animosity of one party against another; foments occasional riot and insurrection."

John Adams agreed in 1808: "Neither party will ever be able to pursue the true interest, honor, and dignity of the nation. I lament the narrow, selfish spirit of the leaders of both parties. . . . They are incorrigible."

But a twentieth century president, Republican Warren Harding, declared in 1923, "I believe in political parties. These were the essential agencies of the popular government that made us what we are. We were never perfect, but under our party system we wrought a development under representative democracy unmatched in all proclaimed liberty."

Lyndon B. Johnson, a staunch Democrat, nevertheless reminded votes of a higher loyalty. "All of us are Americans," he said, "before we are members of any political organization."

More and more Americans today are moving away from rigid party loyalty. A Michigan study made during the 1970s found that only 24 percent of that state's voters considered themselves Republicans and only 42 percent called themselves Democrats. Among voters under 30 it was found that Independents outnumbered both parties together. These findings dramatized the change since a 1958 survey found that 74 percent of voters had voted for the same party their parents had.

The new independent trend has resulted in much split-ticket voting for a presidential team on one ticket and congressmen on both tickets. This is how in 1980 voters elected Republican Reagan president, yet voted for a Democratic House.

Because TV now projects candidates into the nation's living rooms, voters can rely less and less on party affiliations and more on their own perceptions of how the candidates look and what they say. Candidate image clearly matters today far more than party image.

The print media are equally influenced. Doris A. Graber's 1972 study of 20 papers covering the 1968 Humphrey-Nixon race found that almost all reportage of the candidates' presidential qualities dealt with their personality traits, rather than with their abilities or beliefs.

The sparkling personalities of candidates like Adlai Stevenson and John F. Kennedy attracted lots of new young people into the Democratic Party. Likewise, the TV images presented by such attractive political candidates as John Lindsay, Charles Percy, Mark Hatfield, and Howard Baker brought many new enthusiasts into the Republican Party.

By the 1980s many voters seemed to have grown more politically sophisticated, more knowledgeable about the issues. Split-ticket voting was especially common among voters dedicated to special causes—for or against equal rights for women, nuclear weapons, abortion, cleaning up the environment, etc. Millions cast their ballots for candidates who had promised to advance their own passionate interests.

The most important elections in our history, in fact, have been those in which voters' choices of the issues clearly turned the country in a new direction.

When voters elected Jefferson over Adams, they opted for weaker government control of the economy and for limiting federal powers. When they voted for Polk over Clay in 1844, they approved of U.S. territorial expansion. When they made Lincoln president, they did so in opposition to slavery. When they chose Roosevelt over Hoover in 1932, they wanted the

Depression ended by government intervention. And when they elected Reagan over Carter in 1980, they agreed with his program to slash federal taxes and spending to "get the government off our backs."

Sometimes a candidate who seizes on an issue becomes a "one-issue candidate" as a way of standing out from rivals and winning media attention. California Senator Alan Cranston did this in his drive for the 1984 Democratic presidential nomination by embracing the nuclear-freeze issue as his own. He won headlines but risked alienating those millions of voters who were opposed to the nuclear freeze.

Many candidates have wooed the anti-communist vote, calling for a tough stand against the Russians. "They will outbid each other in escalating the arms budget and applying a discredited policy around the world," observed Pulitzer Prize winner Robert Lasch, retired editor of the respected *St. Louis Post Dispatch*. "We should demand something more of our leaders. . . . It is long past time that we began . . . leaving it to the people of every country to pursue their own destiny, socialist or otherwise."

Sometimes when a candidate has the courage to take an unpopular stand on a controversial issue, voters respect his integrity enough to vote for him anyhow. That was the case in the 1970s when Ed Koch was running an uphill race to become mayor of New York. Talking to an audience of homeowners who favored a multi-billion-dollar highway project that he opposed, Koch told them, "I am not going to change my mind about it. If it means the difference between getting your vote and losing your vote, then I am not going to get your vote." One man rose to declare he would vote for Koch anyway, primarily because Koch didn't just tell them what they wanted to hear. Koch was elected.

Civil rights have been, and still are, a key issue in American elections. Black voters are determined to enforce those rights by electing black candidates. In 223 cities that have large black populations, there are now black mayors, 17 of them governing

Whether a voter chooses to cast his or her ballot for the party or the candidate, this machine won't be used. It's a ballot box from the late nineteenth century.

When Lincoln was elected in 1860, the nation had made the decision to oppose slavery. Voters' choices of issues often decide elections. HALFTONE REPRODUCTION OF DRAWING.

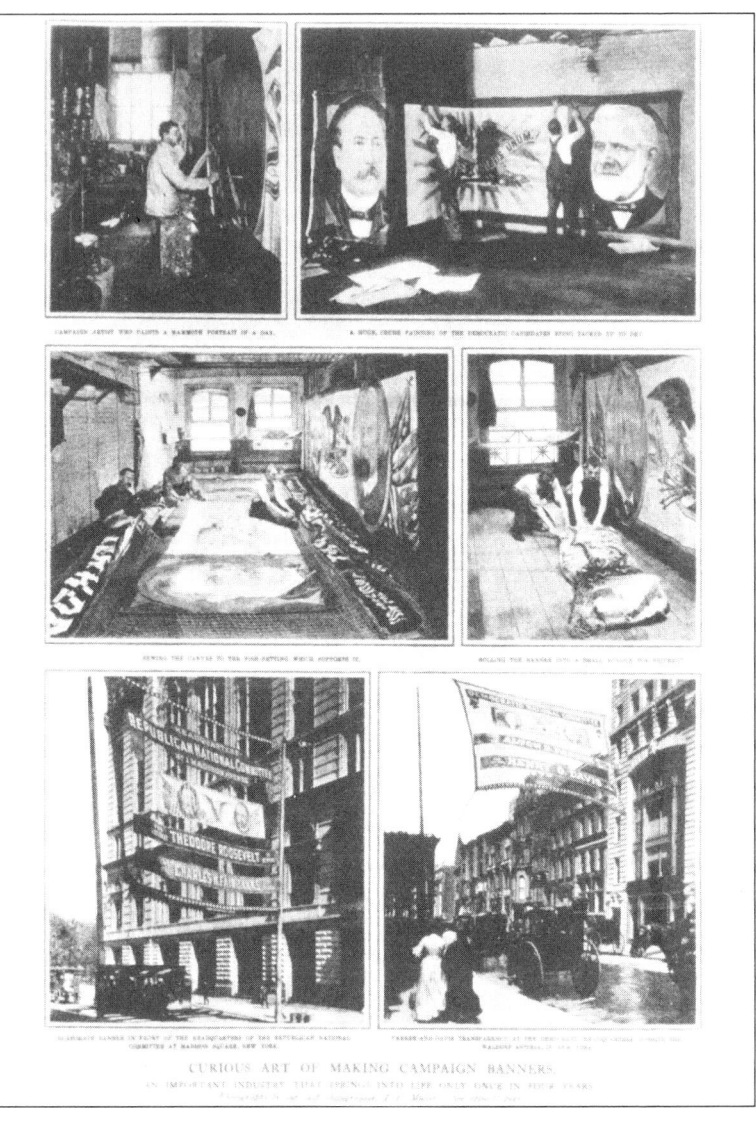

CURIOUS ART OF MAKING CAMPAIGN BANNERS.

Today, television brings candidates into the voter's home, but prior to that, campaigning was conducted via less direct means. This series of 1904 photos shows the process of making campaign banners. REPRODUCTION OF PAGE FROM LESLIE'S WEEKLY, 1904.

cities with populations of over 100,000. The number of black voters has increased by 4 million in the South alone since federal enforcement of voter registration.

"I can remember back in 1968 when Andy Young and I were arrested in Atlanta for lying down in front of some garbage trucks during a strike," recalled Rev. Joseph Lowery, president of the Southern Christian Leadership Conference (SCLC) in the early 1980s. "Today Andy is the mayor and in charge of the garbage trucks."

There are now also 21 black congressmen, over 340 black state legislators, and some 5,000 black local officials. Usually they have won those offices on the Democratic ticket.

Many whites vote for black candidates, either because they agree with the justice of increasing black political power to give them proportionate representation or because they simply agree with the candidates' views. Thus in Missouri, black state legislator Alan Wheat won a congressional seat in a district that was over 75 percent white.

Similarly, blacks will vote for a white candidate, even one running against a black candidate, if they favor his or her stand on the issues. Thus black votes were crucial in electing liberal white Congressman Wyche Fowler Jr. of Georgia over his conservative black opponent.

While issues are emerging increasingly as more important to American voters than party labels, voters are still strongly influenced by a candidate's image. If they are irked by their party's nomination of a candidate they dislike, they are apt to stay home on Election Day or vote for the opposition.

14

How Lobbyists Influence Elections

Railroad barons in the late nineteenth century, who were major sources of campaign funds, exerted tremendous influence over American elections. Candidates they opposed were seldom elected to either state or national office.

James Bryce, an English barrister visiting the United States in 1881, was awed by the railroad lobby. "They have power," he wrote, "more power than perhaps anyone in political life except the president and the speaker, who after all hold theirs only for four years and two years, while the railroad monarch may keep his for life. When the master of one of the greatest Western lines travels toward the Pacific on his palace car, his journey is like a royal progress. Governors of states bow before him; legislatures receive him in solemn session."

Powerful lobbies are still with us today, seeking favors or legislation to benefit their special interests. They pressure legislators who are indebted to them for large campaign contributions and hope to retain their support for reelection.

There is nothing intrinsically evil in lobbying. The right of any group to "petition the government for a redress of grievances" is guaranteed by the First Amendment. But the Bill of Rights never intended the redress of grievances to be influenced by whether or not legislators received campaign contributions from petitioners.

"About 95 percent of campaign funds at the congressional level are derived from business," observed Senator Russell Long, chairman of the Senate Finance Committee. He pointed out that legislators helped their supporters get juicy government contracts, voted to cripple government agencies that regulated industries, blocked agencies seeking to enforce environmental protection laws, and voted to give government subsidies to special interests.

After being in charge of House military budgets for twenty years, Congressman Clarence Long of Maryland accused powerful corporate lobbies of controlling American foreign policy under any administration through campaign contributions. Arms and aid programs adopted by Congress, he charged, were designed to protect corporate investments overseas.

Similar concern was expressed in President Eisenhower's farewell address in 1961, when he voiced his fear that the pressure of lobbies greedy for munitions contracts and fat profits, plus the power of the Pentagon, could stampede Congress into militarizing the nation dangerously. "The potential for the disastrous rise of misplaced power exists," he warned, "and will persist."

Over twenty years later, syndicated columnist Jack Anderson pointed out, "It is doubtful that even Ike foresaw the extent to which the sweetheart relationship between Big Business and the brass has taken control of the single biggest slice of the federal government's budget pie."

In 1979 the *New York Times* reported that in the previous fall's congressional elections, special interests had contributed almost $1 million to the campaigns of just eight congressional leaders. Few realists expected those congressmen to vote against any bills the lobbies wanted passed.

Corporate lobbies exercise even greater power in state legislatures, where they can push their bills through much more easily and cheaply. State legislatures tend to meet infrequently and briefly, because salaries paid are generally so low that the legislators must maintain businesses or careers during their terms in office. Often, in their haste to adjourn, they rush through bills by voice vote—bills they have scarcely read, let alone studied. Many of these bills are written for legislators by the lobbyists.

Philadelphia reporter Bernard McCormick once noted that in the Pennsylvania legislature, the lobbyist for Sun Oil was "often referred to as the fifty-first senator," and the lobbyist for Penn Central Railroad was "considered the fifty-second."

"I have no hesitation in stating my deep conviction," declared Senator Joseph S. Clark of Pennsylvania, "that the legislatures of America . . . are presently the greatest menace to . . . the successful operation of the democatic process."

In 1983 California Secretary of State March Fong Eu warned that if the legislature didn't act to control "the unbelievable spending that is turning elections into auctions," she would introduce a citizens' initiative to control campaign spending. She pointed out that an incredible $150 million had been spent on the state's 1982 elections.

Mark Twain once observed sardonically, "I think I can say, and say with pride, that we have legislatures that bring higher prices than any in the world."

A Ford Foundation study also found that some governors accepted payoffs disguised as campaign contributions from business lobbies, in return for state contracts awarded without competitive bidding. Baltimore contractors testified that they had made such payoffs to Spiro Agnew, when he was governor of Maryland and when he was vice-president. Convicted of tax evasion, he was fined, then forced by Nixon to resign.

As early as 1852, congressional lobbies were a cause for concern. James Buchanan wrote to President Franklin Pierce, who had beaten him for the Democratic nomination, "The host of contractors, speculators, stock-jobbers, and lobby members which haunt the halls of Congress, all desirous . . . on any and every pretext to get their arms into the public treasury are sufficient to alarm every friend of his country."

Three years later a congressional investigation found that lobbyist Samuel Colt, inventor of the Colt .45 pistol, had paid a congressman $10,000 to get him a patent extension and had sought the favors of other congressmen by providing them with food, liquor, and women.

In 1873 Wisconsin Chief Justice Edward Ryan warned, "Money as a political influence is essentially corrupt . . . dangerous to the free and just administration of the law. . . . Who shall fill public stations—educated and patriotic free men, or the feudal serfs of corporate capital?"

The National Association of Manufacturers (NAM) lobby pulled its strings in 1902 to defeat labor bills for an eight-hour workday and a ban on strike injunctions. Congressmen who refused to oblige the lobby were defeated in the 1904 elections by heavy NAM contributions to their rivals' campaigns.

When Theodore Roosevelt sought reelection that year, he received large campaign contributions from the Navy League, made up of munitions makers and industrialists with Navy contracts, as well as from multimillionaires like J. P. Morgan, John D. Rockefeller, and Jay Gould. All were well repaid when Roosevelt revised the Monroe Doctrine to proclaim the right of U.S. armed forces to invade any Latin American country failing to meet its financial obligations to foreign (U.S.) banks and wealthy investors.

A group of investigative reporters whom Roosevelt derisively labeled "muckrakers" exposed the connection between corporate lobbies and the politicians they controlled. Lincoln Steffens declared, "Our political leaders . . . conduct the government of the city, state, and nation, not for the common good, but for the special interests of private business."

Often legislators who were voted out of office were rewarded by the lobbies they had served by being hired, in turn, as lobbyists. They were expected to capitalize on their former associations to influence ex-colleagues.

Thus in 1934 the electric light and power lobby was headed by two former senators. An investigation led by Montana Senator Thomas J. Walsh characterized it as "the most formidable lobby ever brought together . . . representing capital to the amount of nearly ten billion dollars." He predicted wryly that no action would follow his committee's investigation of the lobby's corrupt practices "because it will dry up the sources of campaign funds for the next election."

In 1951 the Kefauver Senate Crime Committee hearings revealed that three men had met in a Florida hotel room to put up $150,000 each as a campaign fund for Fuller Warren's race to be governor. Apart from this half million, Warren received only $15,000 in public contributions. Soon after his election, the partner of one of Warren's three backers wrote a bill that Warren steered through the Florida legislature, freeing the billion-dollar citrus industry from all state taxes.

Look magazine reported in 1960 that lobbyists had scattered a quarter of a million dollars around the Louisiana legislature to assure passage of a right-to-work (anti-union) bill.

The Watergate scandal during the Nixon administration was, in part, about illegal campaign finances. Contributions to Nixon's Committee to Reelect the President (CRP) had been "washed" through a series of banks to conceal their sources.

Big-business lobbies, however, are not the only ones that influence elections. In 1924 organized labor provided large campaign funds that helped elect many congressmen. The new Congress passed the Railway Labor Act, giving labor more latitude in strikes. Similarly, labor's support of Franklin D. Roosevelt's campaigns was rewarded by passage of the Wagner Labor Relations Act, compelling collective bargaining.

In 1943 the Congress of Industrial Organizations (CIO) formed a political action committee (PAC) to mobilize the CIO's 5 million members in electing pro-labor candidates. When the CIO merged with the American Federation of Labor (AFL) in 1955, they organized the Committee on Public Education (COPE), which today is labor's lobby for political action.

Many other lobbies pursue what is called "single-issue politics." The Right to Life (anti-abortion) forces, for example, were responsible for defeating Iowa Democratic Senator Dick Clark's 1978 bid for reelection. Lobbies like Jerry Falwell's Moral Majority, Inc., were active in seeking to defeat congressmen who opposed prayer in the schools or who favored the Equal Rights Amendment.

Crediting lobbying by the Moral Majority for the election of Ronald Reagan in 1980, Falwell proudly asserted that "Christian people came out of the pews into the polls and caused this avalanche."

Single-issue lobbies who came to Washington empty-handed have not always received a cordial welcome. In 1894 when a severe depression led Jacob Coxey to organize a national coalition of the unemployed, Coxey's Army, to march on Washington to demand jobs, Congress turned a deaf ear. Coxey and his lobbyists were jailed for walking on the grass.

And in 1970, when half a million Americans went to Washington to lobby against the Vietnam War, Nixon's Attorney General, John Mitchell, ordered mass arrests that totalled 13,400 people.

Lobbying efforts by Common Cause in the 1970s and 1980s claimed to have as their objective "returning the government to the people." This organization exposed big corporations with defense contracts that paid off helpful politicians with big campaign contributions. It also exposed how much money candidates were collecting, and from whom. Some senators and congressmen were shown to have received donations from contributors who had business before committees on which they sat in judgment.

Angry business lobbyists pointed out that the Common Cause lobby itself had spent over $442,000 in the 1982 off-year

The powerful lobbies that exist today are a far cry from this 1930s parade in New York City in which children marched for better housing conditions. AN INTERNATIONAL NEWS PHOTO.

Theodore Roosevelt, here with Admiral Evans aboard the *Mayflower*, repaid the Navy League for its large campaign contributions in 1904 by revising the Monroe Doctrine to increase the rights of U.S. armed forces. PHOTO BY WILLIAM H. RAN, COPYRIGHT 1908.

elections, almost 25 percent more than any other registered lobby. Its president, Fred Wertheimer, replied, "Many of the organizations that spend substantially more money than we do don't report at all." Other lobbies, he said, used loopholes in the disclosure law to conceal expenditures.

Some lobbies that reported spending over $100,000 each on the 1982 campaign included Handgun Control Inc., the American Petroleum Institute, the Sierra Club, the American Postal Workers Union, the American Medical Association, the Citizens Committee for the Right to Keep and Bear Arms, the U.S. League of Savings Associations, the AFL-CIO, the American Farm Bureau Federation, and the National Rifle Association (which also gave $85,000 to members of the Senate Judiciary Committee the year before it approved a bill making it easier to buy and sell firearms).

Some lobbies contribute campaign funds to both major candidates in an election, so that no matter which one wins, the lobbies are guaranteed the ear of the winner.

The political action committees, or PACs, were set up by lobbies to get around laws setting limits on a candidate's contributions from single sources. The PACs spend funds on behalf of favored candidates, ostensibly without the knowledge or control of those candidates' official campaigns. The use of PACs allows lobbies to put ten or more times the money behind a candidate than the law would allow them to contribute to his own campaign fund. During the 1981–82 election period, some 2,000 PACs contributed up to $90 million to congressional campaigns. Corporate and trade association PACs ("big business") contributed over twice as much as labor PACs (unions). PAC spending on federal campaigns was expected to reach half a billion dollars by 1992.

One of the most powerful union PACs is the National Education Association, whose teachers won from President Carter the creation of a Federal Department of Education. In 1982 its

PAC spent nearly $1.5 million to back 334 candidates in the mid-term elections and helped elect 250 of them.

In 1983 Republican Party leaders appealed for a removal of federal limits on political party expenditures for candidates. "Surveys repeatedly show that the public is overwhelmingly opposed to taxpayers' financing of elections," declared Nevada Senator Paul Laxalt, Republican Party chairman.

The change would lessen the influence of PACs, said Indiana Senator Richard Lugar, chairman of the Senate Republican Campaign Committee, and strengthen the role of the parties. Democrats objected because the Republicans, with access to much wealthier private financing, would benefit most.

The Democrats, meanwhile, went to a federal court to try to block conservative PACs from spending tens of millions of dollars to reelect President Reagan in 1984.

In 1983 three of the six declared candidates for the Democratic Party's presidential nomination—former Vice-President Walter Mondale, Colorado Senator Gary Hart, and Florida Governor Reubin Askew—declared they wanted no PAC support. "A president who owes his election to narrow interests," Hart explained, "risks an administration that is owned by them."

It is unquestionably true that lobbies can, through campaign contributions, affect the outcome of elections. And to the extent that they can claim credit for a candidate's victory, they can influence his decisions while in office.

The problem may never be solved until the amount of money that can be spent on election campaigns is strictly curbed by law. This change would probably require a rigid shortening of the campaign period to reduce expenses; a ban on private contributions or PACs; public funding of candidates; and apportioned free TV time for political speeches and debates.

Such reforms might mean the saving of vast millions in unnecessary expenses, fairer opportunities for all candidates, and more honest representative government for all of us.

15

Stealing Votes

In a special Georgia election held shortly after World War II to replace deceased Governor Eugene Talmadge, his son Herman was elected. *Presumably* elected, that is. It turned out that 32 votes for him were cast by the same man under 32 different names. Only 10 of 48 write-in votes for him were legitimate; at least two voters were dead men; five had moved away; five said they hadn't voted; and another dozen voters couldn't be found. The *Atlanta Journal* won a Pulitzer Prize for exposing Herman Talmadge's stolen election.

There are many ways to steal votes. Some candidates' supporters have done it by outright fraud; some by frightening opposition voters away from the polls; some by using technicalities to disenfranchise the opposition; some by rigging election results.

Stealing votes has a long and dishonorable tradition. Colonial parties in America used mobs to terrorize opposition voters away from the polls. One of the first election riots occurred in 1742 in the Pennsylvania colony, when Scotch-Irish frontiersmen making up the Proprietary Party sought to disenfranchise Quakers. They organized a mob of 70 sailors, arming them with clubs that they "flourished over their heads with loud huzzas, and in a furious and tumultuous manner approached the place of election."

The polls were on a courthouse balcony, to which voters mounted from a street staircase. Rushing the staircase, the mob clubbed and drove off all Quakers seeking to vote. But the ordinarily non-violent Quakers quickly organized their own mob.

Throwing the sailors off the staircase, they locked up 50. The election then proceeded peacefully, with a Quaker victory.

Federalist President John Adams feared the votes of French and Irish immigrants who favored Jefferson over him. So he passed the Alien and Sedition Acts to prevent aliens from becoming citizens for 14 years. Anyone daring to criticize this theft of votes was thrown in jail. Becoming president, Jefferson instantly made the Acts dead letters, so that it was easier for aliens to become citizens and vote.

In the first half of the nineteenth century, as Democrats succeeded in organizing the immigrant vote in the big cities, members of the Know-Nothing Party intensified their efforts to keep foreign-born voters from the polls. The immigrants fought back. Killings on Election Day were commonplace during the 1840s and 1850s.

In 1855, Know-Nothing mobs in Louisville, Kentucky, took control of the polls, beating, shooting, and stabbing Irish and German immigrants seeking to vote. When some Irish killed several rioters, enraged mobs invaded their neighborhoods, burning buildings and shooting down fleeing tenants. Twenty people died. Know-Nothing candidates swept the elections, with almost no Irish or German votes recorded.

In New York City from 1860 to 1871, police looked the other way when Boss Tweed's gangs of Tammany toughs invaded election precincts to frighten off or beat up opposition voters. Tweed also bought and bribed votes and rigged elections, until the Tammany machine was finally overthrown.

During that same period down South, it was the Ku Klux Klan that stole elections. In 1868 a congressional investigation found that in the three weeks prior to Election Day, 2,000 blacks had been murdered, wounded, or flogged in Louisiana. The message to blacks was loud and clear.

In the late nineteenth century, organizations proliferated whose aim was to stop "undesirables" from voting. These included the Immigration Restriction League in the East; the

American Protective Association in the Midwest and Far West; the Klan and similar organizations in the South. They sought to drive away from the polls not only immigrants and blacks, but also Catholics, Jews, Mexican Americans, and Chinese.

In some cities, political bosses stole elections by outright fraud. Shortly after the turn of the century, muckraker Lincoln Steffens reported that St. Louis boss Edward R. Butler would walk out of a polling place and call across a cordon of police to men lounging at the curb, "Are there any more repeaters out here that want to vote again?"

Fraud was even more blatant among Philadelphians. Steffens reported that they had "no more rights at the polls than the Negroes down South. . . . The machine controls the whole process of voting, and practices fraud at every stage. The assessor's list is the voting list, and the assessor is the machine's man." A Municipal League report revealed 250 votes cast in a ward with less than 100 registered voters, the list padded with the names of dead and imaginary persons.

In one Philadelphia election, some 80,000 out of 204,000 votes were found to be fraudulent. Police had enabled repeaters to vote "without intimidation," arresting only voters who dared to protest. With the machine's own officials counting the ballots, there was no way its candidates could lose.

During the Prohibition era in Chicago, Al Capone and other gangsters contributed $300,000 to the reelection of Republican Mayor William Hale Thompson in 1927. On Election Day two Democratic precinct clubs were bombed, two election judges kidnapped and beaten, and voters driven from the polls by gangsters opening fire. Other voters prudently stayed home as police squads cruised the city with machine guns and tear gas. There were very few votes against Mayor Thompson.

In 1948 stealing votes was routine in Louisiana's Plaquemine Parish, bossed by Leander Perez. When Russell Long won election to the Senate that year, he freely admitted receiving several thousand votes stolen for him by Perez. When Perez introduced a law letting him plunder the local treasury, the parish's 3,000-odd registered voters were credited with 5,361 votes in favor and 3 votes against.

During U.S. Senate Judiciary Committee hearings on why so few blacks were registered to vote in his parish, Perez explained that some white Louisiana voters charged $10 for their votes, and others charged $5, while blacks and poor whites could be bribed for only $2. "People of low character," he said, "are a little cheaper. . . . The $5 and $10 voters would not ride in the same automobile with the $2 voters when they are being brought to the polls. It was beneath their dignity."

The astonished investigator asked, "You segregated the voters according to how much you paid them?"

"Yes, sir," replied Perez blandly. He denounced any federal intervention to protect the rights of black voters as both "un-American" and "communistic."

"That," snapped Republican Senator Everett Dirksen, "is as stupid a statement as has ever been uttered in this hearing!"

Stealing elections in the old South was routine until the Civil Rights Act of 1957 established a Federal Civil Rights Commission to investigate complaints and report to the president and congress. Before then, even in communities where blacks far outnumbered whites, white officials won almost all public offices by the simple expedient of barring black voters through poll taxes that they could not afford and through hard literacy tests that only blacks were compelled to take.

Literacy tests were also used in California to exclude Hispanic citizens who didn't speak English. Ironically, the original U.S.-Mexican treaty required all California laws and proceedings to be in both Spanish and English, with the rights of Spanish-speaking citizens respected. The law that kept them from voting was passed "to protect the purity of the ballot box from the corrupting influences of the disturbing elements that come from abroad." The California Supreme Court finally set this law aside as unconstitutional in 1970.

One of the oldest and most skillful methods of stealing votes is called "gerrymandering." It was named after a signer of the Declaration of Independence, Massachusetts Governor Elbridge Gerry, who re-districted his state in 1812 in such a way that his party could win more seats in the legislature with far fewer voters than the opposition needed.

Gerrymandering works this way: Voting-district boundary lines are redrawn so that, say, a district of 40,000 largely Republican voters can elect only one representative, while another district carved out of only 3,000 largely Democratic voters is given one representative also. In effect, the voting power of 37,000 voters has been stolen.

When Gerry re-carved voting districts for this purpose, the boundaries of one had so curious a shape that a legislator suggested it resembled a salamander. "No," replied one wit dryly, "a Gerrymander." The name stuck to the political trick.

In the late 1950s a group of blacks charged Alabama with gerrymandering the election district of Tuskegee from a square shape "into a strangely irregular 28-sided figure," which had the effect of "fencing Negro citizens out of Tuskegee."

The Supreme Court rejected Alabama's claim that it had the right to shape its political subdivisions as it saw fit. No state legislature, said Justice Felix Frankfurter in 1960, could isolate "a racial minority for special discriminatory treatment." Three years later, Justice William O. Douglas upheld the right of the federal government to rule on the fairness of districting. "The conception of political equality . . . can mean only one thing—one person, one vote," he declared. Otherwise, he pointed out, a resident of Georgia's smallest county would have 99 times the political power and influence of a citizen of Atlanta.

All state legislatures were finally forced to undertake reapportionment on a one-person, one-vote basis. District boundaries were redrawn to equalize the number of people in each election district, regardless of geographical size.

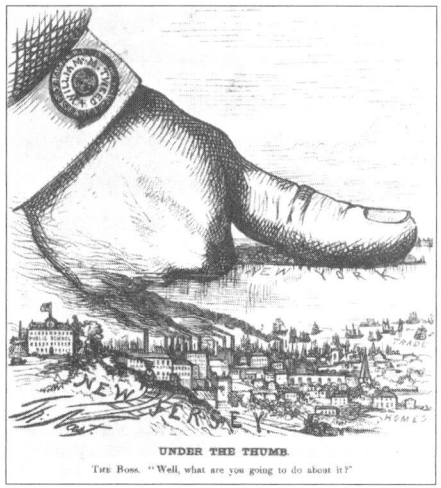

From 1860 to 1871, Boss Tweed bought and bribed voters in New York and New Jersey, putting voters "under his thumb." WOOD ENGRAVING AFTER THOMAS NAST IN *HARPER'S WEEKLY*, JUNE 10, 1871.

Fraud was blatant in Philadelphia, Pennsylvania elections in the late 1800s and early 1900s. In one election, some 80,000 of 204,000 votes were fraudulent. Voting lists were sometimes supplemented by the names of dead or nonexistent men. WOOD ENGRAVING FROM SKETCHES BY BERGHAUS IN FRANK LESLIE'S ILLUSTRATED NEWSPAPER, 1872.

The voter in this 1837 cartoon could well have been a 1948 voter, for that was when Louisiana Plaquemine Parish boss Leander Perez went so far as to segregate bribed voters by how much he had paid them. The range was from two dollars to ten dollars.

LITHOGRAPH BY N. SARONY.

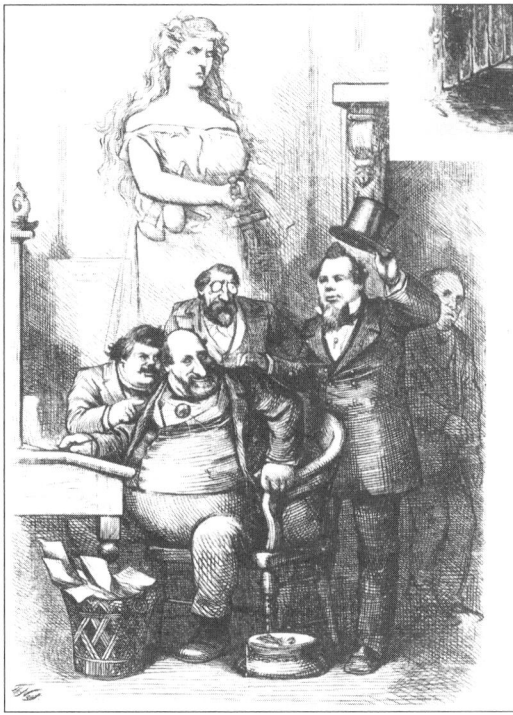

This cartoon shows the 1871 arrest of Boss Tweed, with the ghostly figure of an avenging Justice standing over him.

WOOD ENGRAVING AFTER THOMAS NAST IN *HARPER'S WEEKLY*, 1871.

Politicians still sought to carve election districts in such a way as to tip the balance of power in them as far as possible in favor of one or the other party. In 1983 Republican George Deukmejian of California threw Democrats into an uproar by announcing a special election to try to redistrict the state so that the Republicans could win the legislature.

No other group of Americans was rendered as powerless through having their votes stolen as Southern blacks, even as late as the 1960s. After the passage of civil rights acts, when Northern sympathizers went South to aid in black voter-registration drives, many were terrorized and beaten. Some were murdered.

Fannie Lou Hamer, a black militant, reported in 1964, "I tried to register in 1962. I was fired the same day, after working on the plantation for eighteen years. . . . When my employer found out I'd been down to the courthouse, she said I'd have to withdraw or be fired. 'We are not ready for this in Mississippi' she said. 'Well, I wasn't registering for you,' I told her, 'I was trying to register for myself.'"

One voter-registration drive was mounted in 80 percent black Lowndes County, Alabama, in the spring of 1965, because out of 15,000 resident blacks, not a single one had been allowed to register.

The Voting Rights Act of 1965 suspended literacy tests and other means used to bar blacks from the polls. Federal examiners were appointed for all voting districts where less than half the population was registered to vote. Anyone trying to stop a citizen from registering or voting was made subject to arrest on criminal charges. Shortly afterward the Supreme Court ruled all poll taxes unconstitutional.

The effect of the Voting Rights Act in Mississippi was impressive. Before its passage, only 35,000 blacks had been registered in the whole state; after passage, the number jumped to

Elbridge Gerry, looking rather satisfied in this portrait, redistricted his state of Massachusetts in 1812 so that his party would win more seats in the legislature. Gerrymandering is one of the most effective ways of stealing elections, but no state can get away with it today. ENGRAVING BY J. B. LONGAGRE FROM A DRAWING BY VANDERLYN.

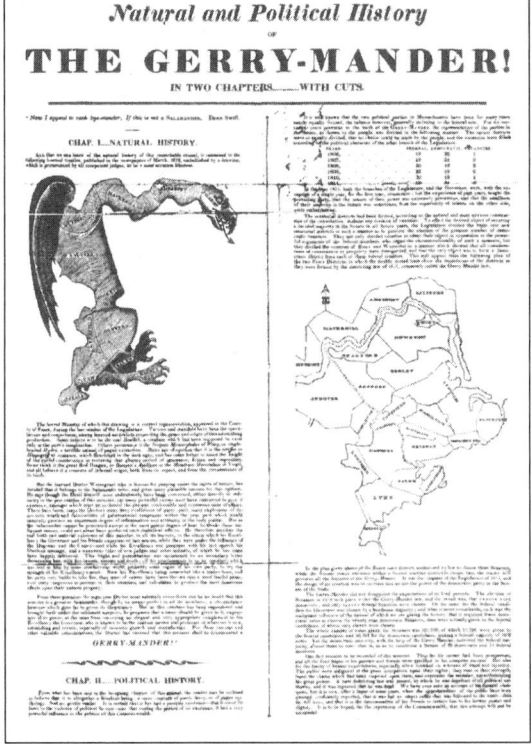

When a legislator suggested in 1812 that the boundaries of one newly founded district resembled a salamander, someone else dubbed it a "Gerrymander." Gerrymandering became the subject of political cartoons such as this. BROADSIDE, 1815.

President Lyndon Johnson signed the Voting Rights Act in 1965, which suspended literacy tests used to bar blacks from the polls.

200,000. By November, 1967, they were able to elect 22 blacks to public office in the state.

Even so, black votes were still being stolen by 1983, when black leader Rev. Jesse Jackson challenged William Reynolds, chief of the Justice Department's Civil Rights Division, to join him in rural Mississippi for a firsthand look at voting rights abuses. Reynolds discovered registration offices that closed at county officials' whims; employers who refused to let blacks leave work to register; polling places moved from black to white neighborhoods without notice; black voters turned away by white imposters posing as federal officials.

"I never heard of anything like that before," Reynolds admitted. He dispatched federal examiners to five Mississippi counties to stop such abuses and register black voters.

Today, because of changes in the law and stricter enforcement, elections are generally more honest, for the most part, than they were in darker periods of our history. There will always be some vote stealing here and there, just as there is some dishonesty in law, medicine, business, or any other facet of American life. But the vast majority of us can count on voting, and on our vote counting—unless we rob ourselves of our vote by failing to go to the polls.

16

"What Difference Does My Vote Make?"

Ever hear of President Charles Evans Hughes?

You would have, if just one more voter in each California district had voted for him, sending him to the White House instead of letting Woodrow Wilson remain in it in 1916.

Many Americans don't bother exercising their franchise, feeling that the vote of one more person isn't going to make any difference in the results of an election. Some explain that they're too busy or have more important things to do. Others shrug and say that they're simply not interested in politics.

In 1964 a public-opinion poll found that three out of four Americans trusted the government to do what was right most of the time. But another poll in 1978 found only 28 percent expressing such trust, with 65 percent by then convinced that the government was run on behalf of a few big interests.

One might have expected such disillusionment to result in a widespread determination to "vote the rascals out." Instead, 65 percent expressed the belief that ordinary people had little to say about what the government does. Their apathy was reflected by a sharp decline in registration and voting.

Yet even presidential races have often been so close that they were decided by the few extra votes of citizens who cared enough to cast their ballots. In 1884 Grover Cleveland was elected over James G. Blaine when, out of over a million New Yorkers who voted, just 1,149 more chose Cleveland.

And in 1960 John F. Kennedy was sent to the White House instead of Richard Nixon by an average of less than a single vote per election precinct.

Even world history could have been changed by a single vote. That was the margin by which Adolf Hitler was elected leader of the Nazis in a 1932 party election. Had he lost by a single vote instead, there might have been no World War II.

Sometimes minorities feel discouraged from voting because they are always outnumbered. Then something happens that lets them discover their strength when anger drives them to vote.

After the Civil War, President Andrew Johnson sought to pacify white Southerners by weakening the Civil Rights Act. In 1868 angry blacks went to the polls in record numbers to vote against him. The black vote proved decisive in sending Ulysses S. Grant to the White House.

Since 1872, there have been eight presidents who went to the White House with less than a majority of the popular vote— Hayes, Garfield, Cleveland, Harrison, Wilson, Truman, Kennedy, and Nixon. The significance of this is that had the small number of third-party votes gone to their opponents instead, those eight presidents would not have been elected. The importance of even a handful of votes cannot be overestimated.

While your vote may or may not be crucial in an election, casting it gives you the healthy satisfaction of acting out your convictions. "Always vote for a principle, though you vote alone," advised John Quincy Adams, "and you may cherish the sweet reflection that your vote is never lost."

Some citizens who ignore the polls on Election Day feel that it doesn't matter because plenty of others will be voting. If everyone felt the same way, of course, there would be no elections and, in a little while, no more democracy.

"The whole system of American government rests on the ballot box," President Calvin Coolidge declared in 1926. "Unless citizens do their duties there, such a system of government is doomed to failure."

One might expect young Americans who pass their eighteenth birthdays to rush enthusiastically to the ballot box in an election year to exercise their right to choose the leaders they want. Ironically, records show that young people 18 through 25 have the poorest voting turnout of any age group. A 1974 Census study found only about 40 percent registered to vote.

This lack of participation disturbed presidential candidate Hubert Humphrey, who resented criticism of American politics by youths who failed to vote. "If you think politics is a little dirty," he challenged them, "why don't you get a bar of Ivory soap and get in and clean it up instead of sitting out there in the bleachers?"

At a 1980 rally of Reagan supporters, Paul Weyrich, director of the Committee for the Survival of a Free Congress, admitted frankly, "I don't want everyone to vote. Our leverage in the election quite candidly goes up as the voting populace goes down. We have no responsibility, moral or otherwise, to turn out our opposition. It's important to turn out those who are with us."

If you have the vote and fail to use it, you may allow a candidate you oppose to slip into office by a slim margin. Then, despite barely escaping defeat, he may claim that his election represents a "mandate from the people" to put into effect the very laws you fear and oppose, ignoring the fact he was elected by only a minority of registered voters.

One of the most valuable services any young American can perform, whether of voting age or below, is to help get out the vote, making certain that as many eligible voters as possible register and express their choices at the polls. The larger the turnout, the more the results will represent the true will of the majority. The smaller the turnout, the easier it is for pressure groups to steamroller an election.

"A registration and get-out-the-vote drive is hard work," admitted John Bailey, a past chairman of the Democratic National Committee. "There is little glamour in it. But it is the most essential of all political activity. It is what puts the votes in the ballot box on Election Day."

There is a wide choice of volunteer jobs awaiting those willing to join in getting out the vote. Needed are checkers to work at the polls and note registered voters who haven't shown up; messengers to convey this information; telephoners to contact the absentees; drivers to take voters to the polls; and baby-sitters to take care of youngsters while their parents vote.

When racist opposition was intense in the South during the early 1960s, many idealistic Northern youths volunteered to go South in buses to help get out the black vote. They persisted in the drive even when some were shot, beaten, gassed, whipped, and jailed. One youth, his arm in a sling after being beaten by a police baton, told a reporter, "If blacks can't register to vote, then what's all this democracy we hear so much about?" Since that drive, the number of black voters in the South has jumped to over 4 million.

More and more American blacks up North, too, were realizing that the answer to many of their problems lay in getting a better deal from their local, state, and federal governments. And the only way to do that was to get out the black vote to support candidates who would work toward that goal.

When black Harold Washington ran for mayor of Chicago in 1983, his campaign attracted a huge black voter turnout. Among black youths 18 to 25, only 10 percent of whom normally voted, fully 90 percent flocked to the polls. Washington's election thrilled and inspired blacks everywhere.

As a direct result, over 100 black young volunteers showed up in Boston to organize voter-registration drives for the 1984 presidential election, even though this was 19 months off.

What difference can one vote make? In 1932, Adolf Hitler was elected leader of the Nazi Party by only one vote. In a less spectacular but nevertheless close election, Grover Cleveland was elected president in 1884. PHOTO COPYRIGHT APRIL 1, 1908.

Like Cleveland, President John F. Kennedy was elected to the office by less than a majority of the popular vote. Other presidents with this distinction: Hayes, Garfield, Harrison, Wilson, Truman, and Nixon.

"It's unheard of," marveled black City Councilor Bruce Boiling. "Generally people don't think about registration until two months before the election."

Other ethnic groups like Mexican Americans and Cuban Americans were impressed. They began cooperating with blacks to support candidates pledged to help minorities. All political parties began paying more attention to the minority vote.

"In the final analysis, it is up to you," Patrick J. McGarvey, a former CIA agent, reminded American voters. "It is the boom of your voice that will bring about the necessary changes. As an individual you no doubt have a feeling of impotence when it comes to influencing your government. Collectively, however, you have tremendous impact. It requires only that you get a slight ground swell started."

Turning out the vote is one way to do that. Any citizen of any age with a burning desire to stop injustice and a willingness to get others to sign on is a one-person dynamo.

"What old people say you cannot do, you try and find that you can," Thoreau advised youth in Walden. "Old deeds for old people, and new deeds for new."

Thomas Carlyle reminded us, "Every new opinion, at its starting, is precisely in a minority of one." And as Henrik Ibsen pointed out, the majority of today was the minority of twenty years ago, because it takes that long for progressive ideas to prevail and transform popular opinion.

If you want to participate in getting out the vote, you can join 120,000 Teen Age Republicans in any of 50 states, or the Young Democrats of America in over 40 states. The American Student Association has branches in many colleges. COPE, the AFL-CIO's political-action arm, recruits young volunteers. The League of Women Voters is a nonpartisan organization devoted to working for open and responsive government. The National Organization for Women (NOW) works for policies that will bring women into the mainstream of American society. And there are many third parties that would eagerly welcome the aid of as many young volunteers as they can get.

Check your local phone book for the names and phone numbers of the organization you'd like to work with. If it isn't listed, phone the local office of your state or federal representative for this information.

It's your country. If you care about it, use your vote when you have it, and help your fellow citizens use theirs.

Or would you rather turn the country over to political bosses to run it as they please?

17

Is Your Job Done When Your Candidates Win?

In 1964, while the Vietnam civil war raged, Americans voted for Lyndon Johnson as president because of his promise of a "Great Society" program, which would end poverty in America, and his assurances about Vietnam: "We don't want our American boys to do the fighting for Asian boys. We don't want to get . . . tied down in a land war in Asia."

Yet Johnson let his Great Society program go by default, throwing America's resources instead into sending half a million American boys to fight the most unpopular war in our history. His broken promises outraged millions of Democrats who had voted for him. They flooded the White House with tons of protesting mail and staged huge anti-war demonstrations.

Johnson did not dare to run for another term

As when your favorite baseball, football, or basketball team wins the season's honors, it's highly satisfying when your favorite candidate or political party wins an election. But the consequences are vastly more important. One week after a sports team is victorious, the event is ancient history and has no further impact on your life. But for the length of an election term, the victorious candidates or party will affect your life by the laws they pass.

If you have voted for or helped get out the vote for the winning side, you may feel that your job is done. Your choices are in place, and now it's up to them to do all the things they promised during the campaign. It's okay now to sit back and "let George do it." Right?

Wrong. Often much of what has been promised during a campaign turns out to be empty oratory. Elected officials or the party may give halfhearted lip service to the goals they promised to the electorate, but then they take no real action to achieve them through legislation. Or they may enact a watered-down, weak, ineffective law that is really a betrayal of their pledge.

Moreover, as new problems arise, a candidate you elected may take a position in dealing with them that you strongly oppose. Just because you've elected leaders to represent you, does that mean you're obligated to support everything they do? Those in office are responsible to the people who elected them. They need to hear from their constituents when their decisions are disappointing, especially in issues of such life-and-death importance as peace and war.

A case in point was the decision of President James Polk to declare war on Mexico in 1846 in order to seize huge areas of Mexican land. Far from docilely accepting this decision, the voters of every New England state reprimanded him sharply. The Massachusetts legislature even flirted with charges of treason by resolving that it was the patriotic duty of "all good citizens to join in efforts to arrest this war."

Similarly, in 1916 Woodrow Wilson campaigned on the slogan, "He kept us out of the war." And just one year earlier he had promised, "We will not ask our young men to spend the best years of their lives making soldiers of themselves!"

Then in 1917 Wilson reversed himself and took the country into World War I. There was deep bitterness among those who had voted for him to keep America at peace, and many dared to speak out openly against the war. Hundreds, including Eugene Debs, were imprisoned under a new Sedition Act rushed through Congress to make "disloyal language" a felony.

No group of Americans is better qualified to testify as to the broken promises of government officials than Native Americans. Despite dozens of treaties signed with Native American tribes, the government has broken almost every one, seizing their best lands and driving them onto arid reservations.

Government officials turned a deaf ear to their complaints until finally Senator Robert Kennedy headed a new subcommittee to investigate conditions on the reservations. "I am doing my best," he told a group of Native American students in one state, "to get you your civil rights."

"Never mind our civil rights, Senator," one young man replied wryly. "Just get us back our country!"

Voters weary of being deceived about Vietnam under the Johnson administration listened to Republican candidate Richard Nixon promise, "It's time we once again had an open administration—open to the ideas from the people and open in its communication with the people—an administration of open doors, open eyes, and open minds." He also promised voters an administration dedicated to "law and order."

Voters elected him in 1968, only to get an administration that proved one of the most dishonest and lawless administrations in the history of the country—the administration that expanded the Vietnam War for four more years and that ended in the Watergate scandal.

But as Nixon himself noted in his book *Six Crises,* "Voters quickly forget what a man says." He proved it by winning a second term despite his broken promises, largely because the full extent of his criminal behavior had not yet been exposed by Election Day of 1972. When it was, however, public outrage was so great that an avalanche of angry mail forced even Republican congressmen to announce they would vote for his impeachment.

The media serve America well when they remind voters of the discrepancy between what politicians say and what they do. This makes it more difficult for them to shift positions when it is politically expedient. When California Senator Alan Cranston announced his candidacy for the 1984 Democratic presidential nomination, he sought to unite all the nuclear-freeze forces behind him. He declared himself "convinced that, in the long run, we cannot revive our economy—or save our society—until we end the incredibly dangerous, shamefully expensive arms race." That won much liberal support.

But the media pointed out that Cranston had supported President Reagan's decision to revive the costly B-1 bomber, which would be built in Cranston's home state. Was expediency, the media asked, more important than principle?

Australian correspondent Elisabeth Wynhausen, stationed in Washington, found discrepancies between President Reagan's claims and his performance. Checking on his claim that as governor of California he had reduced the public payroll, she found that during his governorship, the number of state public servants had increased by 21 percent instead.

Campaigning for president, he had promised a balanced budget by 1984. Elected, he declared that it was unrealistic not to expect a national deficit of $100 billion at least. He had campaigned with promises to weed out "waste, fraud, and mismanagement." Elected, he had demanded record billions for the Pentagon, which all government agencies agreed was the worst culprit in waste, fraud, and mismanagement. Campaigning, he had attacked arms control negotiations with the Soviet Union as "appeasement." Elected, he promised to speed up arms control talks with the Russians.

Widespread public protest forced Reagan to backtrack on some of his initiatives. When he violated the 1980 Republican platform plank opposing the withholding of a percentage of interest and dividends for the Internal Revenue Service, a deluge of protest mail caused Congress to delay his proposal indefinitely.

Even *Reader's Digest*, an enthusiastic Reagan supporter, criticized him for his appointees to head the Environmental Protection Agency (EPA), whom he praised as well qualified to provide the nation with clear air and water. The *Digest* revealed that, by secret agreement with White House officials, the agency's assignment to clean up dangerous dumps and spills was sabotaged, protecting the industries responsible.

A different Republican president, Dwight D. Eisenhower, had declared, "There may be some cynics who think that a platform is just a list of platitudes to lure the naive voter—a sort of facade behind which candidates sneak into power and then do just as they please. I am not one of these."

Most historians agreed that he was not.

It needs to be pointed out that some candidates do honestly try to keep their campaign promises when they win election. Often, however, they depend heavily on campaign funds contributed by special interests that expect legislation favoring them. Such candidates have to weigh conscience against practicality. They may listen to their conscience if enough voters pressure them to vote in the public interest.

There are several ways you can try to hold elected candidates to their campaign promises, forcing them to pay attention to your disagreement with their policies. The easiest and best is to write them letters. Representatives and senators, state as well as national, are sensitive to voter reactions in their mail. So are presidents, governors, and state, county, and local officials. They also pay attention to letters to the editors of newspapers and magazines, because such letters are read and considered by thousands of voters.

Public officials pay particular attention to letters of protest from those who have helped to elect them, whether by contributions, votes, or helping in their campaigns. They hope that they can count on the same support for their reelection campaigns. Thus it becomes important for them either to change their stand or to persuade dissatisfied supporters that their stand is a correct one.

Another way to express disapproval of elected officials' behavior in office is through state primary elections. When you vote against a president, governor, senator, representative,

A vote for James Polk in 1844 was a vote for U.S. territorial expansion, but when he declared war on Mexico in 1846 so the U.S. could seize Mexican land, every New England state opposed his decision. LITHOGRAPH BY P. HAAS, 1844.

When the Narragansett Indians offered shelter to Roger Williams, little did the Native Americans realize what was to follow. Despite dozens of treaties that U.S. government officials signed, the government broke almost every one and stole the Indians' land, confining them to reservations. ENGRAVING BY J. C. ARMYTAGE AFTER A. H. WRAY.

mayor, or other elected official in a state primary, you are sending that candidate a message. The size of the official's reduced vote lets him know clearly how much he has failed to live up to his constituents' expectations.

If enough voters are disillusioned, and the official is defeated, his successor will also get the message. The chances are then brighter that this time you will get the kind of administration you voted for.

18

How Other Countries Choose Their Leaders

An intriguing view of early American elections through European eyes was provided in 1835 by a young Frenchman, Count Alexis de Tocque-ville, when he wrote a book about his visit to America four years earlier. Tocqueville was dubious about French interest in borrowing the American practice of universal suffrage. He felt that the animosity of the masses toward the better-educated classes would result in the election of uneducated incompetents to public office.

That had already happened in America, he noted. The election of roughnecks like Andrew Jackson, Sam Houston, and Davy Crockett to public office showed "how far wrong the people can go . . . to be represented by people of their own kind." It was deplorable that a "David Crockett, who has no education, can read with difficulty, has no property, no fixed residence, but passes his life hunting," should be considered qualified to help make the nation's laws in Congress.

Tocqueville sympathized with leading Americans who refused to seek public office: "To win votes one has to descend to maneuvers that disgust distinguished men. You have to haunt the taverns and dispute with the populace: That's what they call *electioneering* in America."

He expected all New World democracies to become tyrannies through the abuse of power by their elected incompetents.

"It's through this . . . evil," Tocqueville predicted darkly, "that the American republics will perish."

The election of President Andrew Jackson horrified French Count Alexis de Tocqueville, who wrote that it exemplified "how far wrong the people can go . . . to be represented by people of their own kind." This picture is of Jackson's inaugural reception in 1828. COLONIAL AQUA-TINT BY ROBERT CRUIKSHANK IN THE PLAYFAIR PAPERS, 1841.

The secret ballot is as old as the ancient Roman Republic, where it was first adopted in 139 B.C. But the kings who ruled Europe for centuries afterward did not take kindly to any kind of ballot, secret or otherwise. Prince Clemens von Metternich, who forged the Holy Alliance of European monarchs in 1815, warned them that a growing demand for popular elections threatened their thrones.

"Rule must come from above, not below," he cautioned.

But the spread of the Industrial Revolution doomed the old order. Constitutional government gradually spread throughout Europe in the nineteenth century, even though many monarchs were allowed to remain on their thrones as figureheads.

For the first half of the century, votes had to be cast openly under the grim observation of powerful monarchist factions, who could mark opposing voters for reprisal. Finally public pressure forced France to adopt the secret ballot in 1852. Italy followed the trend in 1859. England resisted secret voting at parliamentary and municipal elections until 1872.

The twentieth century saw the rise of a new threat to the institution of free elections in Europe—dictatorship.

When the old Czarist regime in Russia was overturned by revolution in 1917, the Russian people won the right to vote for the first time in their history. But not for long. The Bolshevik Party soon seized power, substituting a "dictatorship of the proletariat" for elected public officials. Only a small band of dedicated Marxists, the communists insisted, was qualified to govern a nation for the benefit of the masses. Elections were scorned as a bourgeois system by which the ruling classes deceived and controlled the people for profit.

The next important challenge to free elections came in the Italy of King Victor Emmanuel, when Fascist leader Benito Mussolini ran for a seat in the Chamber of Deputies in 1921. His Blackshirt followers organized torchlight parades, tossed bombs into socialist meetings, and beat up opponents and forced castor oil down their throats. A year later, Mussolini led a march on Rome, seizing power as prime minister. "We Fascists throw poisonous ideas about liberty on the rubbish heap!" he roared in a balcony speech to a huge crowd. "Italians are tired of liberty. They want and need order, authority, discipline!" Although he scoffed at voting as a "childish game," Mussolini held fraudulent elections in 1924 to "prove" to the world that the Italian people supported his dictatorship. His Blackshirt squads broke up rival meetings, terrorized voters at the polls, stuffed the ballot boxes, then tallied the votes and announced their leader's "victory."

From then until Mussolini's downfall during World War II, the only elections held were those in which Fascists alone were permitted to run. "I prefer fifty thousand rifles to five thousand votes," Mussolini once cried. "A party in power has the duty to defend itself against all!"

Mussolini's example inspired Germany's Adolf Hitler, leader of the Nazi Party, whose Brownshirts waged street warfare against working-class and Jewish districts. By 1932 Hitler had captured over a third of the popular electoral vote and was able to compel his appointment as chancellor of Germany. He lost no time in seizing total power as dictator.

"The man who feels called upon to govern a people has no right to say, 'If you want me or summon me, I will cooperate, '" he explained. "No! It is his duty to step forward!"

That was the end of free elections in Nazi Germany.

Another dictatorship arose in Spain, when Generalissimo Francisco Franco, with military aid from Hitler and Mussolini, led a revolt against the legally elected republican (Loyalist) government in 1936. After the Fascists had shot their way to power three years later, Franco proclaimed himself Caudillo, Chief of State for Life. His firing squads executed 30,000 republican prisoners. He ruled Spain with an iron fist until his death in 1975, when liberal King Juan Carlos took power and subsequently restored free elections to Spain.

Portugal became a republic after the overthrow of its monarchy in 1910. But in the next sixteen years, there were 24 revolutions and 44 changes of government. Finally, in 1926 the military seized power, establishing a dictatorship under Antonio de Oliveira Salazar. When several thousand Portuguese signed a petition urging free elections, Salazar had his secret police locate these "Red intellectuals"[5] for "correction."

Pressured by Portugal's Western allies, Salazar announced elections for 1949. When a political opponent took him seriously and tried to run, Salazar denounced him as a public enemy, compelling him to withdraw his candidacy. The tactic was repeated in 1951. Unopposed, Salazar "won" each time.

Not until 1958 did an air force general, Humberto Delgado, dare defy Salazar by stumping the country to campaign against him. Rigging the election as usual, the dictator declared Delgado the loser. The Bishop of Oporto indignantly cried fraud. Salazar promptly went on TV to announce that he was abolishing popular elections and punishing all "agitators." Delgado, who prudently fled to Brazil, was subsequently murdered.

Illness forced Salazar's retirement in 1968. After several succeeding military dictatorships, popular discontent finally restored elections to Portugal in 1975.

For centuries most Asian people were governed by either autocratic monarchs or Western colonial powers. The first break in this pattern came in 1912, when forces led by republican Sun Yat-sen finally overthrew the Manchu dynasty in China. But his republic was quickly subverted by warlords and their ally, Chiang Kai-shek, who kept China a dictatorship.

In 1948 communist forces led by Mao Tse-tung overthrew Chiang and the warlords, only to establish a Marxist dictatorship under which free elections were still forbidden. That situation still prevails in the China of today.

In 1954, inspired by Mao, Vietnam communist leader Ho Chi Minh led Vietminh revolutionists against ruling French colonial forces and defeated them. A peace settlement at Geneva was guaranteed by the British, the Russians, the Chinese, and the Americans, who withdrew, however, while promising not to interfere with the Geneva Accords.

This agreement decreed that the French were to withdraw to the south, and Ho Chi Minh's forces to the north, to prepare for nationwide elections two years later that would determine a unified government for all Vietnamese.

"I have never talked or corresponded with a person knowledgeable in Indochinese affairs," President Eisenhower subsequently admitted, "who did not agree that had the elections

Italian dictator Benito Mussolini held fraudulent elections in 1924 to prove that people supported him. His Blackshirt squads terrorized voters and counted the votes themselves to guarantee his victory. Mussolini's tactics were a source of inspiration to Adolf Hitler and his Brownshirts. PHOTO BY UNDERWOOD & UNDERWOOD.

Hitler and Mussolini aided Generalissimo Francisco Franco in establishing his dictatorship in Spain. Franco proclaimed himself Chief of State for Life, and he had 30,000 republican prisoners executed to seal that proclamation. He died in 1975, after ruling Spain for almost 40 years. PHOTO BY ALFONSO.

been held as of the time of the fighting, possibly 80 percent of the population would have voted for Ho Chi Minh."

They never got the chance because Eisenhower's secretary of state, John Foster Dulles, was determined to sabotage the Geneva Accords. He set up a puppet government in South Vietnam, which rejected the scheduled elections. The result was the disastrous Vietnam War, involving an American intervention with troops that was denounced by most nations in the world.

When outraged American public opinion finally forced the Nixon administration to sign a peace that extracted U.S. forces from the Vietnamese quagmire, North Vietnam quickly overran and defeated South Vietnam. They could then have held the long-postponed national elections and probably have won. The elections were never held. As in other countries where the communists won power militarily, there were no further free elections. Elections represented a dangerous precedent for the future.

After World War II, African nations began to fight off the yoke of colonialism. The first to succeed was the Belgian Congo, now called Zaire, which won its freedom and the right to hold its first election in 1960. Almost 200 tribes speaking 400 different languages and dialects participated. Murders of each other's candidates were not uncommon. Polling booths were wrecked, election officials beaten. Rival tribes speared each other in the streets. The elections left some 60 dead, hundreds wounded.

The omens were not too bright for the peaceful transition of other former African colonies to new democracies.

Closer to home, the Cuban people had suffered under the tyrannical and corrupt rule of U.S.-supported dictator Fulgencio Batista until 1959, when he was overthrown by a popular revolution led by Fidel Castro. Castro instituted sweeping reforms benefiting the poor Cuban masses at the expense of the middle classes, many of whom fled to the United States.

Most journalists who covered the Cuban revolution agreed that if elections had been held, Castro would have been the overwhelming choice of the people. But he resisted all demands for elections, saying, "They would be unfair because I would be swept into office."

At a May Day rally in 1961, he told a huge crowd that elections were unnecessary: "A revolution expressing the will of the people is an election every day, not every four years; it is a constant meeting with the people, like this meeting. The old politicians could never have gathered as many votes as there are people here tonight to support the revolution."

When he asked the crowd to express their will, they roared back the answer he wanted: "No elections!"

One bitter opponent, Urrutia Lleo, declared, "Castro's maneuver was successful. He knew that the people would reject the kind of elections that had been held so often before in Cuba, and he did not offer them better ones, democratic, honest elections."

The U.S. State Department cited Castro's refusal to hold elections as proof that Cuba was a communist state. But Castro did not turn to the Soviet Union for aid until Washington had rejected his appeal for a U.S.-Cuban accord and had instead sought to overthrow him by the Bay of Pigs invasion.

In India, Prime Minister Indira Gandhi was found guilty in 1975 of violating the election laws to win her seat in Parliament. Faced with demands for her resignation, she declared a state of emergency instead and assumed dictatorial powers. Tens of thousands of her political opponents were jailed. Censoring the press, she suspended further elections. Angry dissenters fought running gun battles with police.

Turmoil in India grew so great that Gandhi was finally forced to dissolve Parliament in 1977 and announced new elections for March. She tried to rig them against the opposition, but she failed. Voted decisively out of office, she sought to mollify the citizens by restoring civil liberties, abolishing censorship, freeing political prisoners, and then resigning. But she was imprisoned awhile for her misdeeds.

Nevertheless three years later the Indians forgave her, electing her to a second chance as prime minister. This time, she promised, India would continue to operate as a democracy.

Fresh political storms brewed in 1983 over a scheduled election in the state of Assam, where Hindus were enraged over the heavy immigration of Muslim Bengalis from Bangladesh. Boycotting the election, which the Bengalis were expected to win, the Hindus demanded that Gandhi cancel it. Perhaps because her party would gain from the Bengali vote, she refused. The result was a horrifying massacre.

Ten thousand Hindus in Assam marched with guns, spears, and arrows against 50 Muslim villages. They burned huts, chased the villagers into cornfields, and hunted them down like rabbits. Women and children were killed. As village after village burned to the ground, the death toll exceeded 3,000.

Such are the lethal passions that can swirl around foreign elections deciding supremacy between mortal enemies.

The British electoral system differs from ours in a number of significant ways. We vote for a president. The English vote for a party; the party that wins the most seats in Parliament forms a government, and its leader becomes prime minister. Our president's term is four years. Each Parliament sits for five years, but it can be dissolved by a vote of no confidence in the government or by new elections called sooner by the prime minister.

Traditionally, Britain has given its voters a choice between the Conservative Party and the Labor Party. A split in Labor's ranks, however, has produced a third-party alliance of Social Democrats and Liberals. This split allowed Conservative Prime Minister Margaret Thatcher to remain in power in a 1983 election with only 43.1 percent of the total vote.

Britain also has its share of tiny splinter parties, many of them expressing the British sense of humor at the cost of a $240 filing fee. There are the Nobody Party, the Independent Mushroom Party, the Ban the Old Fogeys Party, the Best Party I've Ever Been To Party, Freddie's Alternative Medicine Party, and Jim the Fish Conservative Independent Party.

The Official Monster Raving Looney Party ran against Thatcher in her own home constituency. Its leader, Screaming Lord Sutch, campaigned with the slogan: "Give a vote for insanity. You know it makes sense!"

Australia offers its voters a choice between the Labor Party and the conservative Liberal/Country Party. Voting is compulsory, with fines for any citizen who fails to vote in a national election. In 1983 an Australia newspaper accused the American CIA of secretly interfering in a previous election in order to defeat the Labor Party.

The French elect their president for a seven-year term. He appoints the premier. The French Parliament consists of a National Assembly and Senate. The president has the right to dissolve the Assembly and call for new elections.

There are many different French parties, no one of which holds a majority in Parliament. Most laws are passed by a coalition between parties. France turned socialist in the spring of 1981 with the election of Frangois Mitterand as president. In municipal elections 22 months later, the dissatisfied French voted heavily anti-socialist. But like him or lump him, Mitterand would remain their president for another five years.

After World War II, a defeated Germany was divided into the Federal Republic of Germany (West Germany), a democracy allied to Europe and the U.S.; and the German Democratic Republic (East Germany), a communist state linked to the Soviet Union. More than the ugly Berlin Wall erected by East Germany divides the two German governments.

West Germany is governed by a Parliament, whose *Bundestag* members are elected for four-year terms. Together with an appointed upper chamber, the *Bundesrat*, they elect a president for a five-year term. The *Bundestag* alone chooses the chancellor, or prime minister. The major parties are the Social Democratic Party and the Christian Democratic Union/Christian Social Union Party.

Something of a stir was created in 1983 when a new party called the Greens, supported by German youth, won five seats in the *Bundestag*. They marched to Parliament wearing jeans and sweaters, in a festive parade featuring banners, bongo drums, and flowers. The Greens vowed to work against nuclear power plants, acid rain, the East-West arms race, and NATO.

West German elections have a remarkably high voluntary voter turnout. A European Community study found the levels of political discussion in West Germany to be the highest on the continent, a remarkable turnaround for a people who, under the Nazis, did not dare express a controversial opinion.

East German citizens have little to say about how they are governed. That is determined by the Socialist Unity (communist) Party, which handpicks the 500 deputies who are "elected" to the People's Chamber for five-year terms. The Chamber chooses the Council of State and Council of Ministers who carry on executive functions. But the real power in East Germany is suggested by 400,000 Soviet troops garrisoned there.

On the other hand, in communist Yugoslavia, non-communists can run for office. There is also relative freedom to criticize the government, unusual in a communist society, although advocating its overthrow could result in arrest.

Yugoslavs vote for delegates, who then vote for the councils that run the nation's six republics and the federal government. A policy of rotating the national leadership annually gives each republic's council representative a chance to be president. This system prevents any one official from becoming a dictator or any one republic from becoming dominant.

Hungary, too, is liberalizing its regime. Non-communist candidates have been permitted to run for office in 39 of the nation's 352 parliamentary districts. Under new proposals for 1985 sponsored by communist officials, up to 85 percent of seats in the National Assembly will be open to non-communists.

From 1967 to 1974 Greece was a dictatorship ruled by a military regime known as "the Colonels," who seized power. A public uproar finally compelled them to agree to elections, which brought about a socialist government. Most Greeks I spoke to during my visit there in 1983 told me that it had made little difference in their lives, except that they now felt free to say anything they pleased in the daily political discussions that go on in the *tavernas*.

Television plays a major role in many West European countries. Britain, Sweden, Denmark, Norway, the Netherlands, and West Germany give generous TV coverage to important political debates. No political advertising is permitted at election time, but free time is made available for party broadcasts.

Twelve political parties in the Dutch Parliament are given ten minutes of TV time four times a year, with extra time at elections. In Britain political broadcasts are shown on all channels, so that viewers cannot escape exposure.

No elections have been more controversial than those in Central America. In El Salvador revolutionists sought to overthrow a brutal government that used army troops and rightist "death squads" to murder dissenters and innocent villagers. Despite its persistent human rights violations, which included the murders of four American nuns, the government was supported by the Reagan administration.

In 1982 the junta in power, prodded by President Reagan, staged elections in El Salvador, which, however, were supervised by its brutal troops. The rebels led a boycott of the election, warning that leftists who tried to vote were likely to be seized and shot. The junta assured a large turnout by letting it be known that Salvadorans who couldn't show proof of having voted might be suspected of being rebel supporters.

The junta won the election, which the rebels disdained as unfree and unrepresentative. President Reagan sought to increase military and economic aid to El Salvador, calling it a vital ally in fighting the spread of communism in Central America. But Congress was appalled when the junta arrested 23 Salvadoran teachers for "terrorism," while the army also kidnapped scores of trade-union and political leaders. Amnesty International protested the junta's capture and torture of political prisoners.

Refusing to increase any aid to the brutal regime until there was proof it was reforming, Congress also demanded that President Reagan compel the junta to enter into negotiations with the rebels for a peaceful solution to the civil war.

What about elections in the nation that is the leading challenger of the United States for world influence?

In the Soviet Union, nomination is tantamount to election. One candidate for each local post is chosen in small, closed meetings controlled by the Communist Party, the union committee in a factory or commune, or often by both together.

Asked why two or more candidates were not nominated for a post, a Soviet official replied, "It would mean you think one of them is not good enough for the office. We don't want to insult our candidates."

Nominations for deputies to the Supreme Soviet take place at a club or Palace of Culture. Officials in the Communist Party apparatus indicate who is to be nominated. Speeches are made on behalf of the candidates. Their nomination, voted on by a show of hands, is always approved unanimously.

Candidates chosen are usually Party members who excel in their jobs and in demonstrated civic concern. Nominated because of the respect they command in their communities, they often have little knowledge of the workings of government.

This is not considered important as long as they follow the Party line. Important legislation does not originate with the Supreme Soviet, which is largely a rubber stamp for decisions made by the Party's *Politburo,* the ruling body of the Soviet Union. Deputies facilitate execution of policy, not its formulation.

"The old deputies will tell me what to do," one newly elected deputy explained, "and I'll carry out my assignments."

During the last ten days of election campaigns, voters are visited by candidates and Party workers speaking in their behalf. These occasions also allow voters to voice grievances they would like the candidates to take care of.

Elections are viewed basically as a public vote of confidence in the Soviet regime. As Election Day draws closer, scarce food items suddenly become abundant in the stores. Soviet papers overflow with praise for communist accomplishments since the Revolution. Bookstores display brochures attacking Western bourgeois elections. These charge that monopolists manipulate and control those elections through fraud and bribery; that blacks and minorities are prevented from voting; and that candidates can be elected by a minority vote, unlike Soviet candidates, who usually get 100 percent of the vote.

On Election Day, polls are set up in schools, Palaces of Culture, and other public places. They are usually decorated with flowers, pictures of Lenin, and red banners with communist slogans. Sometimes there are refreshments and a brass band to reward voters. There are no voting machines. Since there is usually only one candidate for each post, voters can either mark their ballots or just drop them in an urn.

All voters have their names checked off a voting list that tells poll watchers who has failed to vote. By mid-afternoon nonvoters are contacted and reminded of their civic duty. This follow-up has different implications in the Soviet Union than in Western democracies like ours. Soviet elections have something like a 99 percent turnout because few Russians care to attract suspicion, by refusing to vote, that they are dissenters.

On the rare occasions when an angry Russian may enter a voting booth, scratch off the name of the official candidate, and write in his own choice, his vote is invalidated because his candidate has not been nominated and approved.

Soviet elections cost only a tiny fraction of what is spent on American elections. Most campaign workers are unpaid volunteers. Candidates pay nothing in campaign expenses.

The significant difference between Soviet and American elections is, of course, that Russian voters never have the option of turning out one government and installing a new one. They cannot reject and reverse a government policy they don't like. And they have no real choice of candidates to represent them. No free elections, in the Western sense, can be said to exist in the Soviet Union.

It would boggle the mind if 70 percent of American candidates elected to Congress were suddenly to be arrested and executed by the president of the United States. Yet former Premier Nikita Khrushchev revealed that in 1934 Josef Stalin had done just that to Soviet deputies: "It was determined that of the 139 members and candidates of the Party's Central Committee who were elected at the Seventeenth Congress, 98 persons, i.e., 70 percent, were arrested and shot."

Western democracies, with all their shortcomings, still offer their citizens a free choice of candidates and programs.

Dictatorships have an advantage in that their unlimited powers enable them to act more swiftly than democracies. It only takes a change of mind by one person or a few people to change the whole course of government.

A constitutional democracy, on the other hand, is deliberately slowed down by checks and balances. Power and authority are divided among a president, Congress, and Supreme Court; or a prime minister, Parliament, and High Court.

These precautions also make it difficult for any one person or group in a democracy to gain enough power to impose a dictatorship upon its people. That is the great strength of all democratic electoral systems, including our own.

19

What's Good and What's Bad About Our System

No one would claim that our electoral system is perfect.

We have had notable presidents like Thomas Jefferson, Abraham Lincoln, and Franklin D. Roosevelt. But our system has also put into the White House presidents who were "eminently forgettable" mediocrities like Millard Fillmore, Franklin Pierce, and James Buchanan; and presidents like Ulysses S. Grant, Warren Harding, and Richard M. Nixon whose administrations were corrupt.

Certainly no electoral system can guarantee that only the finest, most intelligent and honest chief executive will emerge victorious. But one has to question why Americans have so often made poor choices.

During the Nixon administration, the American public was shocked by disclosure of the Watergate scandal. They were stunned further when tapes of conversations within the White House were made public, revealing the president and his aides as cynical, vulgar, dishonest, and corrupt. After Nixon was forced to resign and many of his aides went to jail, millions wondered how they could have been so misled as to have voted for such an administration not just once, but twice.

Perhaps we need to pay less attention to political propaganda and self-serving pitches by candidates and parties, and more to factual campaign information provided by such organizations as the League of Women Voters and Common Cause.

Some voters are dissatisfied with the convention system of the two major parties because often the candidates chosen, instead of being the best each party can offer, represent a compromise between opposing factions within each party. The electorate is then faced with a choice of two unexciting major candidates. Consequently, many disgusted voters either stay home on Election Day or protest by voting for a third party.

During the 1960s and early 1970s, voters became disillusioned about professional politicians after Vietnam and Watergate. Democrat Jimmy Carter won election promising that his administration would stay close to the people because he was not part of the Washington Establishment. Similarly, Republican Ronald Reagan won election by promising voters to "get the federal government off our backs."

The election of presidents who lack national experience is a mistake, argues Nelson W. Polsby of the University of California at Berkeley in his book *Consequences of Party Reform*. "That our two most recent presidents [Carter and Reagan] should be arguably the two most nationally inexperienced in American history," he declares, "cuts directly across the grain of common sense that tells us that duties of the presidency are not smaller today than when more seasoned candidates . . . were routinely the only ones considered qualified for the job."

Our turnout at the polls, poor at best in the past, seems gradually to be growing even worse. In 1960 slightly over 3 in 5 citizens voted in a presidential election. This percentage steadily declined until the 1980 election, when only 53.9 percent of the population—slightly over half—bothered going to the polls. Thus Ronald Reagan was elected president by less than 28 percent of Americans eligible to vote.

Perhaps one reason is that we're too engrossed in our private affairs to pay attention to shaping the government we live under. As long ago as 1896, M. I. Ostrogorski, a Russian visitor observing American politics, reflected, "The desperate race for wealth has absorbed the citizen and has not left him time

THE CRADLE OF THE G.O.P.

FIRST REPUBLICAN CONVENTION HELD AT LAFAYETTE HALL, PITTSBURG, PA, FEB, 22ᴰ 1856.

LITHOGRAPH BY ARMOR LITHOGRAPH COMPANY, 1897

GET OUT !!

G.O.P. PROTECTION

FREE TRADE DEMOCRACY

FULL DINNER PAIL

TRYING TO KICK IT OVER.

POLITICAL CARTOON BY LEON BARRITT, OCTOBER 1, 1904

Perhaps voters should turn their attention from political propaganda and self-serving campaign speeches to factual information provided by organizations such as the League of Women Voters and Common Cause.

BEN SHAHN PHOTO

LITHOGRAPH PRINTED BY B. THURSTON, 1856

to attend to the public welfare; it even encouraged his want of public spirit and converted it almost into a virtue."

George E. Reedy, former press secretary to President Lyndon B. Johnson, thinks the problem lies in public dissatisfaction with mediocre, muddling White House leadership. Perhaps we need to shake off resignation and apathy by getting mad instead—mad enough to "turn the rascals out."

On Election Day, that is our time-honored form of peaceful revolution, one of the great strengths of our electoral system. As long as we enjoy the right to vote against candidates, parties, and programs we oppose, we can feel confident of living in freedom. Even if our choices are mistaken, as they often are, we will always have another opportunity to reverse them at the next regular election . . . if only we take it.

One serious defect in our electoral system is the advantage large campaign funds give to some candidates. As the law presently operates, huge sums can be spent on behalf of a candidate's campaign as long as he presumably does not have control of those expenditures himself.

Trade association, labor union, corporation, and other PACs were revealed to have spent $83 million on behalf of 1982 congressional candidates. "When PACs give money they expect something in return other than good government," observed Republican Senator Robert Dole, chairman of the Senate Finance Committee.

Democrat Representative Thomas Downey declared, "You can't buy a congressman for five thousand dollars, but you can buy his vote on a particular issue." There are 3,371 PACs of all kinds, only a quarter of them pro-labor.

"The financing of elections must be altered if there is to be authenticity in our society," insists Professor Art Pearl. "A campaign *by* Big Money must also be a campaign run *for* Big Money. That leaves us no alternative but to think small—to spend no more money than needed, to build a mass base of large numbers of persons contributing modest amounts. . . . If contribution is monopolized by the few, the quality of life must suffer for the majority."

England's campaign period is only one month. If we could shorten ours, the cost of running for election could be reduced tremendously. There would be many benefits. Candidates would have less need of PACs. Money would be less of an obstacle to running for office. Fewer voters would be bored by yearlong campaigning, and more would be willing to pay attention during the month before Election Day.

On the other hand, our present lengthy campaigns do serve to help educate voters. During the 1960s, for example, the clashing campaigns of Barry Goldwater and Lyndon Johnson made voters think deeply about the issues of nuclear war. The campaigns of George Wallace, Strom Thurmond, and Robert Kennedy made voters sensitive to racial issues. The campaigns of Hubert Humphrey, George McGovern, and Richard Nixon made them think deeply about the Vietnam War. Such campaigns serve to crystalize views of controversial problems.

Public-opinion polls are both a minus and a plus in our electoral process. Critics charge that they don't merely sample public opinion, but also create or change it. A poll may ask a loaded question that elicits answers favoring one candidate or position. Polls also create a "bandwagon effect." People like to vote with a winner, to bet on a favorite.

If polls show a candidate in the lead for either nomination or election, a certain number of voters are likely to be influenced to jump on that bandwagon. That candidate also finds it easier to win financial support from PACs, which desire to back a winner who will be obligated to them.

Polls can't, of course, be outlawed. They're part of a free press, of the people's right to know. And they do satisfy public curiosity about how well candidates are doing, who seems to be forging ahead, and which issues are prevailing. In that sense they serve the electoral process well, because they contribute to the interest in a campaign race.

Perhaps what's needed is greater public awareness that polls are only straws in the wind. Voters' minds change from week to week with new developments. Schools could also help by educating tomorrow's voters to think for themselves, rather than follow the herd just to "be with a winner."

There is controversy over the role of the media in our elections. Conservatives accuse them of being biased in favor of liberal candidates because many reporters and editors are liberals. On the other hand, liberal and radical candidates accuse the media of being under the thumb of their wealthy owners and big advertisers, slanting campaign coverage to favor conservative candidates.

Presidential candidates have often complained about the media's scrutiny, which Democratic Senator George McGovern labeled often "beyond reason." When he had delivered a major campaign address, the media had largely ignored it, playing up instead a personal feud between two of his staff members.

When a newspaper had attacked the wife of Democratic Senator Edmund Muskie in 1972, he was moved to tears of outrage in public.

The media blew up the incident as an alleged indication of instability, and Muskie's presidential candidacy was destroyed.

When Republican Governor George Romney reversed his support of the Vietnam War, explaining that he had been previously "brainwashed" by the administration's "snow job," the media ended his chances by calling him "the brainwashed candidate."

When Republican President Jerry Ford sought to be elected to a term of his own, he said, in answer to a question, that he didn't think the Polish people considered themselves dominated by the Soviet Union. His error was magnified by the media into an indictment that he was totally ignorant about foreign affairs. It helped defeat his candidacy.

Presidents complain, too, about media reportage once they are elected. But with all their faults, the American media are still free—which means free to make mistakes and free to be unfair from time to time. Would anyone trade them for controlled media that report only what the government allows?

A major flaw in our electoral system is its discrimination against women. They have a hard time unseating male officials in office, who have decided advantages as incumbents—name recognition, party support, favors done for constituents, easy access to campaign funds. They are also handicapped by the myth that women aren't qualified to be politicians.

PACs contribute to far more men than women. One reason is contacts made by men on golf links, at business lunches, at fraternal organizations, at the Chamber of Commerce, etc.—opportunities that are mostly closed to women. When women do get contributions, those are usually only a fraction of the money given to male candidates.

One of the more urgent needs for reforming our electoral system, most political experts agree, is the abolition of the Electoral College, so that citizens can vote directly for their presidential choice instead of for electors with that power.

Unless we make that change, it is quite possible that a candidate may become president even though most of us vote for his opponent. If he wins a state's popular vote by just a single ballot, he gets that state's entire electoral vote. Many similar slim wins give him a lot of electors. Thus he may win the election with a majority of Electoral College votes, even though his opponent gets a majority of the popular vote.

Countless efforts have been made in Congress to abolish the Electoral College, but none have succeeded to date because of reluctance to tamper with our traditional electoral machinery. We can expect a fresh public uproar, however, the next time a candidate wins the White House while losing the popular vote.

The increasing practice of American voters in splitting their tickets, instead of voting for all candidates of a single party, has resulted in what some see as a weakness of our electoral system, while others regard it as a strength.

A president may be of one party, while the majority of one or both houses of Congress may be of the other. The same is true of a governor and his legislature. This can create serious problems if what a president or governor wants, the Congress or state legislature doesn't. Or vice versa. Thus there may be constant squabbles, a series of executive vetoes, and legislation piling up un-passed.

On the other hand, this division of power also provides a series of checks and balances. Neither the chief executive nor the legislators get their way entirely. Often they are compelled to compromise, so that the final legislation that emerges does not ride roughshod over the wishes of the voters who support either party.

The quality of our elections might improve if some way could be found to make voters blind to the color of a candidate's skin. Too often the campaigns of black or Hispanic candidates provoke a backlash of racism, with many voters casting ballots out of prejudice, regardless of the candidates' qualifications or the excellence of their programs.

It is understandable that such prejudice would anger blacks and Hispanics into voting as a bloc for minority candidates. But one can only hope for the day when *all* of us vote for candidates purely on the basis of their character, qualifications, and record, and what they pledge to accomplish in office.

A minor flaw in our electoral system is the time difference in reporting election results, because of the three-hour lag between closing of the polls in the East and on the West Coast. In 1980, when it became clear that Republican Ronald Reagan had won decisively over Democrat Jimmy Carter, Carter graciously and publicly acknowledged defeat soon after early results began coming in, and while the West Coast was still voting.

California's Democratic candidates were furious. They lost votes when many of the state's Democratic voters, hearing Carter's concession on TV, didn't bother going to the polls. They demanded that, in the future, either no election results be broadcast until California voting had ended or all polls shut down at the identical moment, regardless of the different time zones. This would require a compromise as to the hours all polls would be open.

The United States has probably the most elaborate, complicated, and expensive electoral system in the world. It operates according to a kaleidoscope of national, state, and local party rules, state statutes, and special rulings by federal, state, and local courts.

Political maneuvering also goes on for much longer than in any other country. Some critics complain that no sooner is an administration elected than it prepares for the next election.

Yet, with all its shortcomings, our system is recognized as one of the best and most flexible in the world. Consider how we have been able to transfer power peacefully in the most turbulent of times, as during the Vietnam War, civil rights riots, and the Watergate crisis, instead of by violence or armed insurrection. Even when America has been at war abroad, or within itself as during the Civil War, we have continued to hold our elections on schedule. And each time, citizens have been free to vote whether to continue an administration in office or to end it.

When a dictator or junta seizes power, the people of that country have no voice in their own destiny. Even when a coup or uprising with sincerely patriotic motives overturns a tyrannical government, the longer the new dictatorship remains in power without free elections, the more it begins to resemble the tyranny it overthrew. "Power tends to corrupt," said the British historian Lord Acton; "absolute power corrupts absolutely."

That is why, in the United States, we give no presidential administration longer than four years in office without compelling it to submit to new elections. As President Wilson once said, "America is safe only because we do not know who the presidents of the United States are going to be."

In his book *Landslide*, Professor Art Pearl urges students—the voters of tomorrow—to get involved in the electoral process as early as possible. This requires, he says, that "everyone gets with some *political* organization, pays dues, and gets involved in policy determination and candidate selection. . . . *Now* is the time to be involved . . . in your community."

To participate properly in the machinery of our democracy, we need to attend political meetings and work for causes and candidates we believe in. If we don't, a handful of activists are likely to operate and control our governments—local, state, and national. We need to understand the direct link between politics and our personal benefit. If we fail to look after our own interests, why should we expect strangers with different goals to do it for us?

When there is misgovernment in Washington, state capitols, or local offices, it is easy to blame political leaders. But those leaders did not get in power without our votes. As Lincoln Steffens once observed, "The misgovernment of the American people is misgovernment *by* the American people."

We need to work inside the political parties to help select candidates of the highest integrity, instead of permitting political bosses to foist their choices on us. To keep the power out of their hands, more of us have to seek election as convention delegates.

We need to be aware, moreover, that there are among us some who would like to see elections outlawed. They are not many, but they are often tightly organized in paramilitary groups seeking to establish an American dictatorship.

For example, in California, John Capricorn heads a paramilitary group called Orion Nebula 18. "The military order will take possession of the government," he predicts. "What this country needs is a good military dictatorship . . . to straighten out people's perspective."

The only way to keep groups like this at bay is to make certain, by our participation, that the electoral system remains the only way to change our government. "The ballot," Lincoln said, "is stronger than the bullet."

Another way you can participate in the political process is through writing your local officials, state legislators, Senators, and Representatives, letting them know what you think about the issues that concern you. This is an excellent way of making your voice and your views heard, and you don't have to be of voting age. Even if a thirteen-year-old youth writes, an elected official needs to pay attention, because that youth probably has at least two adult voters in the family.

"I read every letter written me by a constituent," declared Arizona Representative Morris K. Udall. "A staff member may process it initially, but it will be answered and I will insist on reading it and personally signing the reply."

Sometimes the candidates we vote for turn out to be terrible choices. As one wit put it wryly, "I'm superstitious—I believe that voting brings four years of bad luck." But lots of other decisions we make also turn out wrong. That doesn't stop us from trying to make better decisions in the future.

And we *have* had some outstanding Americans serving us in the White House, Congress, governor's mansions, and city halls. If we learn all we can about the candidates and the issues and get involved in the electoral process, we're bound to elect a lot more fine leaders.

One of them, in fact, might eventually be you.

ACKNOWLEDGMENTS

For their generous assistance in helping me to shed light on our intricate electoral system, to make it understandable and entertaining without being simplistic, I wish to thank:

My friend Professor Arthur Pearl of the University of California, himself once a candidate for Governor of Oregon; Jean G. Birch, Secretary, and William I. Greener III, Director of Communications, of the Republican National Committee; the National Teen Age Republicans (TARS); Rick Boylan of the Democratic National Committee; the Young Democrats of America; Raymond O. Heaps, G. W. Brown, and William K. Shearer of the American Independent Party; Donald Davis of the Socialist Workers Party; the Young Socialist Alliance; Robert Bills, National Secretary of the Socialist Labor Party; the AFL-CIO Committee on Political Education; and various individuals in Greece, Yugoslavia, France, Northern Ireland, England, and West Germany who discussed their countries' electoral systems with me.

My appreciation, too, to the Knight Publishing Corporation for allowing me to adapt my article "The Man Who Clowned His Way to the State Capitol" (ADAM Magazine), in somewhat different form, for Chapter 12 of this book.

Jules Archer
Santa Cruz, California

APPENDIX

Presidential Winners and Losers

DATE	WINNER	LOSER
1789	George Washington (F)	John Adams (F)
1792	George Washington (F)	John Adams (F)
1796	John Adams (F)	Thomas Jefferson (D-R)
1800	Thomas Jefferson (D-R)	Aaron Burr (D-R)
1804	Thomas Jefferson (D-R)	Charles C. Pinckney (F)
1808	James Madison (D-R)	Charles C. Pinckney (F)
1812	James Madison (D-R)	De Witt Clinton (F)
1816	James Monroe (D-R)	Rufus King (F)
1820	James Monroe (D-R)	John Quincy Adams (N-R)
1824	John Quincy Adams (N-R)	Andrew Jackson (D)
1828	Andrew Jackson (D)	John Quincy Adams (N-R)
1832	Andrew Jackson (D)	Henry Clay (N-R)
1836	Martin Van Buren (D)	William Henry Harrison (W)
1840	William Henry Harrison (W), replaced by Vice-President John Tyler (W) in 1841	Martin Van Buren (D)
1844	James K. Polk (D)	Henry Clay (W)
1848	Zachary Taylor (W), replaced by Vice-President Millard Fillmore (W) in 1850	Lewis Cass (D)
1852	Franklin Pierce (D)	Winfield Scott (W)
1856	James Buchanan (D)	John Charles Fremont (R)
1860	Abraham Lincoln (R)	Stephen A. Douglas (D)

1864	Abraham Lincoln (R), replaced by Vice-President Andrew Johnson (R) in 1865	George B. McClellan (D)
1868	Ulysses S. Grant (R)	Horatio Seymour (D)
1872	Ulysses S. Grant (R)	Horace Greeley (D/Lib. R)
1876	Rutherford B. Hayes (R)	Samuel Jones Tilden (D)
1880	James A. Garfield (R), replaced by Vice-President Chester A. Arthur (R) in 1881	Winfield Scott Hancock (D)
1884	Grover Cleveland (D)	James Gillespie Blaine (R)
1888	Benjamin Harrison (R)	Grover Cleveland (D)
1892	Grover Cleveland (D)	Benjamin Harrison (R)
1896	William McKinley (R)	William Jennings Bryan (D, Pop.)
1900	William McKinley (R), replaced by Vice-President Theodore Roosevelt (R) in 1901	William Jennings Bryan (D)
1904	Theodore Roosevelt (R)	Alton Brooks Parker (D)
1908	William H. Taft (R)	William Jennings Bryan(D)
1912	Woodrow Wilson (D)	Theodore Roosevelt (Prog.)
1916	Woodrow Wilson (D)	Charles Evans Hughes (R)
1920	Warren G. Harding (R), replaced by Vice-President Calvin Coolidge (R) in 1923	James Middleton Cox (D)
1924	Calvin Coolidge (R)	John William Davis (D)
1928	Herbert Hoover (R)	Alfred Emanuel Smith (R)
1932	Franklin D. Roosevelt (D)	Herbert Hoover (R)
1936	Franklin D. Roosevelt (D)	Alfred M. Landon (R)
1940	Franklin D. Roosevelt (D)	Wendell Willkie (R)
1944	Franklin D. Roosevelt (D), replaced by Vice-President Harry S. Truman (D) in 1945	Thomas Edmund Dewey (R)
1948	Harry S. Truman (D)	Thomas Edmund Dewey (R)
1952	Dwight D. Eisenhower (R)	Adlai Ewing Stevenson II (D)
1956	Dwight D. Eisenhower (R)	Adlai Ewing Stevenson II (D)
1960	John F. Kennedy (D), replaced by Vice-President Lyndon B. Johnson (D) in 1963	Richard Milhous Nixon (R)

1964	Lyndon B. Johnson (D)	Barry Morris Goldwater (R)
1968	Richard M. Nixon (R)	Hubert Horatio Humphrey, Jr. (D)
1972	Richard M. Nixon (R), replaced by Vice-President Gerald R. Ford (R) in 1974	George Stanley McGovern (D)
1976	James E. Carter (D)	Gerald R. Ford (R)
1980	Ronald Reagan (R)	James E. Carter (D)

POLITICAL PARTY LEGEND

F = Federalist

D-R = Democratic-Republican

N-R = National-Republican

W= Whig

R = Republican

D = Democrat

Prog. = Progressive

Pop. = Populist

Lib. R = Liberal Republican

BIBLIOGRAPHY AND
RECOMMENDED READING

Archer, Jules. *Angry Abolitionist: William Lloyd Garrison*. New York: Julian Messner, 1969.

————. *Battlefield President: Dwight D. Eisenhower*. New York: Julian Messner, 1967.

————. *Colossus of Europe: Metternich*. New York: Julian Messner, 1970.

*————. *The Dictators*. New York: Hawthorn Books, Inc., Publishers, 1967.

*————. *The Extremists: Gadflies of American Society*. New York: Hawthorn Books, Inc., Publishers, 1969.

————. *Famous Young Rebels*. New York: Julian Messner, 1973.

————. *Fighting Journalist: Horace Greeley*. New York: Julian Messner, 1966.

————. *Hawks, Doves, and the Eagle*. New York: Hawthorn Books, Inc., Publishers, 1970.

————. *Ho Chi Minh: The Legend of Hanoi*. New York: Crowell-Collier Press, 1971.

————. *Indian Foe, Indian Friend*. New York: Crowell-Collier Press, 1970.

————. *Laws That Changed America*. New York: Criterion Books, 1967.

*————. *1968: Year of Crisis*. New York: Julian Messner, 1971.

*————. *The Plot to Seize the White House*. New York: Hawthorn Books, Inc., Publishers, 1973.

---

* Indicates recommended reading.

*————. *Police State.* New York: Harper & Row, Publishers, 1977.

*————. *Resistance.* Philadelphia: Macrae Smith Company, 1973.

*————. *Revolution in Our Time.* New York: Julian Messner, 1971.

*————. *Riot! A History of Mob Action in the United States.* New York: Hawthorn Books, Inc., Publishers, 1974.

————. *The Russians and the Americans.* New York: Hawthorn Books, Inc., Publishers, 1975.

————. *Strikes, Bombs, and Bullets: Big Bill Haywood and the I.W.W.* New York: Julian Messner, 1972.

————. *Superspies: The Secret Side of Government.* New York: Delacorte Press, 1977.

————. *Thorn In Our Flesh: Castro's Cuba.* New York: Cowles Book Company, Inc., 1970.

————. *They Made a Revolution: 1776.* New York: Scholastic Book Services, 1973; St. Martin's Press, 1975.

————. *Treason in America: Disloyalty Versus Dissent.* New York: Hawthorn Books, Inc., Publishers, 1971.

————. *Twentieth-Century Caesar: Benito Mussolini.* New York: Julian Messner, 1964.

————. *Uneasy Friendship: France and the United States.* New York: Four Winds Press, 1972.

————. *The Unpopular Ones.* New York: Crowell-Collier Press, 1968.

*————. *Washington vs. Main Street.* New York: Thomas Y. Crowell Company, 1975.

*————. *Watergate: America in Crisis.* New York: Thomas Y. Crowell Company, 1975.

*————. *Who's Running Your Life?* New York and London: Harcourt Brace Jovanovich, 1979.

*————. *World Citizen: Woodrow Wilson.* New York: Julian Messner, 1967.

*————. *You and the Law.* New York and London: Harcourt Brace Jovanovich, 1978.

*————. *You Can't Do That to Me!* New York and London: Macmillan Publishing Co., Inc., 1980.

*Atkins, Chester G. *Getting Elected: A Guide to Winning State and Local Office.* Boston: Houghton Mifflin Company, 1973.

Bailey, Thomas A. *Presidential Greatness.* New York: Applet on-Century, 1969.

Baker, Kendall L., Russell J. Dalton, and Kai Hildebrandt. *Germany Transformed.* Cambridge and London: Harvard University Press, 1981.

*Barber, James David, ed. *Choosing the President.* Englewood Cliffs, N.J.: Prentice Hall, Inc., 1974.

*Broder, David and staff of the *Washington Post.* *The Pursuit of the Presidency: 1980.* New York: Berkley Books, 1980.

*Bruno, Jerry and Jeff Greenfield. *The Advance Man.* New York: William Morrow and Company, Inc., 1971.

Clavir, Judy and John Spitzer, eds. *The Conspiracy Trial.* Indianapolis/New York: The Bobbs-Merrill Company, 1970.

*Deuel, Wallace R. *People Under Hitler.* New York: Harcourt Brace and Company, 1942.

*Domhoff, G. William. *Fat Cats and Democrats: The Role of the Rich in the Party of the Common Man.* Englewood Cliffs, N.J.: Prentice Hall, 1972.

*Dorman, Michael. *Under 21.* New York: Dell Publishing Co., Inc., 1970.

*Douglas, William O. *The Right of the People.* New York: Arena Books, 1972.

Durant, John and Alice. *Pictorial History of American Presidents.* New York: A. S. Barnes and Company, 1955.

*Ferguson, Thomas and Joel Rogers, eds. *The Hidden Election.* New York: Pantheon Books, 1981.

Gosnell, Harold F. and Richard Smoka. *American Parties and Elections.* Columbus, Ohio: C. E. Merrill, 1976.

Green, Timothy. *The Universal Eye.* New York: Stein and Day, Publishers, 1972.

*Greenfield, Jeff. *Playing to Win: An Insider's Guide to Politics.* New York: Simon &, 1980.

*Gregory, Dick. *Dick Gregory's Political Primer.* New York: Harper & Row, Publishers, 1972.

Haldeman, H. R. *The Ends of Power.* New York: Times Books, 1978.

Harnsberger, Caroline Thomas. *Treasury of Presidential Quotations.* Chicago: Follett Publishing Company, 1964.

*Hoopes, Roy. *Getting With Politics.* New York: Dell Publishing Company, 1968.

Johnston, Mary. *Roman Life.* Chicago: Scott Foreman and Company, 1975.

*Lebedoff, David. *Ward Number Six.* New York: Charles Scribner's Sons, 1972.

Leinwand, Gerald, ed. *Civil Rights and Civil Liberties.* New York: Washington Square Press, Inc., 1968.

Leish, Kenneth W. *The American Heritage Pictorial History of the Presidents of the United States* (3 vols.). New York: American Heritage Publishing Co., Inc., 1968.

Levy, Mark R. *The Ethnic Factor: How America's Minorities Decide Elections.* New York: Simon and Schuster, 1972.

*Mandel, Ruth B. *In the Running: The New Woman's Candidate.* New Haven and New York: Ticknor & Fields, 1981.

Martin, Michael and Leonard Gelber, eds. *The New Dictionary of American History.* New York: Philosophical Library, 1965.

Masters, Nicholas A. and Mary E. Baluss. *The Growing Power of the Presidency.* New York: Parents' Magazine Press, 1968.

*McGinnis, Joe. *The Selling of the President: 1968.* New York: Trident Press, 1969.

Morris, Richard B., ed. *Encyclopedia of American History.* New York: Harper & Row, Publishers, 1965.

*Mote, Max E. *Soviet Local and Republic Elections.* Stanford: Stanford University Press, 1965.

*Murphy, William T. Jr. and Edward Schneier. *Vote Power: How to Work for the Person You Want Elected.* Anchor Press, 1974.

Nash, Gerald D. *The Great Transition.* Boston: Allyn and Bacon, Inc., 1971.

*Neuborne, Burt and Arthur Eisenberg. *The Rights of Candidates and Voters.* New York: Avon Books, 1976.

*Nie, Norman H., Sidney Verba and John R. Petrocik. *The Changing American Voter.* Cambridge & Boston: Harvard University Press, 1979.

*Paizis, Suzanne. *Getting Her Elected: A Political Woman's Handbook.* Sacramento, Calif.: Creative Editions Publishing Co., 1977.

*Papele, Henry. *Banners, Buttons, and Songs: A Pictorial Review of America's Presidential Campaigns.* Cincinnati: World Library Publications, Inc., 1968.

*Pearl, Arthur. *Landslide.* Secaucus, N.J.: The Citadel Press, 1973.

*Polsby, Nelson W. and Aaron Wildausky. *Presidential Elections: Strategies of American Electoral Politics.* New York: Charles Scribner's Sons, 1980.

Quigley, Charles N., exec. dir. *On Participation.* Los Angeles: Law In A Free Society, 1973.

Reedy, George E. *The Twilight of the Presidency.* New York and Cleveland: The World Publishing Company, 1970.

Rosenbloom, David Lee. *The Election Men: Professional Campaign Managers and American Democracy.* New York: Quadrangle, 1973.

*Roseboom, Eugene Holloway and Alfred E. Eckes. *A History of Presidential Elections.* New York: Macmillan Publishing Co., Inc., 1979.

*Russell, Francis. *The President Makers.* Boston/Toronto: Little Brown and Company, 1976.

Saul, Mort. *Heartland.* New York and London: Harcourt Brace Jovanovich, 1976.

*Sandoz, Ellis and Cecil V. Crabb, eds. *A Tide of Discontent: The 1980 Elections and Their Meaning.* Washington, D.C.: Congressional Quarterly Press, 1981.

Seldes, George. *Freedom of the Press.* Indianapolis/New York: The Bobbs-Merrill Company, Publishers, 1935.

*Sherrill, Robert. *Gothic Politics in the Deep South.* New York: Grossman Publishers, 1968.

Sinkler, George. *The Racial Attitudes of American Presidents.* Garden City, New York: Doubleday & Company, Inc., 1971.

*Spero, Robert. *The Duping of the American Voter.* New York: Lippincott & Crowell, Publishers, 1980.

Steam, Gerald Emanuel, ed. *Broken Image: Foreign Critiques of America.* New York: Random House, 1972.

*Steffens, Lincoln. *The Shame of the Cities.* New York: Hill and Wang, 1957.

*Thompson, Hunter S. *Fear and Loathing on the Campaign Trail '72.* New York: Popular Library, 1974.

*Weingast, David E. *We Elect a President.* New York: Julian Messner, 1966.

*White, Theodore. *America in Search of Itself: The Making of the President 1956–1980.* New York: Harper & Row, Publishers, 1982.

*Wolfinger, Raymond E. and Stephen J. Rosenstone. *Who Votes?* New Haven: Yale University Press, 1980.

Also consulted were issues of *Newsweek, The Nation, Reader's Digest, Life, Commonsense, Variety,* the *Australian National Times,* American Civil Liberties Union reports, and political materials provided by various political parties.

INDEX

Abel, Jules, 126, 134

Abolitionists, 23, 89–90, 106–107

Abortion, 20, 100, 116, 118, 169, 179

Acid rain, 218

Acton, Lord, 233

Adams, John, 5, 7, 40–42, 75, 168–169, 184

Adams, John Quincy, 37, 39, 43, 46, 195

Adamson Act, 74

AFL-CIO Committee on Public Education (COPE), 13, 181, 199

Africa, 214

Afro-American Unity Party, 113

Agnew, Spiro T., 54, 56, 176

Alabama, 9, 16, 30, 54, 78, 115, 187, 190

Alaska, 3

Aldrich, Winthrop W., 65

Alexander, Herbert, 65

Alien and Sedition Acts, 5, 184

Allen, George, 51

American Beat Consensus, 113

American Civil Liberties Union (ACLU), 13

American Farm Bureau Association, 181

American Federation of Labor, 112, 178

American and Foreign Christian Union, 105

American Government: Democracy at Work, 129

American Independent Party, 54, 103, 115–116

American League Against War and Fascism, 22

American Medical Association (AMAJ), 181

American Party, 89–90

American Party of the United States, 103

American Protective Association, 185

American Protestant Society, 105

American Railway Union (ARU), 111

American Revolution, 75

American Student Association, 199

American Vegetarian Party, 113

Amnesty International, 220

Anderson, Jack, 175

Anti-draft demonstrations (see Anti-war rallies)

Anti-Federalist Party, 41, 73, 104

Anti-Mason Party, 126

Anti-Saloon League of America, 110, 161

Anti-semitism, 113

Anti-war rallies, 55, 83, 115, 132, 201

Appraisal of U.S. electoral system, 224–235
Arizona, 32, 67, 88, 235
Arms race, 204, 218
Asians, 10, 34, 53, 201, 212
Askew, Reubin, 182
Assassinations, 53, 71, 83, 92
A Tide of Discontent, 26
Australia, 22, 217
    Labor Party, 217
    Liberal/Country Party, 217

Bailey, John, 197
Baker, Howard, 13, 169
Bangladesh, 216
Barnburners Party, 106
Batista, Fulgencio, 214
Bayh, Birch, 12, 86
Bay of Pigs invasion, 83, 215
B-1 bomber, 204
Bedford, Roger, 16
Belgian Congo (*see* Zaire)
Berkeley High School, 14
Berlin Wall, 217
Big business, 26, 64, 66, 73, 88, 92, 107–108, 175, 178, 181
Bilbo, Theodore, 142, 154
Bill of Rights, 2, 174
Birney, James G., 106
Blacks, 6, 9, 34–35, 45, 53, 58, 85, 145, 156, 170, 173, 184–187, 190, 192, 197, 232
    mayors, 58, 156, 170
    vote, 9, 34–35, 85, 156, 170, 173, 186, 190, 192, 195, 197
Blackshirts, 210, 213

Blaine, James G., 194
"Bloody Sixth" ward, 76
Boling, Bruce, 199
"Boll Weevil" Democrats, 54, 56, 81, 100
Bolsheviks, 210
Bonus Army march, 95
Borah, William E., 120
Boray, Alvin, 89
Boston Irish, 77
Bouchet, Edward, 13
Breckinridge, John C., 44, 78, 82
Bridges, Harry, 154
Brown, G.W., 116
Brown, Edmund G., 53
Brown, Pat, 154
Brownshirts, 211, 213
Bryan, William Jennings, 47–48, 50, 78–79, 82, 92, 108, 128, 130
Bryant, William Cullen, 90
Bryce, James, 174
Buchanan, James, 90, 176, 224
Bular, William J., 140
Bull Moose Party, 78, 94
Burr, Aaron, 42–43, 46, 47
Bush, George, 29
Busing, 100, 116
Butler, Edward R., 185
Byrne, Jane, 70

Cajuns, 35
California, 3, 4, 9, 14, 17, 23, 35, 53, 63, 70, 77, 90, 101, 116, 124, 141, 145, 146, 154, 170, 176, 186, 190, 194, 203, 204, 225, 233, 234
    Supreme Court, 10, 186

Campaigning, 15, 20, 29, 48, 52, 60, 67, 70, 84, 85, 94, 134–137, 145, 148, 149, 155, 156, 163, 204
funds, 55, 58, 59, 64, 65, 66, 85, 174, 178, 181, 205, 228, 231
Candidate requirements, 57–72, 167–173
Capitalism, 80, 110–111, 118, 134, 139
Capone, Al, 185
Capricorn, John, 234
Carlyle, Thomas, 199
Carter, Jimmy, 3, 26, 29, 56, 58–60, 63, 66, 69, 84, 133, 151–152, 170, 181, 225, 232–233
Cass, Lewis, 78, 107
Castro, Fidel, 214–215
Castro, Genoveva, 9
Catholics, 5, 31, 48, 58, 74, 105–106, 141, 143, 144, 156, 185
Celler, Emanuel, 117
Censorship, 100
Central America, 219, 220
Chappaquiddick incident, 67
"Checkers" speech, 146
Chiang Kai-shek, 212
Chicago, 13, 54–55, 58, 70, 85, 111, 113, 124, 126, 128–129, 132, 141, 144, 150, 156, 167, 185, 197
Chicanos (see Mexican Americans)
Child Labor, 112
China
Manchu dynasty, 212
People's Republic, 99

Chinese, the, 185, 212
Chisholm, Shirley, 68, 70
Chotiner, Murray, 145, 146
Christian Front, 142
CIA, 199, 217
Civil rights, 6, 34, 54, 80, 85, 115, 170, 186, 203, 233
Acts, 6, 74, 145, 186, 190, 195
Commission, 186
Civil War, 5, 44, 54, 61–62, 78, 83, 91, 107, 201, 220, 233
Clark, Dick, 179
Clark, Champ, 130
Clark, James, 78, 79, 130
Clark, Joseph S., 176
Clay, Henry, 43, 106, 135, 169
Cleveland, Grover, 38, 47, 78, 107, 137, 194, 195, 198
Cold war, 83, 145
Collective bargaining, 48, 112, 178
Collins, Lisa, 119
Colombia, 92
"Colonels, the," Greece, 219
Colonialism, 212, 214
Colt, Samuel, 177
Committee to Reelect the President (CRP), 55, 178
Common Cause, 179, 224, 226
Communism, 51, 80, 97, 99, 101, 104, 111, 113, 116–118, 134, 142, 146–148, 210, 212, 214–215, 217–221
Communist International, 112
Communist Party, U.S.A., 103, 111, 117

Congress, 2, 3, 5, 6, 9, 17, 23, 29, 30, 35, 37, 42–44, 47, 56, 59, 65, 66, 68, 80, 81, 92, 96–98, 100, 104, 106–108, 110, 114, 117, 135, 145, 149, 154, 175–179, 202, 204, 208, 220, 222, 231–232, 235
Congress of Industrial Organizations (CIO), 178
Connecticut, 4, 70, 132
Consequences of Party Reform, 225
Conservation, 88
Conservative Party, 104, 113, 116, 216
Conservatives (*see* Right Wing)
Constitution, 1, 2, 7, 9, 13, 41–42, 110
Constitutional Convention, 40
Constitutional Party, 116
Conventions, political, 40, 68, 122–133
Cook County, 129
delegates, 32, 48, 122–133, 234
Coolidge, Calvin, 63, 94–95, 112, 140, 195
Costigan, Howard, 165
Cotton, Douglas MacArthur, 34
Coughlin, Charles E., 113
Cox, James, 139
Coxey's Army march, 179
Cranston, Alan, 63, 170, 203–204
Crockett, Davy, 136, 208
Croker, Richard, 139
"Cross of Gold" speech, 48, 50, 128
Cuba, 78, 83, 92, 105, 118, 215

Cuban missile crisis, 83
Cuban Americans, 3, 199
Czarist Russia, 210

Daley, Richard J., 54, 132
"Dark-horse" candidates, 48, 67, 85
Davis, Bob, 138
Davis, John W., 140
Dayton, Mark, 65
"Debategate" controversy, 151
Debs, Eugene, 109, 111, 139–140, 143, 202
Decatur, Stephen, 45
Defenders of the Christian Faith, 142
Defense, 80, 88, 179
Delaware, 40, 78
Delegates (*see* political conventions)
Delgado, Humberto, 212
De Leon, Daniel, 110
Democratic Party, 12, 31, 40, 42, 43, 58, 70, 73, 74, 79–81, 83–84, 86, 88, 90, 97, 99, 101, 117, 145, 154, 155, 169, 182
National Committee, 86, 153, 197
1968 Chicago convention, 132
reforms, 74
Democratic-Republican Party, 5, 41–43, 46, 73, 75, 104
Denmark, 219
Denver, 3
Depression, 51, 79, 95, 112, 141, 169, 179
Deukmejian, George, 190

Dewey, Thomas, 81, 96, 122, 144–145, 147
Dictatorships, 23, 88, 168, 210–213, 219, 222–223, 233–235
Dirksen, Everett, 186
Disarmament conference, 94
Discrimination, 5, 74, 100, 119, 231
Dix, I. F., 163
Dixiecrat Party, 80
Dole, Robert, 228
Dore, John F., 158–158, 162
Douglas, Helen Gahagan, 145–146
Douglas, Stephen, 44, 78, 82, 90
Douglas, William O., 187
Downey, Thomas, 228
Draft resistance (see Anti-war rallies)
Dulles, John Foster, 96, 214
Durenberger, David, 65
Dyke, William, 16

East Germany, 217
People's Chamber, 218
Socialist Unity (communist) Party, 218
Education, 14, 15, 35, 89, 101, 104–105, 118, 120
Eighteenth Amendment (see Prohibition)
Eisenhower, Dwight D., 35, 51–52, 59, 61, 64–65, 81, 96–98, 118, 146, 148–149, 166, 175, 205, 212, 214

Elections, 21–28
close, 194–200
costs, 222, 229
election day, 1, 36, 91, 139, 146, 154, 173, 184–185, 195, 197, 203, 221, 225, 228
fraud, 185, 188, 204, 221
procedures, 22, 40, 43, 75, 113, 123, 229, 234
riots, 183
Electoral College, 35, 37–44, 47, 52, 78, 111, 231
El Salvador, 100, 105, 118, 219–220
"death squads," 219
Enforcement Act of 1870, 45
England, 210, 216, 229
Conservative Party, 216
Labor Party, 216
Parliament, 216
Social Democrat-Liberal Party, 216
Environment, 28, 116, 169, 175
Environmental Protection Agency (EPA), 204
Epton, Bernard, 156
Equal Rights Amendment (ERA), 20, 71, 100, 118, 179
Equal Rights Party, 44
Eskimos, 3, 34
Eu, March Fong, 70, 176
Europe, 4, 94, 96, 209–210, 217
Extremists, 77, 88–89, 97, 100, 105, 120, 150

Fala, 144

Falwell, Jerry, 179
Farenthold, Frances, 68
Farley, Jim, 165
Farm aid, 79
Farmer Labor Party, 112–113
Farm relief, 107
Fascism, 22, 113, 142
"Favorite son" candidates, 124–125
FBI harassment, 117
Federal budget deficit, 100
Federal Communications Act, 119
Federal Election Campaign Act of
    1971, 55
Federal Election Campaign Reform
    Act of 1974, 119
Federal Election Commission, 65
Federalists, 41–42, 46, 75, 104, 184
Feinstein, Dianne, 70
Fifteenth Amendment, 4–5, 45
Fillmore, Millard, 90, 106, 109, 224
Financing the 1980 Election, 65
Fitzgerald, "Honey Fitz," 77
Flexner, Abraham, 120
Florida, 4, 35, 45, 78, 137, 178,
    182
Ford, Gerald, 56, 69, 84, 99
Foreign policy, 88, 92, 175
Founding Fathers, 2, 30
Fowler, Wyche, Jr., 173
France, 210, 217
Franco, Francisco, 211, 213
Frankfurter, Felix, 187
Freedom Rides, 6
Free enterprise (*see* Capitalism)
Free silver, 47, 107, 128
Free Soil Party, 89, 106–107

Fremont, John C., 90–91, 93
French Canadians, 35
French Parliament, 217
French Revolution, 75
Fusion Party, 103

Gandhi, Indira, 215
Gang wars, 48, 110, 114
Garfield, Arthur, 195, 198
Garner, John, 71
Garrison, William Lloyd, 23, 107
Geneva Accords, 212, 214
Geocaris, John, 156
George, Henry, 110
Georgia, 40, 56, 58, 70, 78, 173,
    183, 187
German-American Bund, 142
Germany, 140, 217
    Nazis, 21, 80, 96, 113, 142,
        195, 211, 218
Gerry, Elbridge, 187, 191
Gerrymandering, 187, 191
Getting Her Elected, 68
Ghetto riots, 53
Glenn, John, 66
Gold standard, 47, 116
Goldwater, Barry, 88, 115, 150, 229
Gould, Jay, 177
Gould, Simon, 113
Government
    ownership, 108, 112
    regulation, 94, 118, 175
    spending, 99, 116, 170
Graber, Doris A., 169
Grant, Ulysses S., 44–45, 61, 137,
    195, 224

Grasso, Ella, 70
Great Society, the, 53, 83, 201
Greece, 219
    Ancient Greece, 22
    Greeks, the, 35
Greeley, Horace, 62, 76–77, 89–91,
    93, 105, 136–137
Greenback Party, 107, 113
Gregory, Dick, 27
Grenada invasion, 101, 118
Guam, 92
Gun control, 116, 181

Hague, Frank, 21–22, 24
Haiti, 6, 105
Hall Leonard, 73, 154
Hamer, Fannie Lou, 190
Hamilton, Alexander, 2, 41–43, 46
Hanna, Mark, 91, 128
Harding, Warren G., 63, 94, 98,
    130, 139, 140, 143, 168, 224
Harper's Weekly, 189
Harrison, Benjamin, 38, 47, 198
Harrison, William, 61, 62, 136
Hart, Gary, 66, 182
Hart, Philip, 15
Harvard, 52
Hatfield, Mark, 16, 169
Hay, John, 91
Hayes, Rutherford B., 37, 45, 49,
    195, 198
Haymarket Square incident, 111
Hepburn Act, 92
Hicks, B.N., 161
Hindo-Muslim riots in Assam,
    216

Hispanics, 10, 34, 35, 74, 123, 186,
    232
Hitler, Adolf, 142, 195, 198, 211, 213
Ho Chi Minh, 212, 214
Holy Alliance, 209
Homosexuals, 100
Hone, Philip, 137
Hoover, Herbert, 11, 16, 48, 51, 79,
    95, 112, 141, 143, 169
Housing Acts, 74
Houston, Sam, 208
Hughes, Charles Evans, 112, 194
Humphrey, Hubert, 32, 53, 54, 55,
    116, 132, 150, 196, 229
Hungarians, 64

Ibsen, Henrik, 199
Idaho, 4
Illinois, 12
Immigrants, 3, 5, 64, 74, 77, 105,
    106, 184, 185
Independent vote, 120, 168, 173
India, 215–216
Indiana, 47
Indians, 9, 61, 163, 206, 216
Industrial Revolution, 209
Inflation, 83, 87, 100
Iran hostages, 56, 84
Irish, the, 35, 76, 77, 184
Isolationism, 96
Israel, 35
Italian Americans, 35
Italy, 96, 210

Jackson, Andrew, 37, 39, 40, 43, 46,
    61, 73, 126, 135, 208, 209

Jackson, Jesse, 58, 192

Jackson State demonstrations, 55

Japan, 96

Jefferson, Thomas, 5, 40–42, 46, 52, 63, 73, 75, 76, 104, 169, 184, 224

Jersey City, 21

Jews, 35, 74, 185, 211

Johnson, Andrew, 44–45, 195

Johnson, Lyndon B., 6, 16, 18, 35, 53, 54, 83, 88, 101, 115, 150, 168, 192, 201, 203, 28

Juan Carlos, King, 211

Kansas, 90, 108, 142

Kefauver Senate Crime Committee, 32, 178

Keyserling, Harriet, 17

Kennedy, Edward, 26, 67

Kennedy, John F., 31, 35, 52, 57, 63, 81, 130, 149, 169, 195, 198

Kennedy, Robert, 53, 58, 203, 229

Kent State demonstrations, 55

Khrushchev, Nikita, 222

King, Martin Luther, 28

Kings, 209–210

Know-Nothings (*see* American Party)

Koch, Ed, 170

Korean War, 79, 97

Krajewski, Henry, 113

Ku Klux Klan, 6, 184

Labor Party, 107

Labor unions, 26, 66, 74, 88, 110, 116, 228

La Follette, Robert, 112, 114, 140

La Guardia, Fiorello H., 103

Landon, Alf, 142, 154

Landslide, 234

La Plante, Laura, 161

Lasch, Robert, 170

"Law and order," 55, 104, 115, 203

Laxalt, Paul, 182

League of Nations, 79, 140

League of Women Voters, 17, 20, 27, 32, 199, 224, 236

Lease, Mary Ellen, 108

Lebanon, 100

Lee, Robert E., 61

Lefkowitz, Louis J., 15

Left Wing, 88, 117, 154

Lemke, William, 112–113

Lenin, Vladimir Ilyich, 221

Lewelling, L.D., 108

Liberal Party, 104

Liberalism, 74, 75, 81, 84, 100, 125, 140, 167, 204, 230

Liberal Republican Party, 137

Libertarian National Committee, 104

Lincoln, Abraham, 1, 44, 54, 62–63, 67, 68, 89, 90, 91, 106, 120, 126, 169, 171, 224

Lindblom, Louise, 30

Lindsay, John, 169

Linton High School, 14

Lippmann, Walter, 146

Literary Digest poll, 154

Lleo, Urrutia, 215

Lobbyists, 174–182

Long, Clarence, 175

Long, Huey "Kingfish," 142
Long, Russell, 174, 185
Longworth, Alice Roosevelt, 145
Louisiana, 35, 45, 78, 142, 178, 184, 186
Lowery, Rev. Joseph, 173
Lugar, Richard, 182

Madison, James, 16, 39, 40, 41, 75, 151
Maine, 28, 35, 142, 157
Manatt, Charles, 153
Manchu dynasty, 212
Manifest Destiny, 77, 145
Mao Tse-tung, 212
Marcantonio, Vito, 146
Marines, the, 100–101
Massachusetts, 35, 67, 84, 106, 187, 191, 202
Massachusetts Bay Colony, 5
Masters, Edgar Lee, 128
McCarthy, Eugene, 32, 54
McCarthy, Joseph, 80, 97
McClesky, Clifton, 26
McCombs, William, 130
McCormick, Bernard, 176
McGarvey, Patrick, 199
McGary, Thomas, 144
McGovern, George, 13, 55, 66, 83, 84, 132, 133, 229, 230
McKinley, William, 47, 48, 62, 91, 92, 108, 128,
McLuhan, Marshal, 167
Mechanics Union, 104
Medical care, 74, 119
Metternich, Clemens von, 209

Mexico, 77, 78, 105, 202, 206
Mexican Americans, 9, 185, 199
Mexican War, 77, 106
Meyers, Vic, 158–166
Miami, 3
Michigan, 3, 15, 56, 78, 114, 168
Military-industrial complex, 97, 177
Minimum Wage Act, 74
Mississippi, 3, 6, 34, 53, 55, 78, 142, 154, 190, 192
Mississippi delegation fight of 1968, 124
Mitchell, John, 179
Mitterand, Frangois, 217
Mondale, Walter, 59, 182
Monopolies, 104, 107, 112
Monroe Doctrine, 177, 180
Monroe, James, 40, 75
Montana, 3
Montgomery, Robert, 52
Moral Majority, Inc., 179
Morgan, J. Pierpont, 79, 177
Moriarty, Charles, 163
Morrison, Cameron, 140
Morton, Thruston, 150
Moss, Frank, 16
Muckrakers, 92, 177
Muskie, Edmund, 150, 230
Mussolini, Benito, 210, 211, 213

NAACP, 144, 156
National Anti-Monopoly Party, 107
National Association of Manufacturers (NAM), 177

National Association of Student Governments, 25

National debt, 83, 95

National defense (*see* Defense)

National Education Association, 181

National Guard, 55

National Organization for Women (NOW), 20, 199

National Republicans, 42, 126

National Rifle Association, 181

National States Rights Party, 104, 113, 115

National Teen Age Republicans (TARS), 12, 101, 236

National Union Party, 44, 91

National Women's Political Caucus, 20, 70

National Youth Administration, 16

National Youth Caucus, 25

Nation, Carrie, 110

NATO, 218

Navy League, 177, 180

Nazi Party, 80, 96, 113, 142, 144, 195, 198, 211, 218

Netherlands, the, 219

New Deal, the, 51, 79, 84, 113, 141, 142

New England Association of Farmers and Mechanics, 105

New Hampshire, 35, 67, 85, 132

New Jersey, 3, 21, 22, 24, 26, 40, 79, 113, 138, 139, 188

News media, 116, 119, 144, 155, 169, 205, 217, 230–231

New York, 3, 11, 12, 14, 15, 21, 22, 30, 33, 35, 36, 40, 43, 47, 54, 65, 68, 76–79, 81, 88, 89, 90, 93, 103–105, 110, 113, 117, 139, 170, 184

Board of Education, 14

General Organization Council, 14

Legislature, 15

Supreme Court, 15

Nicaragua, 100, 118

Nineteenth Amendment, 4

Nixon, Richard M., 7, 25, 26, 52–56, 63, 65, 84, 97, 99, 115, 116, 145–155, 167, 178, 179, 195, 198, 203, 214, 224, 229

Northern states, 6, 77–78, 81, 85, 197

Norway, 219

Nuclear freeze, 170, 204

Nuclear power plants, 28, 119, 218

Nuclear war, 27, 62, 83, 150, 229

Ohio third party controversy, 117

O'Neill, Thomas P. ("Tip"), Jr., 71

Order of the Star-Spangled Banner, 105

Order of United Americans, 105

Oregon, 12, 16, 236

Orion, Nebula Eighteen, 234

Ostrogorski, M.I., 129, 225

O'Sullivan, John L., 77

Paderewski, Ignace Jan, 163

Paizis, Susanne, 68

Panama Canal, 92, 98

Peace movement, 88, 113, 132, 184, 202

Pearl, Art, 23, 101, 153, 228, 234, 236

Pearl Harbor, 96

Pennsylvania, 3, 176, 183, 188

Pentagon, the, 175, 204

People's march on Washington, 47, 53, 179

People's Party (*see* Populists)

Pepper, Claude, 138

Percy, Charles, 12, 88, 169

Perez, Leander, 185–186, 189

Philippines, the, 92

Pierce, Franklin, 176, 224

Pilgrims, the, 9, 44

Plunkett, 33

Political Action Committees (PACs), 66, 178, 181, 182, 228, 229, 231

Polk, James K., 77, 78, 106, 137, 169, 202, 206

Poles, the, 39

Police brutality, 119

Polsby, Nelson W., 225

Poor Man's Party, 113

Poor, the, 5, 10, 39, 41, 53, 61, 74, 83, 87, 104, 106, 107, 128, 186, 224, 225

Pope, the, 48, 106

Populists, 107, 108

Portugal, 211, 212

Portuguese, the, 35

Prayer in schools, 20, 100, 179

Precinct caucuses, 32

Primary elections, 6, 12, 123, 160, 205

Private enterprise (*see* Capitalism)

Progressive Party, 81, 112, 114, 130

Prohibition, 48, 89, 110, 161, 185

Prohibition Party, 108, 113, 114

Proprietary Party, 183

Protective tariffs, 116

Protestants, 31, 89, 106

Public opinion polls, 32, 58, 64, 115, 194, 229

Puerto Rico, 92, 105

Pullman railroad strike, 111

Pure Food and Drug Act, 92

Puritans, the, 5

Quakers, the, 183–184

Quay, Mat, 47

Racism, 156, 197, 229, 232

Radical Republican Party, 45, 91

Railroads, 92, 108, 111, 112, 174, 176

Railway Labor Act, 178

Ray, Dixie Lee, 70

Rayburn, Sam, 122

Reader's Digest, 204

Reagan, Ronald, 4, 12, 29, 54, 56–60, 63, 66, 81, 85, 86, 89, 99, 100, 101, 133, 151, 152, 156, 169, 179, 182, 186, 204, 219, 220, 225, 232

Recession, 100

Reed, Thomas Brackett, 157

Reedy, George E., 88, 238

Reeves, Donald St. George, 14

Republican Party, 5, 41, 42, 44, 45, 54, 73, 75, 78, 85–97, 101, 103, 104, 128, 141, 152, 169, 182
  National Committee, 47, 51, 73, 148, 153, 154, 236
Revolution, 23, 56, 75, 80, 111, 118, 139, 210, 214, 215, 221, 228
Reynolds, Robert, 140
Reynolds, William, 192
Rhode Island, 5, 13, 35
Ribicoff, Abraham, 132
Right Wing, 64, 88, 89, 100, 133, 150
Rockefeller, John D., 177
Rockefeller, Nelson, 12, 54, 65, 88
Rogers, Will, 87
Roman Republic, 57, 209
  Senate, the, 57
Romney, George, 230
Roosevelt, Franklin D., 16, 51, 57, 59, 71, 79, 83, 84, 86, 112, 124, 141, 142, 154, 178, 224
Roosevelt, Theodore, 6, 57, 64, 78, 91, 92, 98, 100, 111, 129, 139, 177, 180
Root, Elihu, 129
Rural Electrification Act, 74
Ryan, Edward, 177

Salazar, Antonio de Oliveira, 211–212
Salem, Eric, 1
San Francisco, 3, 70, 88
Schroeder, Pat, 71

Schurz, Carl, 45
Seattle campaigns, 158–166
Secret ballot, the, 40, 42, 209, 210
Sedition Act, World War I, 202
Senate Judiciary Committee hearings, 181, 186
Seward, William H., 126
Shakespeare's *Coriolanus*, 57
Share the Wealth program, 142
Sheridan, Phil, 61
Sherman, William Tecumseh, 61
Sherman Anti-Trust Act, 107
Sierra Club, 181
"Silent Majority, the," 55
Single Tax Party, 110
Six Crises, 203
Slavery issue, 41, 44, 78, 89, 90, 106, 169, 171
Slum Clearance Act, 74
Smathers, George, 137–138
Smith, Al, 11, 48, 103, 141, 143
Smith, Margaret Bayard, 40
Smith, "Sugar Jim," 138
Social Security, 74, 79, 111, 141
Socialism, 51, 104, 108, 111, 134
Socialist Labor Party, 104, 110, 111, 113, 115, 236
Socialist Party, 104, 109, 110, 111, 112
Socialist Workers Party, 104, 113, 117, 118, 236
Soglin, Paul, 16
South Carolina, 4, 17, 45, 78, 80, 145
Southern Christian Leadership Conference (SCLC), 173

"Southern strategy," 54

Southern Democrats (*see* Boll Weevils and Democratic Party)

Southern states, 5, 44, 45, 47, 54, 78, 80, 81, 85, 91, 108, 115, 137, 145, 173, 190, 195

Soviet Union, 83, 96, 150, 204, 215, 217, 220, 221, 222, 230

elections, 220–222

Politburo, 221

Supreme Soviet, 220

Spain, 91, 211, 213

Spanish-American War, 91, 92

Spencer, Susan, 14

Split tickets, 168, 169

Stalin, Josef, 222

Stanton, Elizabeth Cady, 43, 46

State conventions, 37, 126

State elections, 205

State legislatures, 30, 104, 105, 175, 187, 232

Steffens, Lincoln, 177, 185, 234

Stevenson, Adlai, 32, 51, 52, 58, 59, 64, 135, 148, 169

Stock market, 95

Strikes, 111–112, 173, 177, 178

Student Non-Violent Coordinating Committee (SNCC), 34

Student revolts, 53

Suffragettes, 43

Sun Oil Company, 176

Sunset High School, 12

Sun Yat-sen, 212

Supreme Court, 3, 13, 15, 47, 65, 112, 117, 186, 187, 190, 222

Sutch, Lord, 217

Sweden, 219

Taft, Robert A., 96, 122

Taft, William H., 78, 92, 129, 139

Talmadge, Eugene, 183

Talmadge, Herman, 183

Tammany Hall, 33, 47, 78, 111, 139

Taylor, Zachary, 78, 107

Tax Cut Party, 113

Taxes, 4, 6, 27, 28, 74, 89, 95, 100, 107, 110, 113, 116, 158, 170, 176, 178, 186, 190

Teapot Dome scandal, 94

Teel, Steven, 14

Teen Dem Clubs, 12, 86

Television, 26, 52, 54, 63, 65, 69, 119, 122, 123, 132, 146, 150, 151, 153, 155, 167, 172, 182, 212, 219, 233

Television debates, 52, 63, 69, 151, 167, 182

Tennessee, 13, 116

Tennessee Valley Authority (TVA), 74

Territorial expansion (*see* Manifest Destiny)

Terrorists, 100

Texas, 3, 16, 68, 78, 113, 124

Thatcher, Margaret, 216, 217

Third parties, 80, 84, 85, 89, 90, 94, 103–121, 141, 195, 216, 225

Thomas, Norman, 112

Thompson, Hunter S., 25

Thompson, William Hale, 185

Index

Thoreau, Henry, 199
Thurmond, Strom, 80, 145, 229
Tilden, Samuel J., 37, 45, 47, 49
"Tippecanoe and Tyler, tool"
    campaign, 136
Tocqueville, Alexis de, 208, 209
Tories, 75
Townsend Plan, 141
"Trickle down" theory, 89
Truman, Harry S, 32, 51, 61, 62,
    67, 72, 73, 80–82, 96, 97, 145,
    195
Truth Squad, the, 148
Twain, Mark, 176
Tweed, Boss, 184, 188, 189
Twenty-fourth Amendment, 4, 6
Twenty-sixth Amendment, 1–2, 7, 8
"Twenty years of treason," 80
Tyler, John, 136

Udall, Morris K., 67, 235
Unemployment, 74, 79, 80, 100,
    112, 142
Unemployment insurance, 74, 120
Union Party, 112
Unions, 74, 79, 88, 220, 228
United Nations, 116
United States Bank, 105
USSR (see Soviet Union)
Utah, 16, 113
Utilities, 120

Van Buren, Martin, 107, 135, 136,
    152
Van Rennselaer, Steben, 43
Vatican, the, 141, 143

Vermont, 4, 142
Victor Emmanuel, King, 210
Vietnam War, 1, 25, 26, 53–55, 83,
    99, 132, 150, 179, 203, 214,
    229, 230, 233
Virginia colony, 5
Volstead Act, 110
"Voodoo economics," 29
Voting
    compulsory, 23, 217
    districts (precincts), 32–33
    fraud, 77, 80, 108, 155, 183,
        185, 188, 204, 212, 221
    registration, 6, 13, 31, 173, 190,
        192, 194, 197
    requirements, 4, 6, 30, 39, 77,
        119
    student vote, 4, 14, 234
    turnout, 22, 85, 196, 197, 218,
        219, 222, 225
Voting Rights Act of 1965, 190,
    192
wards, 32, 76, 77, 156
write-in votes, 183
youth vote, 2, 11, 25, 26, 196,
    199, 235

Wagner Labor Relations Act, 178
Walker, Felix, 135
Wallace, George, 54, 112, 115–117,
    229
Wallace, Henry, 80
Wall Street, 108
Walsh, Thomas J., 178
War, 94
War Democrats, 44, 91

Warren, Fuller, 178

Washington Commonwealth
    Federation, 165

Washington, state of, 159, 166

Washington, George, 5, 61, 75, 168

Washington, Harold, 85, 156, 197

Washington Post, 50, 55, 99

Watergate scandal, 26, 84, 99, 151,
    178, 203, 224

Webster, Daniel, 40

Welch, Doug, 159

Welfare, 25, 74, 88, 111, 228

Wertheimer, Fred, 181

Western states, 47, 108, 174, 211,
    212, 221, 222

West Germany, 217–219
    Christian Democratic-Social
        Union Party, 218
    Green Party, 218
    Parliament, 217–218
    Social Democratic Party, 218

West Virginia, 31

Weyrich, Paul, 196

Wheat, Alan, 173

Whigs, 42, 44, 75, 76, 77, 89, 90,
    93, 104, 136, 137

White Citizens Councils, 115

White House, 7, 16, 23, 31, 37–40,
    48, 51–53, 55–57, 59, 61–65,
    67, 72, 75, 77, 80, 81, 85, 94,
    95, 99, 111, 120, 136, 137, 139,
    141, 143, 145, 151, 152, 194,
    195, 201, 205, 224, 231, 235

White, Robert, 129

Wicker, Tom, 83

Williams, Roger, 5, 206

Wilson, Woodrow, 26, 52, 64, 78,
    79, 94, 101, 111, 130, 138–140,
    143, 194, 198, 202, 234

Winrod, Gerald B., 142, 144

Wisconsin, 16, 80, 148

Women candidates, 17, 20, 27, 68,
    231

Women's Rights Convention, 44

Women's vote, 5, 68, 74, 111, 161

Woodhull, Victoria Claflin, 44

Workingman's Labor Party, 104,
    105, 110, 118

World War I, 79, 94, 111, 139, 143,
    202

World War II, 51, 79, 80, 96, 145,
    183, 195, 210, 214, 217

Wynhausen, Elisabeth, 204

Young, Andy, 173

Young Democrats of America, 199,
    236

Young Socialist Alliance, 117, 119,
    236

Yugoslavia, 218, 236

Zaire, 214